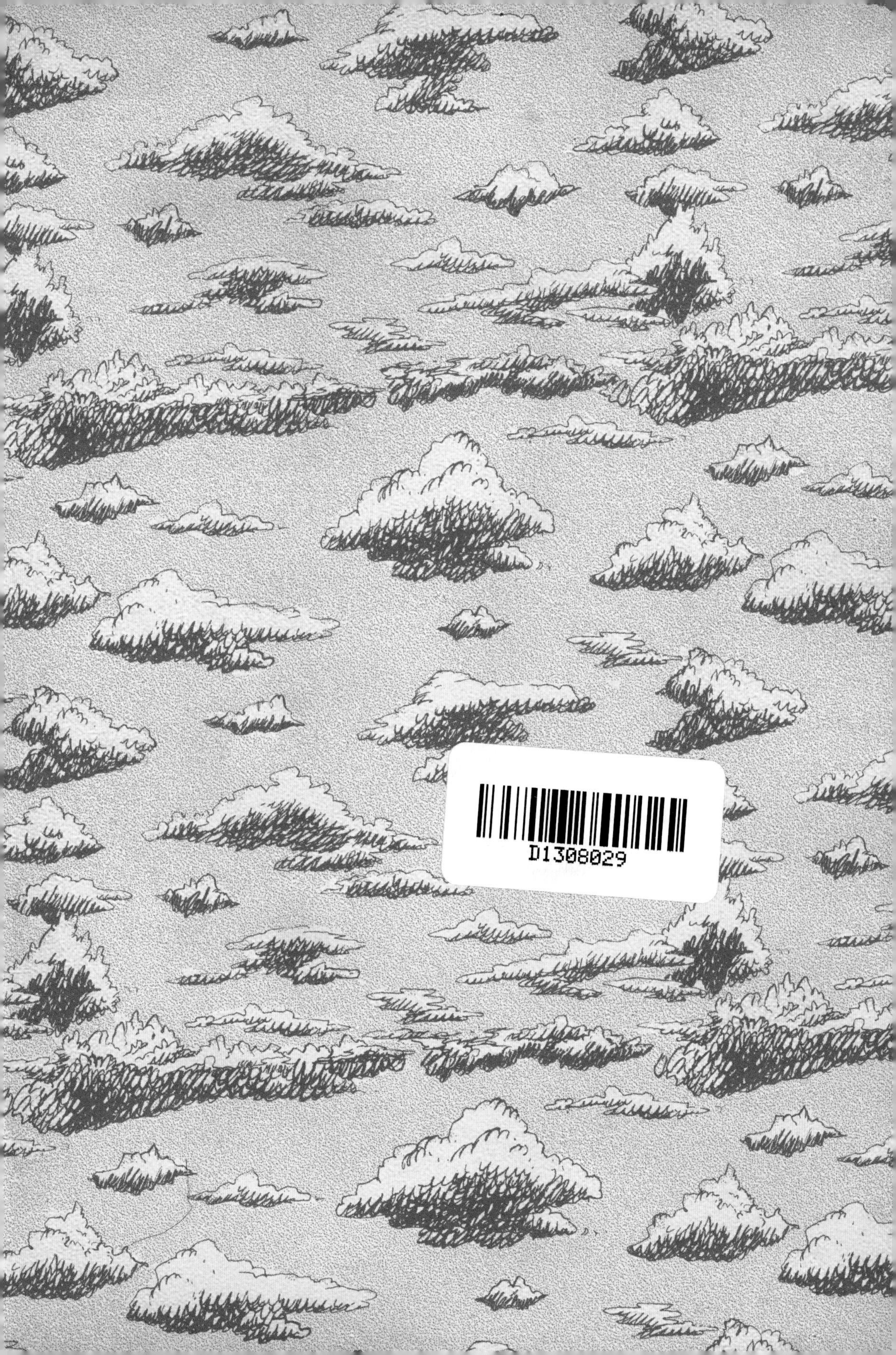

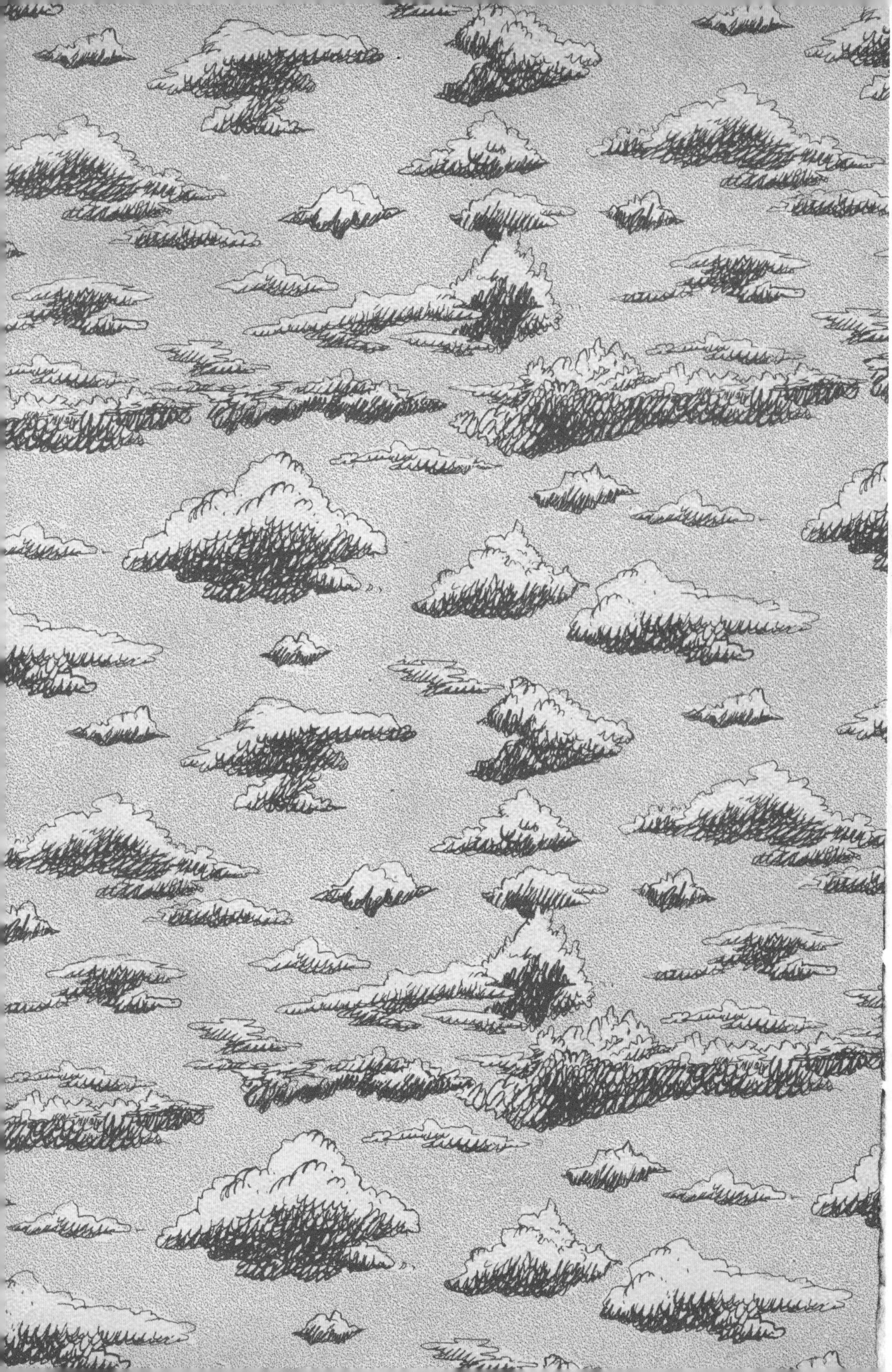

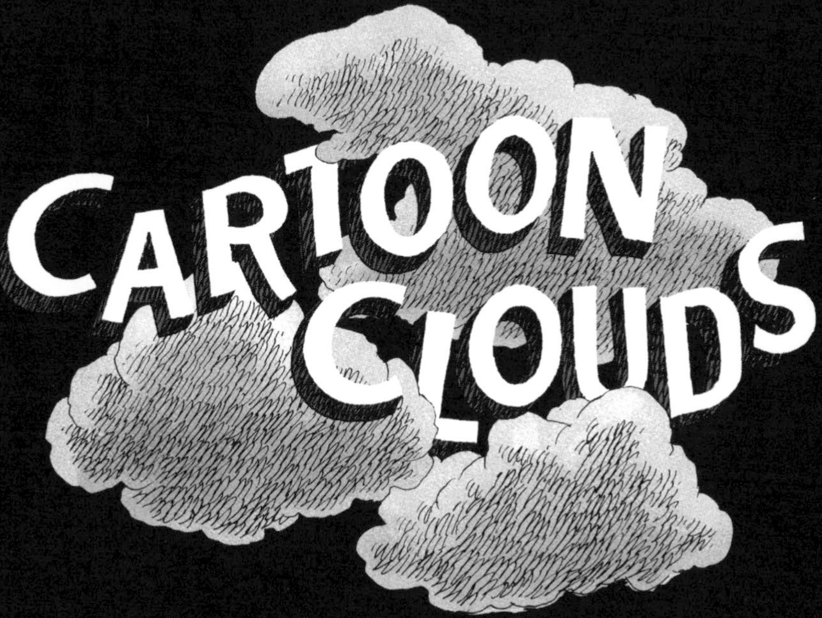
CARTOON CLOUDS

Joseph Remnant

FANTAGRAPHICS BOOKS
Seattle, Washington

For Hilary

Editor: Gary Groth
Designer: Sean David Williams
Production: Paul Baresh
Associate Publisher: Eric Reynolds
Publisher: Gary Groth

Fantagraphics Books, Inc.
7563 Lake City Way NE
Seattle, WA 98115

ISBN: 978-1-606999-394
Library of Congress Control Number: 2017938230
First Printing: October
Printed in China

3 9547 00435 5801

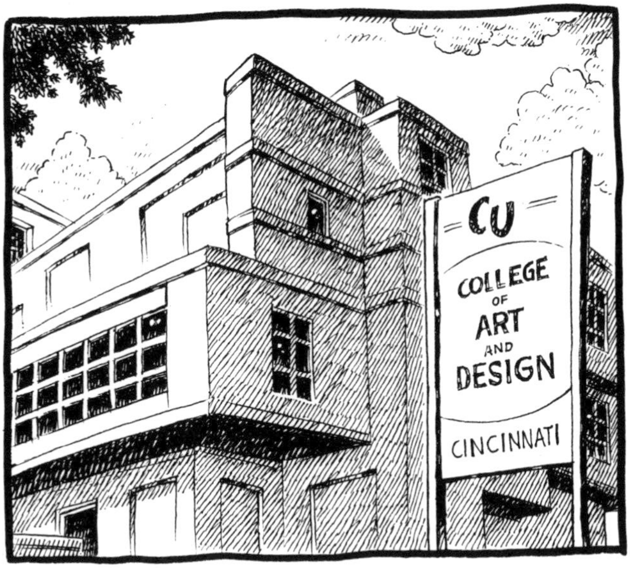
CU
COLLEGE OF ART AND DESIGN
CINCINNATI

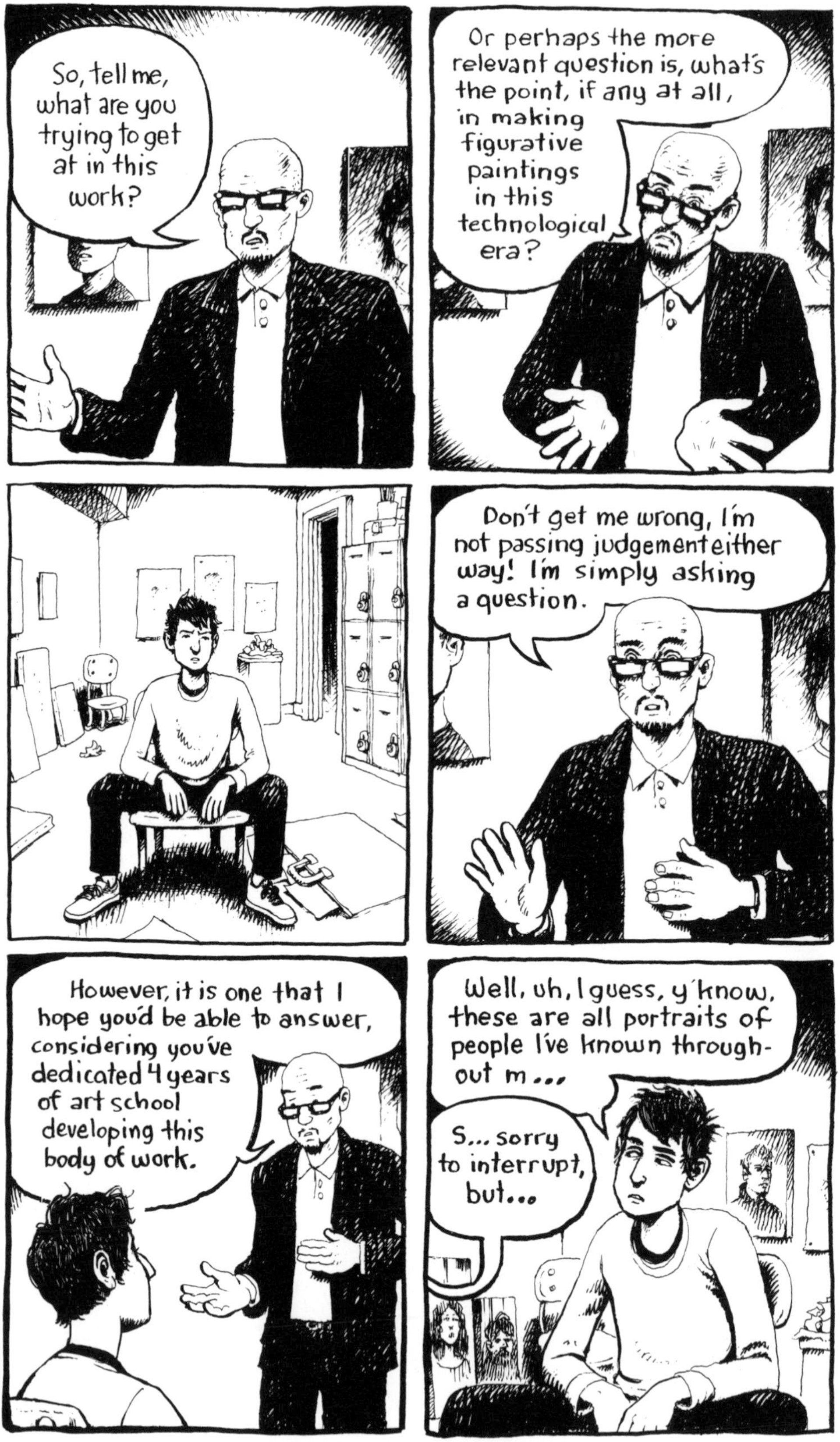
So, tell me, what are you trying to get at in this work?
Or perhaps the more relevant question is, what's the point, if any at all, in making figurative paintings in this technological era?
Don't get me wrong, I'm not passing judgement either way! I'm simply asking a question.
However, it is one that I hope you'd be able to answer, considering you've dedicated 4 years of art school developing this body of work.
Well, uh, I guess, y'know, these are all portraits of people I've known throughout m...
S... sorry to interrupt, but...

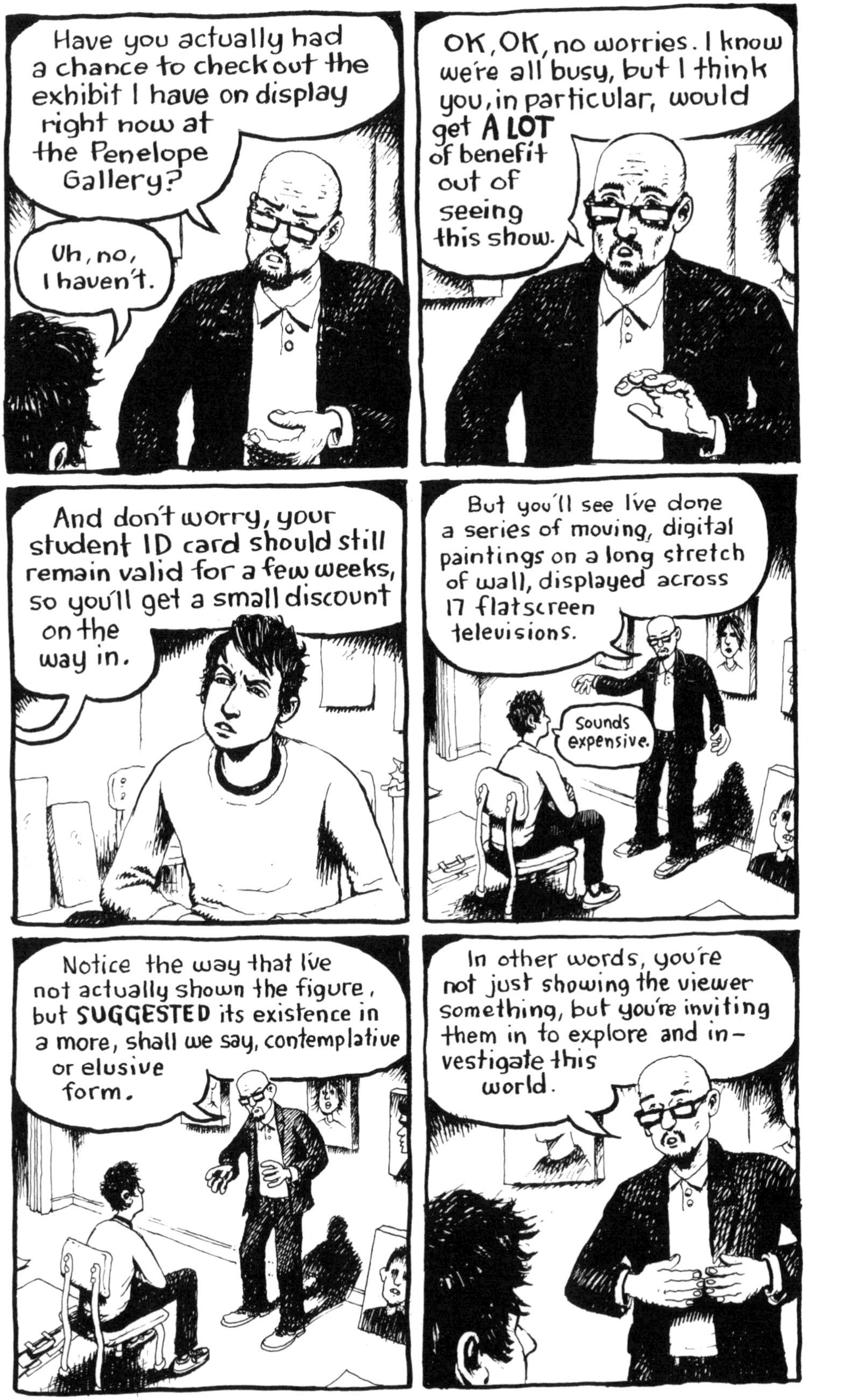
Have you actually had a chance to check out the exhibit I have on display right now at the Penelope Gallery?
Uh, no, I haven't.
OK, OK, no worries. I know we're all busy, but I think you, in particular, would get **A LOT** of benefit out of seeing this show.
And don't worry, your student ID card should still remain valid for a few weeks, so you'll get a small discount on the way in.
But you'll see I've done a series of moving, digital paintings on a long stretch of wall, displayed across 17 flatscreen televisions.
Sounds expensive.
Notice the way that I've not actually shown the figure, but **SUGGESTED** its existence in a more, shall we say, contemplative or elusive form.
In other words, you're not just showing the viewer something, but you're inviting them in to explore and in-vestigate this world.

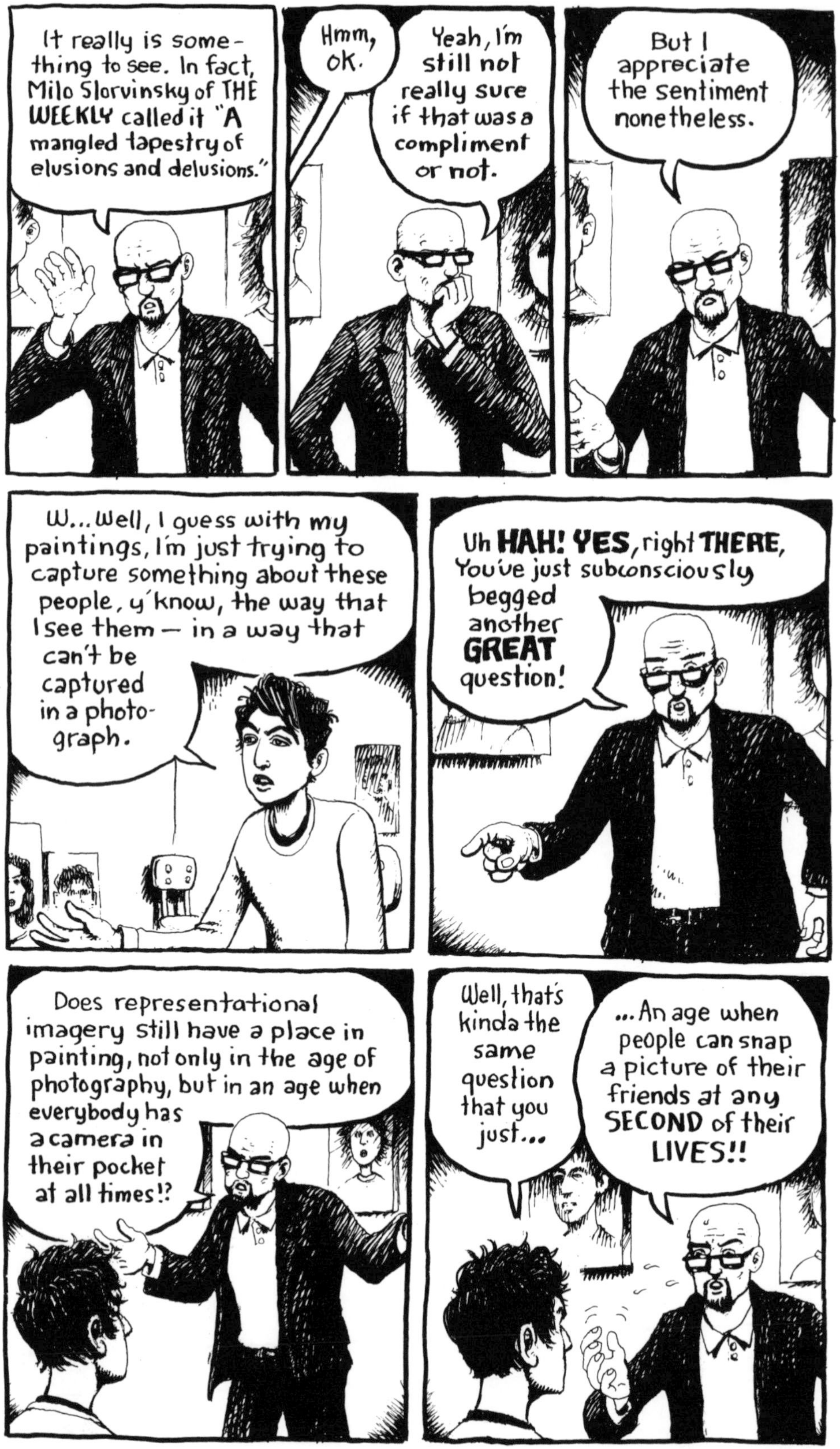
It really is something to see. In fact, Milo Slorvinsky of THE WEEKLY called it "A mangled tapestry of elusions and delusions."
Hmm, OK.
Yeah, I'm still not really sure if that was a compliment or not.
But I appreciate the sentiment nonetheless.
W... Well, I guess with my paintings, I'm just trying to capture something about these people, y'know, the way that I see them — in a way that can't be captured in a photograph.
Uh HAH! YES, right THERE, You've just subconsciously begged another GREAT question!
Does representational imagery still have a place in painting, not only in the age of photography, but in an age when everybody has a camera in their pocket at all times!?
Well, that's kinda the same question that you just...
...An age when people can snap a picture of their friends at any SECOND of their LIVES!!

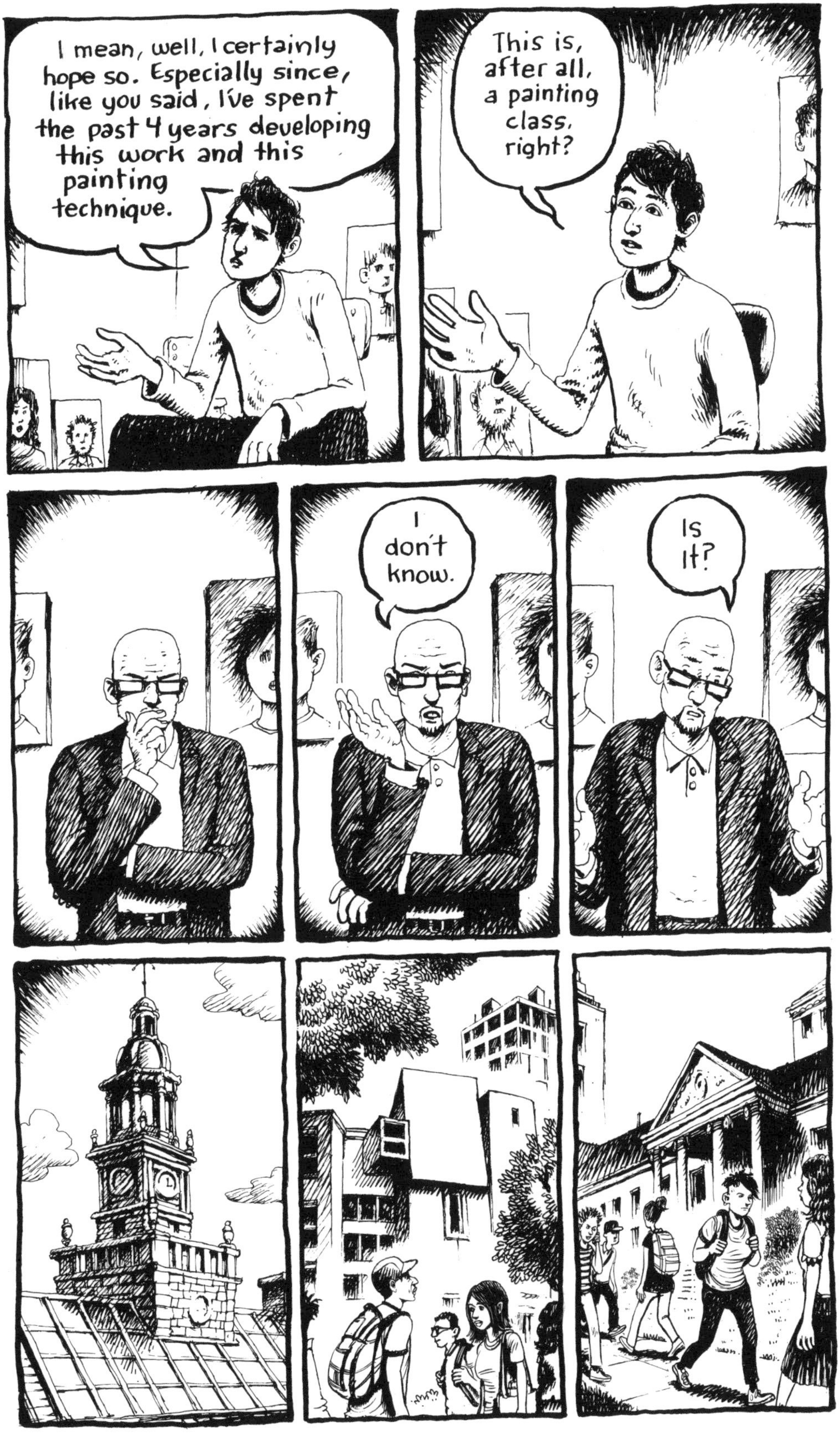
I mean, well, I certainly hope so. Especially since, like you said, I've spent the past 4 years developing this work and this painting technique.
This is, after all, a painting class, right?
I don't know.
Is it?

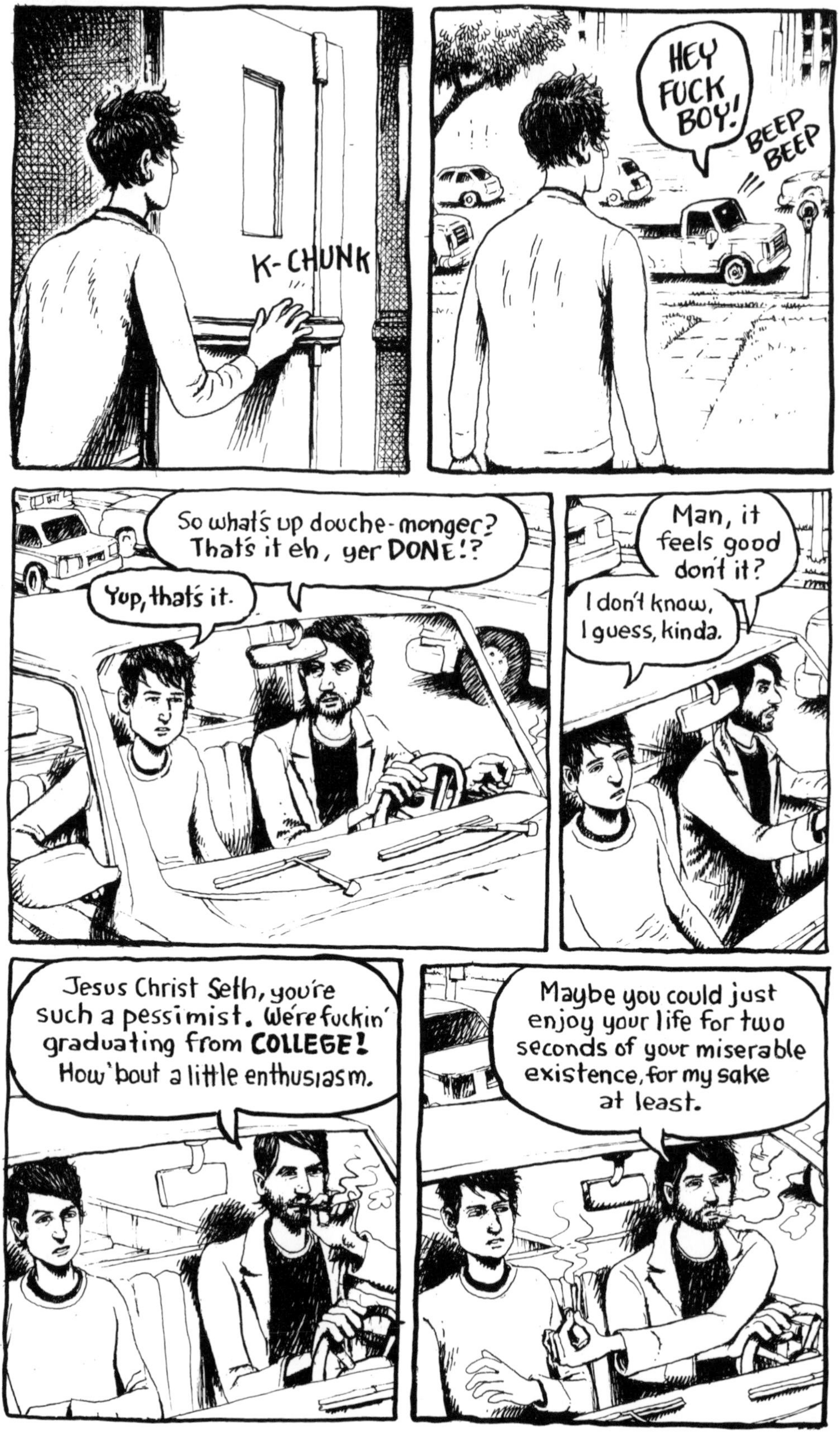
K-CHUNK
HEY FUCK BOY!
BEEP BEEP
So what's up douche-monger? That's it eh, yer DONE!?
Yup, that's it.
Man, it feels good don't it?
I don't know, I guess, kinda.
Jesus Christ Seth, you're such a pessimist. We're fuckin' graduating from COLLEGE! How 'bout a little enthusiasm.
Maybe you could just enjoy your life for two seconds of your miserable existence, for my sake at least.

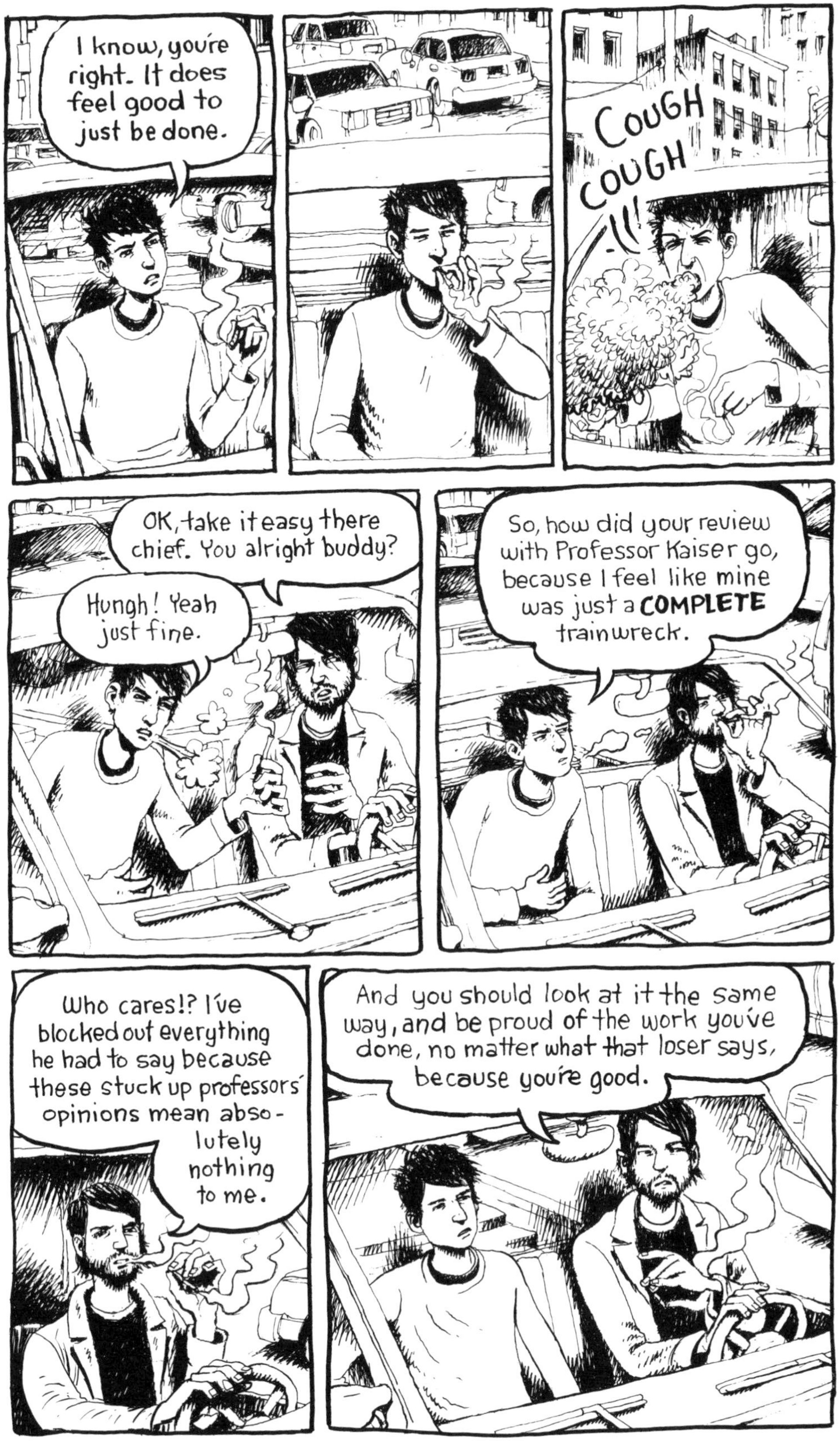
I know, you're right. It does feel good to just be done.
COUGH
COUGH
-!!!
OK, take it easy there chief. You alright buddy?
Hungh! Yeah just fine.
So, how did your review with Professor Kaiser go, because I feel like mine was just a **COMPLETE** trainwreck.
Who cares!? I've blocked out everything he had to say because these stuck up professors' opinions mean abso-lutely nothing to me.
And you should look at it the same way, and be proud of the work you've done, no matter what that loser says, because you're good.

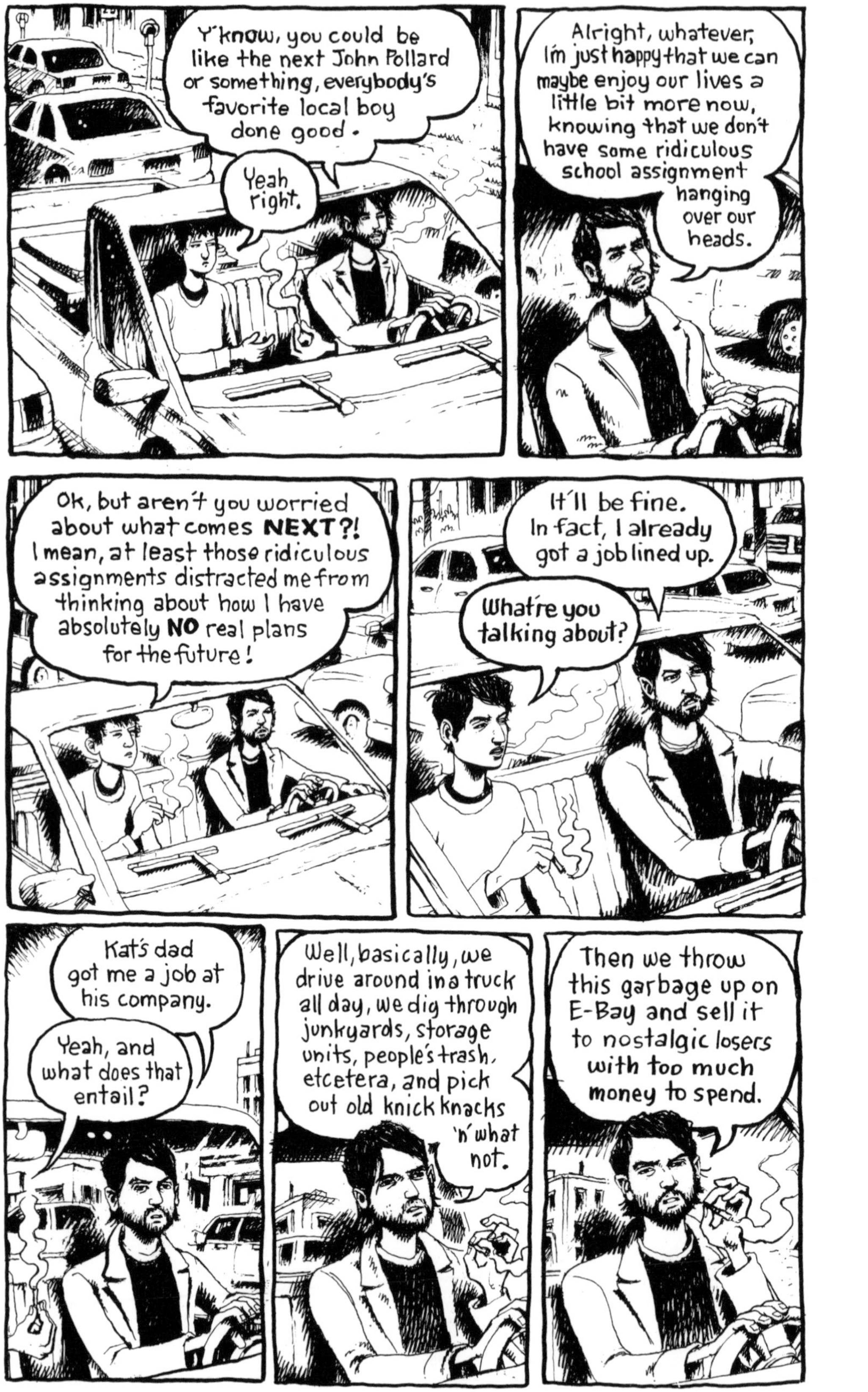
Y'know, you could be like the next John Pollard or something, everybody's favorite local boy done good.
Yeah right.
Alright, whatever, I'm just happy that we can maybe enjoy our lives a little bit more now, knowing that we don't have some ridiculous school assignment hanging over our heads.
Ok, but aren't you worried about what comes NEXT?! I mean, at least those ridiculous assignments distracted me from thinking about how I have absolutely NO real plans for the future!
It'll be fine. In fact, I already got a job lined up.
What're you talking about?
Kat's dad got me a job at his company.
Yeah, and what does that entail?
Well, basically, we drive around in a truck all day, we dig through junkyards, storage units, people's trash, etcetera, and pick out old knick knacks 'n' what not.
Then we throw this garbage up on E-Bay and sell it to nostalgic losers with too much money to spend.

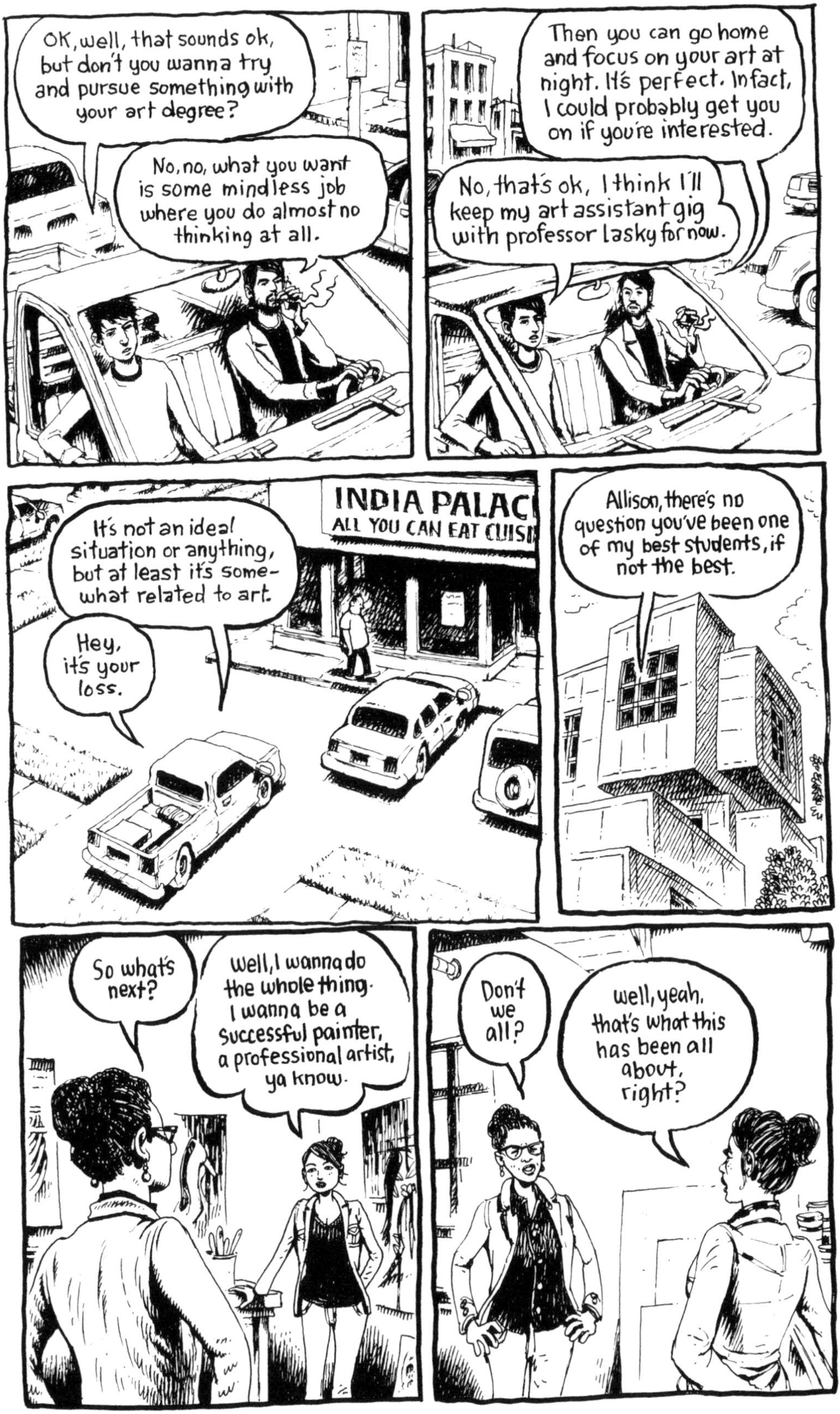
OK, well, that sounds ok, but don't you wanna try and pursue something with your art degree?
No, no, what you want is some mindless job where you do almost no thinking at all.
Then you can go home and focus on your art at night. It's perfect. In fact, I could probably get you on if you're interested.
No, that's ok, I think I'll keep my art assistant gig with professor Lasky for now.
INDIA PALAC
ALL YOU CAN EAT CUISI
It's not an ideal situation or anything, but at least it's somewhat related to art.
Hey, it's your loss.
Allison, there's no question you've been one of my best students, if not the best.
So what's next?
Well, I wanna do the whole thing. I wanna be a successful painter, a professional artist, ya know.
Don't we all?
Well, yeah, that's what this has been all about, right?

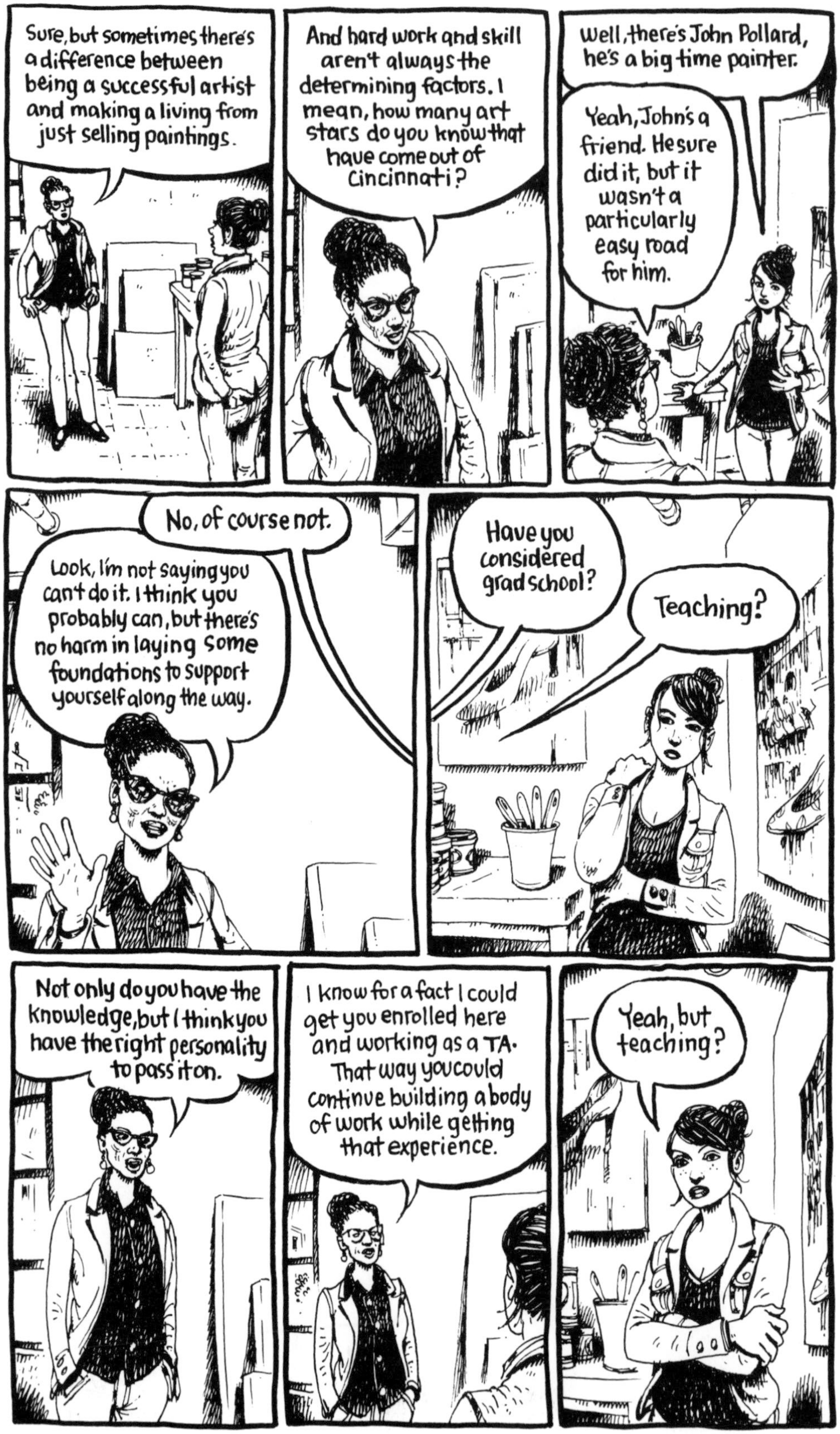
Sure, but sometimes there's a difference between being a successful artist and making a living from just selling paintings.
And hard work and skill aren't always the determining factors. I mean, how many art stars do you know that have come out of Cincinnati?
Well, there's John Pollard, he's a big time painter.
Yeah, John's a friend. He sure did it, but it wasn't a particularly easy road for him.
No, of course not.
Look, I'm not saying you can't do it. I think you probably can, but there's no harm in laying some foundations to support yourself along the way.
Have you considered grad school?
Teaching?
Not only do you have the knowledge, but I think you have the right personality to pass it on.
I know for a fact I could get you enrolled here and working as a TA. That way you could continue building a body of work while getting that experience.
Yeah, but teaching?

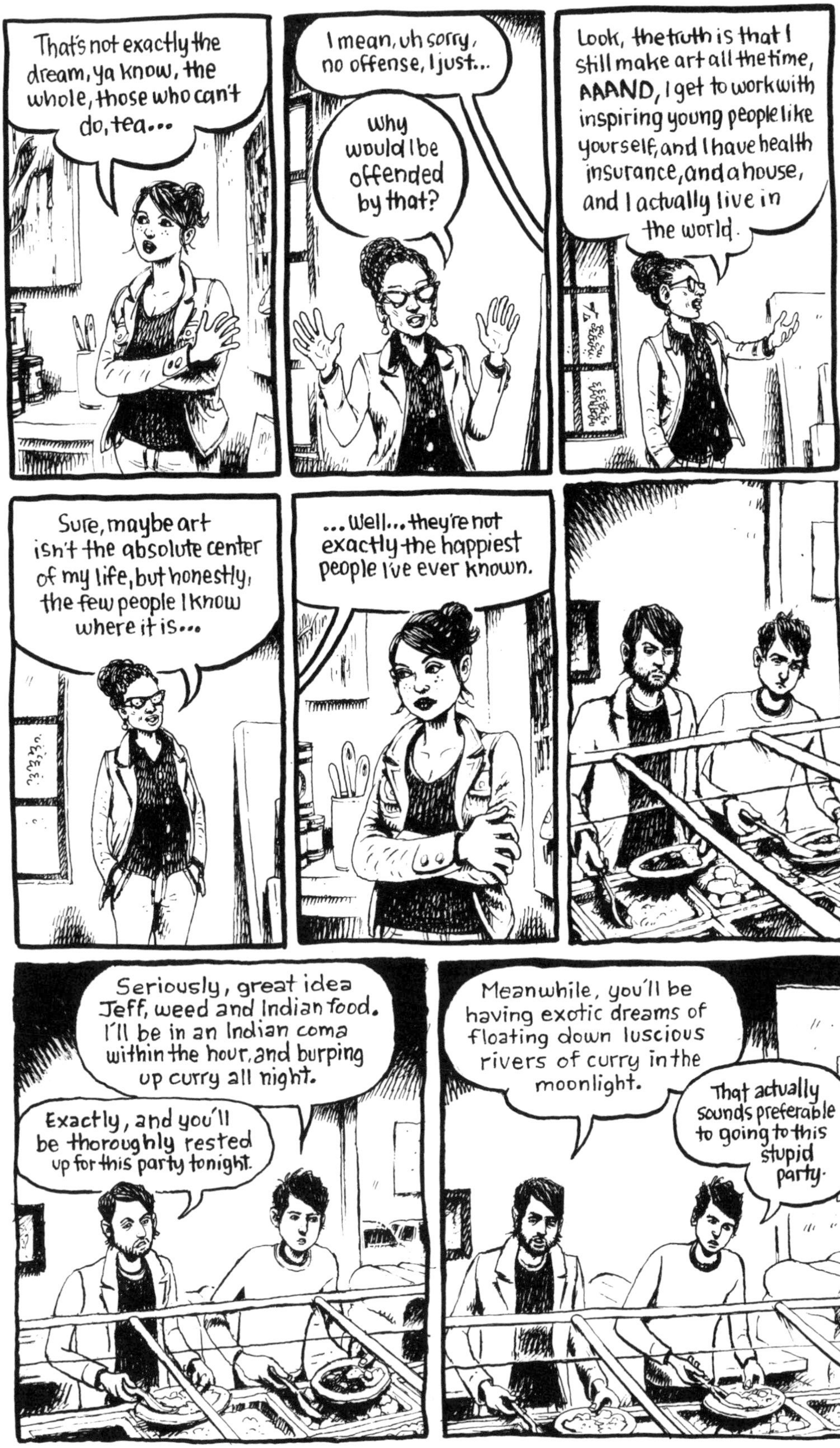
That's not exactly the dream, ya know, the whole, those who can't do, tea...
I mean, uh sorry, no offense, I just...
Why would I be offended by that?
Look, the truth is that I still make art all the time, AAAND, I get to work with inspiring young people like yourself, and I have health insurance, and a house, and I actually live in the world.
Sure, maybe art isn't the absolute center of my life, but honestly, the few people I know where it is...
...Well... they're not exactly the happiest people I've ever known.
Seriously, great idea Jeff, weed and Indian food. I'll be in an Indian coma within the hour, and burping up curry all night.
Exactly, and you'll be thoroughly rested up for this party tonight.
Meanwhile, you'll be having exotic dreams of floating down luscious rivers of curry in the moonlight.
That actually sounds preferable to going to this stupid party.

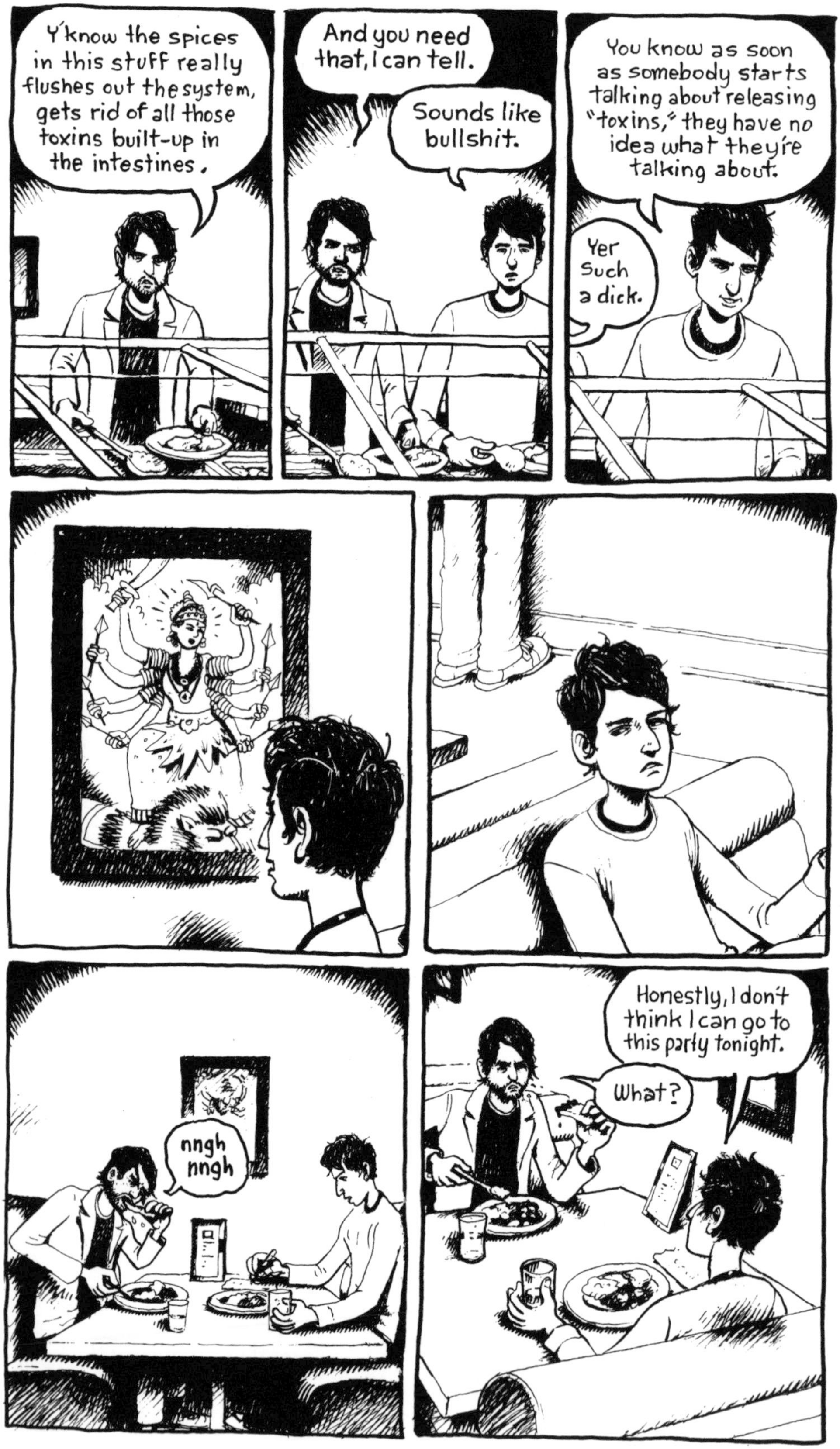
Y'know the spices in this stuff really flushes out the system, gets rid of all those toxins built-up in the intestines.
And you need that, I can tell.
Sounds like bullshit.
You know as soon as somebody starts talking about releasing "toxins," they have no idea what they're talking about.
Yer such a dick.
nngh nngh
Honestly, I don't think I can go to this party tonight.
What?

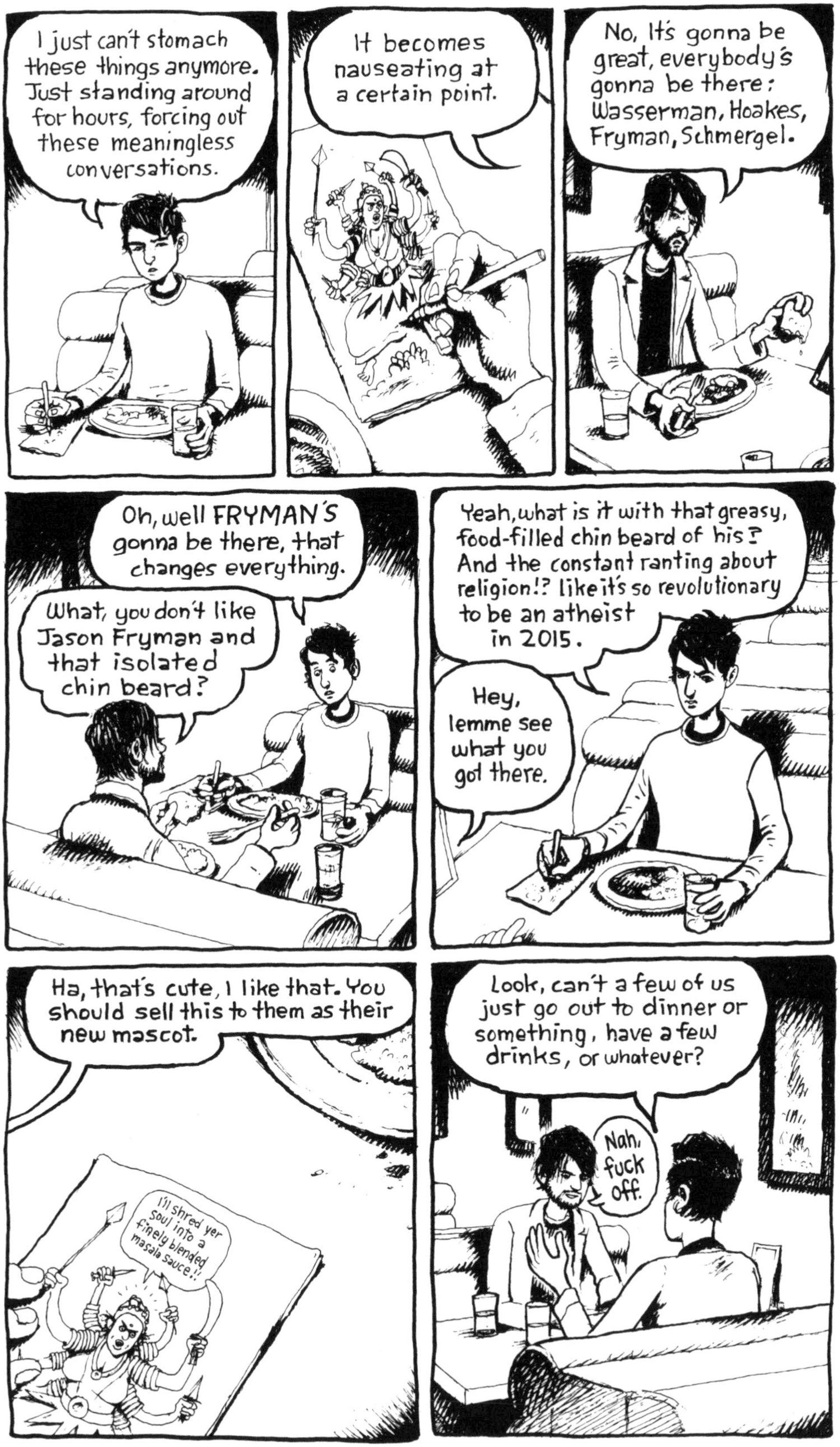
I just can't stomach these things anymore. Just standing around for hours, forcing out these meaningless conversations.
It becomes nauseating at a certain point.
No, It's gonna be great, everybody's gonna be there: Wasserman, Hoakes, Fryman, Schmergel.
Oh, well FRYMAN'S gonna be there, that changes everything.
What, you don't like Jason Fryman and that isolated chin beard?
Yeah, what is it with that greasy, food-filled chin beard of his? And the constant ranting about religion!? like it's so revolutionary to be an atheist in 2015.
Hey, lemme see what you got there.
Ha, that's cute, I like that. You should sell this to them as their new mascot.
I'll shred yer soul into a finely blended masala sauce!!
Look, can't a few of us just go out to dinner or something, have a few drinks, or whatever?
Nah, fuck off.

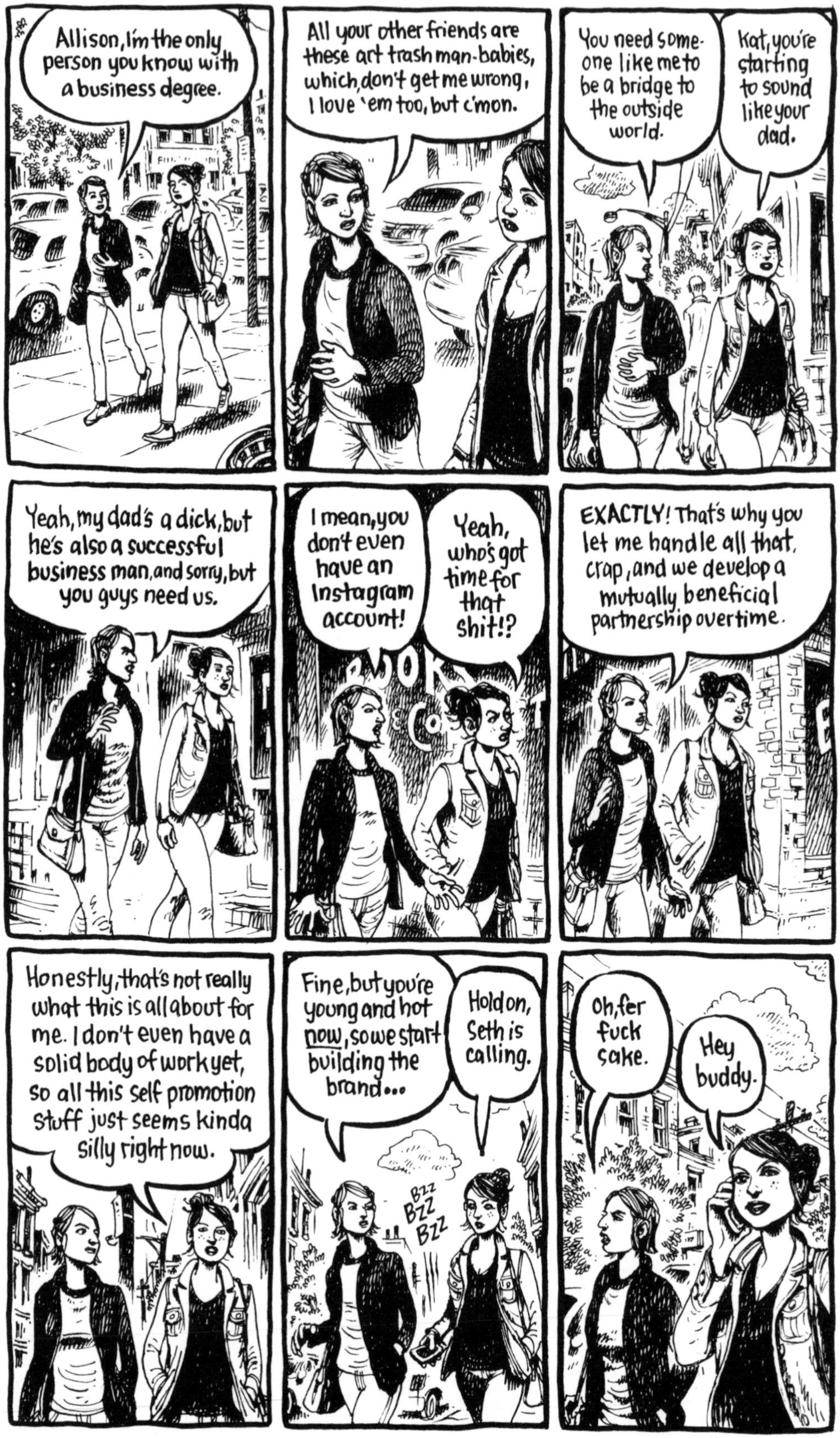

Allison, I'm the only person you know with a business degree.
All your other friends are these art trash man-babies, which, don't get me wrong, I love 'em too, but c'mon.
You need someone like me to be a bridge to the outside world.
Kat, you're starting to sound like your dad.
Yeah, my dad's a dick, but he's also a successful business man, and sorry, but you guys need us.
I mean, you don't even have an Instagram account!
Yeah, who's got time for that shit!?
EXACTLY! That's why you let me handle all that crap, and we develop a mutually beneficial partnership over time.
Honestly, that's not really what this is all about for me. I don't even have a solid body of work yet, so all this self promotion stuff just seems kinda silly right now.
Fine, but you're young and hot now, so we start building the brand...
BZZ BZZ BZZ
Hold on, Seth is calling.
Oh, fer fuck sake.
Hey buddy.

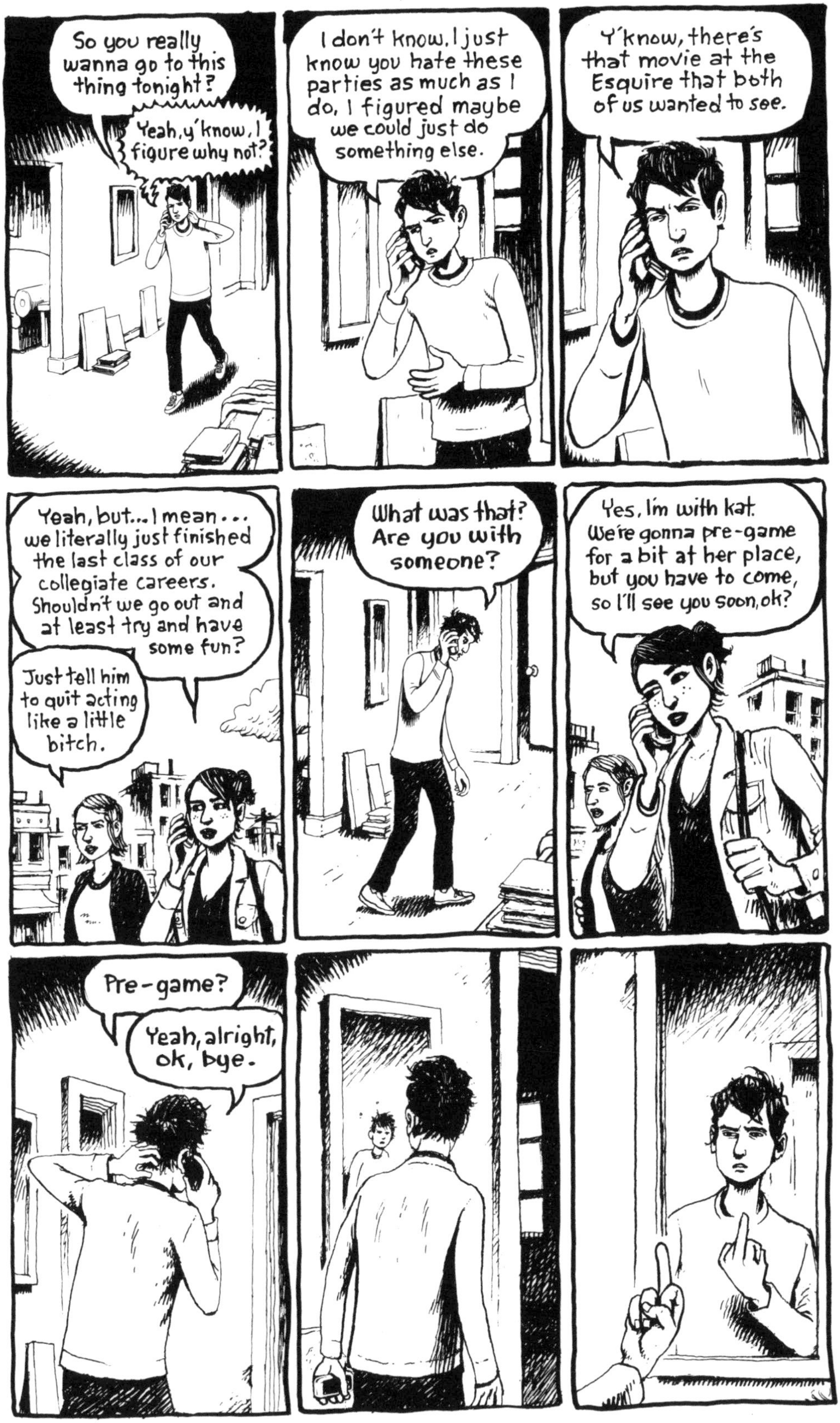
So you really wanna go to this thing tonight?
Yeah, y'know, I figure why not?
I don't know. I just know you hate these parties as much as I do, I figured maybe we could just do something else.
Y'know, there's that movie at the Esquire that both of us wanted to see.
Yeah, but... I mean... we literally just finished the last class of our collegiate careers. Shouldn't we go out and at least try and have some fun?
Just tell him to quit acting like a little bitch.
What was that? Are you with someone?
Yes, I'm with Kat. We're gonna pre-game for a bit at her place, but you have to come, so I'll see you soon, ok?
Pre-game?
Yeah, alright, ok, bye.

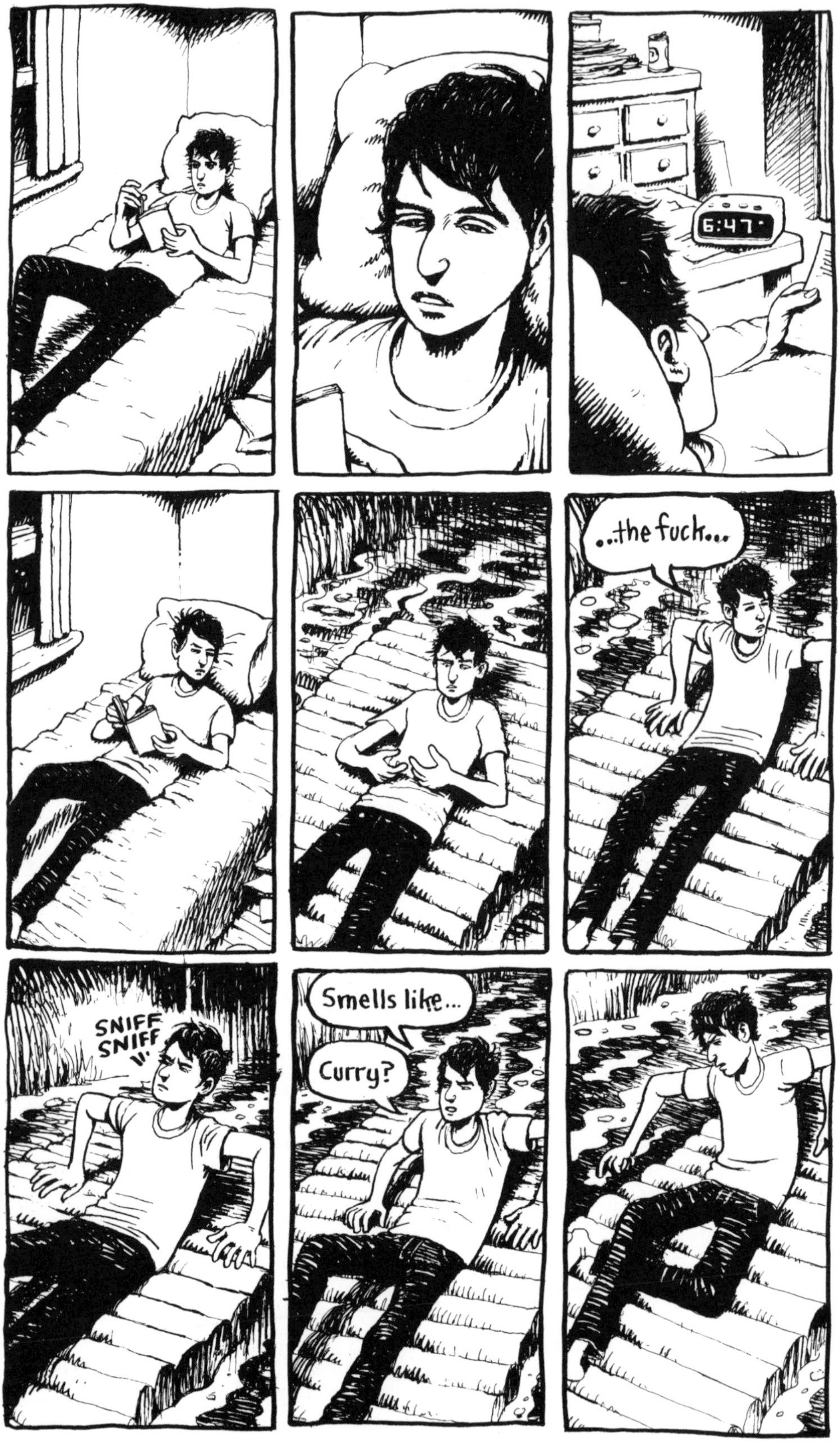
6:47
...the fuck...
SNIFF
SNIFF
Smells like...
Curry?

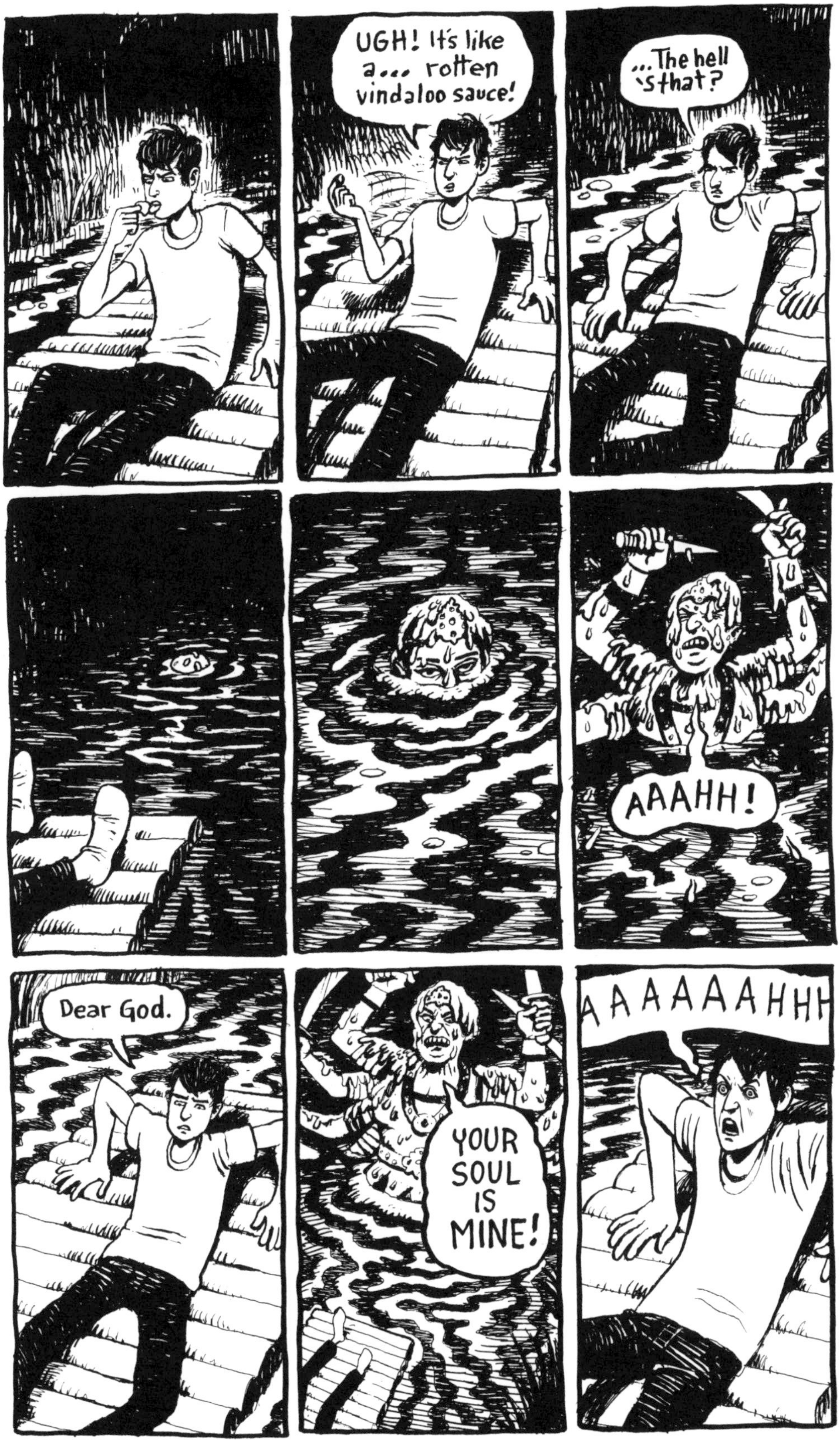
UGH! It's like a... rotten vindaloo sauce!
...The hell 'sthat?
AAAHH!
Dear God.
YOUR SOUL IS MINE!
AAAAAAAHHH

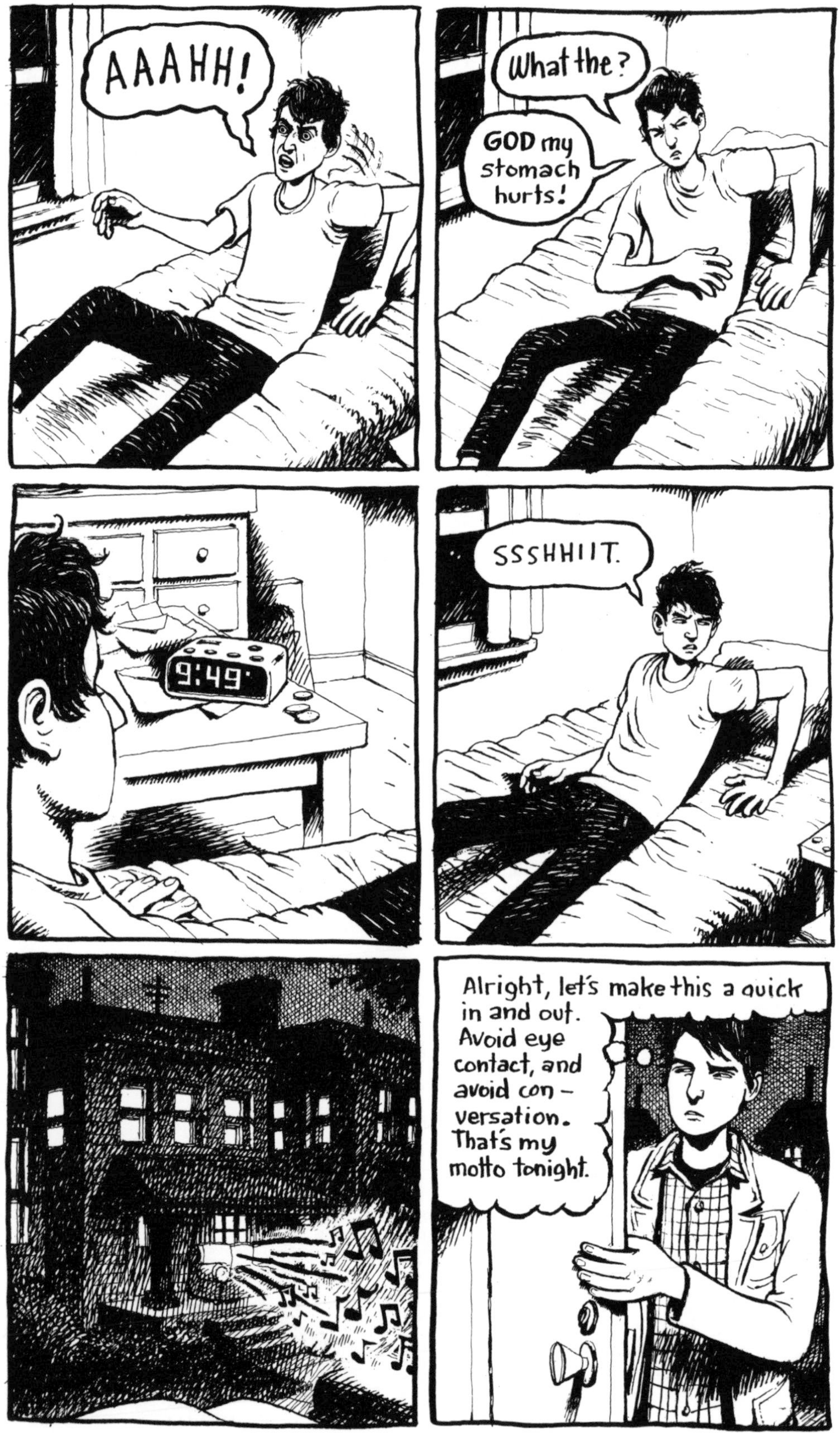
AAAHH!
What the?
GOD my stomach hurts!
9:49
SSSHHIIT.
Alright, let's make this a quick in and out. Avoid eye contact, and avoid con-versation. That's my motto tonight.

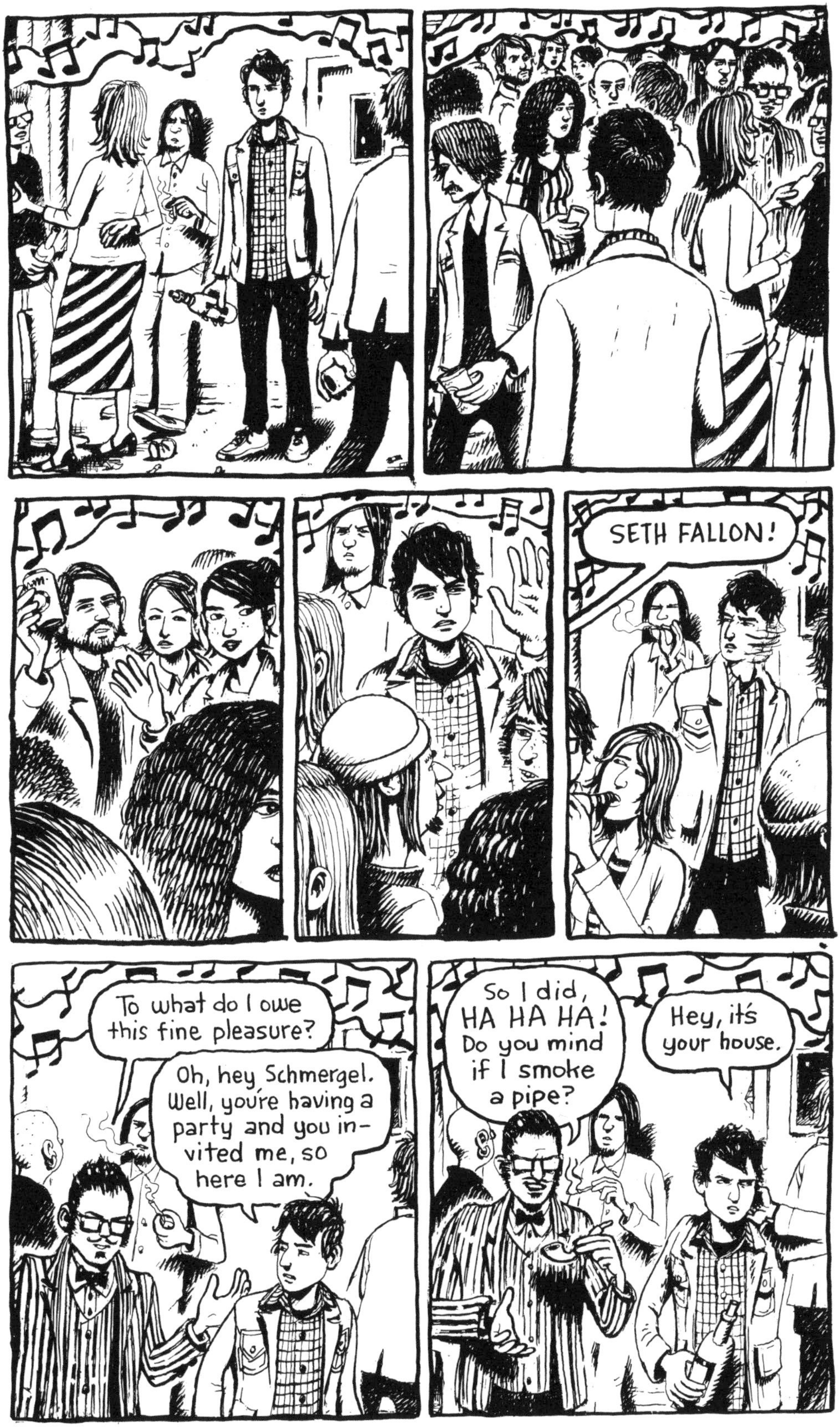
SETH FALLON!
To what do I owe this fine pleasure?
Oh, hey Schmergel. Well, you're having a party and you in-vited me, so here I am.
So I did, HA HA HA! Do you mind if I smoke a pipe?
Hey, it's your house.

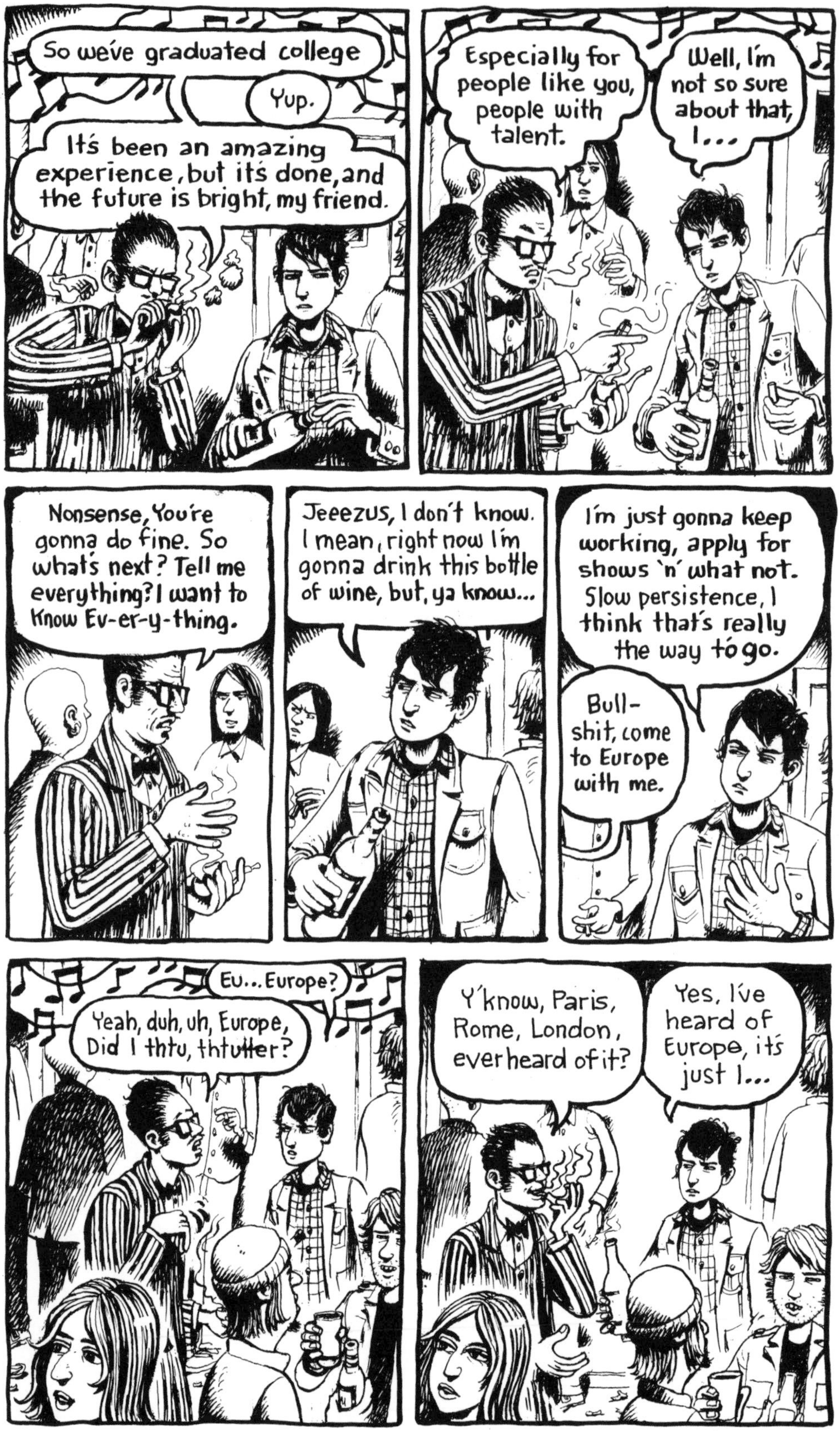
So we've graduated college
Yup.
It's been an amazing experience, but it's done, and the future is bright, my friend.
Especially for people like you, people with talent.
Well, I'm not so sure about that, I...
Nonsense, You're gonna do fine. So what's next? Tell me everything? I want to Know Ev-er-y-thing.
Jeeezus, I don't know. I mean, right now I'm gonna drink this bottle of wine, but, ya know...
I'm just gonna keep working, apply for shows 'n' what not. Slow persistence, I think that's really the way to go.
Bull-shit, come to Europe with me.
Eu... Europe?
Yeah, duh, uh, Europe, Did I thtu, thtutter?
Y'know, Paris, Rome, London, ever heard of it?
Yes, I've heard of Europe, it's just I...

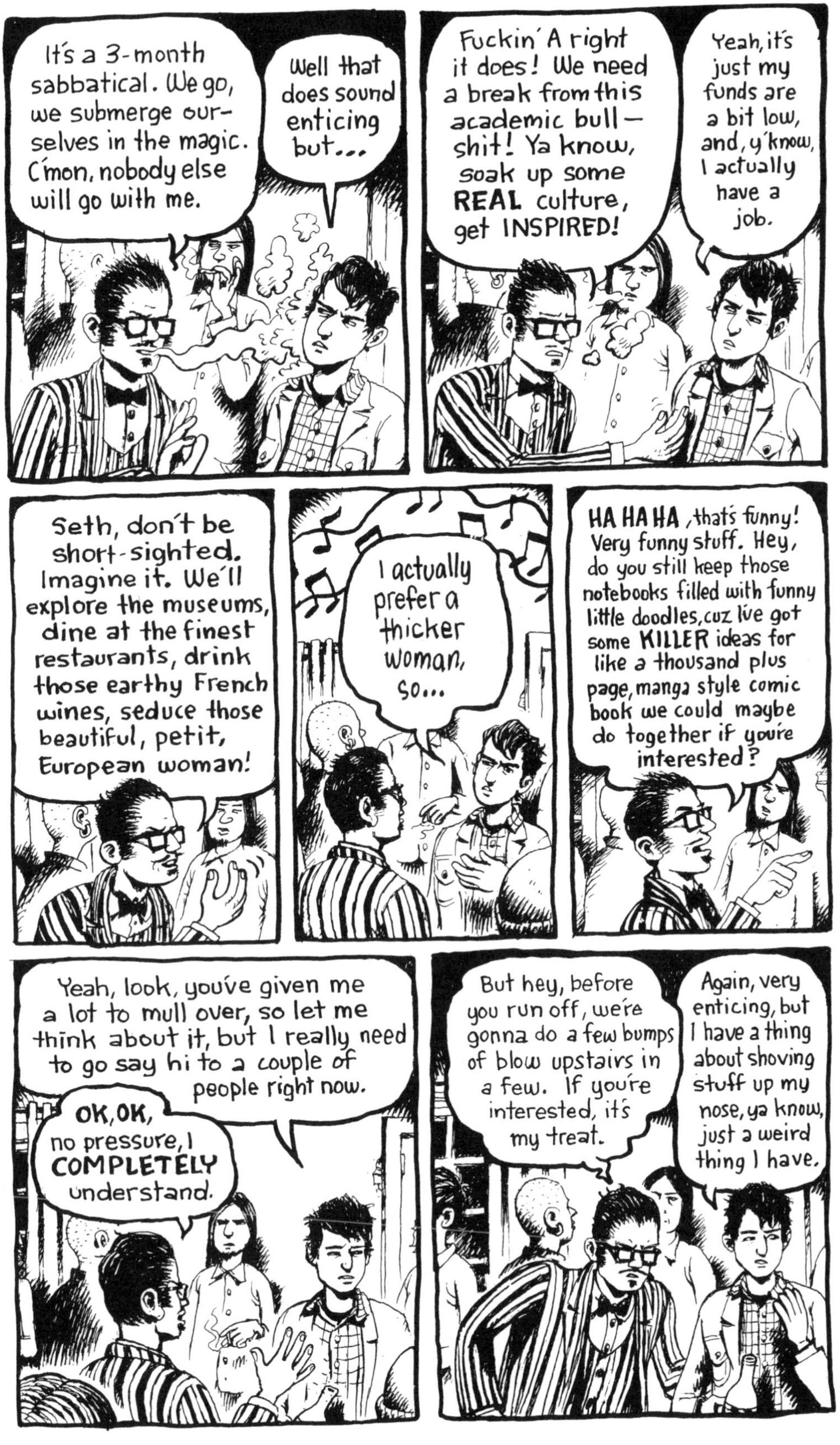
It's a 3-month sabbatical. We go, we submerge our-selves in the magic. C'mon, nobody else will go with me.
Well that does sound enticing but...
Fuckin' A right it does! We need a break from this academic bull-shit! Ya know, soak up some REAL culture, get INSPIRED!
Yeah, it's just my funds are a bit low, and, y'know, I actually have a job.
Seth, don't be short-sighted. Imagine it. We'll explore the museums, dine at the finest restaurants, drink those earthy French wines, seduce those beautiful, petit, European woman!
I actually prefer a thicker woman, so...
HA HA HA, that's funny! Very funny stuff. Hey, do you still keep those notebooks filled with funny little doodles, cuz I've got some KILLER ideas for like a thousand plus page, manga style comic book we could maybe do together if you're interested?
Yeah, look, you've given me a lot to mull over, so let me think about it, but I really need to go say hi to a couple of people right now.
OK, OK, no pressure, I COMPLETELY understand.
But hey, before you run off, we're gonna do a few bumps of blow upstairs in a few. If you're interested, it's my treat.
Again, very enticing, but I have a thing about shoving stuff up my nose, ya know, just a weird thing I have.

Panel 1:

Alright buddy, I'll talk to you soon!

Jesus Christ.

Panel 2:

Did I hear my name?

...the fffuu...

Panel 3:

Oh, hey Fryman.

I'm kidding, you know I don't believe any of that fucking bullshit.

Yeah, I've heard.

Panel 4:

Man, he got caught up with Fryman. We should really go intervene.

Dude, no way am I going over there.

Yeah, me either.

Panel 5:

So, it's good to see you, on the outside, as they say.

Yeah, you too man.

Have you seen my show at the Scum Gallery?

Panel 6:

No, I'm sorry I haven't had a chance to see it yet.

Well do yourself a favor and check it out before it's taken down, because it's stirring up a lot of controversy.

Is that right?

Panel 7:

The Frankford register wrote a story denouncing it because I depicted certain local religious leaders molesting children. Of course, it's all in a metaphorical sense, but now some fucking hick Christian group is all pissed about it.

Wow, what a buncha prudes.

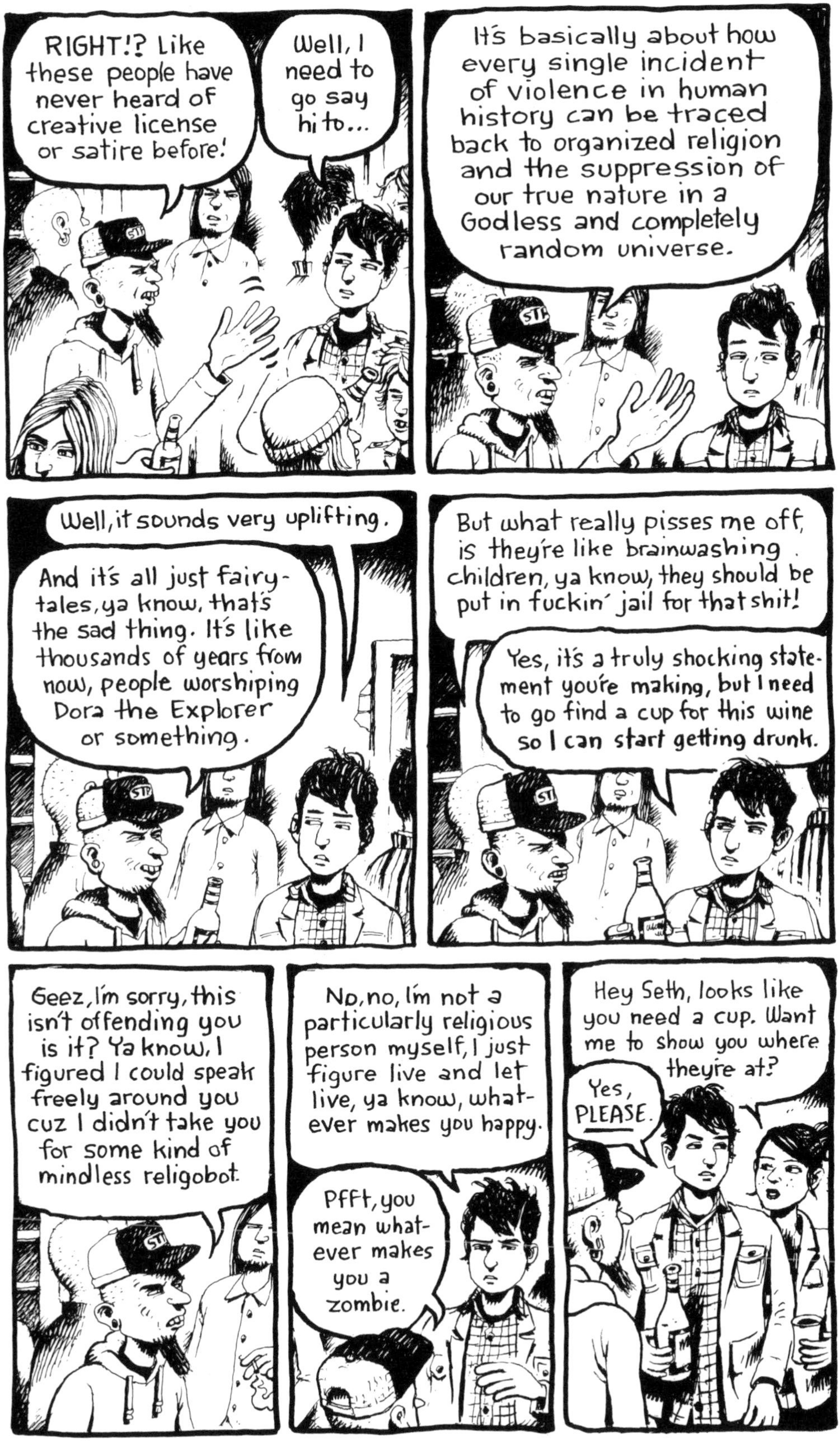
RIGHT!? Like these people have never heard of creative license or satire before!
Well, I need to go say hi to...
It's basically about how every single incident of violence in human history can be traced back to organized religion and the suppression of our true nature in a Godless and completely random universe.
Well, it sounds very uplifting.
And it's all just fairy-tales, ya know, that's the sad thing. It's like thousands of years from now, people worshiping Dora the Explorer or something.
But what really pisses me off, is they're like brainwashing children, ya know, they should be put in fuckin' jail for that shit!
Yes, it's a truly shocking statement you're making, but I need to go find a cup for this wine so I can start getting drunk.
Geez, I'm sorry, this isn't offending you is it? Ya know, I figured I could speak freely around you cuz I didn't take you for some kind of mindless religobot.
No, no, I'm not a particularly religious person myself, I just figure live and let live, ya know, whatever makes you happy.
Pfft, you mean whatever makes you a zombie.
Hey Seth, looks like you need a cup. Want me to show you where they're at?
Yes, PLEASE.

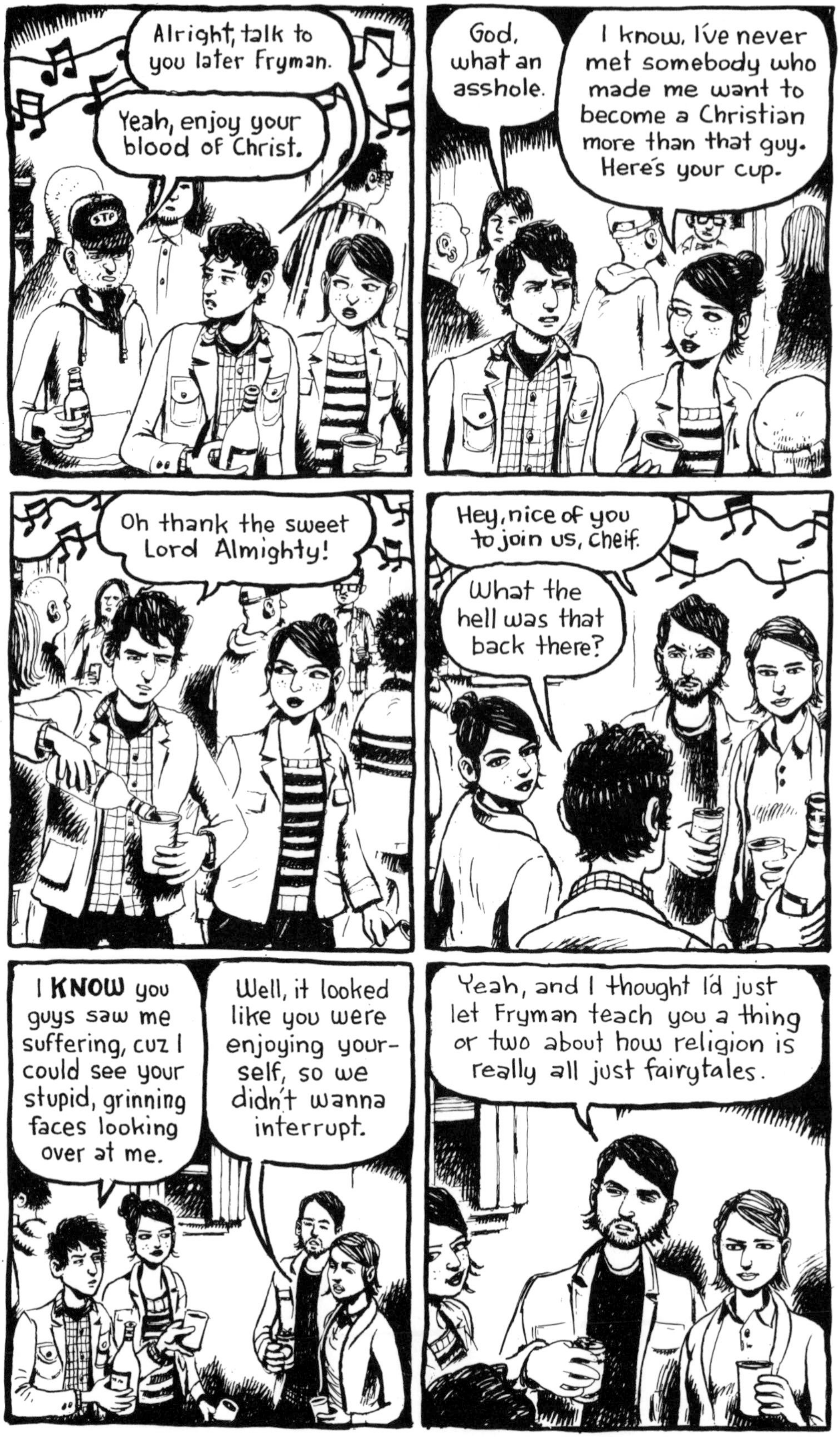
Alright, talk to you later Fryman.
Yeah, enjoy your blood of Christ.
God, what an asshole.
I know, I've never met somebody who made me want to become a Christian more than that guy. Here's your cup.
Oh thank the sweet Lord Almighty!
Hey, nice of you to join us, cheif.
What the hell was that back there?
I **KNOW** you guys saw me suffering, cuz I could see your stupid, grinning faces looking over at me.
Well, it looked like you were enjoying your-self, so we didn't wanna interrupt.
Yeah, and I thought I'd just let Fryman teach you a thing or two about how religion is really all just fairytales.

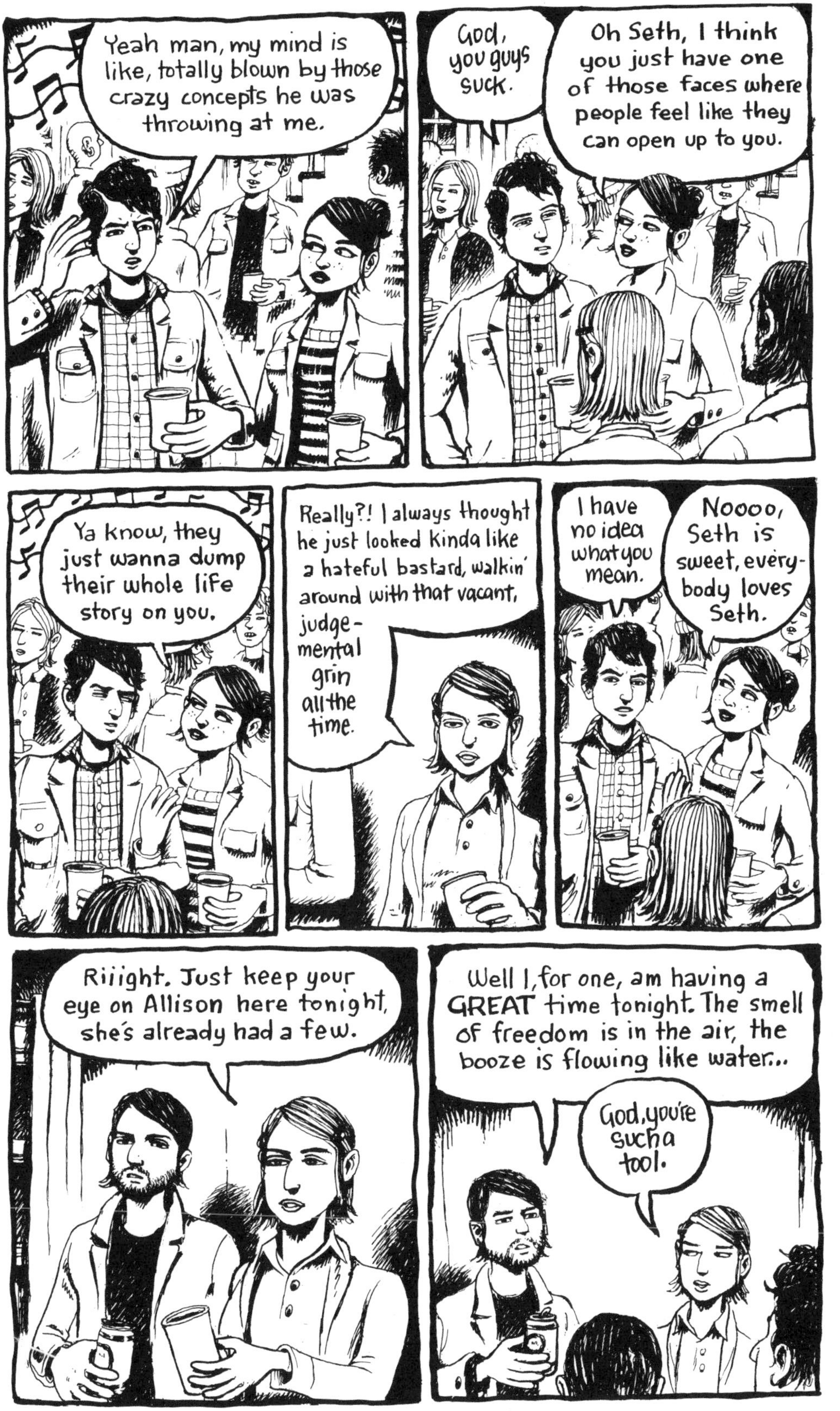
Yeah man, my mind is like, totally blown by those crazy concepts he was throwing at me.
God, you guys suck.
Oh Seth, I think you just have one of those faces where people feel like they can open up to you.
Ya know, they just wanna dump their whole life story on you.
Really?! I always thought he just looked kinda like a hateful bastard, walkin' around with that vacant, judge-mental grin all the time.
I have no idea what you mean.
Noooo, Seth is sweet, every-body loves Seth.
Riiight. Just keep your eye on Allison here tonight, she's already had a few.
Well I, for one, am having a GREAT time tonight. The smell of freedom is in the air, the booze is flowing like water...
God, you're such a tool.

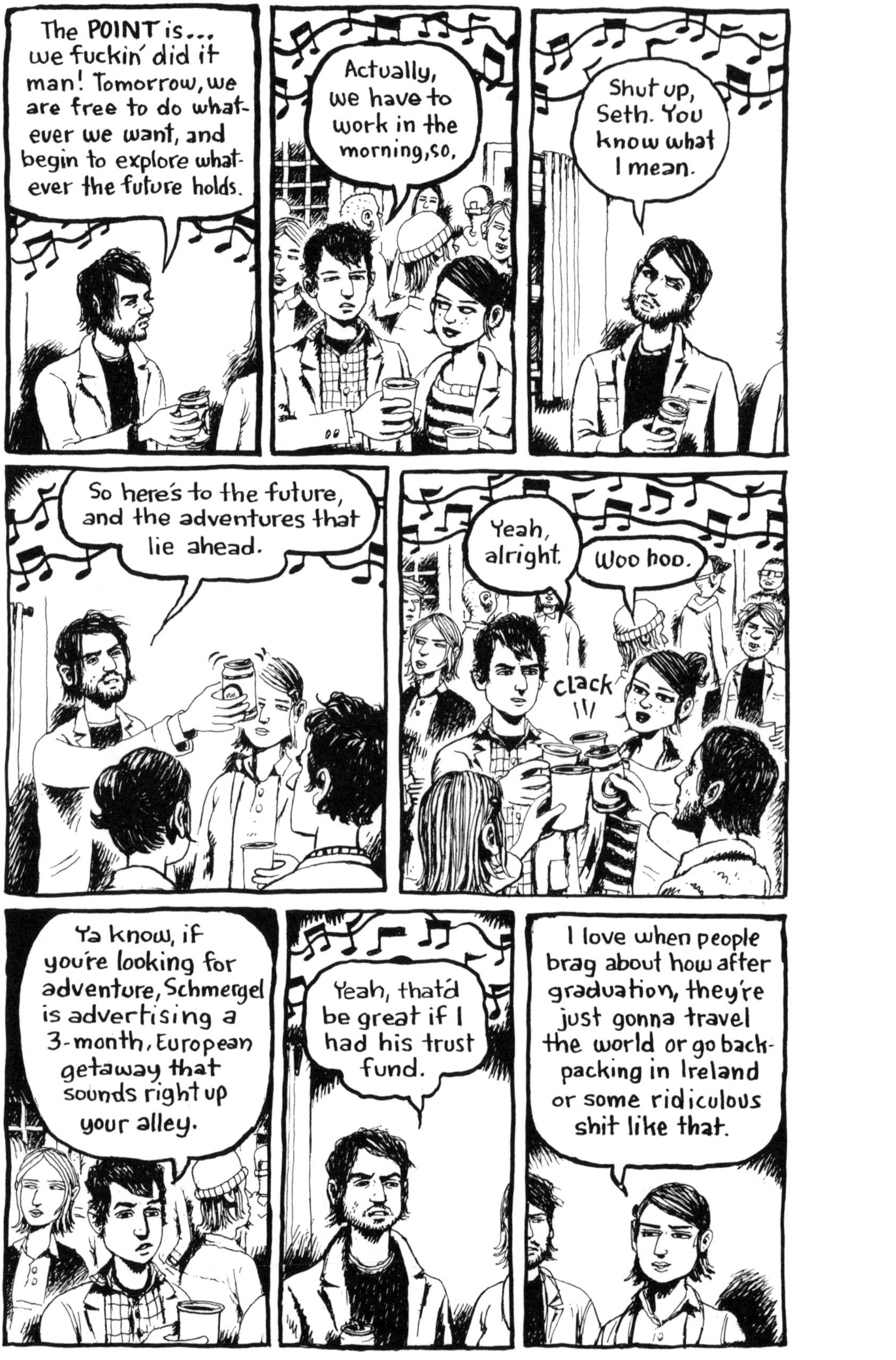
The POINT is... we fuckin' did it man! Tomorrow, we are free to do whatever we want, and begin to explore whatever the future holds.
Actually, we have to work in the morning, so,
Shut up, Seth. You know what I mean.
So here's to the future, and the adventures that lie ahead.
Yeah, alright.
Woo hoo.
CLACK
Ya know, if you're looking for adventure, Schmergel is advertising a 3-month, European getaway that sounds right up your alley.
Yeah, that'd be great if I had his trust fund.
I love when people brag about how after graduation, they're just gonna travel the world or go backpacking in Ireland or some ridiculous shit like that.

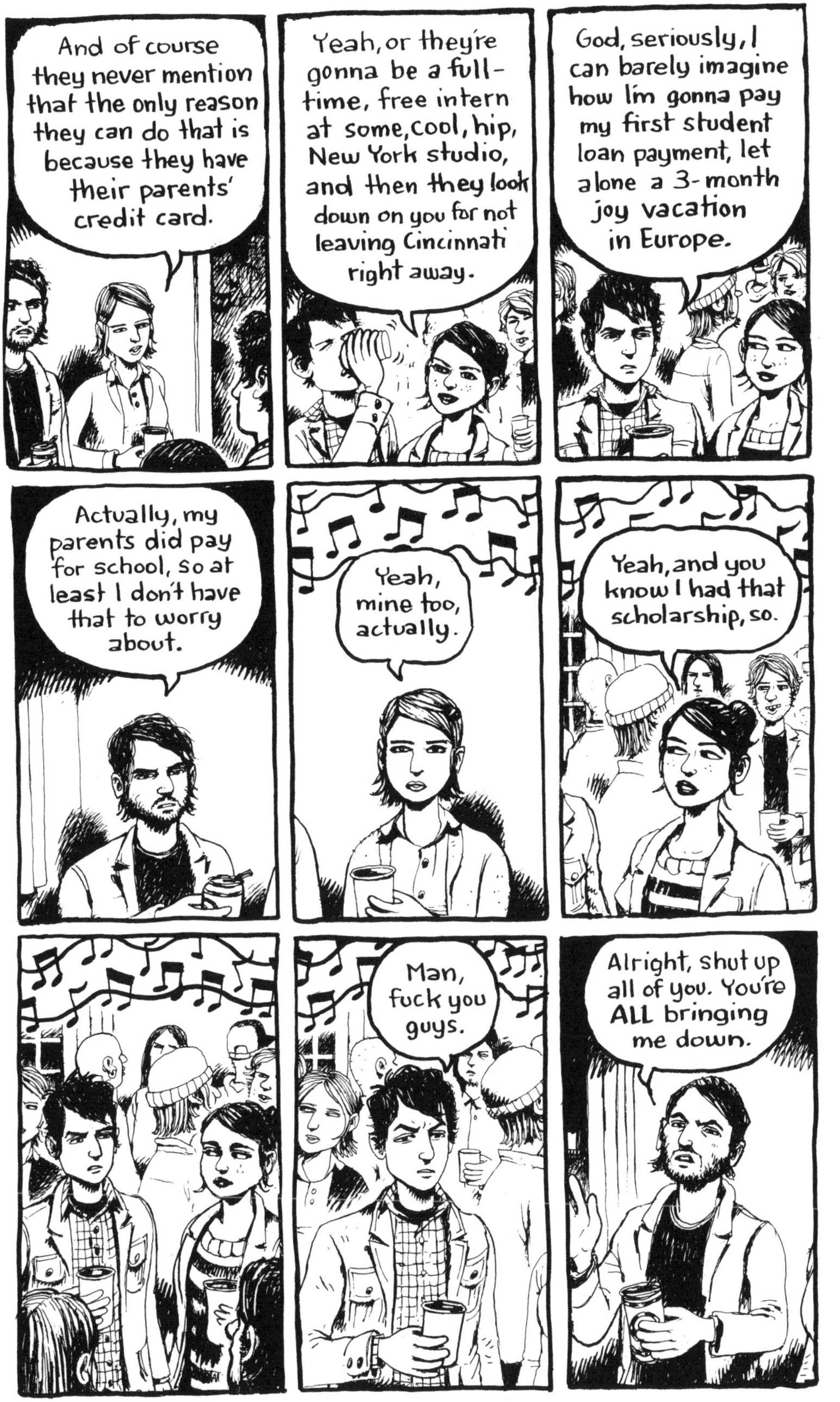
And of course they never mention that the only reason they can do that is because they have their parents' credit card.
Yeah, or they're gonna be a full-time, free intern at some, cool, hip, New York studio, and then they look down on you for not leaving Cincinnati right away.
God, seriously, I can barely imagine how I'm gonna pay my first student loan payment, let alone a 3-month joy vacation in Europe.
Actually, my parents did pay for school, so at least I don't have that to worry about.
Yeah, mine too, actually.
Yeah, and you know I had that scholarship, so.
Man, fuck you guys.
Alright, shut up all of you. You're ALL bringing me down.

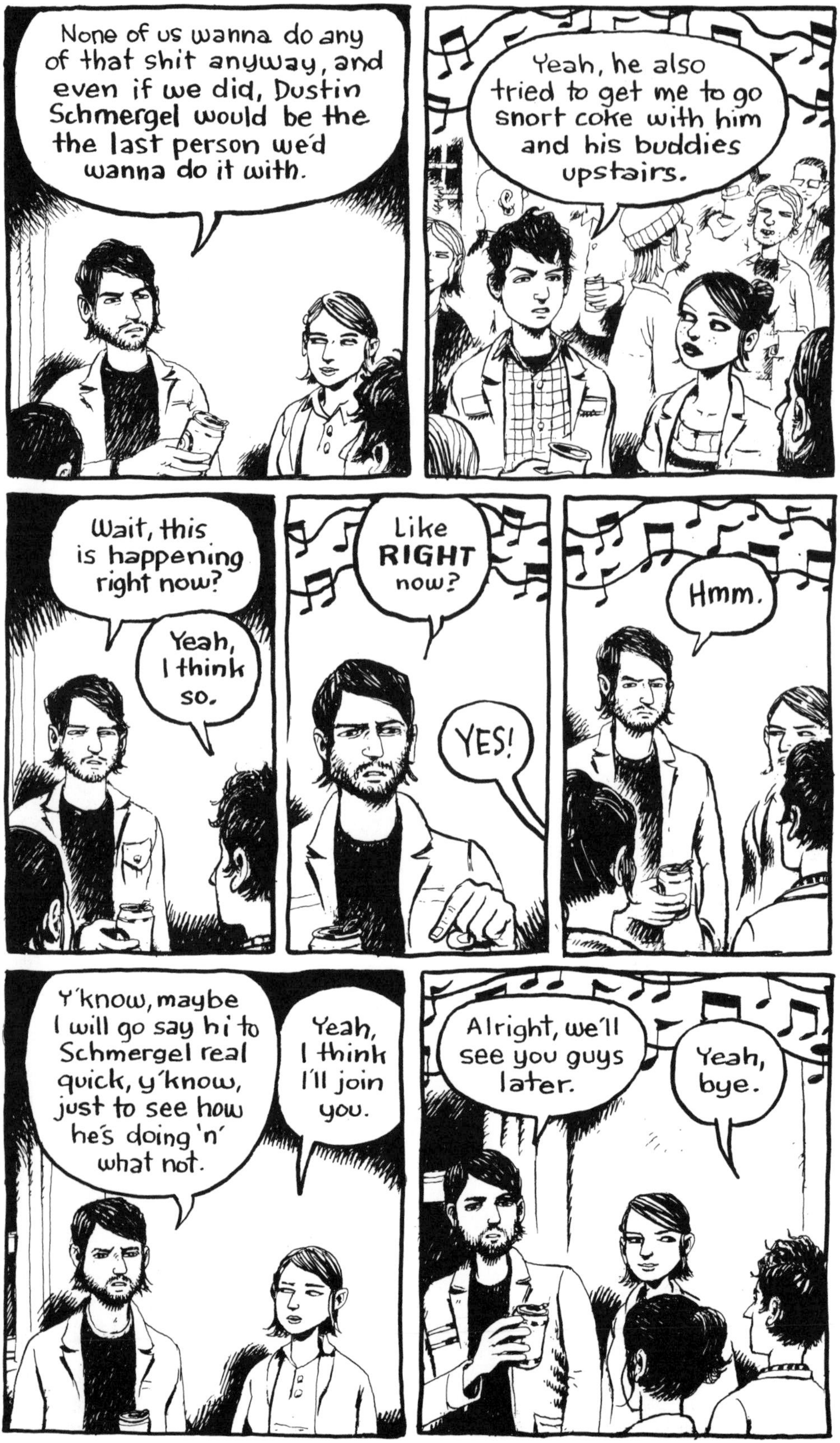
None of us wanna do any of that shit anyway, and even if we did, Dustin Schmergel would be the the last person we'd wanna do it with.
Yeah, he also tried to get me to go snort coke with him and his buddies upstairs.
Wait, this is happening right now?
Yeah, I think so.
Like RIGHT now?
YES!
Hmm.
Y'know, maybe I will go say hi to Schmergel real quick, y'know, just to see how he's doing 'n' what not.
Yeah, I think I'll join you.
Alright, we'll see you guys later.
Yeah, bye.

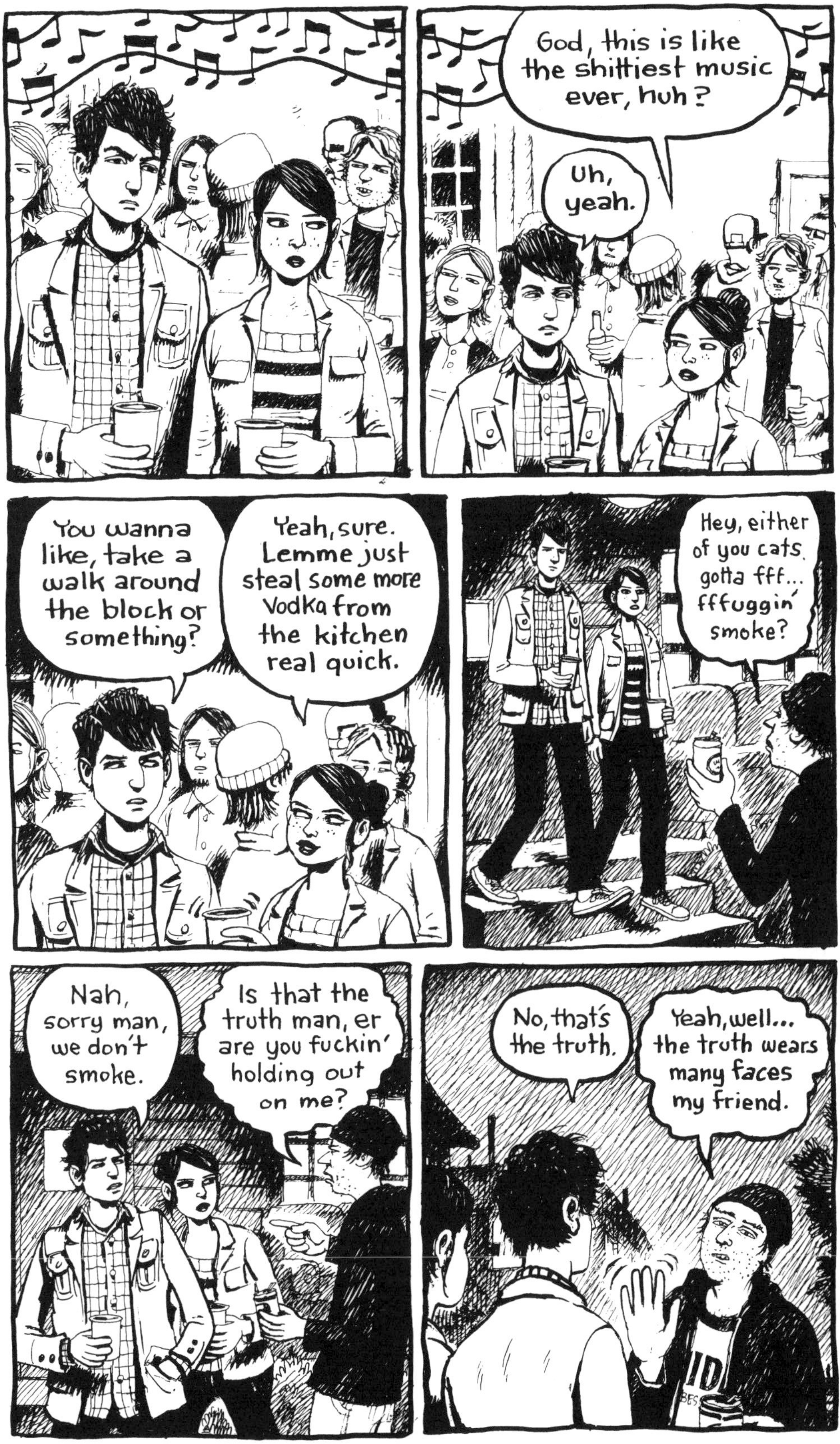
God, this is like the shittiest music ever, huh?
Uh, yeah.
You wanna like, take a walk around the block or something?
Yeah, sure. Lemme just steal some more Vodka from the kitchen real quick.
Hey, either of you cats gotta fff... fffuggin' smoke?
Nah, sorry man, we don't smoke.
Is that the truth man, er are you fuckin' holding out on me?
No, that's the truth.
Yeah, well... the truth wears many faces my friend.

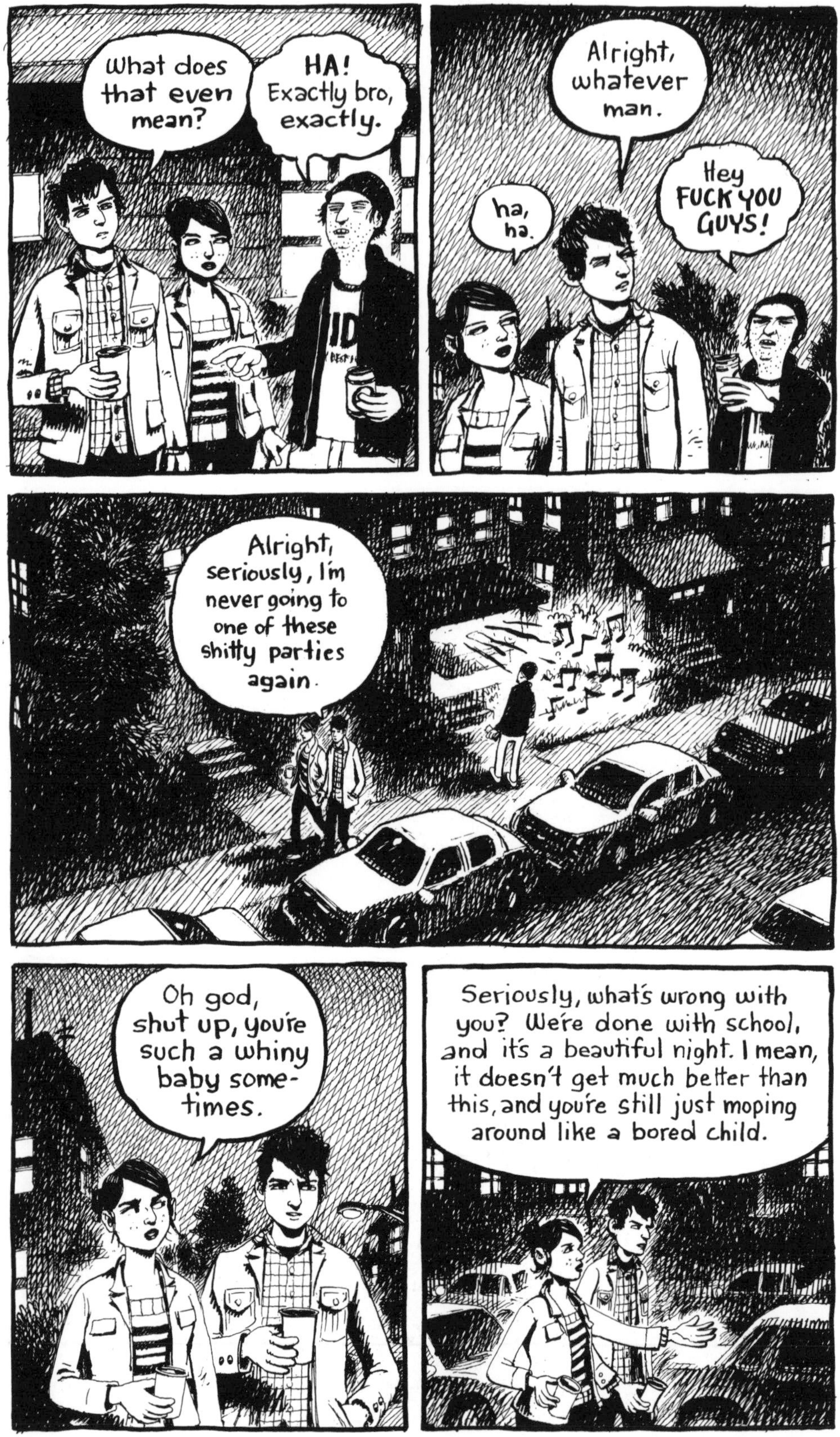
What does that even mean?
HA! Exactly bro, exactly.
Alright, whatever man.
ha, ha.
Hey FUCK YOU GUYS!
Alright, seriously, I'm never going to one of these shitty parties again.
Oh god, shut up, you're such a whiny baby some-times.
Seriously, what's wrong with you? We're done with school, and it's a beautiful night. I mean, it doesn't get much better than this, and you're still just moping around like a bored child.

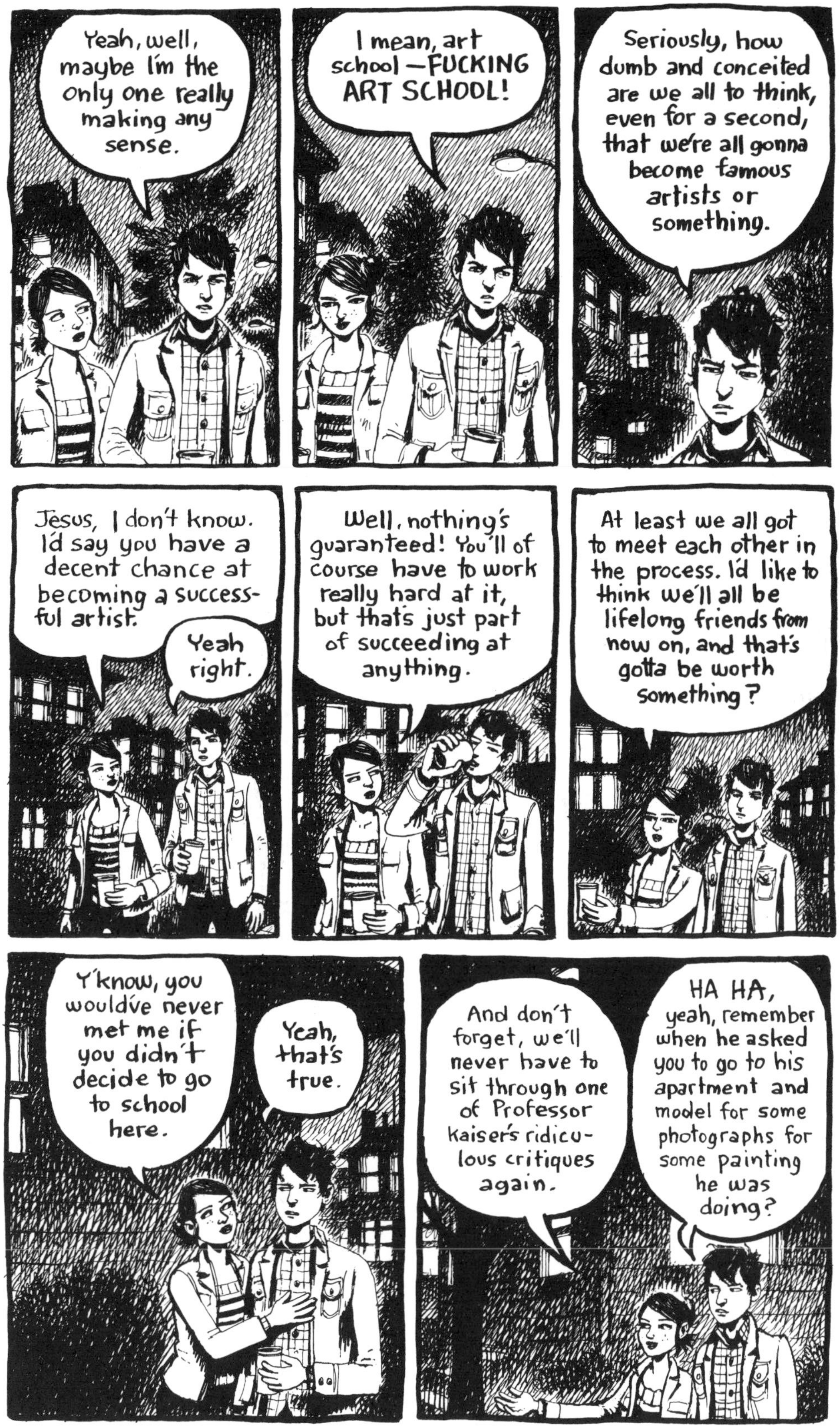
Yeah, well, maybe I'm the only one really making any sense.
I mean, art school—FUCKING ART SCHOOL!
Seriously, how dumb and conceited are we all to think, even for a second, that we're all gonna become famous artists or something.
Jesus, I don't know. I'd say you have a decent chance at becoming a successful artist.
Yeah right.
Well, nothing's guaranteed! You'll of course have to work really hard at it, but that's just part of succeeding at anything.
At least we all got to meet each other in the process. I'd like to think we'll all be lifelong friends from now on, and that's gotta be worth something?
Y'know, you would've never met me if you didn't decide to go to school here.
Yeah, that's true.
And don't forget, we'll never have to sit through one of Professor Kaiser's ridiculous critiques again.
HA HA, yeah, remember when he asked you to go to his apartment and model for some photographs for some painting he was doing?

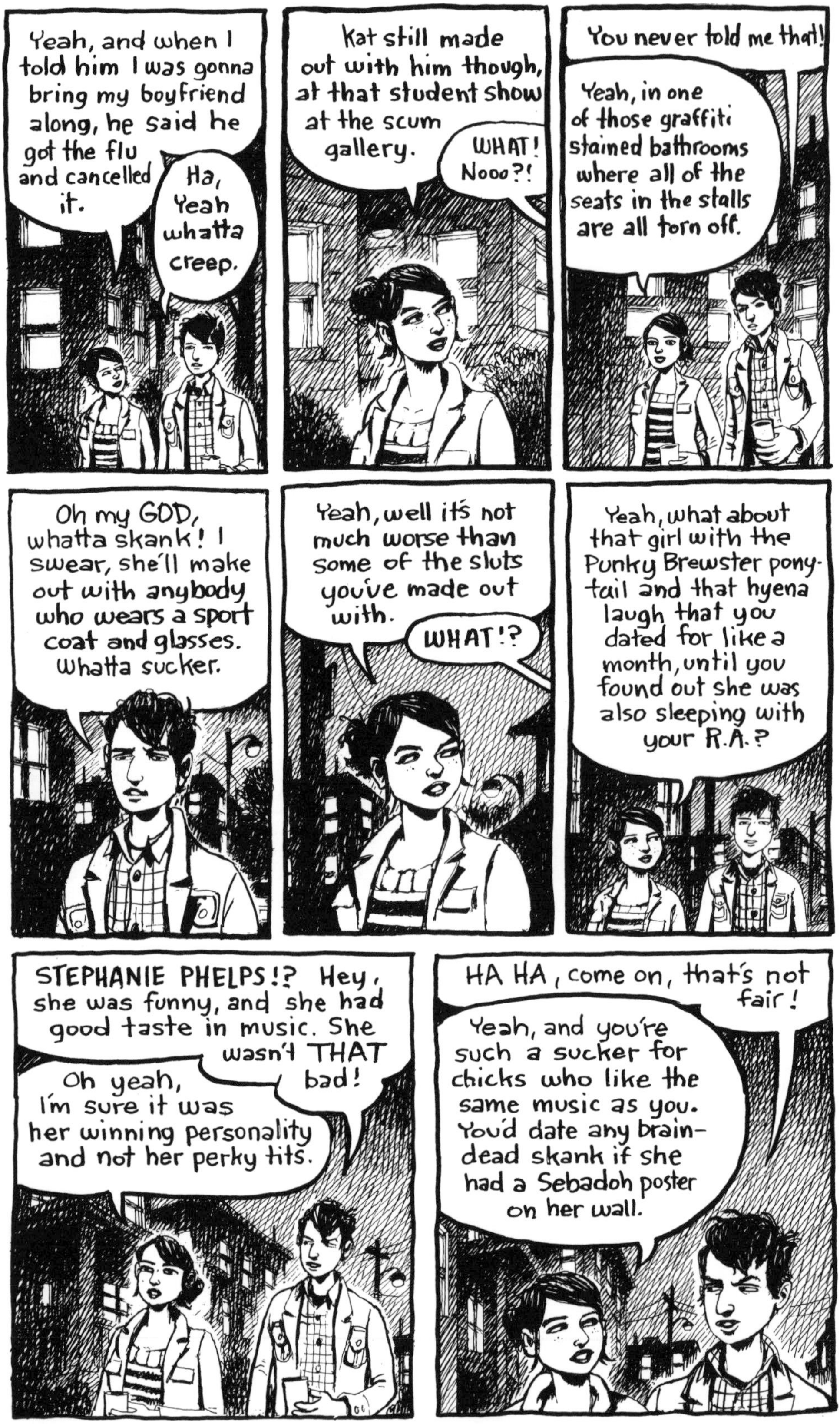
Yeah, and when I told him I was gonna bring my boyfriend along, he said he got the flu and cancelled it.
Ha, Yeah whatta creep.
Kat still made out with him though, at that student show at the scum gallery.
WHAT! Nooo?!
You never told me that!
Yeah, in one of those graffiti stained bathrooms where all of the seats in the stalls are all torn off.
Oh my GOD, whatta skank! I swear, she'll make out with anybody who wears a sport coat and glasses. Whatta sucker.
Yeah, well it's not much worse than some of the sluts you've made out with.
WHAT!?
Yeah, what about that girl with the Punky Brewster pony-tail and that hyena laugh that you dated for like a month, until you found out she was also sleeping with your R.A.?
STEPHANIE PHELPS!? Hey, she was funny, and she had good taste in music. She wasn't THAT bad!
Oh yeah, I'm sure it was her winning personality and not her perky tits.
HA HA, come on, that's not fair!
Yeah, and you're such a sucker for chicks who like the same music as you. You'd date any brain-dead skank if she had a Sebadoh poster on her wall.

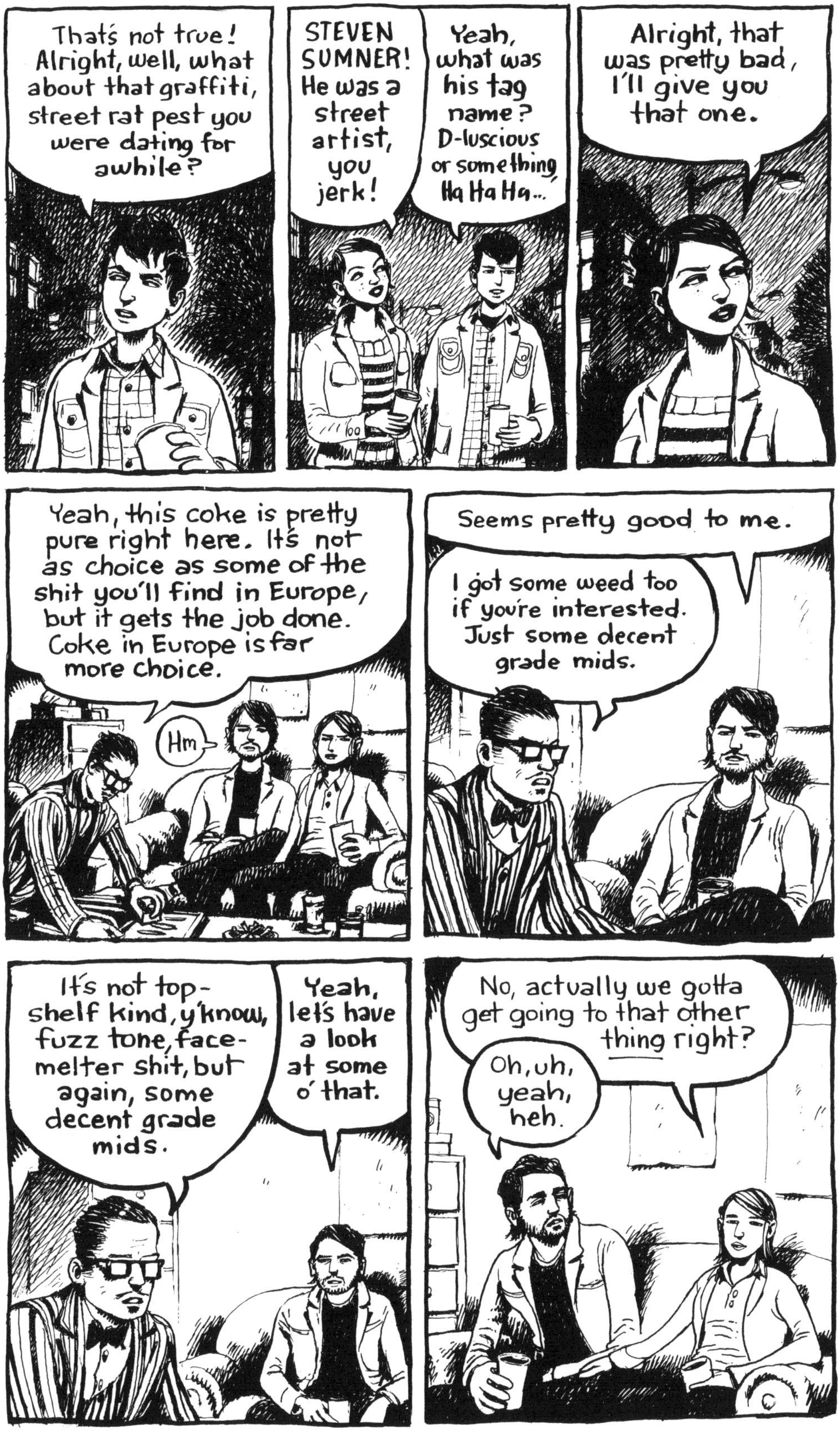
That's not true! Alright, well, what about that graffiti, street rat pest you were dating for awhile?
STEVEN SUMNER! He was a street artist, you jerk!
Yeah, what was his tag name? D-luscious or something, Ha Ha Ha...
Alright, that was pretty bad, I'll give you that one.
Yeah, this coke is pretty pure right here. It's not as choice as some of the shit you'll find in Europe, but it gets the job done. Coke in Europe is far more choice.
Hm
Seems pretty good to me.
I got some weed too if you're interested. Just some decent grade mids.
It's not top-shelf kind, y'know, fuzz tone, face-melter shit, but again, some decent grade mids.
Yeah, let's have a look at some o' that.
No, actually we gotta get going to that other thing right?
Oh, uh, yeah, heh.

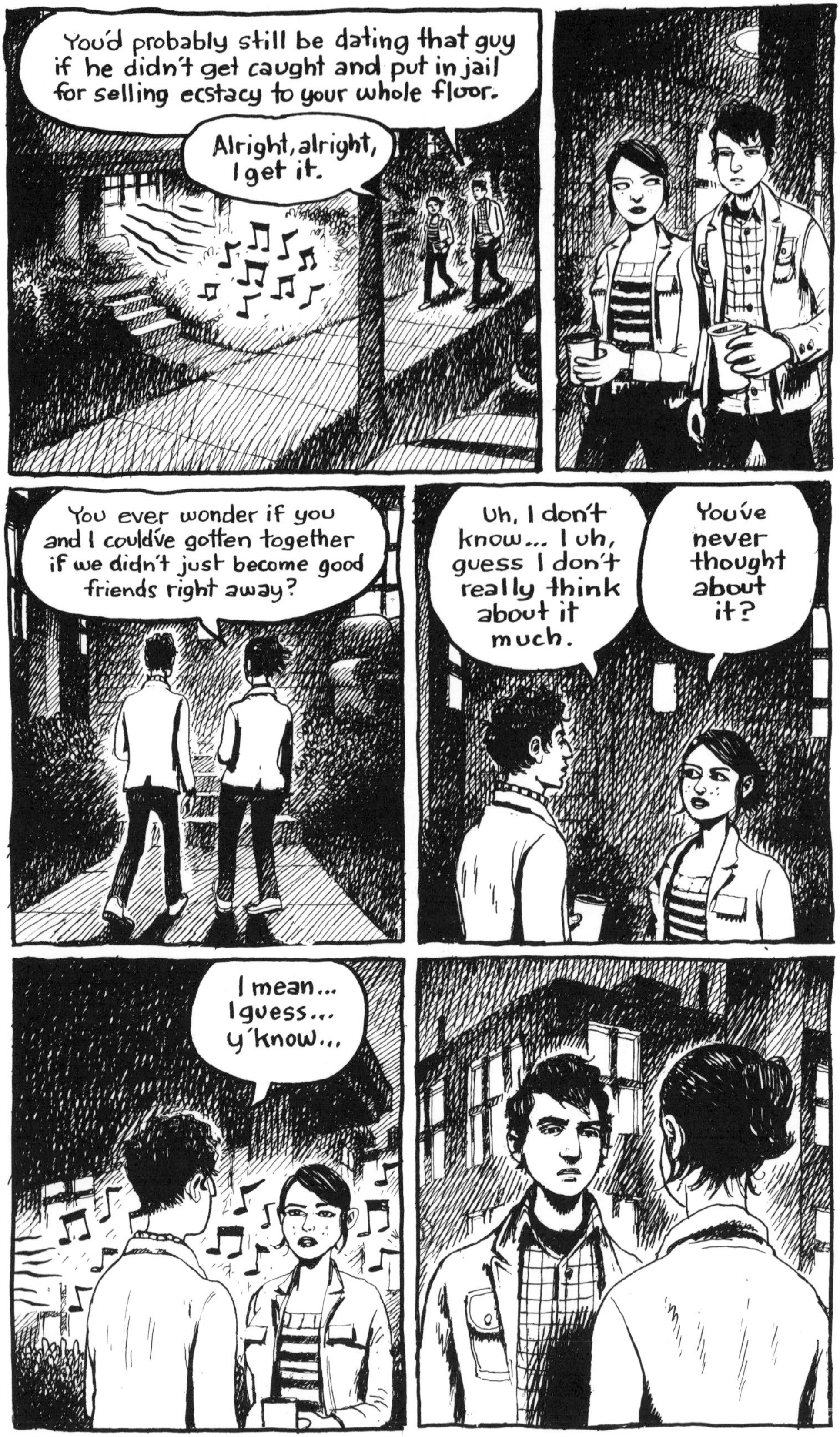
You'd probably still be dating that guy if he didn't get caught and put in jail for selling ecstacy to your whole floor.
Alright, alright, I get it.
You ever wonder if you and I could've gotten together if we didn't just become good friends right away?
Uh, I don't know... I uh, guess I don't really think about it much.
You've never thought about it?
I mean... I guess... y'know...

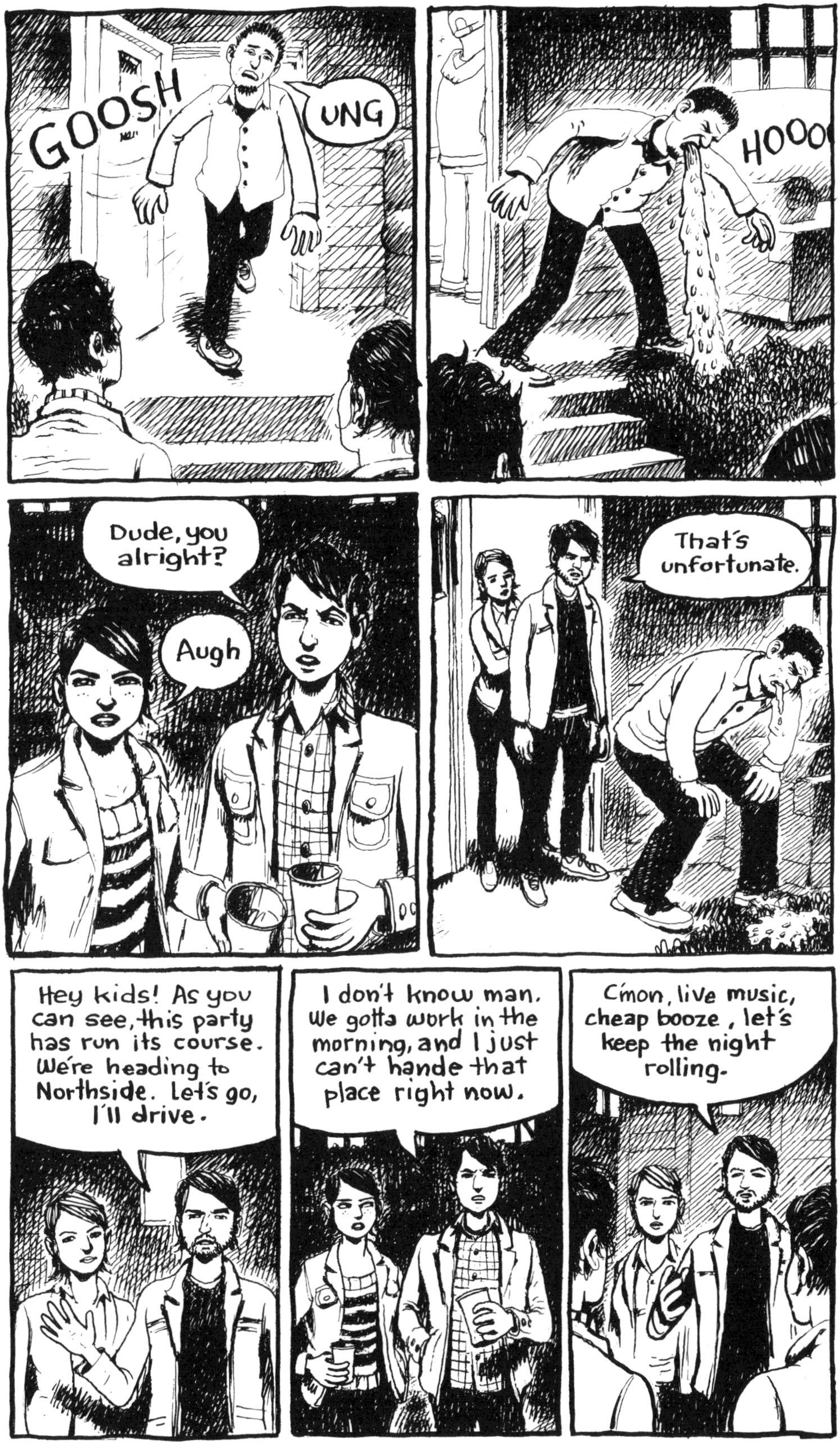
GOOSH
UNG
HOOO
Dude, you alright?
Augh
That's unfortunate.
Hey kids! As you can see, this party has run its course. We're heading to Northside. Let's go, I'll drive.
I don't know man. We gotta work in the morning, and I just can't hande that place right now.
C'mon, live music, cheap booze, let's keep the night rolling.

Allison, you're definitely coming. That cute guy from that film class is gonna be there. His friend just texted me.

You don't wanna go there. Y'know, all that obnoxious music and the guys with the haircuts.

Yeah, I don't know.

Seth, if you don't wanna go, that's fine, but don't ruin everybody else's night just because you hate seeing other people have a good time

Hey, it's up to you, y'know, we just gotta be at the studio by nine, and Professor Lasky has been really cranky ever since his divorce, so we should really get there on time, y'know.

Oh God, let's go already. You guys can have more girl talk at work tomorrow.

Alright, I'm coming. See you in the morning, okay?

Yeah, alright, have fun.

See ya bitch boy!

Yeah, bye.

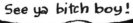

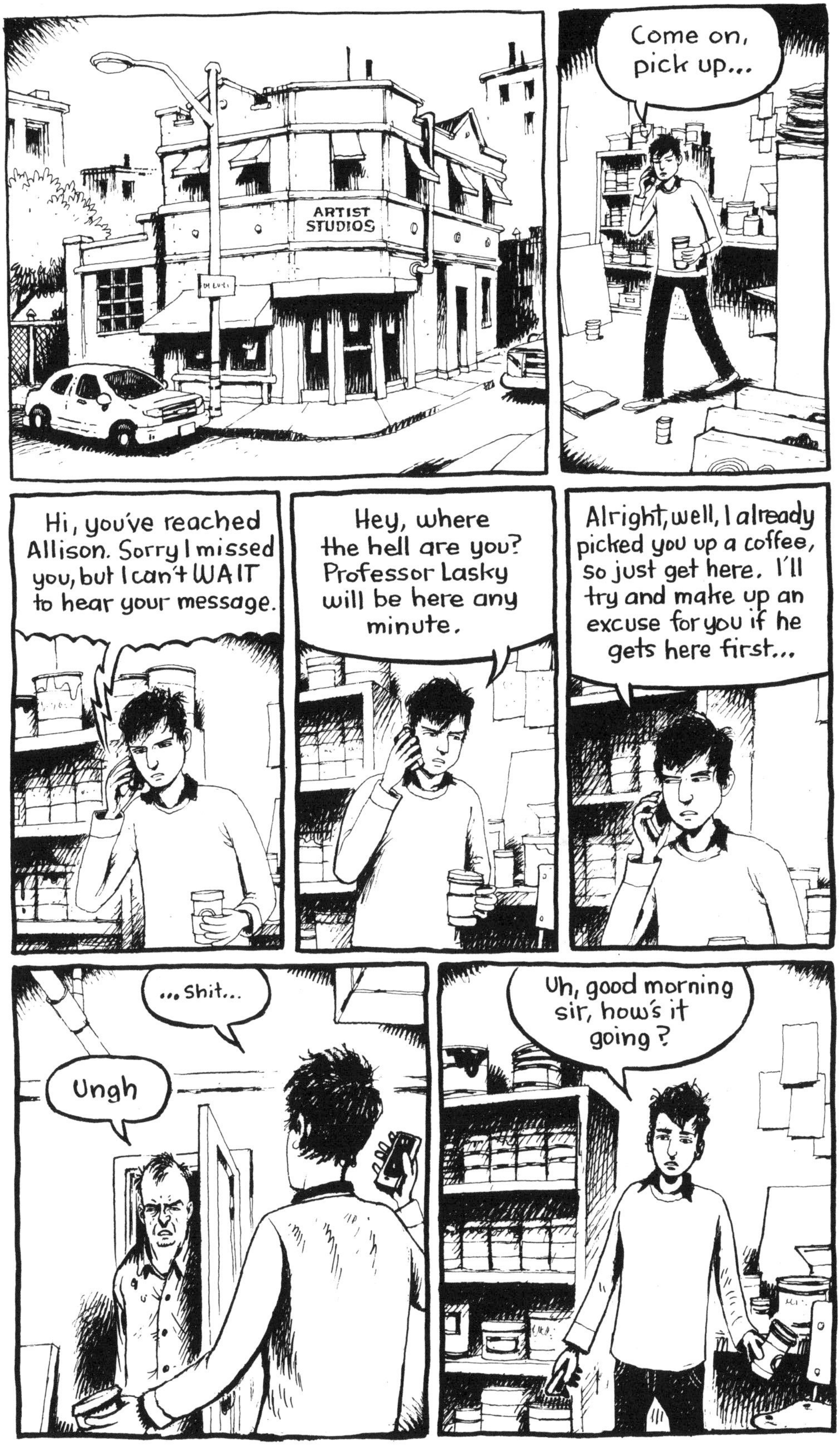
ARTIST STUDIOS
Come on, pick up...
Hi, you've reached Allison. Sorry I missed you, but I can't WAIT to hear your message.
Hey, where the hell are you? Professor Lasky will be here any minute.
Alright, well, I already picked you up a coffee, so just get here. I'll try and make up an excuse for you if he gets here first...
...Shit...
Ungh
Uh, good morning sir, how's it going?

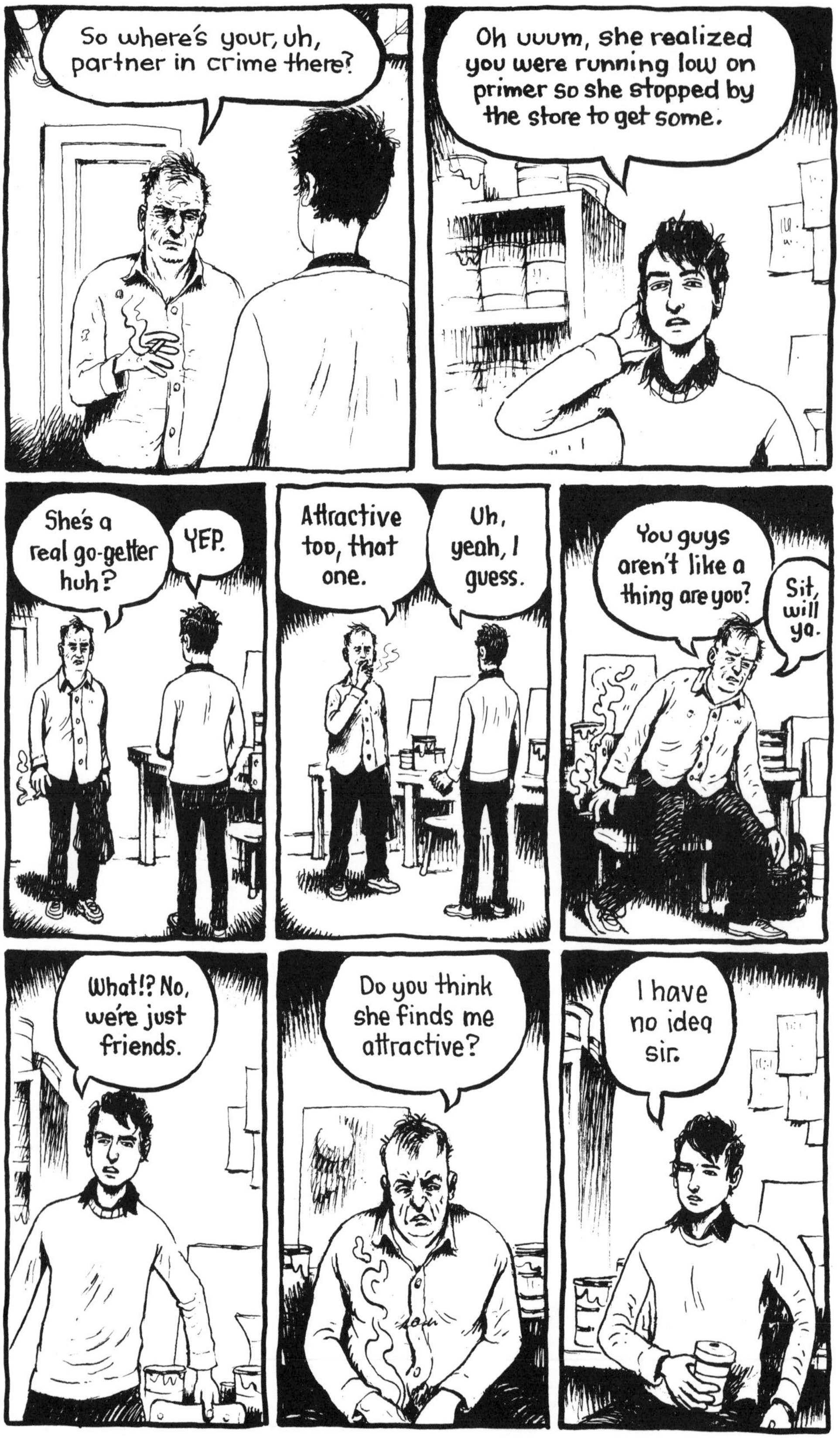

So where's your, uh, partner in crime there?
Oh uuum, she realized you were running low on primer so she stopped by the store to get some.
She's a real go-getter huh?
YEP.
Attractive too, that one.
Uh, yeah, I guess.
You guys aren't like a thing are you?
Sit, will ya.
What!? No, we're just friends.
Do you think she finds me attractive?
I have no idea sir.

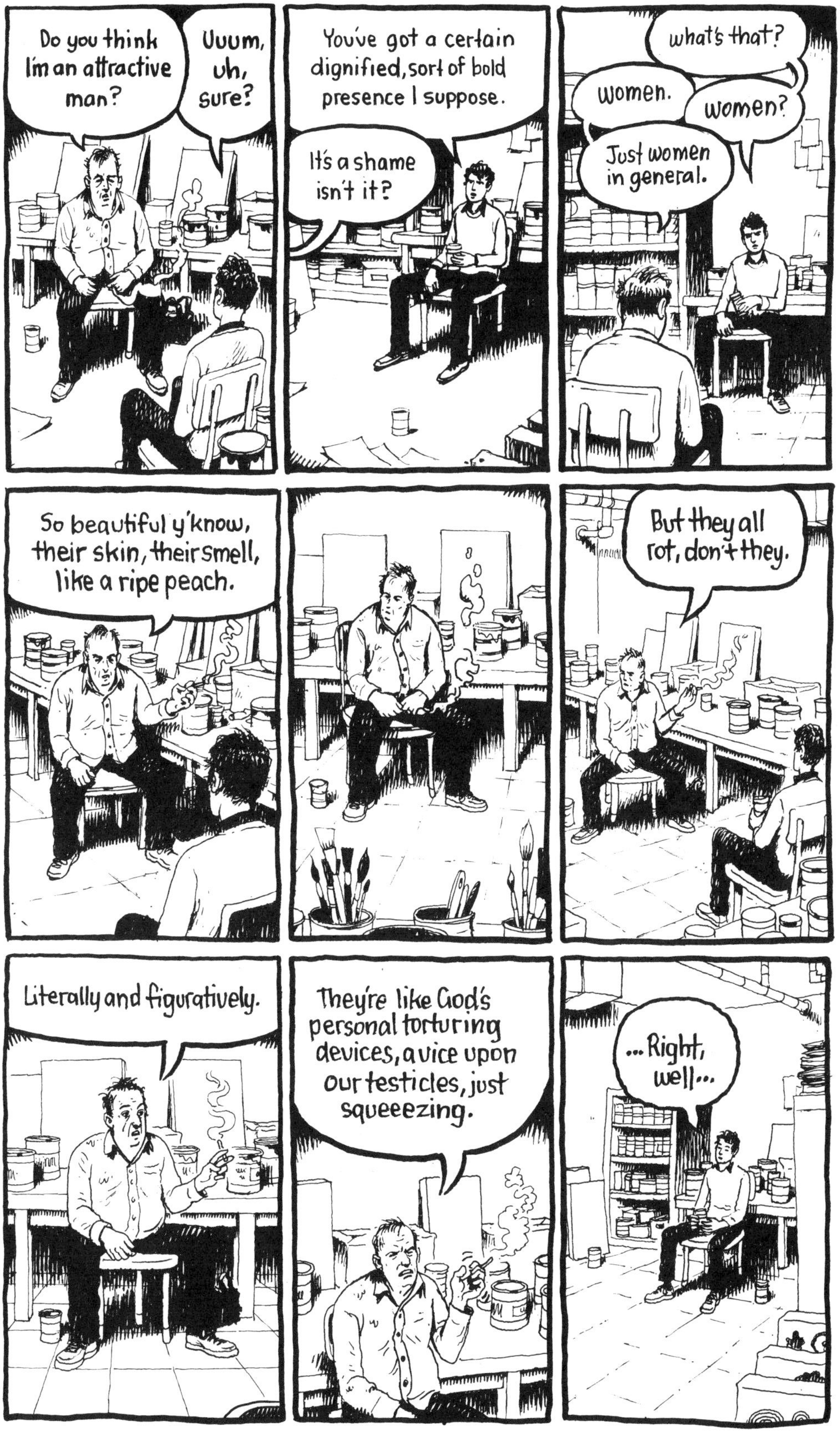
Do you think I'm an attractive man?
Uuum, uh, sure?
You've got a certain dignified, sort of bold presence I suppose.
It's a shame isn't it?
what's that?
women.
women?
Just women in general.
So beautiful y'know, their skin, their smell, like a ripe peach.
But they all rot, don't they.
Literally and figuratively.
They're like God's personal torturing devices, a vice upon our testicles, just squeeezing.
...Right, well...

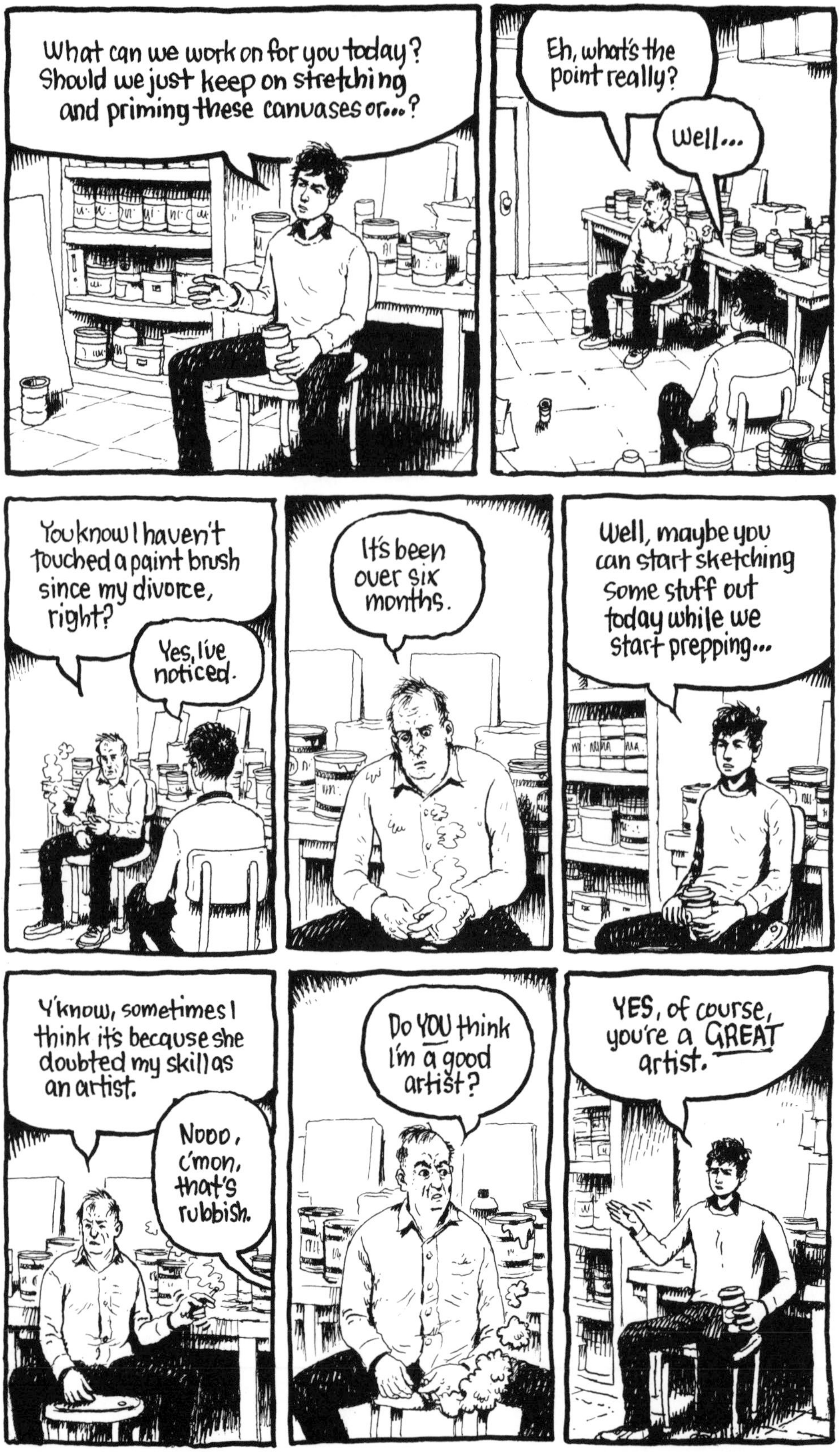
What can we work on for you today? Should we just keep on stretching and priming these canvases or...?
Eh, what's the point really?
Well...
You know I haven't touched a paint brush since my divorce, right?
Yes, I've noticed.
It's been over six months.
Well, maybe you can start sketching some stuff out today while we start prepping...
Y'know, sometimes I think it's because she doubted my skill as an artist.
Nooo, c'mon, that's rubbish.
Do YOU think I'm a good artist?
YES, of course, you're a GREAT artist.

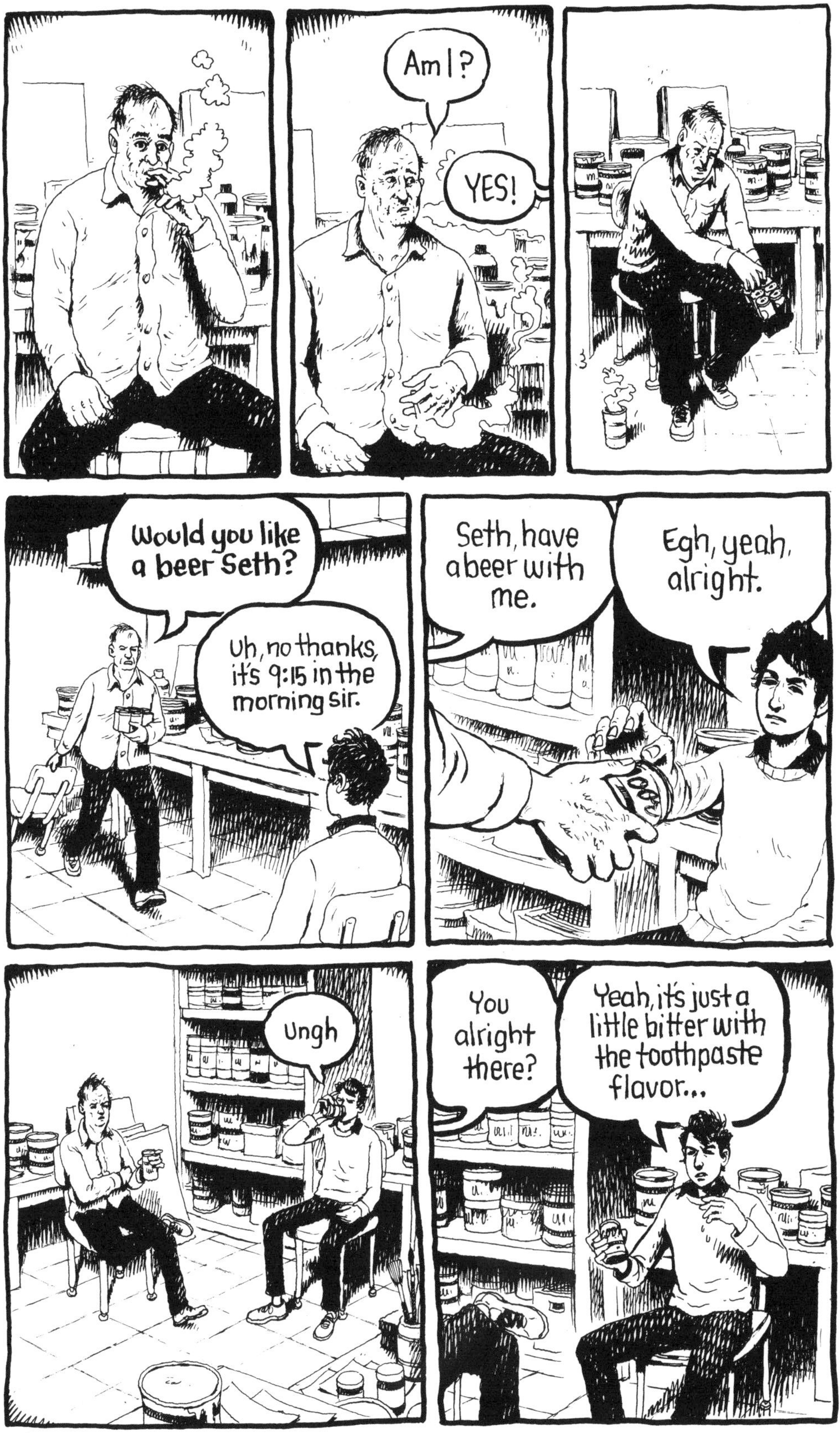
Am I?
YES!
Would you like a beer Seth?
Uh, no thanks, it's 9:15 in the morning sir.
Seth, have a beer with me.
Egh, yeah, alright.
Ungh
You alright there?
Yeah, it's just a little bitter with the toothpaste flavor...

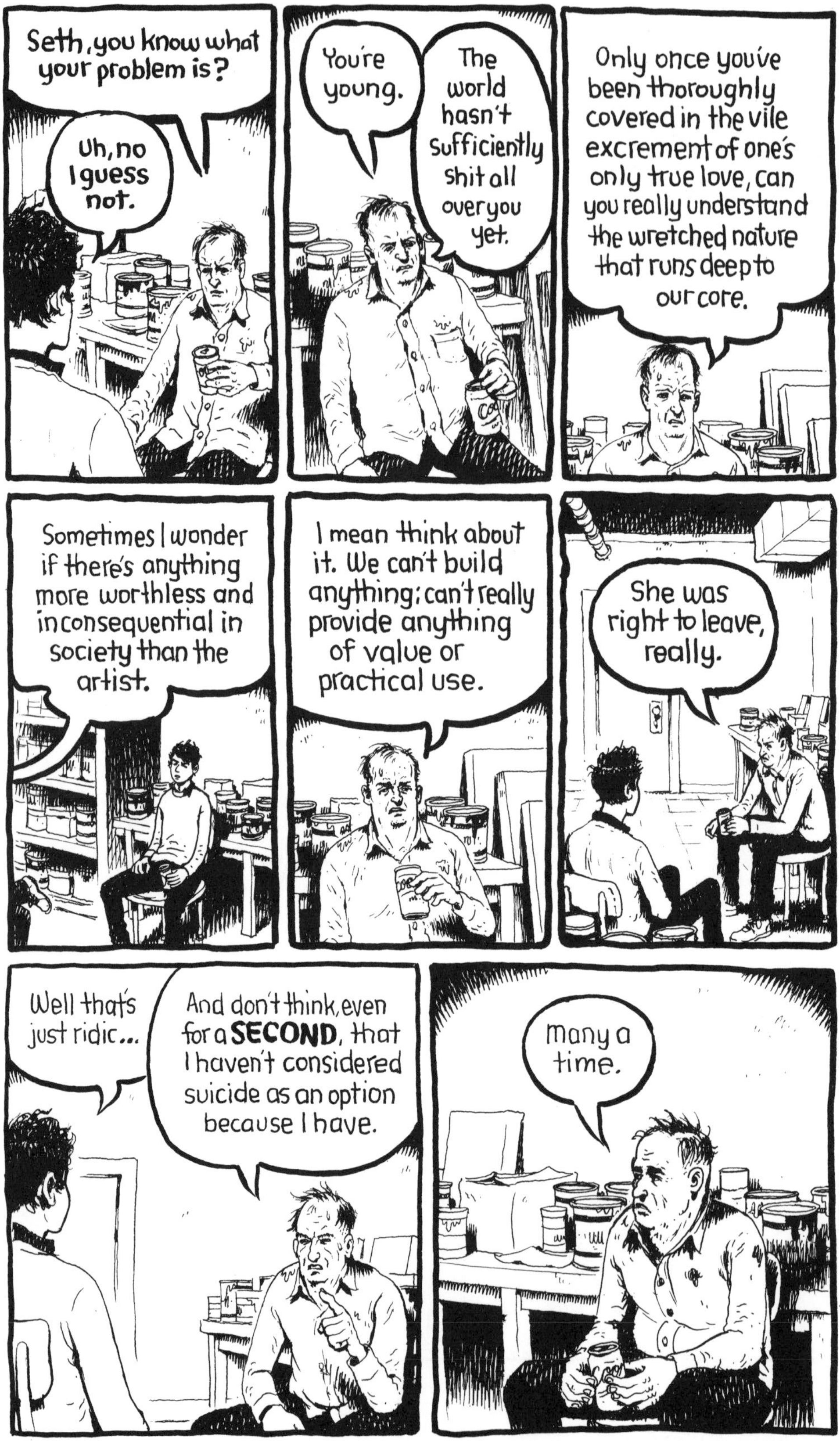

Seth, you know what your problem is?
Uh, no I guess not.
You're young.
The world hasn't sufficiently shit all over you yet.
Only once you've been thoroughly covered in the vile excrement of one's only true love, can you really understand the wretched nature that runs deep to our core.
Sometimes I wonder if there's anything more worthless and inconsequential in society than the artist.
I mean think about it. We can't build anything; can't really provide anything of value or practical use.
She was right to leave, really.
Well that's just ridic...
And don't think, even for a SECOND, that I haven't considered suicide as an option because I have.
Many a time.

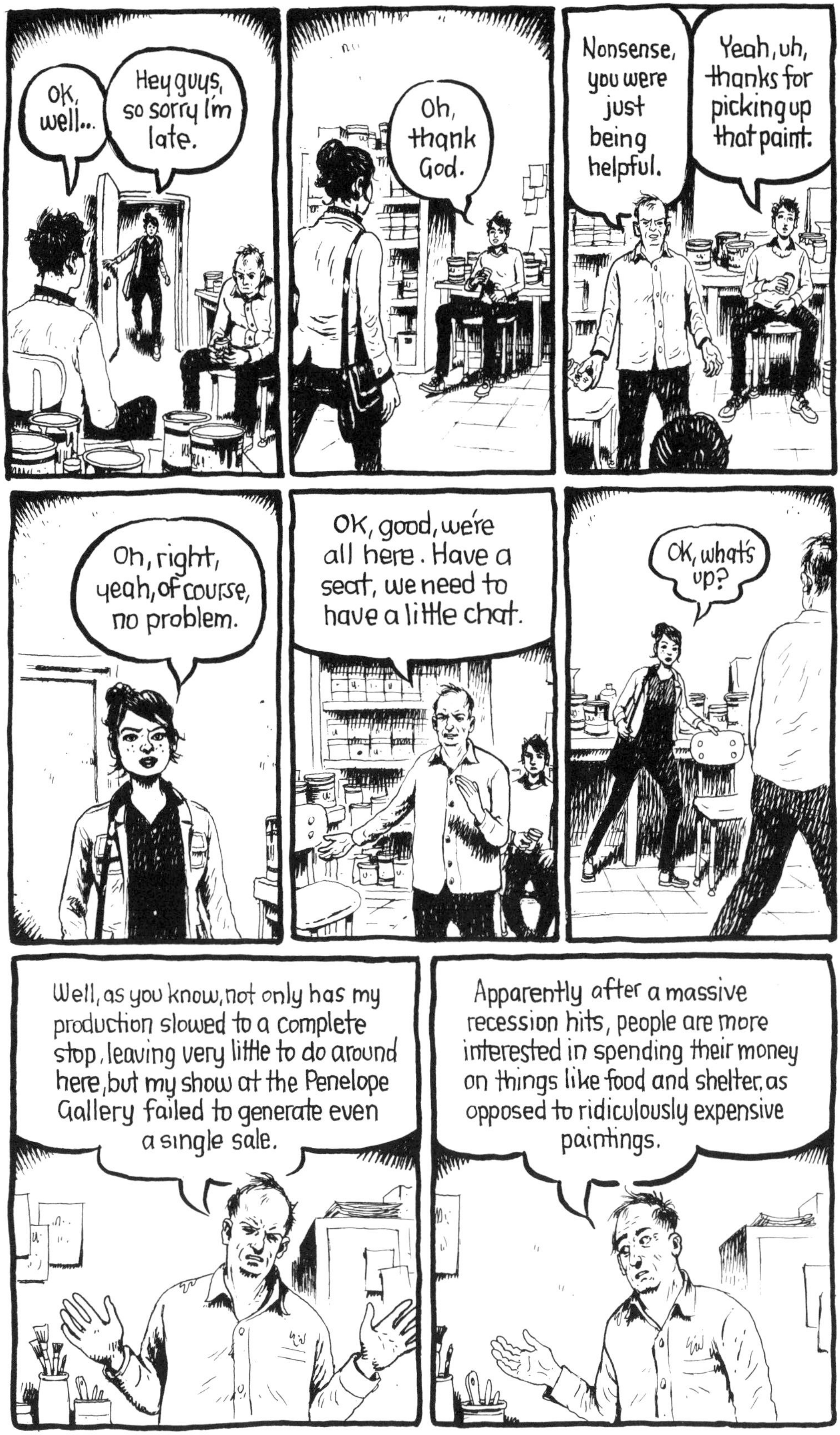
OK, well...
Hey guys, so sorry I'm late.
Oh, thank God.
Nonsense, you were just being helpful.
Yeah, uh, thanks for picking up that paint.
Oh, right, yeah, of course, no problem.
OK, good, we're all here. Have a seat, we need to have a little chat.
OK, what's up?
Well, as you know, not only has my production slowed to a complete stop, leaving very little to do around here, but my show at the Penelope Gallery failed to generate even a single sale.
Apparently after a massive recession hits, people are more interested in spending their money on things like food and shelter, as opposed to ridiculously expensive paintings.

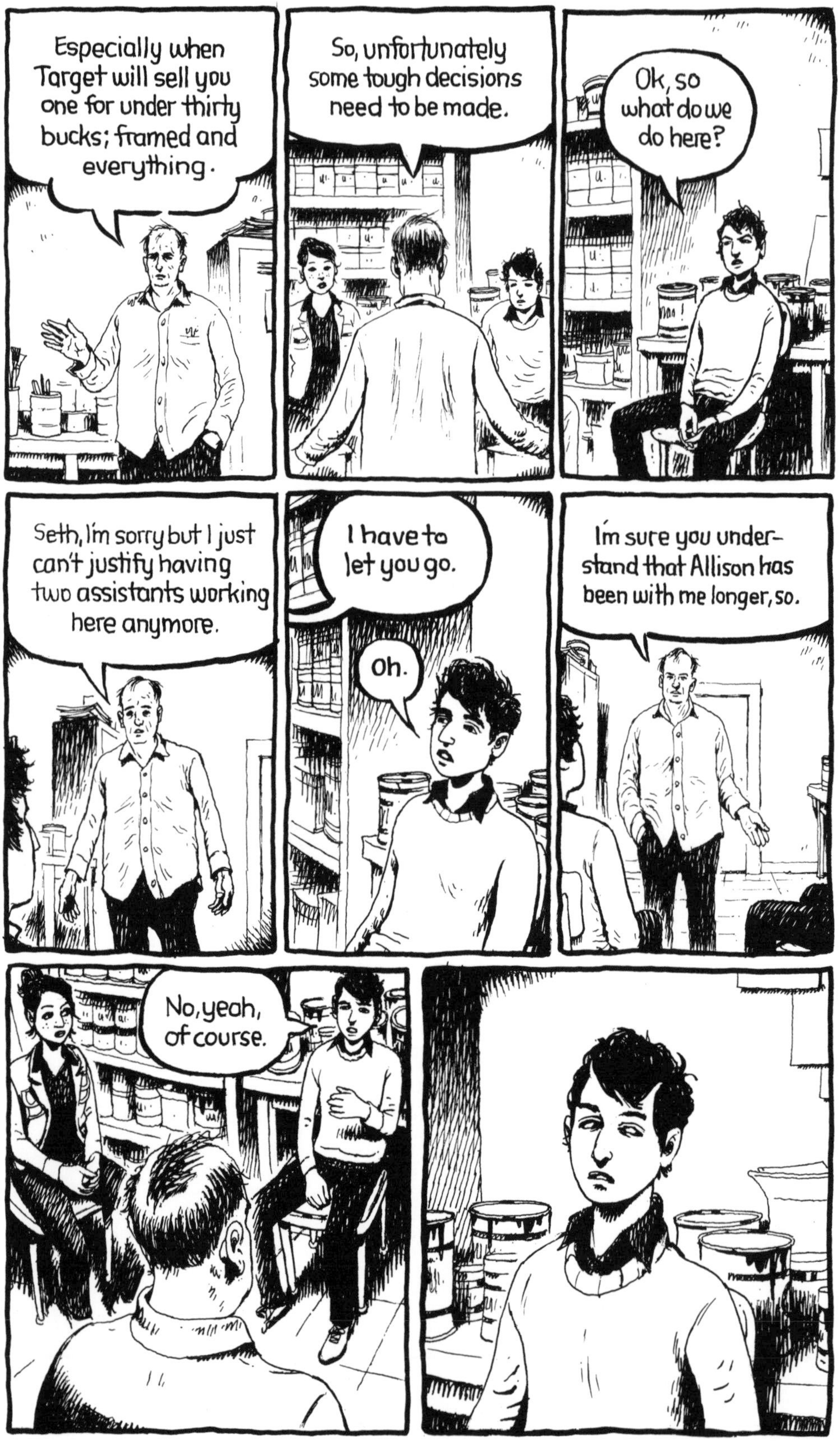
Especially when Target will sell you one for under thirty bucks; framed and everything.
So, unfortunately some tough decisions need to be made.
Ok, so what do we do here?
Seth, I'm sorry but I just can't justify having two assistants working here anymore.
I have to let you go.
Oh.
I'm sure you under-stand that Allison has been with me longer, so.
No, yeah, of course.

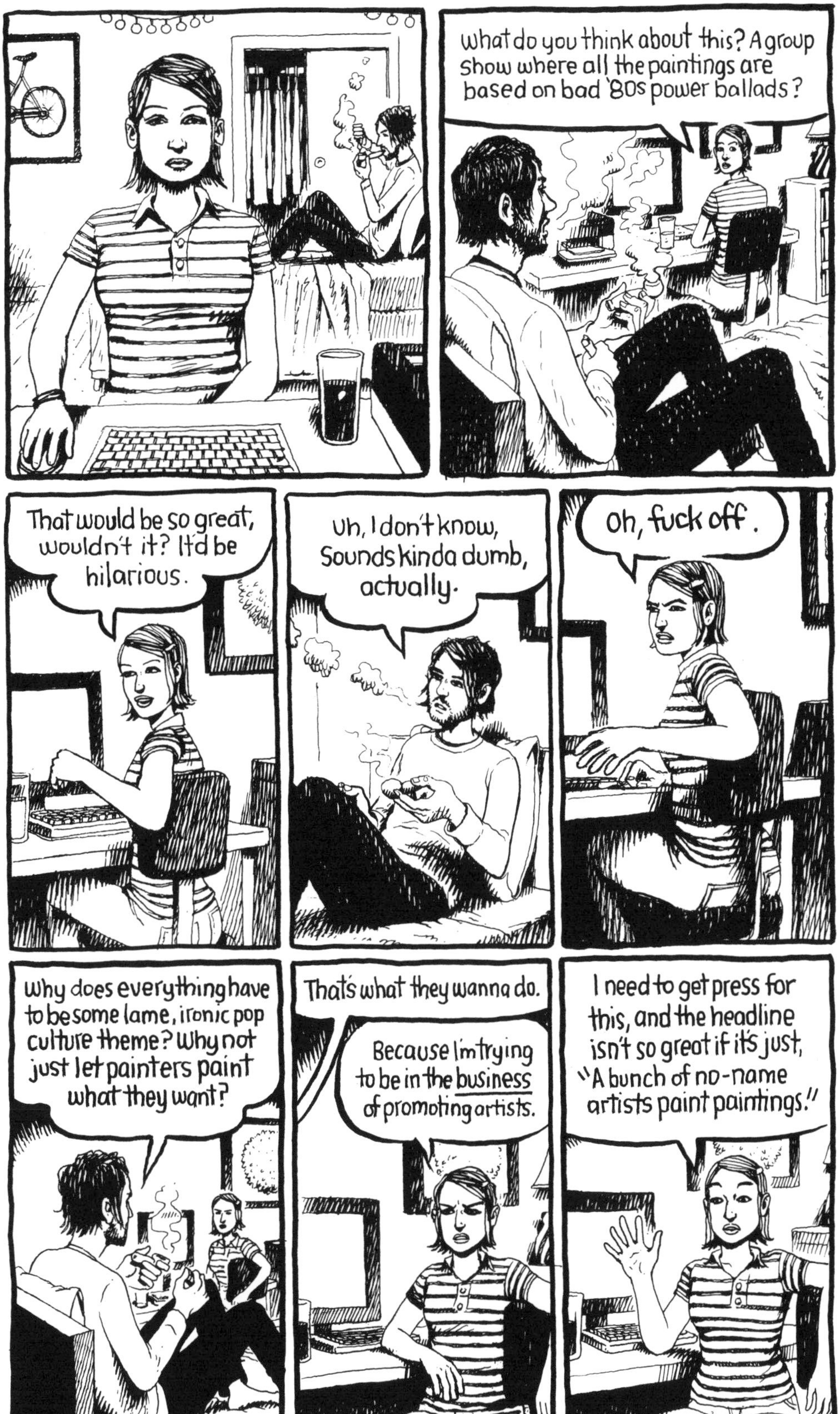
What do you think about this? A group show where all the paintings are based on bad '80s power ballads?
That would be so great, wouldn't it? It'd be hilarious.
Uh, I don't know, Sounds kinda dumb, actually.
Oh, fuck off.
Why does everything have to be some lame, ironic pop culture theme? Why not just let painters paint what they want?
That's what they wanna do.
Because I'm trying to be in the business of promoting artists.
I need to get press for this, and the headline isn't so great if it's just, "A bunch of no-name artists paint paintings."

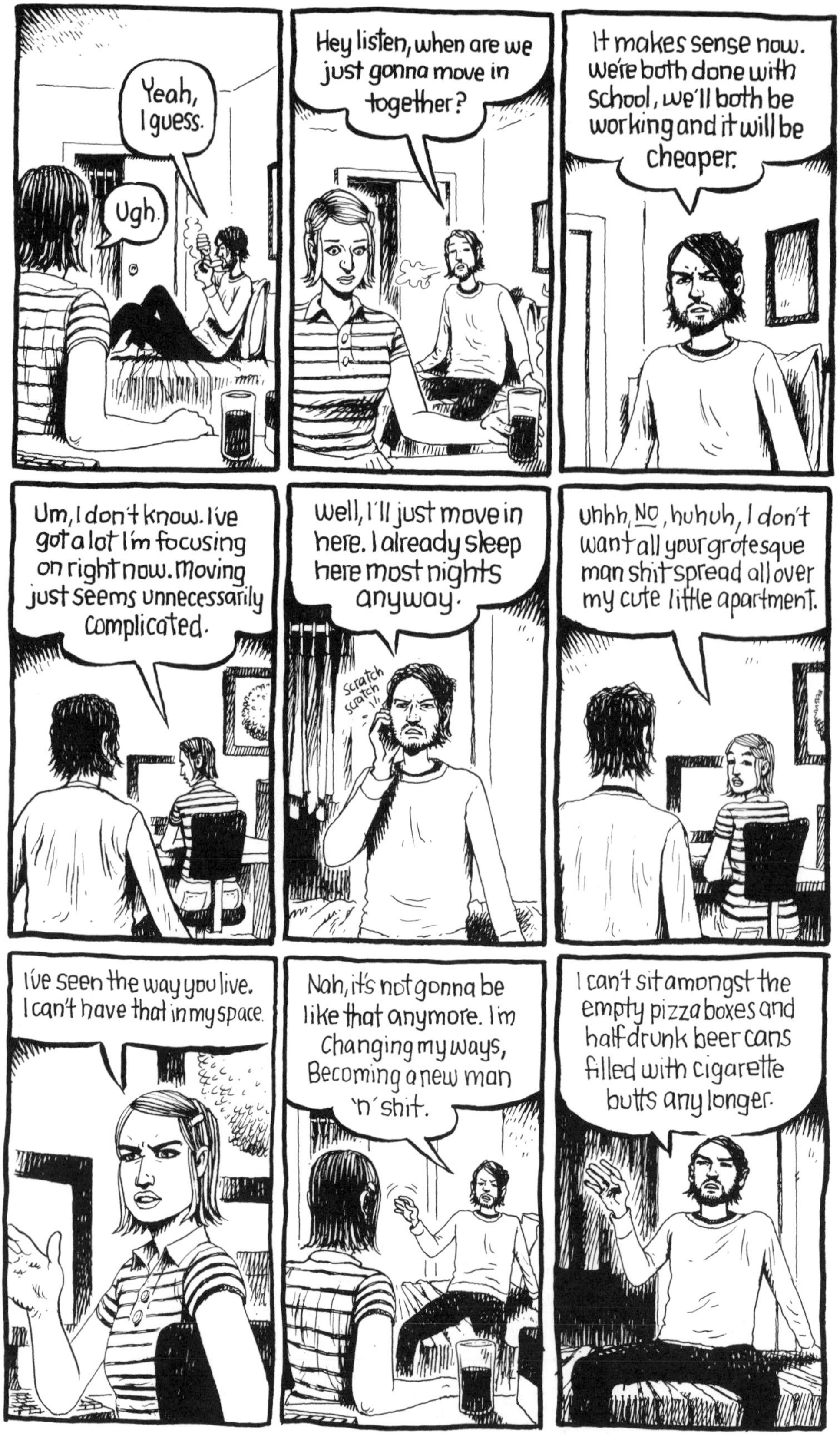
Yeah, I guess.
Ugh.
Hey listen, when are we just gonna move in together?
It makes sense now. We're both done with school, we'll both be working and it will be cheaper.
Um, I don't know. I've got a lot I'm focusing on right now. Moving just seems unnecessarily complicated.
Well, I'll just move in here. I already sleep here most nights anyway.
scratch scratch
Uhhh, NO, huhuh, I don't want all your grotesque man shit spread all over my cute little apartment.
I've seen the way you live. I can't have that in my space.
Nah, it's not gonna be like that anymore. I'm changing my ways, Becoming a new man 'n' shit.
I can't sit amongst the empty pizza boxes and half drunk beer cans filled with cigarette butts any longer.

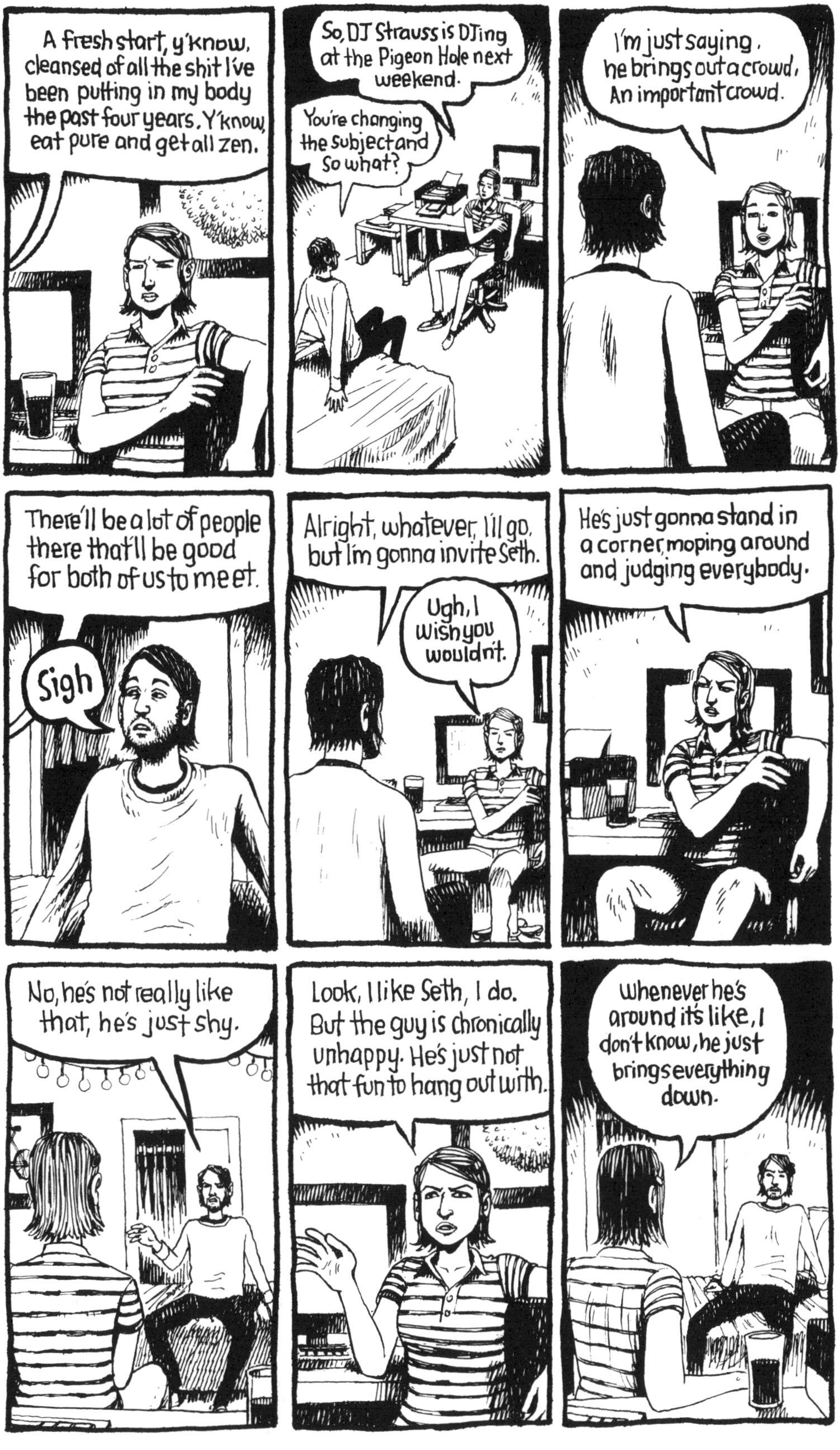
A fresh start, y'know, cleansed of all the shit I've been putting in my body the past four years. Y'know, eat pure and get all zen.
So, DJ Strauss is DJing at the Pigeon Hole next weekend.
You're changing the subject and so what?
I'm just saying, he brings out a crowd, An important crowd.
There'll be a lot of people there that'll be good for both of us to meet.
Sigh
Alright, whatever, I'll go, but I'm gonna invite Seth.
Ugh, I wish you wouldn't.
He's just gonna stand in a corner, moping around and judging everybody.
No, he's not really like that, he's just shy.
Look, I like Seth, I do. But the guy is chronically unhappy. He's just not that fun to hang out with.
Whenever he's around it's like, I don't know, he just brings everything down.

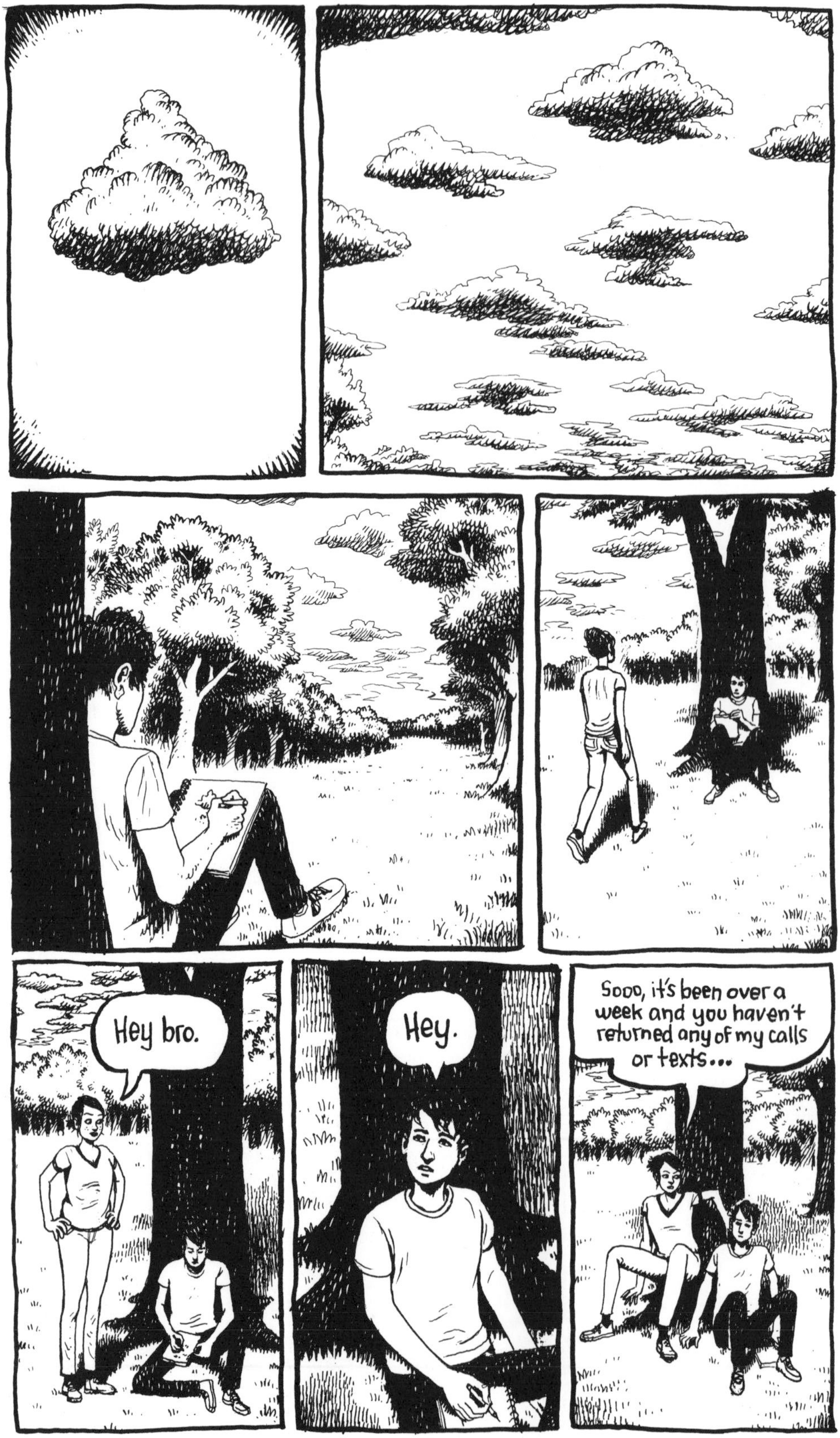
Hey bro.
Hey.
Sooo, it's been over a week and you haven't returned any of my calls or texts...

I was starting to think you've been avoiding me.

Yeah, I don't know. I just haven't felt like talking in general, I guess.

Don't take it personally.

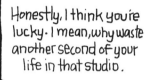

Honestly, I think you're lucky. I mean, why waste another second of your life in that studio.

Working for Mr. Lasky is about as depressing as it gets.

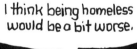

I think being homeless would be a bit worse.

Yeah well, I think my days are numbered too. It's not like he has any use for me either.

Nah, he's too lonely to fire you too. He'll keep you around just to stare at if nothing else.

51

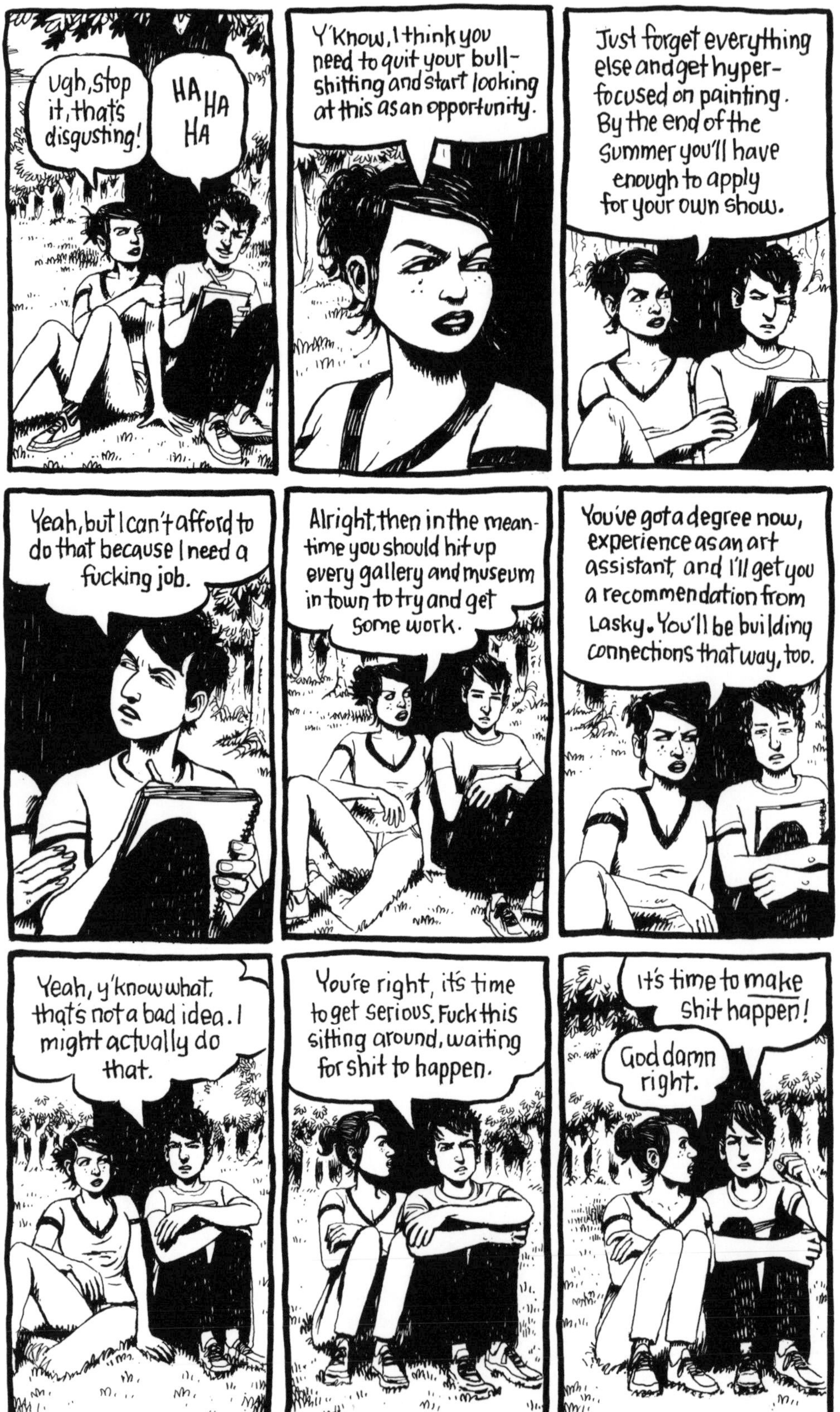
Ugh, Stop it, that's disgusting!
HA HA HA
Y'Know, I think you need to quit your bull-shitting and start looking at this as an opportunity.
Just forget everything else and get hyper-focused on painting. By the end of the summer you'll have enough to apply for your own show.
Yeah, but I can't afford to do that because I need a fucking job.
Alright, then in the mean-time you should hit up every gallery and museum in town to try and get some work.
You've got a degree now, experience as an art assistant, and I'll get you a recommendation from Lasky. You'll be building connections that way, too.
Yeah, y'know what, that's not a bad idea. I might actually do that.
You're right, it's time to get serious. Fuck this sitting around, waiting for shit to happen.
It's time to make shit happen!
God damn right.

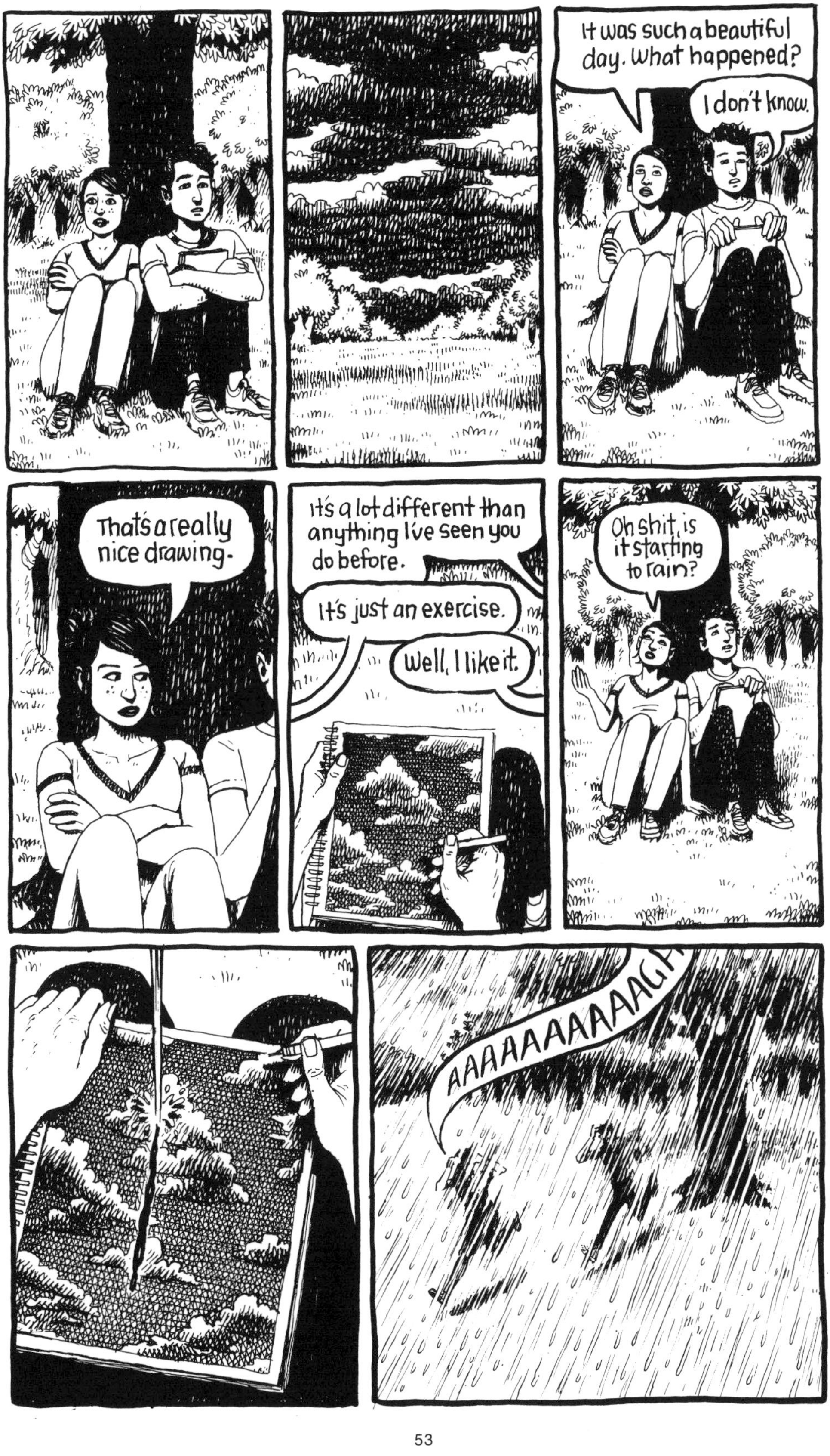
It was such a beautiful day. What happened?
I don't know.
That's a really nice drawing.
It's a lot different than anything I've seen you do before.
It's just an exercise.
Well, I like it.
Oh shit, is it starting to rain?
AAAAAAAAAAGH

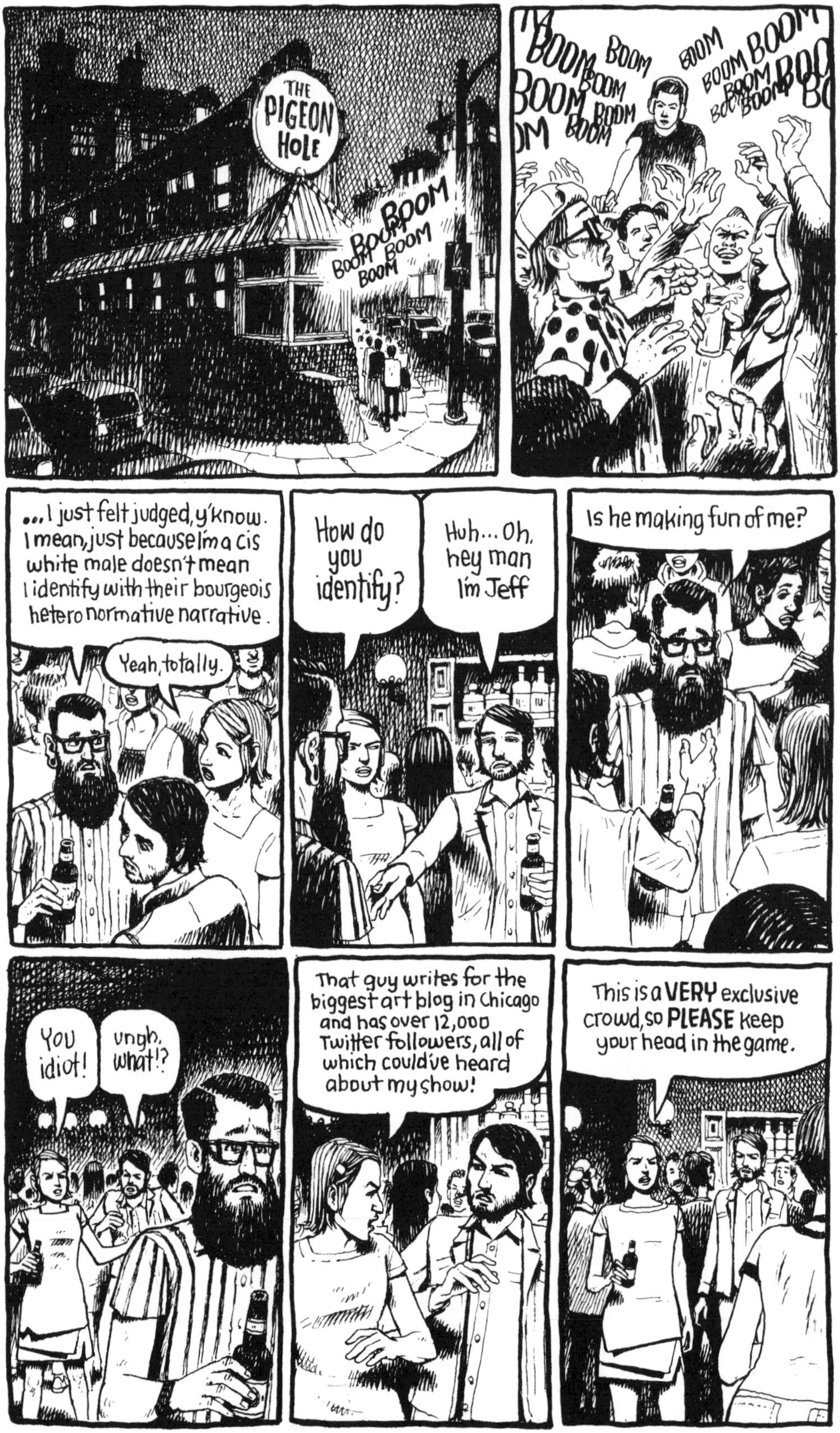
THE PIGEON HOLE
BOOM BOOM BOOM BOOM BOOM
BOOM BOOM BOOM BOOM BOOM BOOM BOOM BOOM BOOM BOOM
...I just felt judged, y'know. I mean, just because I'm a cis white male doesn't mean I identify with their bourgeois hetero normative narrative.
Yeah, totally.
How do you identify?
Huh... Oh, hey man I'm Jeff
Is he making fun of me?
You idiot!
ungh, what!?
That guy writes for the biggest art blog in Chicago and has over 12,000 Twitter followers, all of which could've heard about my show!
This is a **VERY** exclusive crowd, so **PLEASE** keep your head in the game.

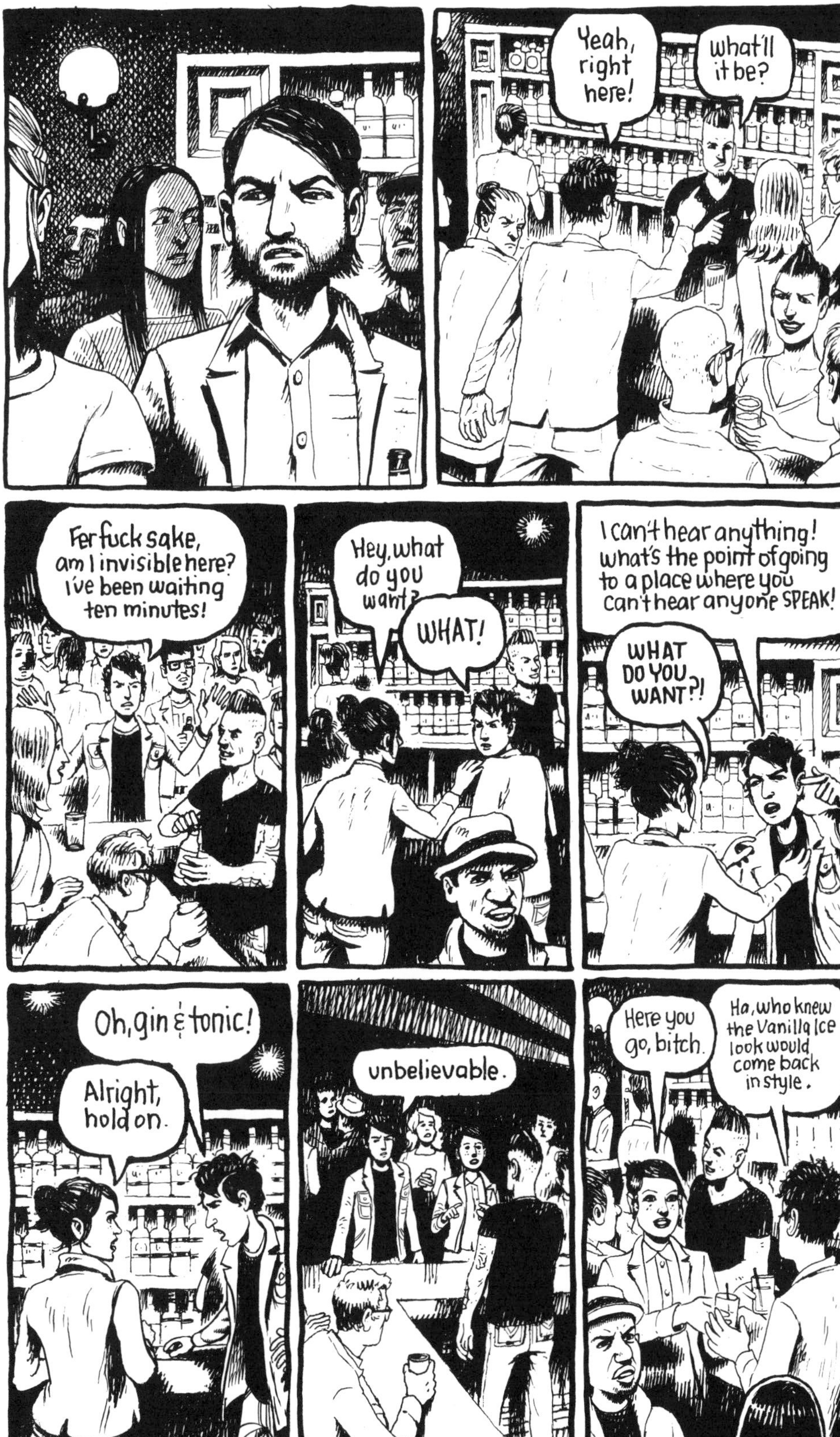
Yeah, right here!
what'll it be?
Fer fuck sake, am I invisible here? I've been waiting ten minutes!
Hey, what do you want?
WHAT!
I can't hear anything! what's the point of going to a place where you can't hear anyone SPEAK!
WHAT DO YOU WANT?!
Oh, gin & tonic!
Alright, hold on.
unbelievable.
Here you go, bitch.
Ha, who knew the Vanilla Ice look would come back in style.

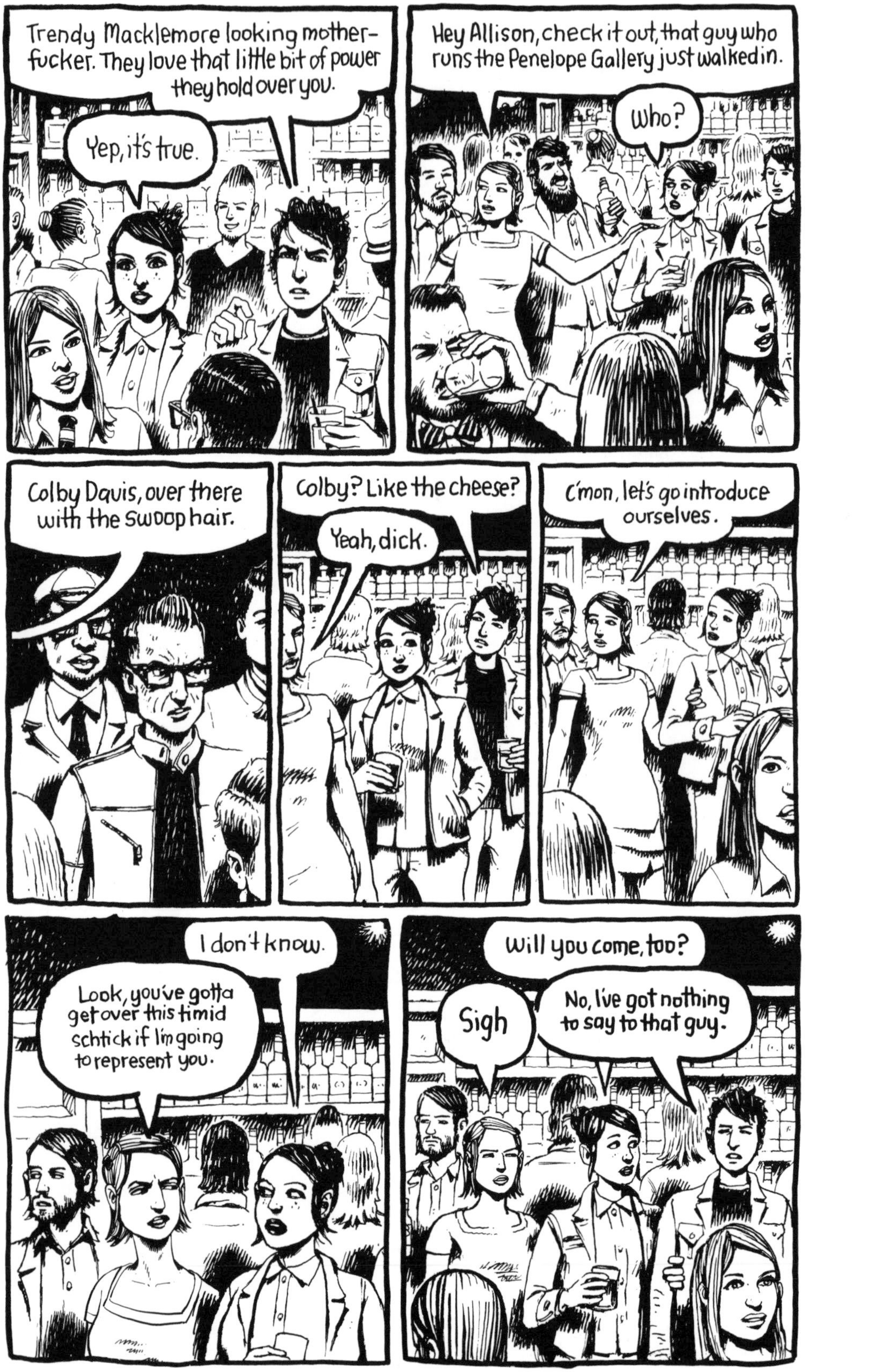

Trendy Macklemore looking motherfucker. They love that little bit of power they hold over you.
Yep, it's true.
Hey Allison, check it out, that guy who runs the Penelope Gallery just walked in.
Who?
Colby Davis, over there with the swoop hair.
Colby? Like the cheese?
Yeah, dick.
C'mon, let's go introduce ourselves.
I don't know.
Look, you've gotta get over this timid schtick if I'm going to represent you.
Will you come, too?
Sigh
No, I've got nothing to say to that guy.

Seth, you don't know anything about that guy.

He's wearing a white leather jacket, what else do I need to know?

ugh, c'mon Allison.

welp, there they go, buddy.

So are you guys gonna move in together?

mmm, no, it's looking like you're gonna be stuck with me for a bit longer, son.

BOOM BOOM BOOM BOOM BOOM BOOM BOOM BOOM

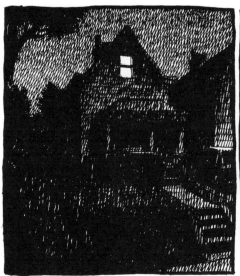

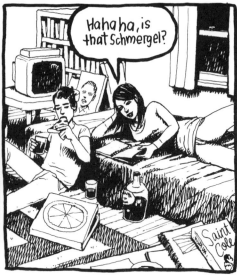

Hahaha, is that Schmergel?
Saint Cole
Who else could it be?
Ha Ha Ha
I only smoke Davidoff's. You have to import them from Italy.
I buy them by the case.
Very expensive
Hey, it's Colby.
Do you have anything in white leather
I'm big into white leather.
Haha, oh yeah.
What's with that guys' "cool guy" look?
John Pollard
Saint Cole
I hate anybody who tries to play themselves up as some kind of "Rock Star" of the art world or any other industry.
Yeah, he's got like a Mark McGrath, slash Delirious era Eddie Murphy look.
Pathetic.

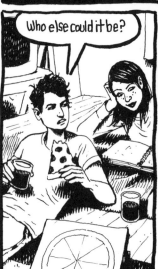

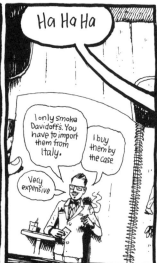

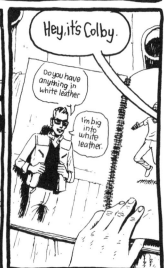

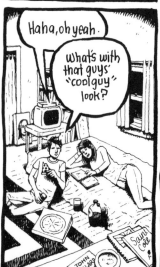

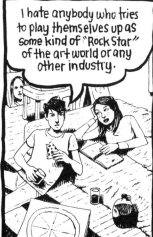

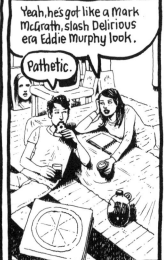

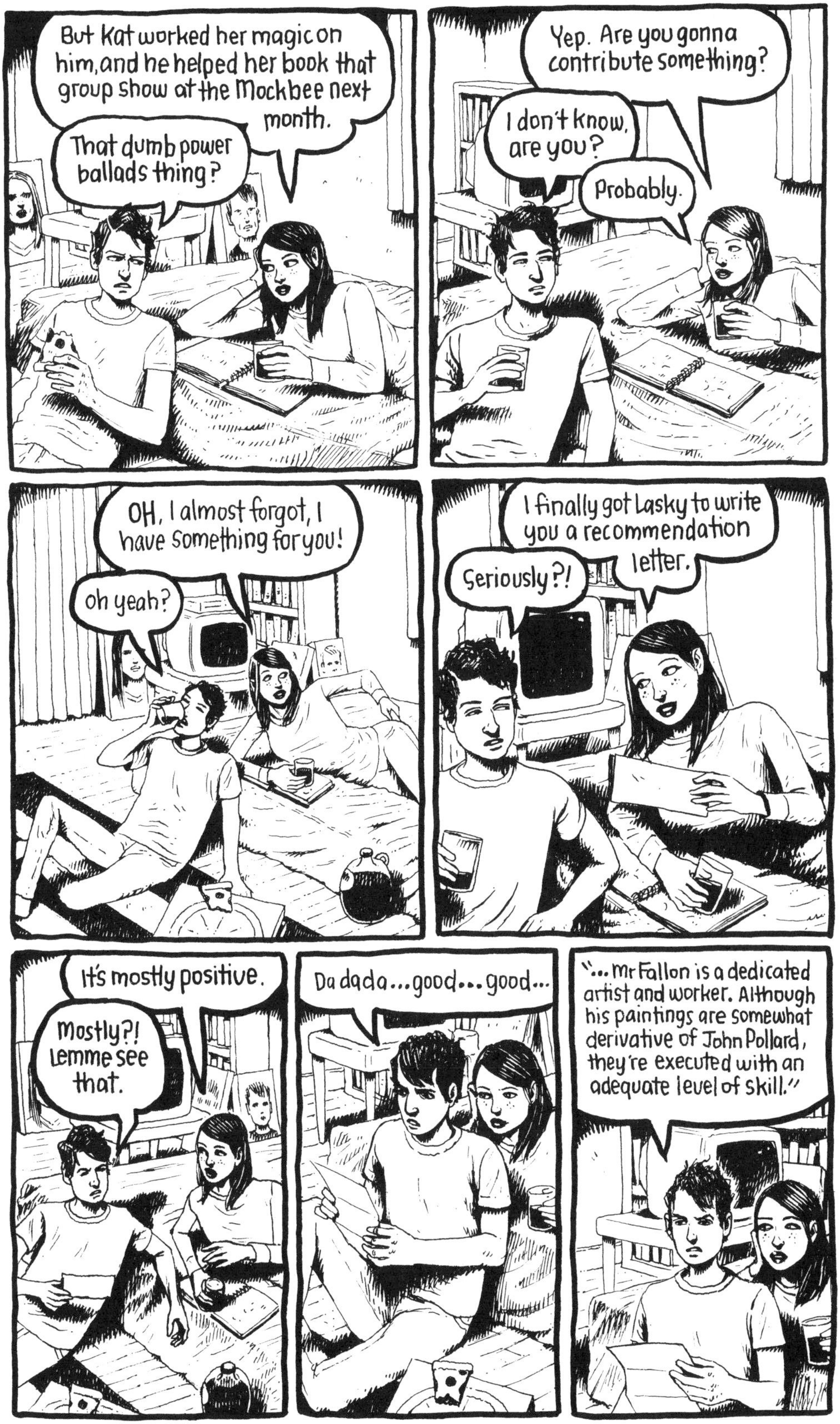
But Kat worked her magic on him, and he helped her book that group show at the Mockbee next month.
That dumb power ballads thing?
Yep. Are you gonna contribute something?
I don't know, are you?
Probably.
OH, I almost forgot, I have something for you!
oh yeah?
I finally got Lasky to write you a recommendation letter.
Seriously?!
It's mostly positive.
Mostly?! Lemme see that.
Da dada...good...good...
"...Mr Fallon is a dedicated artist and worker. Although his paintings are somewhat derivative of John Pollard, they're executed with an adequate level of skill."

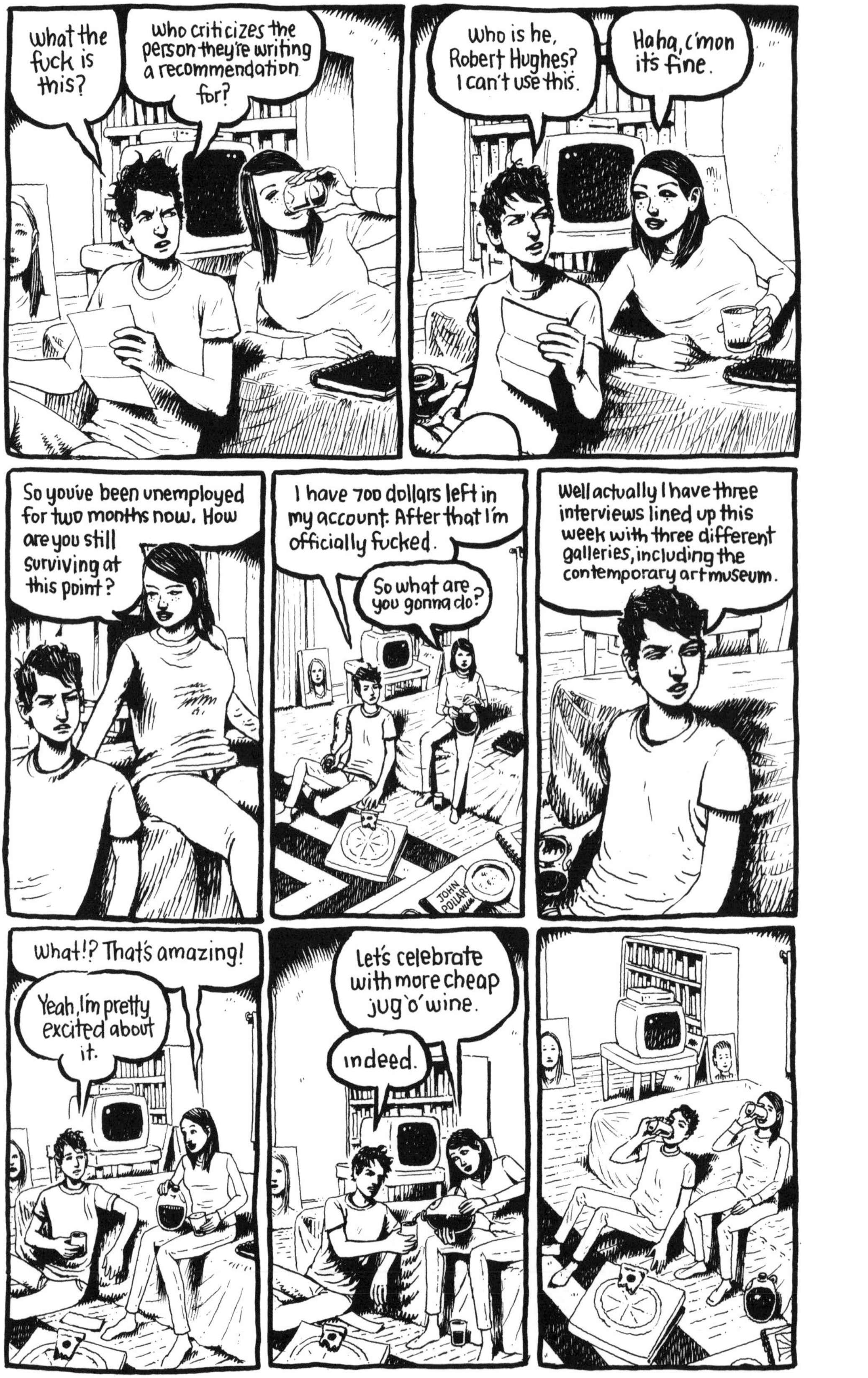
What the fuck is this?
Who criticizes the person they're writing a recommendation for?
Who is he, Robert Hughes? I can't use this.
Haha, c'mon it's fine.
So you've been unemployed for two months now. How are you still surviving at this point?
I have 700 dollars left in my account. After that I'm officially fucked.
So what are you gonna do?
JOHN POLLARD
Well actually I have three interviews lined up this week with three different galleries, including the contemporary art museum.
What!? That's amazing!
Yeah, I'm pretty excited about it.
Let's celebrate with more cheap jug 'o' wine.
Indeed.

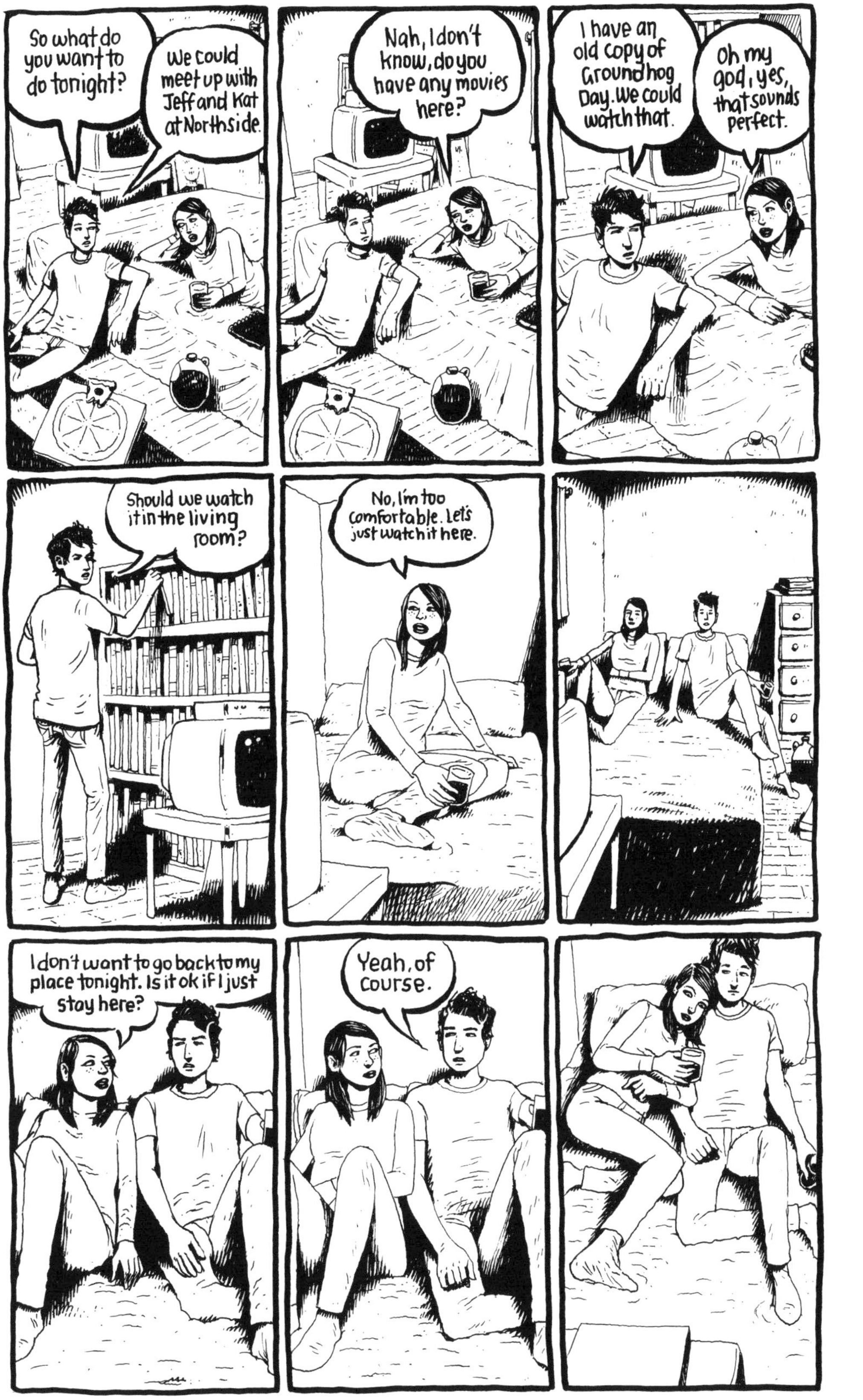
So what do you want to do tonight?
We could meet up with Jeff and Kat at Northside.
Nah, I don't know, do you have any movies here?
I have an old copy of Groundhog Day. We could watch that.
Oh my god, yes, that sounds perfect.
Should we watch it in the living room?
No, I'm too comfortable. Let's just watch it here.
I don't want to go back to my place tonight. Is it ok if I just stay here?
Yeah, of course.

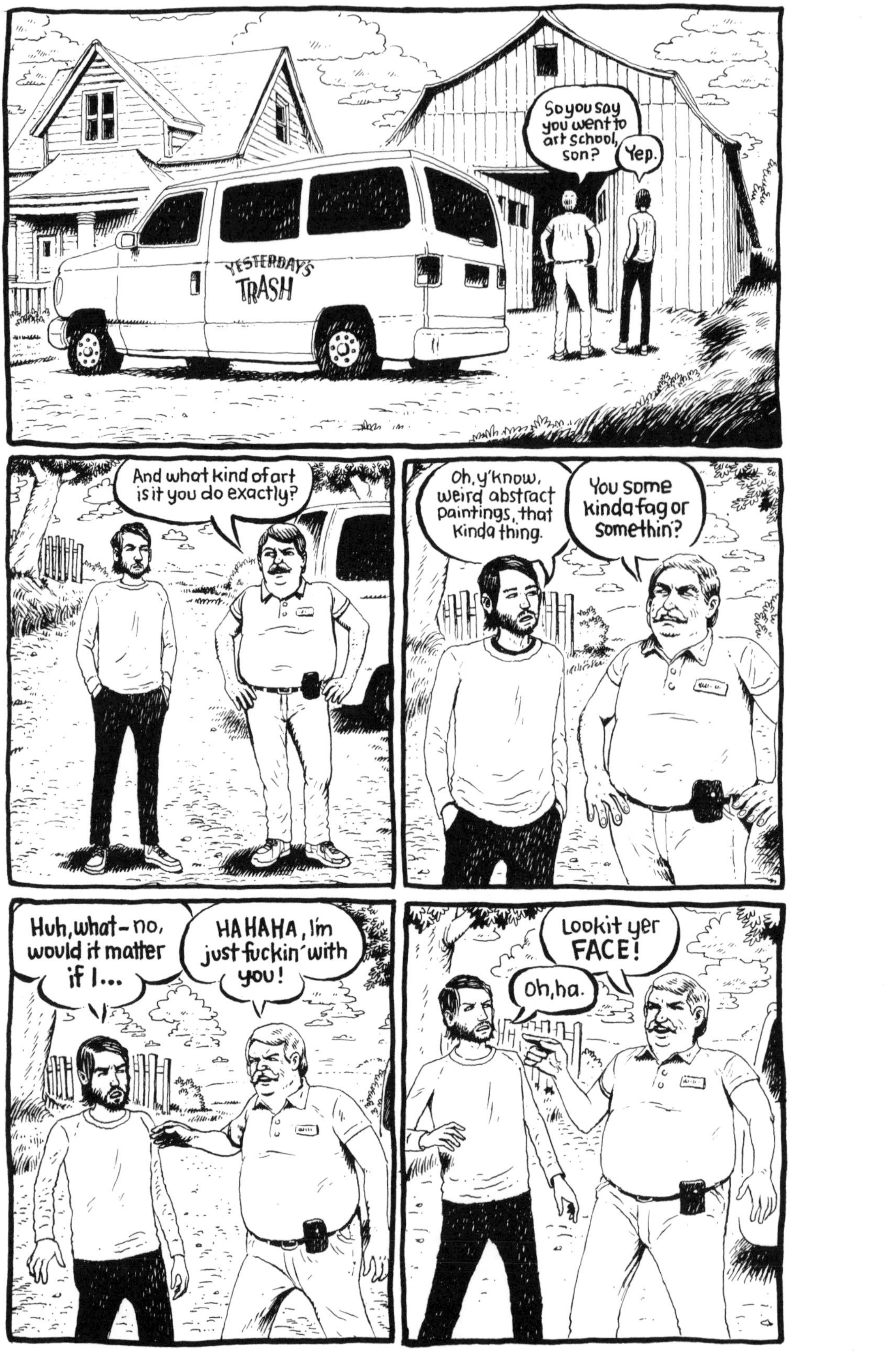
So you say you went to art school, son?
Yep.
YESTERDAY'S TRASH
And what kind of art is it you do exactly?
Oh, y'know, weird abstract paintings, that kinda thing.
You some kinda fag or somethin'?
Huh, what- no, would it matter if I...
HAHAHA, I'm just fuckin' with you!
Lookit yer FACE!
Oh, ha.

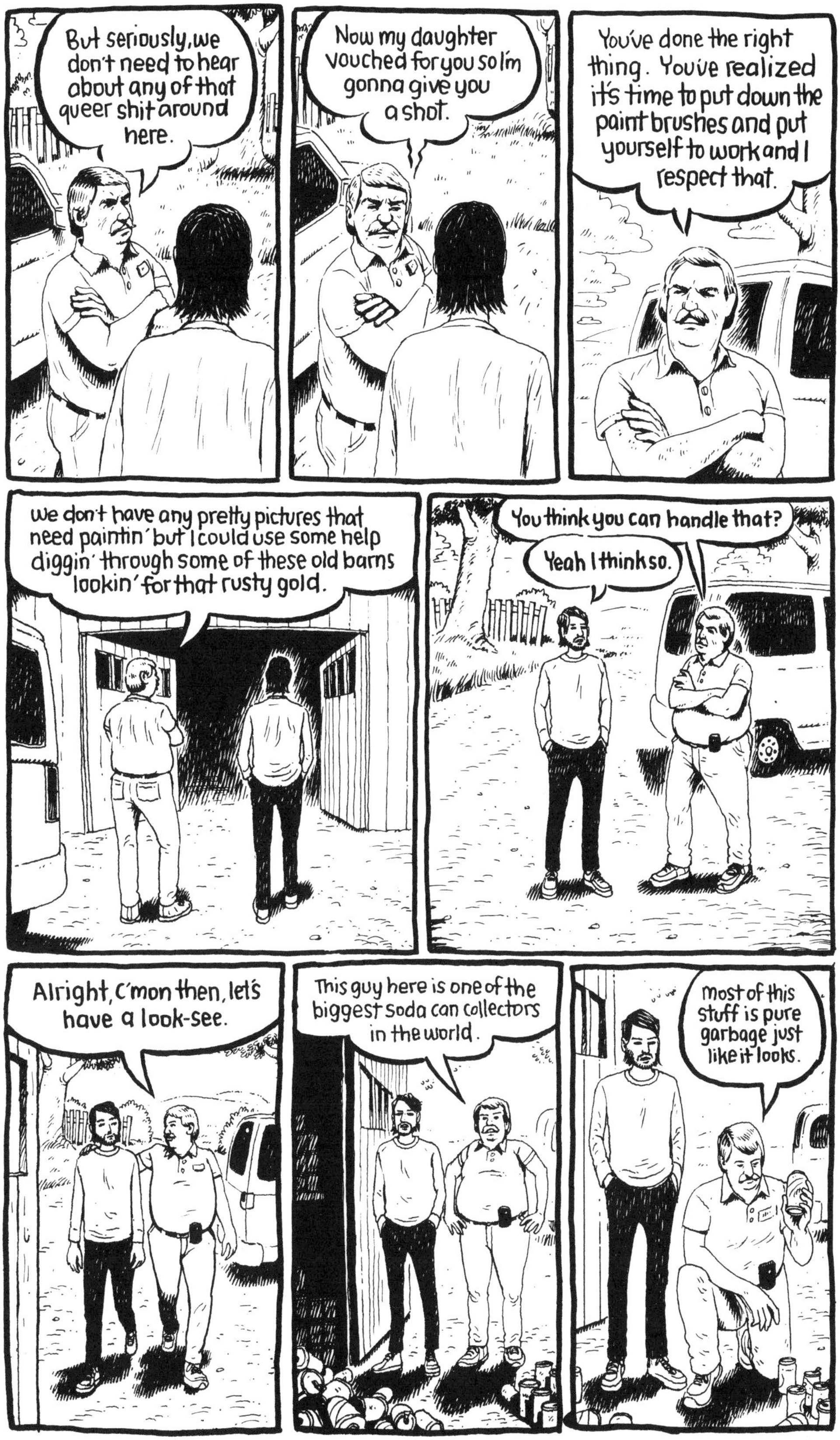
But seriously, we don't need to hear about any of that queer shit around here.
Now my daughter vouched for you so I'm gonna give you a shot.
You've done the right thing. You've realized it's time to put down the paint brushes and put yourself to work and I respect that.
We don't have any pretty pictures that need paintin' but I could use some help diggin' through some of these old barns lookin' for that rusty gold.
You think you can handle that?
Yeah I think so.
Alright, C'mon then, let's have a look-see.
This guy here is one of the biggest soda can collectors in the world.
Most of this stuff is pure garbage just like it looks.

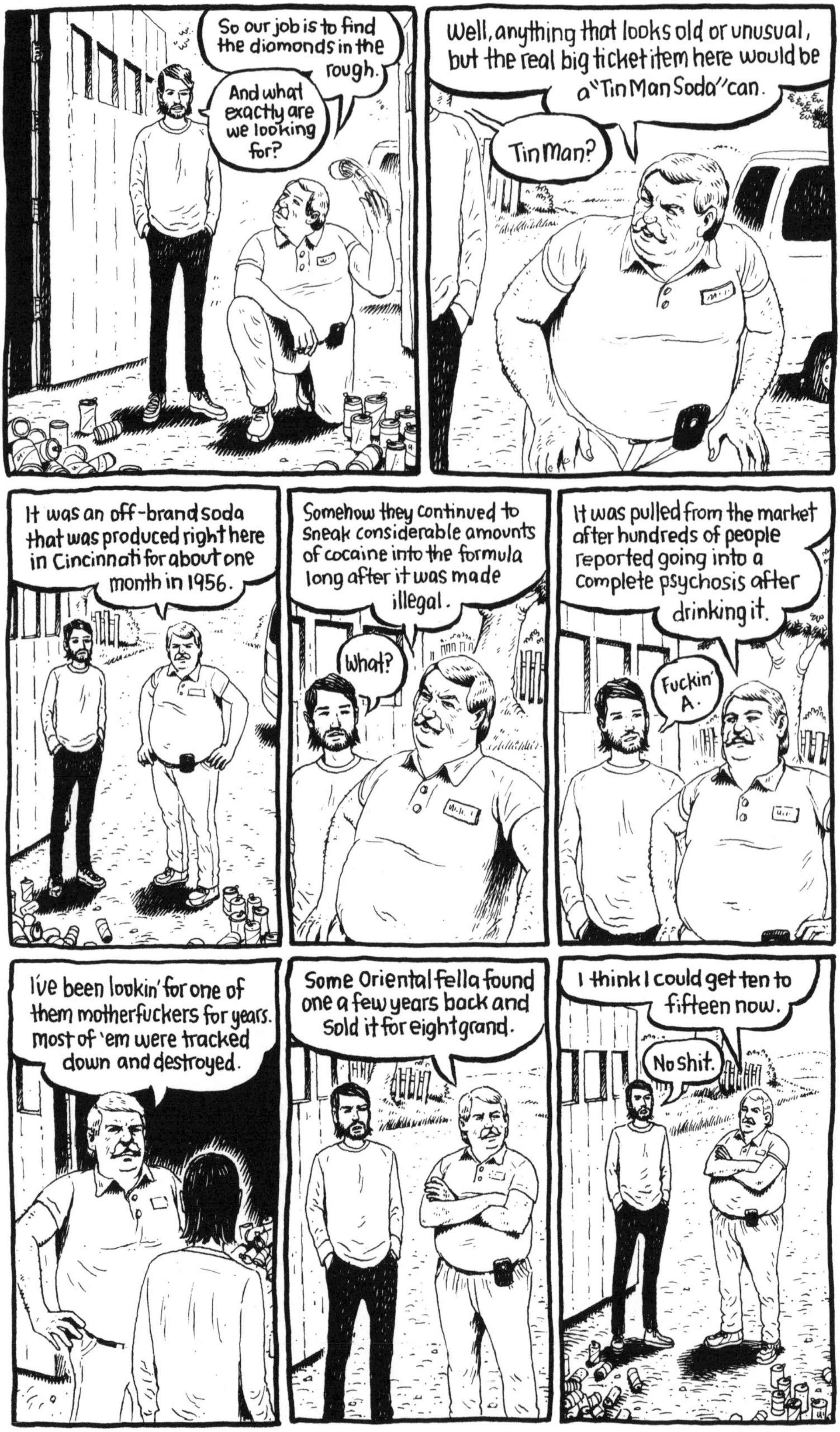
So our job is to find the diamonds in the rough.
And what exactly are we looking for?
Well, anything that looks old or unusual, but the real big ticket item here would be a "Tin Man Soda" can.
Tin Man?
It was an off-brand soda that was produced right here in Cincinnati for about one month in 1956.
Somehow they continued to sneak considerable amounts of cocaine into the formula long after it was made illegal.
What?
It was pulled from the market after hundreds of people reported going into a complete psychosis after drinking it.
Fuckin' A.
I've been lookin' for one of them motherfuckers for years. most of 'em were tracked down and destroyed.
Some Oriental fella found one a few years back and sold it for eight grand.
I think I could get ten to fifteen now.
No shit.

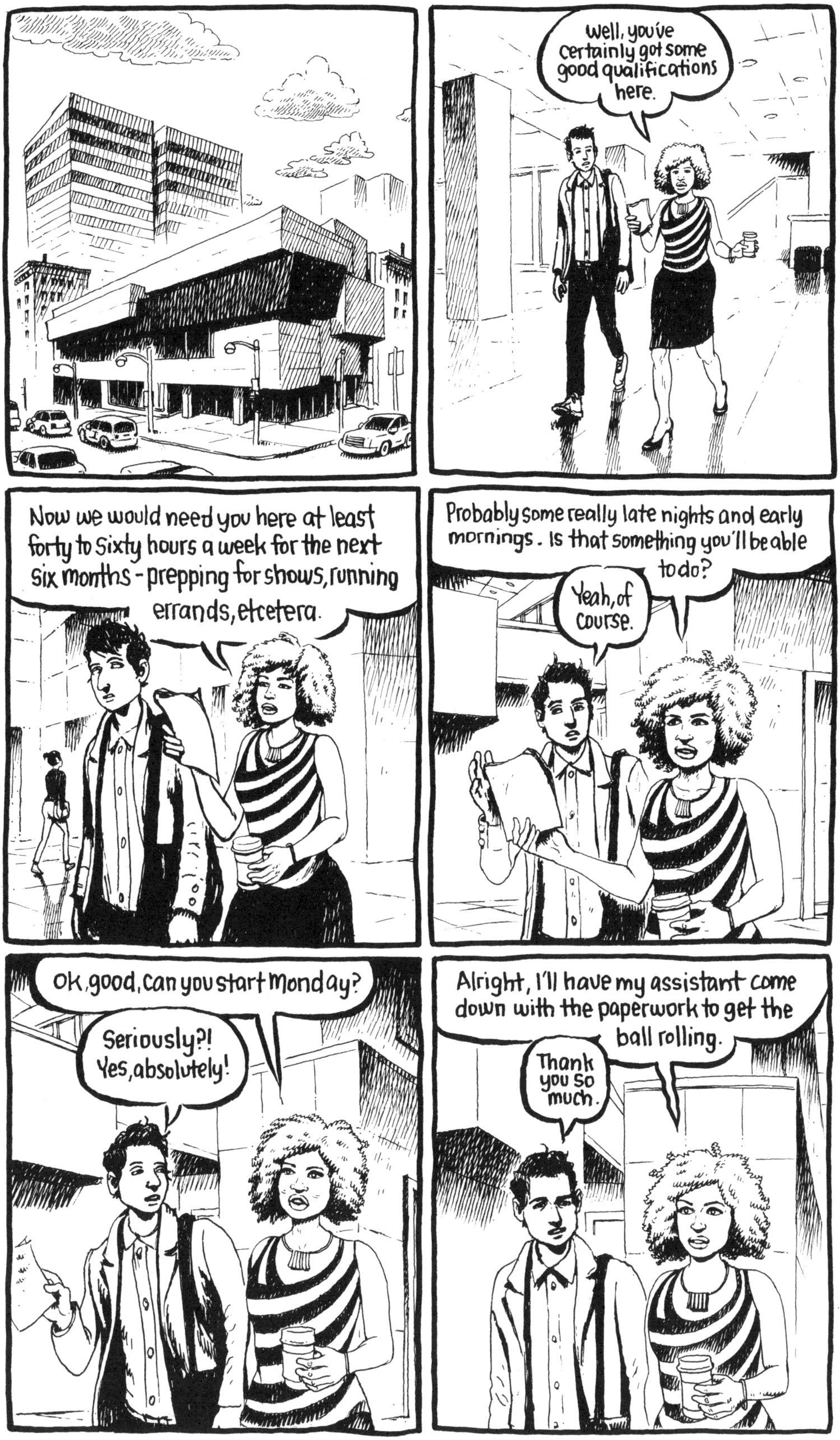
Well, you've certainly got some good qualifications here.
Now we would need you here at least forty to sixty hours a week for the next six months - prepping for shows, running errands, etcetera.
Probably some really late nights and early mornings. Is that something you'll be able to do?
Yeah, of course.
Ok, good, can you start Monday?
Seriously?! Yes, absolutely!
Alright, I'll have my assistant come down with the paperwork to get the ball rolling.
Thank you so much.

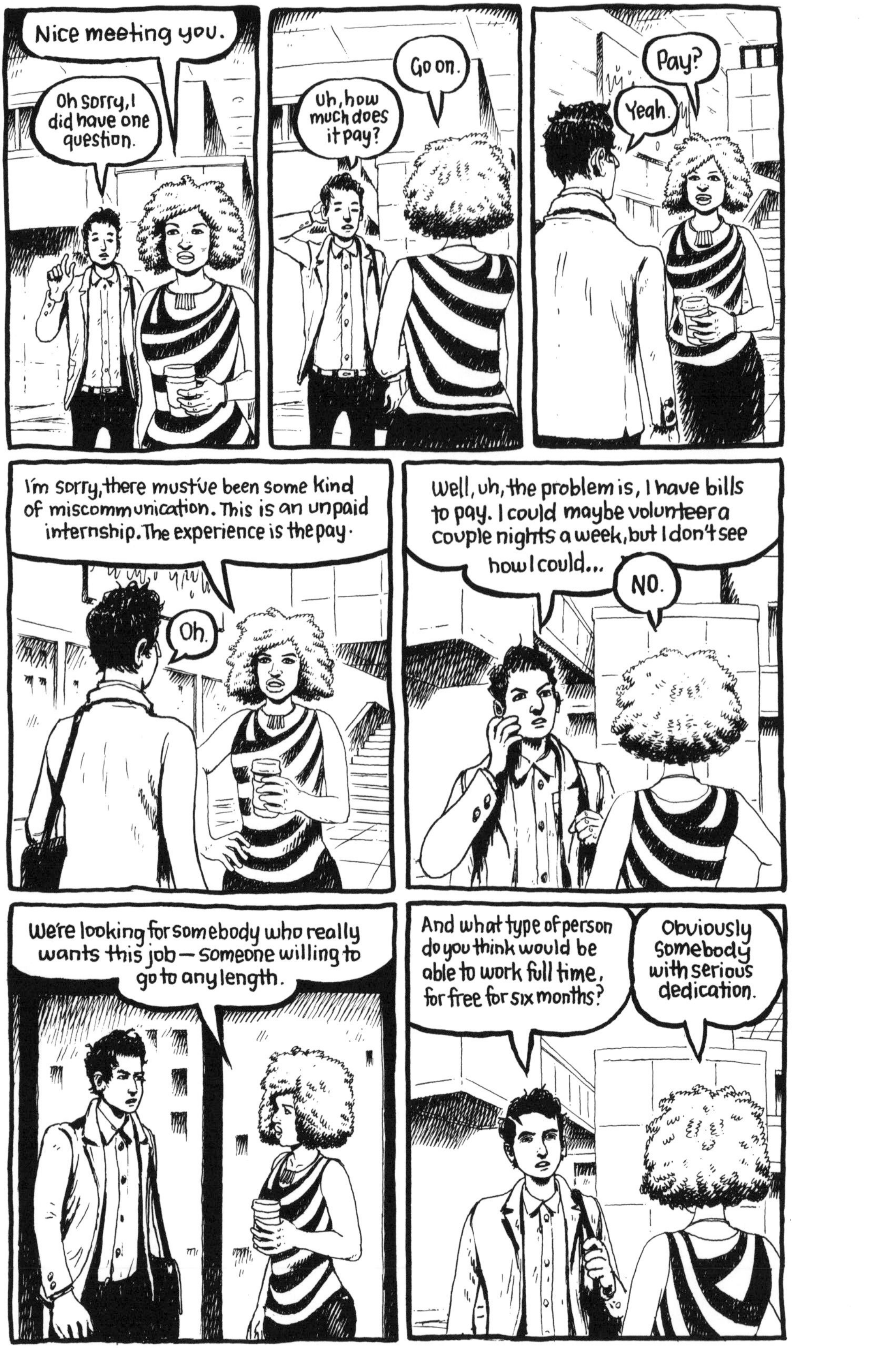
Nice meeting you.
Oh sorry, I did have one question.
Uh, how much does it pay?
Go on.
Pay?
Yeah.
I'm sorry, there must've been some kind of miscommunication. This is an unpaid internship. The experience is the pay.
Oh.
Well, uh, the problem is, I have bills to pay. I could maybe volunteer a couple nights a week, but I don't see how I could...
NO.
We're looking for somebody who really wants this job—someone willing to go to any length.
And what type of person do you think would be able to work full time, for free for six months?
Obviously somebody with serious dedication.

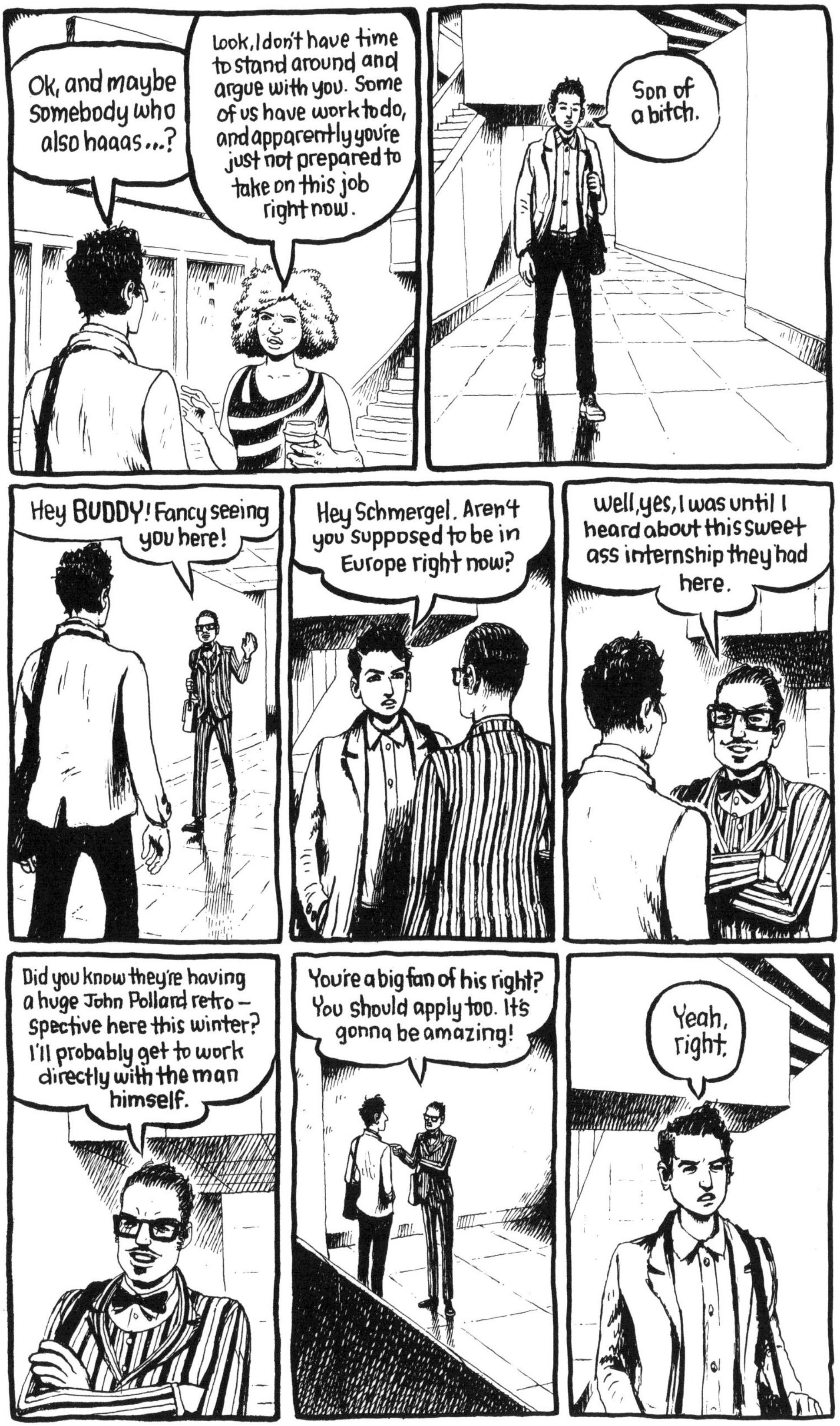
Ok, and maybe somebody who also haaas...?
Look, I don't have time to stand around and argue with you. Some of us have work to do, and apparently you're just not prepared to take on this job right now.
Son of a bitch.
Hey BUDDY! Fancy seeing you here!
Hey Schmergel. Aren't you supposed to be in Europe right now?
Well, yes, I was until I heard about this sweet ass internship they had here.
Did you know they're having a huge John Pollard retro-spective here this winter? I'll probably get to work directly with the man himself.
You're a big fan of his right? You should apply too. It's gonna be amazing!
Yeah, right.

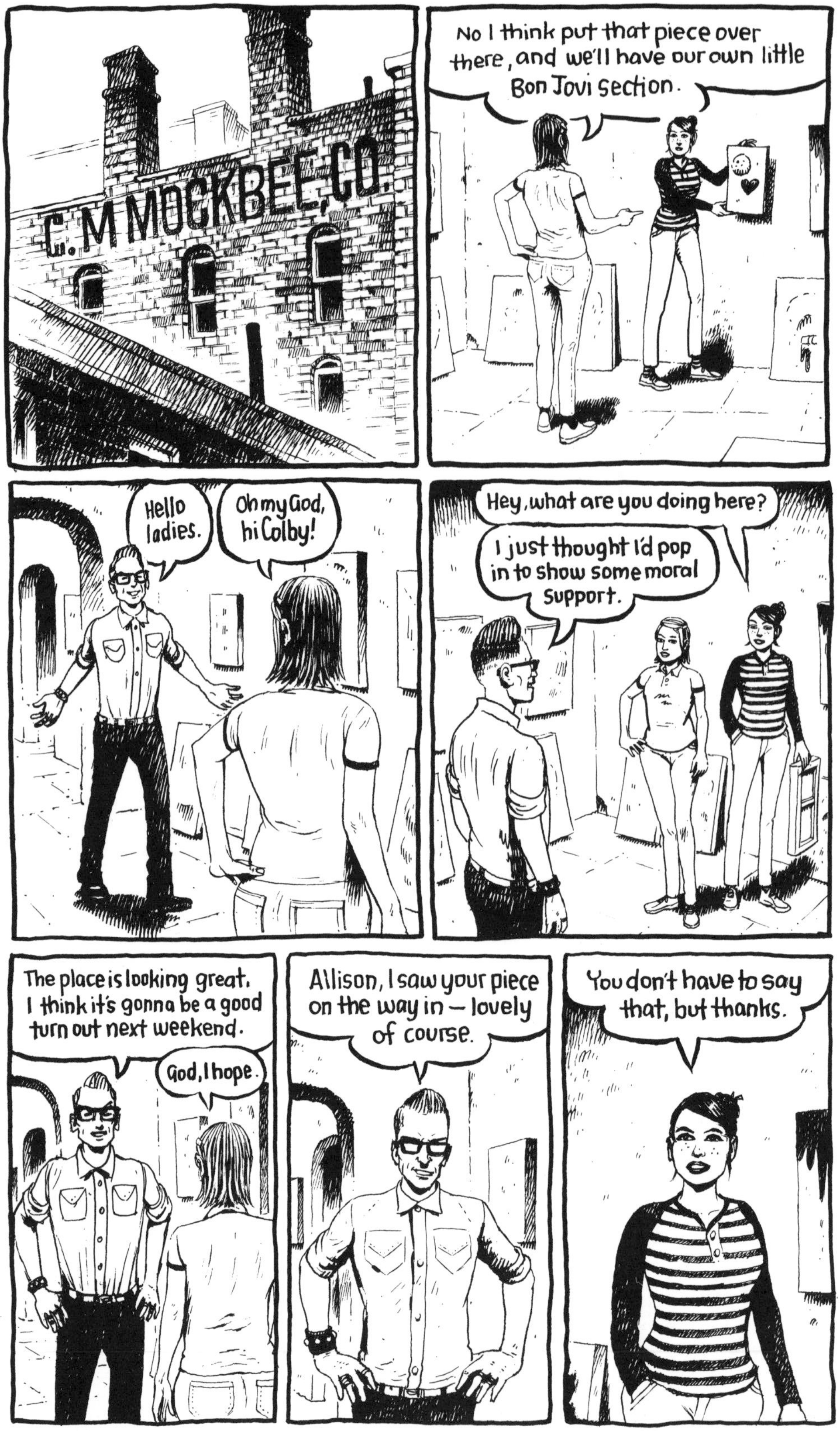
C.M MOCKBEE, CO.
No I think put that piece over there, and we'll have our own little Bon Jovi section.
Hello ladies.
Oh my God, hi Colby!
Hey, what are you doing here?
I just thought I'd pop in to show some moral support.
The place is looking great. I think it's gonna be a good turn out next weekend.
God, I hope.
Allison, I saw your piece on the way in — lovely of course.
You don't have to say that, but thanks.

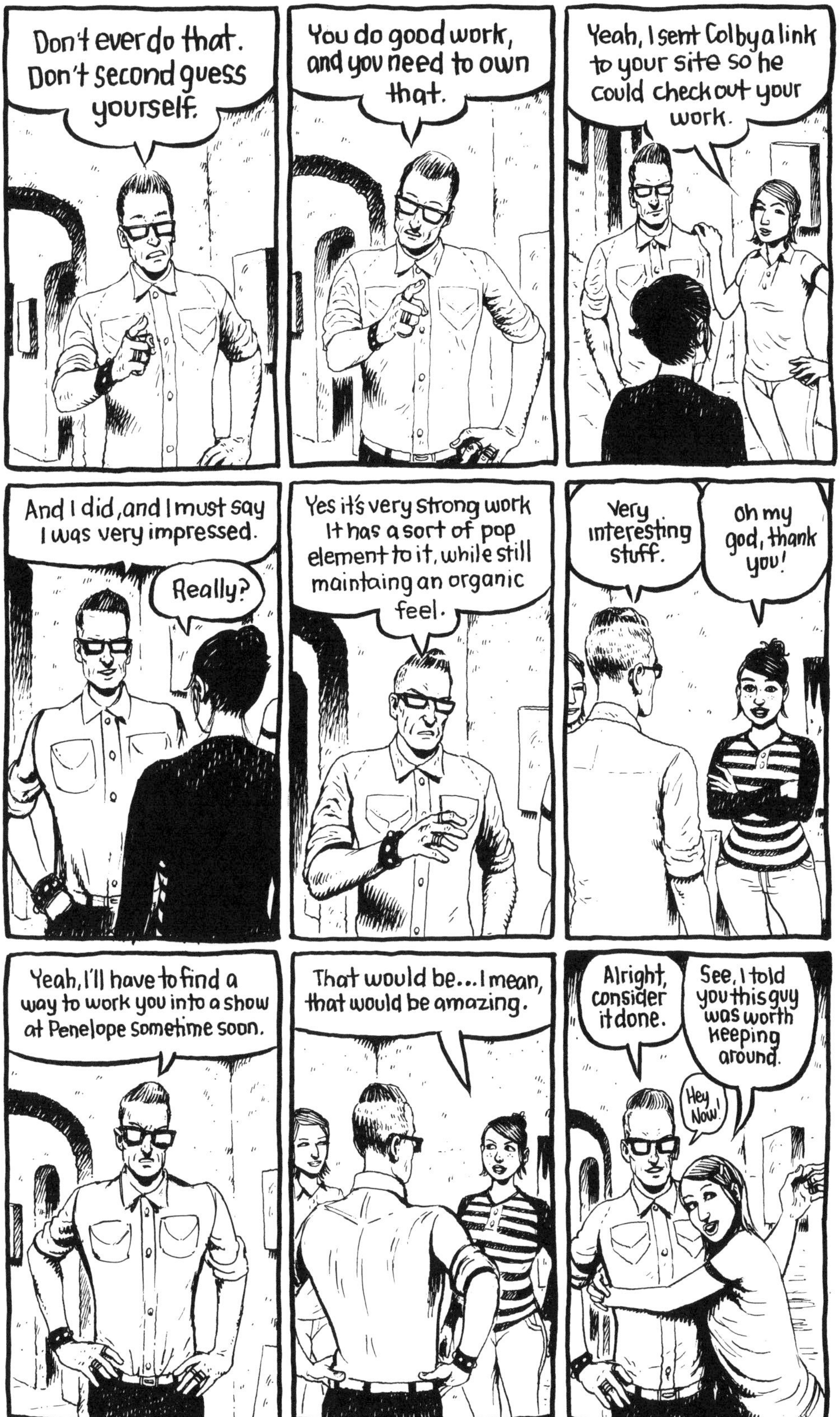
Don't ever do that. Don't second guess yourself.
You do good work, and you need to own that.
Yeah, I sent Colby a link to your site so he could check out your work.
And I did, and I must say I was very impressed.
Really?
Yes it's very strong work It has a sort of pop element to it, while still maintaining an organic feel.
Very interesting stuff.
Oh my god, thank you!
Yeah, I'll have to find a way to work you into a show at Penelope sometime soon.
That would be... I mean, that would be amazing.
Alright, consider it done.
See, I told you this guy was worth keeping around.
Hey Now!

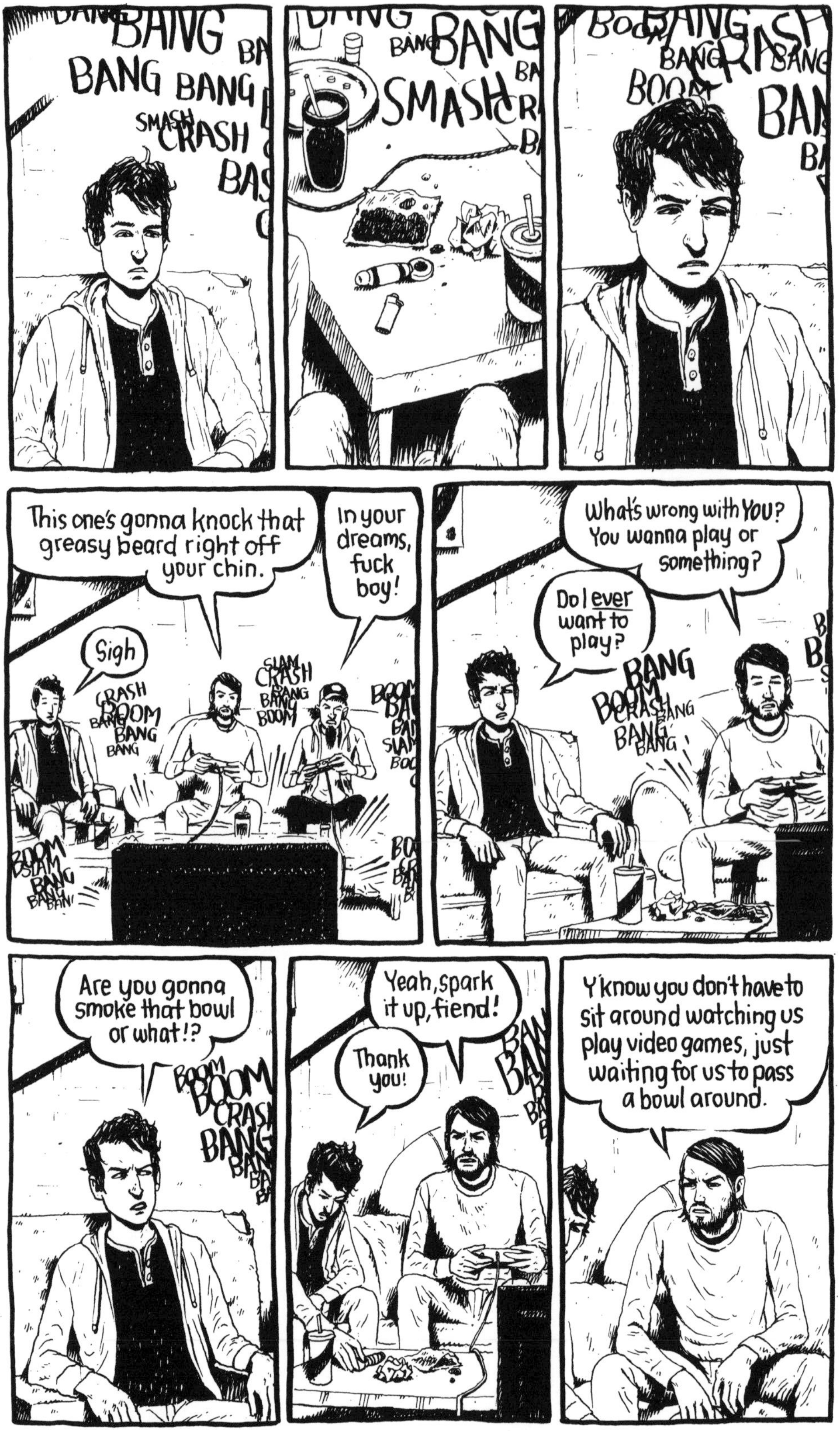
BANG
BANG BANG
SMASH CRASH
BANG
SMASH
BOOM
BANG
BANG
BOOM
BANG
This one's gonna knock that greasy beard right off your chin.
In your dreams, fuck boy!
Sigh
CRASH BOOM BANG BANG
SLAM CRASH BANG BOOM
BOOM SLAM BANG
What's wrong with YOU? You wanna play or something?
Do I ever want to play?
BANG BOOM CRASH BANG BANG BANG
Are you gonna smoke that bowl or what!?
BOOM BOOM CRASH BANG
Yeah, spark it up, fiend!
Thank you!
Y'know you don't have to sit around watching us play video games, just waiting for us to pass a bowl around.

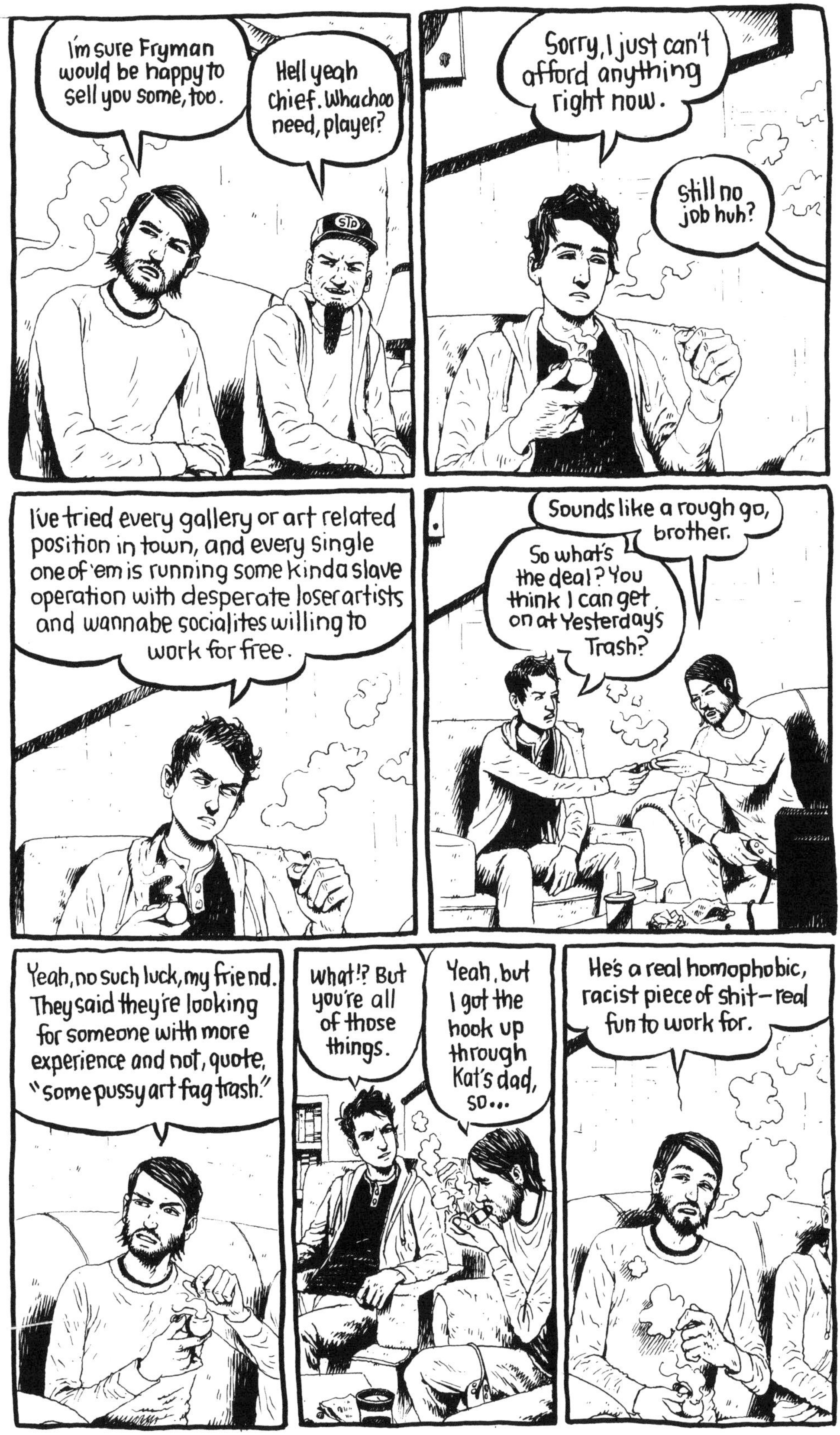
I'm sure Fryman would be happy to sell you some, too.
Hell yeah Chief. Whachoo need, player?
STD
Sorry, I just can't afford anything right now.
Still no job huh?
I've tried every gallery or art related position in town, and every single one of 'em is running some kinda slave operation with desperate loser artists and wannabe socialites willing to work for free.
Sounds like a rough go, brother.
So what's the deal? You think I can get on at Yesterday's Trash?
Yeah, no such luck, my friend. They said they're looking for someone with more experience and not, quote, "some pussy art fag trash."
What!? But you're all of those things.
Yeah, but I got the hook up through Kat's dad, so...
He's a real homophobic, racist piece of shit—real fun to work for.

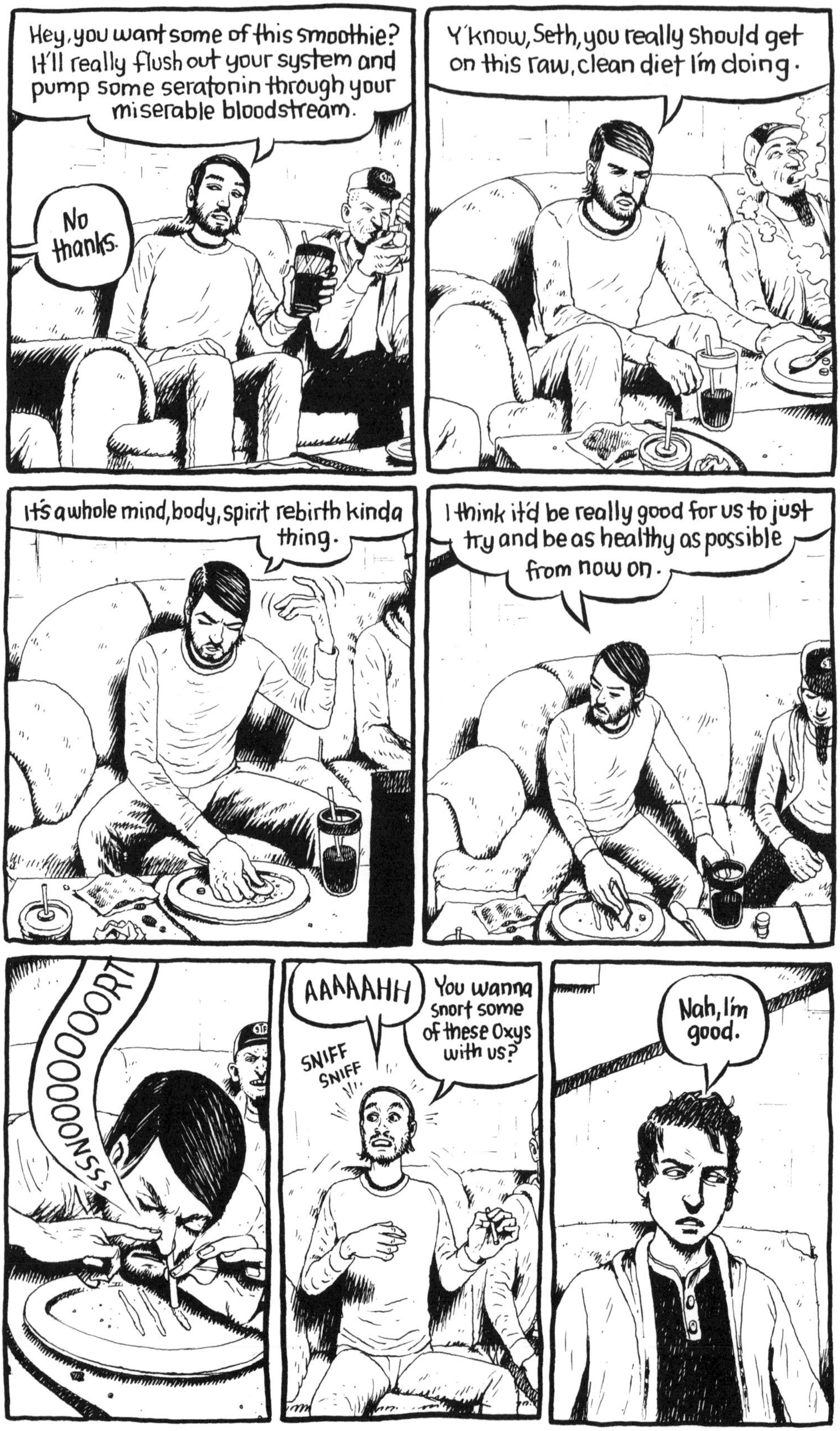
Hey, you want some of this smoothie? It'll really flush out your system and pump some seratonin through your miserable bloodstream.
No thanks.
Y'know, Seth, you really should get on this raw, clean diet I'm doing.
It's a whole mind, body, spirit rebirth kinda thing.
I think it'd be really good for us to just try and be as healthy as possible from now on.
SSNOOOOOOOORT
AAAAAHH
SNIFF SNIFF
You wanna snort some of these Oxys with us?
Nah, I'm good.

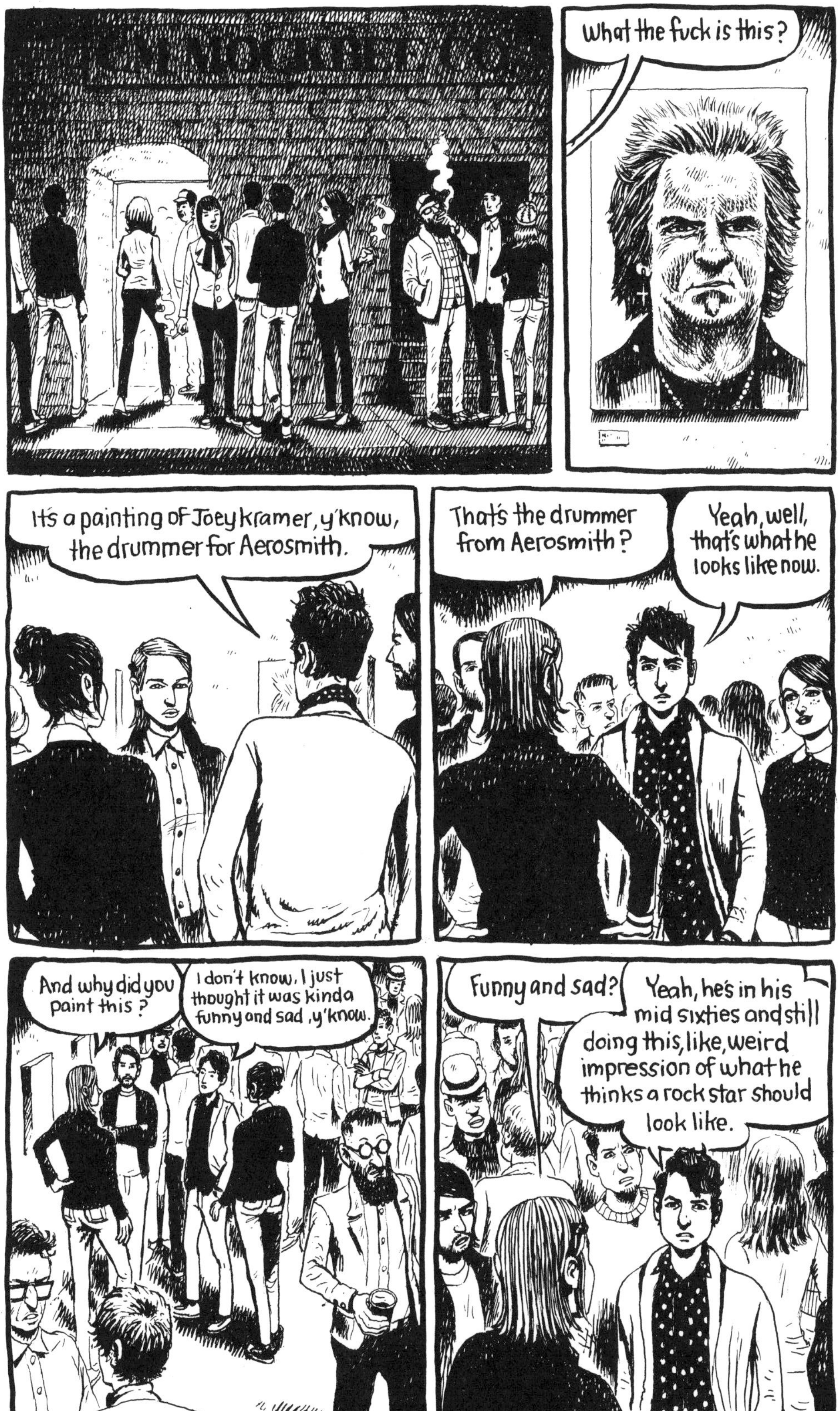
What the fuck is this?
It's a painting of Joey kramer, y'know, the drummer for Aerosmith.
That's the drummer from Aerosmith?
Yeah, well, that's what he looks like now.
And why did you paint this?
I don't know, I just thought it was kinda funny and sad, y'know.
Funny and sad?
Yeah, he's in his mid sixties and still doing this, like, weird impression of what he thinks a rock star should look like.

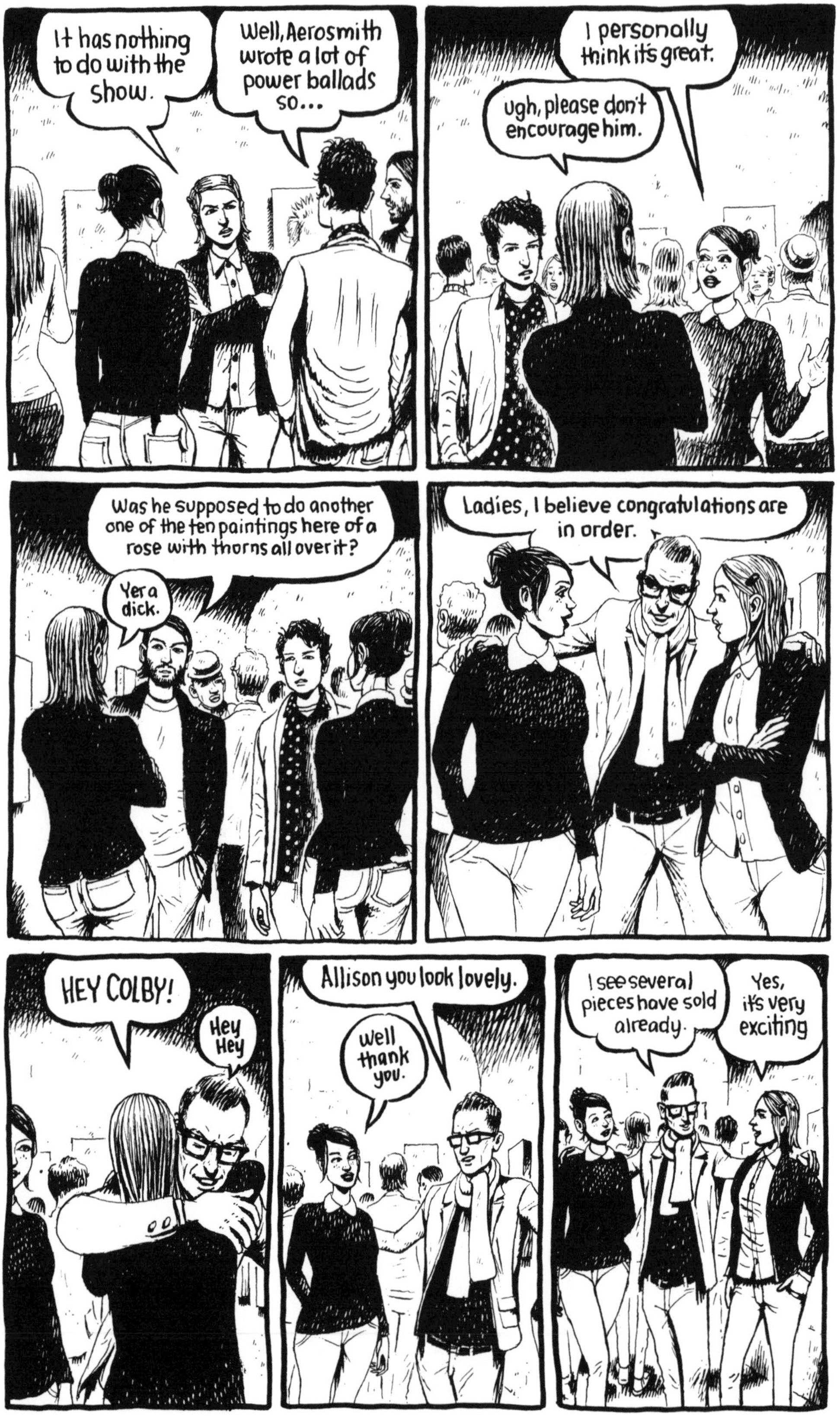
It has nothing to do with the show.
Well, Aerosmith wrote a lot of power ballads so...
I personally think it's great.
Ugh, please don't encourage him.
Was he supposed to do another one of the ten paintings here of a rose with thorns all over it?
Yer a dick.
Ladies, I believe congratulations are in order.
HEY COLBY!
Hey Hey
Allison you look lovely.
Well thank you.
I see several pieces have sold already.
Yes, it's very exciting

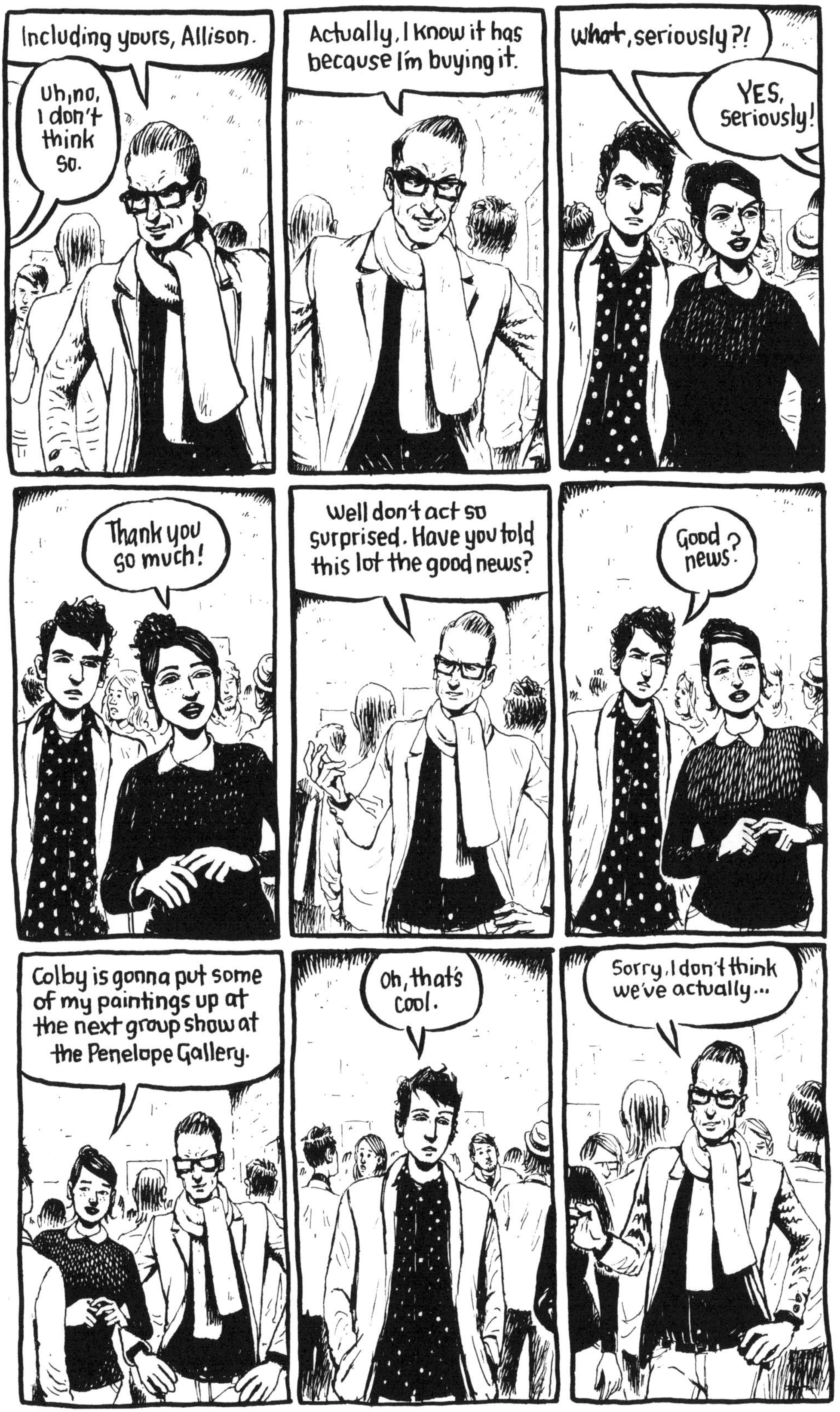
Including yours, Allison.
Uh, no, I don't think so.
Actually, I know it has because I'm buying it.
What, seriously?!
YES, seriously!
Thank you so much!
Well don't act so surprised. Have you told this lot the good news?
Good news?
Colby is gonna put some of my paintings up at the next group show at the Penelope Gallery.
Oh, that's cool.
Sorry, I don't think we've actually...

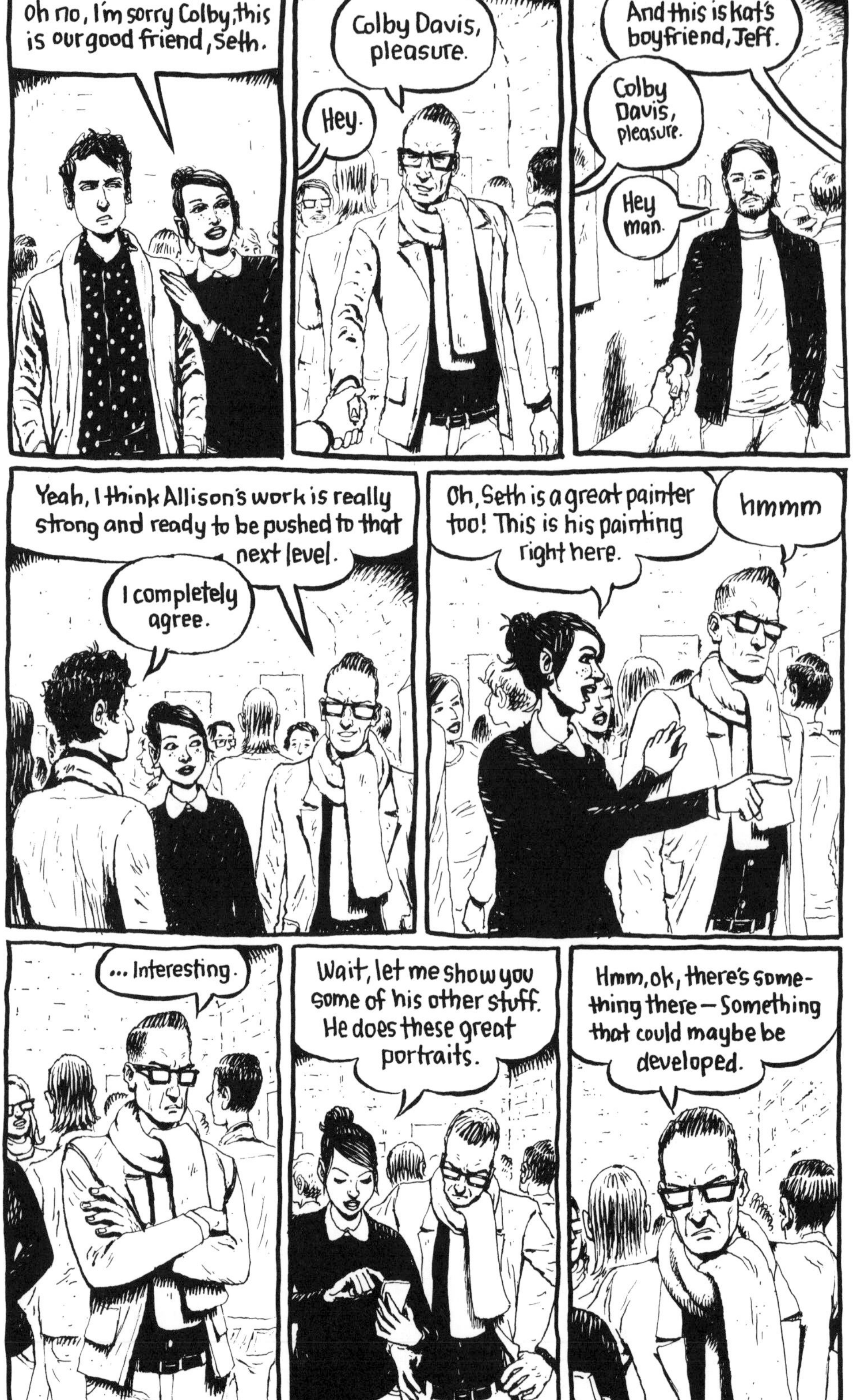
Oh no, I'm sorry Colby, this is our good friend, Seth.
Colby Davis, pleasure.
Hey.
And this is Kat's boyfriend, Jeff.
Colby Davis, pleasure.
Hey man.
Yeah, I think Allison's work is really strong and ready to be pushed to that next level.
I completely agree.
Oh, Seth is a great painter too! This is his painting right here.
hmmm
... Interesting.
Wait, let me show you some of his other stuff. He does these great portraits.
Hmm, ok, there's something there — Something that could maybe be developed.

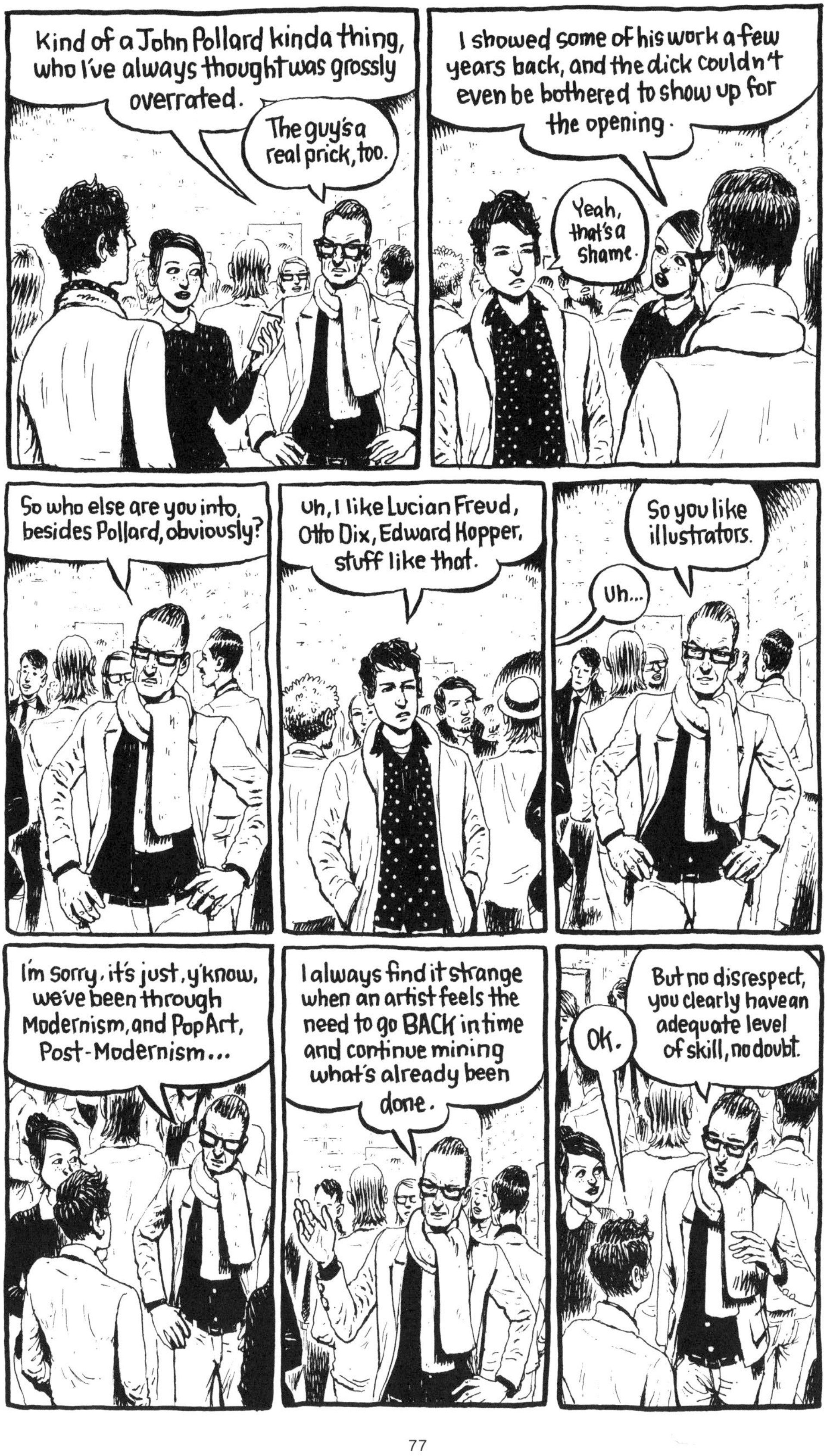

Kind of a John Pollard kinda thing, who I've always thought was grossly overrated.
The guy's a real prick, too.
I showed some of his work a few years back, and the dick couldn't even be bothered to show up for the opening.
Yeah, that's a shame.
So who else are you into, besides Pollard, obviously?
Uh, I like Lucian Freud, Otto Dix, Edward Hopper, stuff like that.
So you like illustrators.
Uh...
I'm sorry, it's just, y'know, we've been through Modernism, and Pop Art, Post-Modernism...
I always find it strange when an artist feels the need to go BACK in time and continue mining what's already been done.
But no disrespect, you clearly have an adequate level of skill, no doubt.
OK.

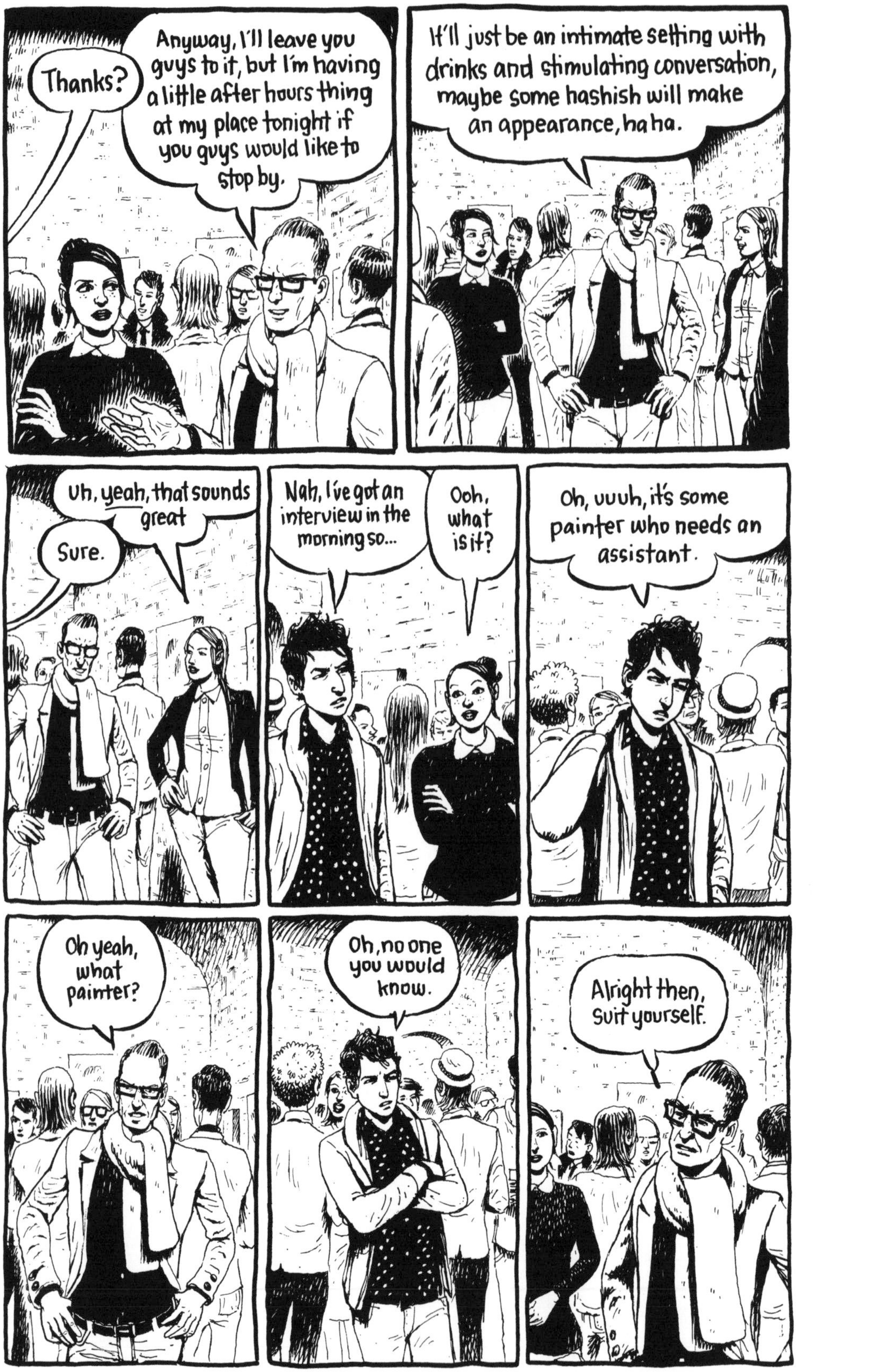
Thanks?
Anyway, I'll leave you guys to it, but I'm having a little after hours thing at my place tonight if you guys would like to stop by.
It'll just be an intimate setting with drinks and stimulating conversation, maybe some hashish will make an appearance, ha ha.
Uh, yeah, that sounds great
Sure.
Nah, I've got an interview in the morning so...
Ooh, what is it?
Oh, uuuh, it's some painter who needs an assistant.
Oh yeah, what painter?
Oh, no one you would know.
Alright then, suit yourself.

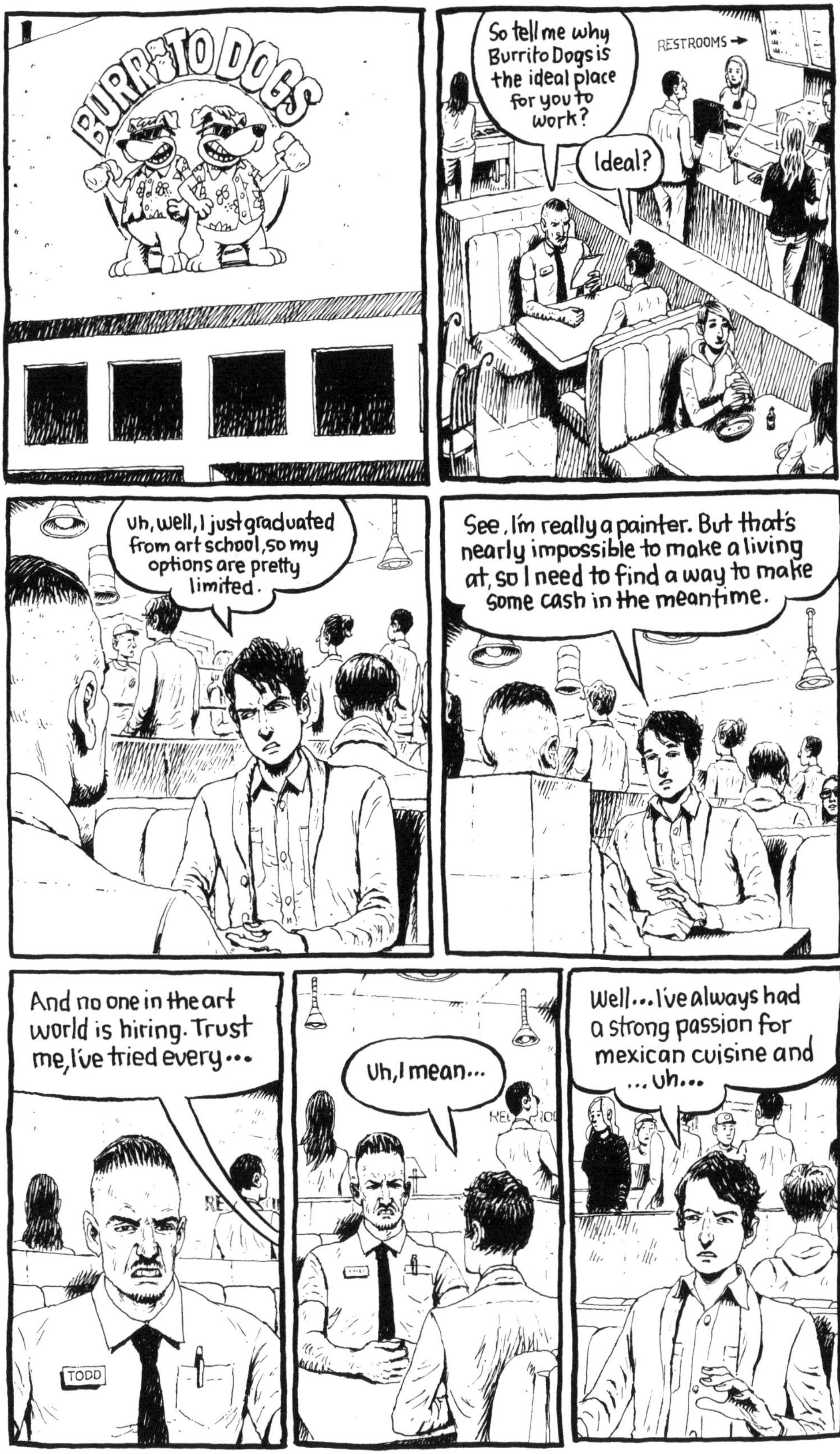
BURRITO DOGS
So tell me why Burrito Dogs is the ideal place for you to work?
RESTROOMS →
Ideal?
Uh, well, I just graduated from art school, so my options are pretty limited.
See, I'm really a painter. But that's nearly impossible to make a living at, so I need to find a way to make some cash in the meantime.
And no one in the art world is hiring. Trust me, I've tried every...
TODD
Uh, I mean...
Well... I've always had a strong passion for mexican cuisine and ...uh...

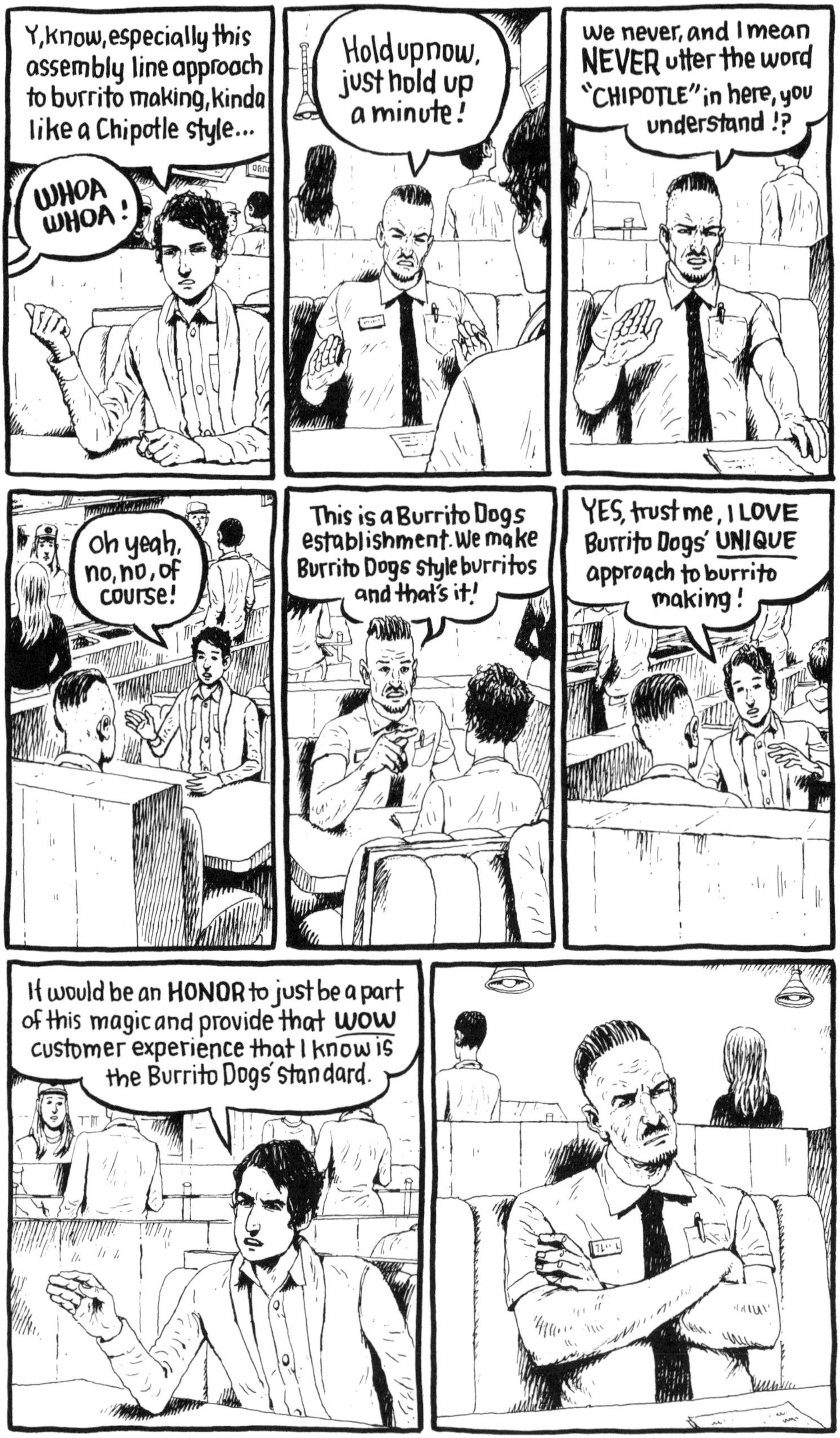
Y,know, especially this assembly line approach to burrito making, kinda like a Chipotle style...
WHOA WHOA!
Hold up now, just hold up a minute!
We never, and I mean NEVER utter the word "CHIPOTLE" in here, you understand !?
Oh yeah, no, no, of course!
This is a Burrito Dogs establishment. We make Burrito Dogs style burritos and that's it!
YES, trust me, I LOVE Burrito Dogs' UNIQUE approach to burrito making!
It would be an HONOR to just be a part of this magic and provide that WOW customer experience that I know is the Burrito Dogs' standard.

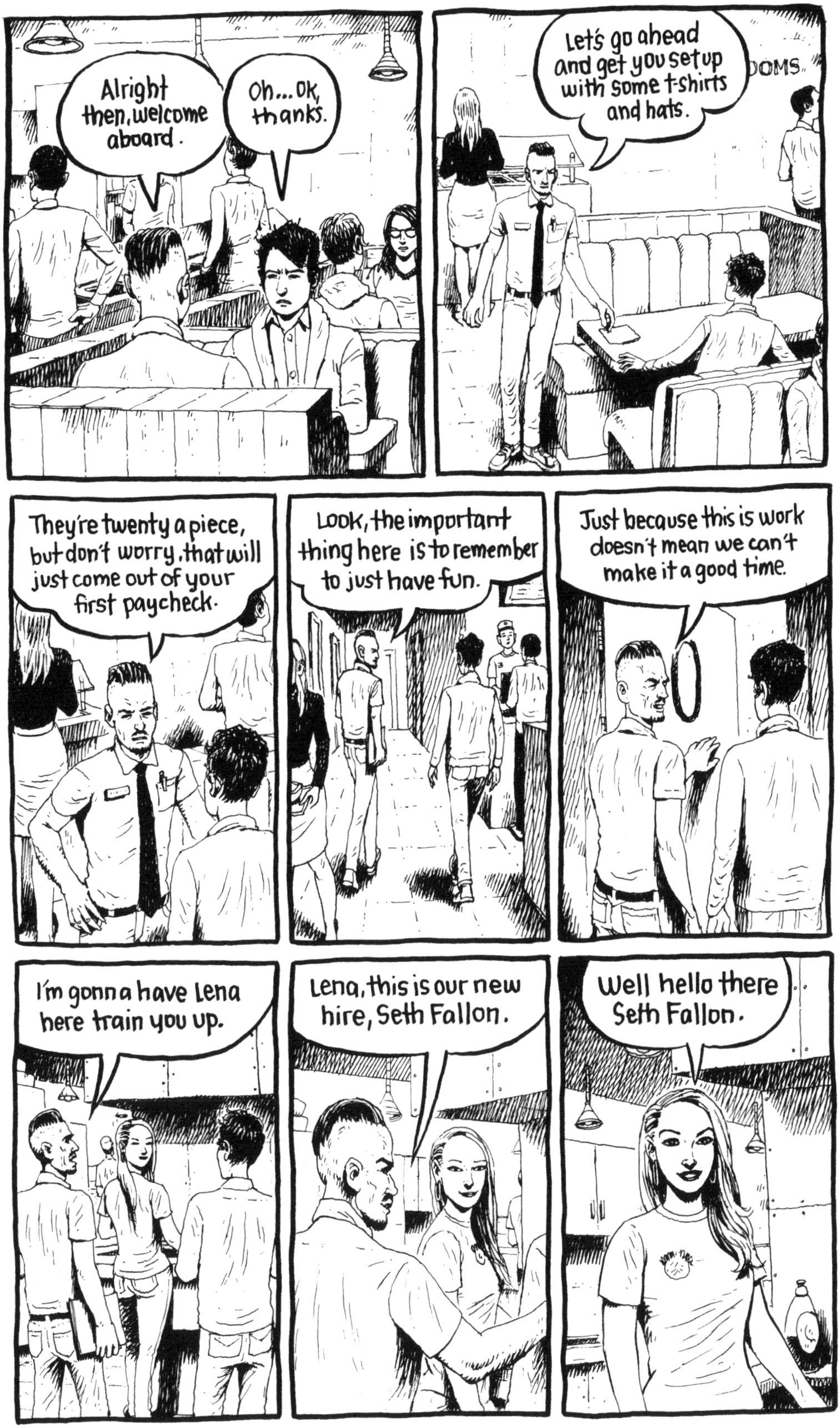
Alright then, welcome aboard.
Oh... ok, thanks.
Let's go ahead and get you set up with some t-shirts and hats.
They're twenty a piece, but don't worry, that will just come out of your first paycheck.
Look, the important thing here is to remember to just have fun.
Just because this is work doesn't mean we can't make it a good time.
I'm gonna have Lena here train you up.
Lena, this is our new hire, Seth Fallon.
Well hello there Seth Fallon.

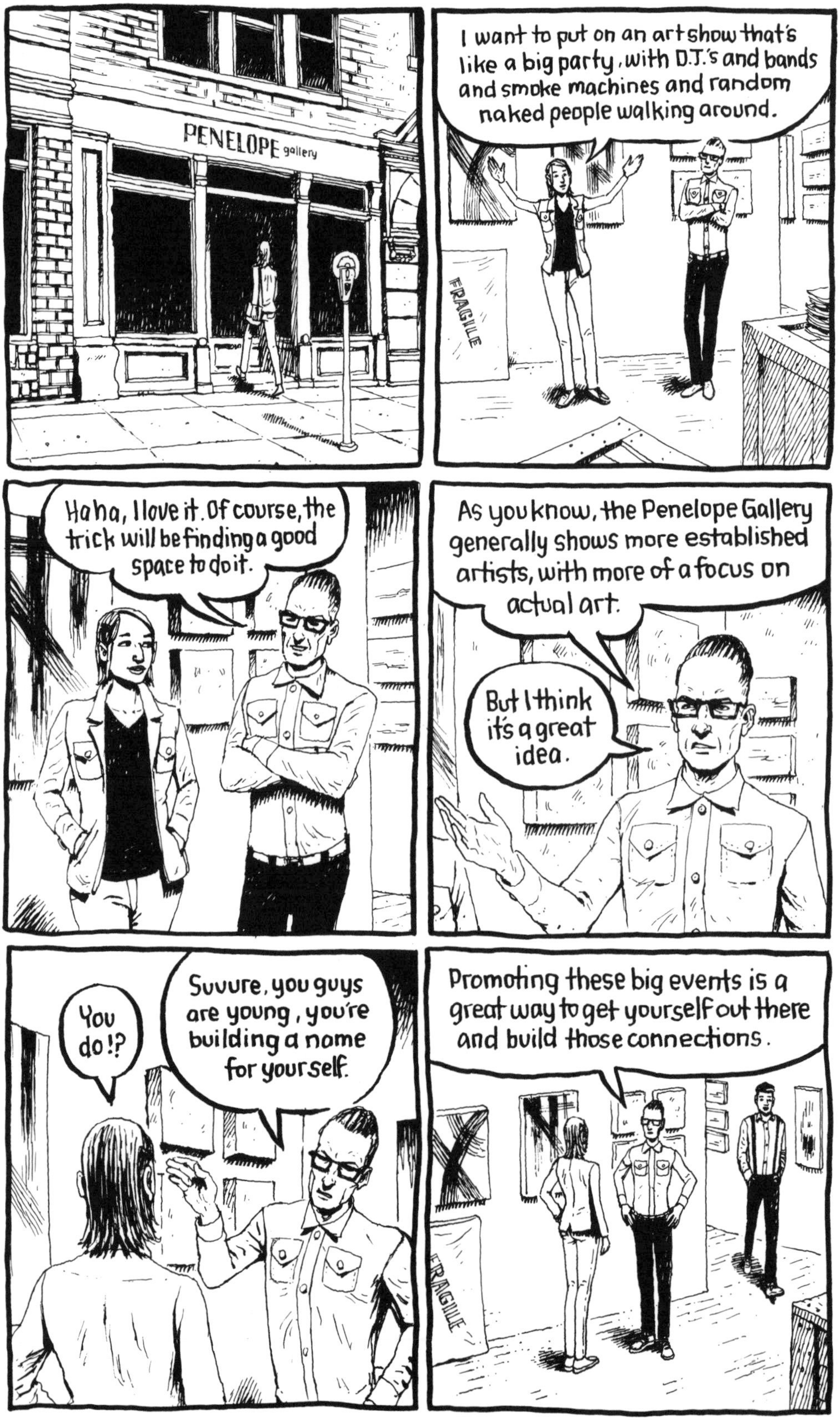
PENELOPE gallery
I want to put on an art show that's like a big party, with D.J.'s and bands and smoke machines and random naked people walking around.
FRAGILE
Haha, I love it. Of course, the trick will be finding a good space to do it.
As you know, the Penelope Gallery generally shows more established artists, with more of a focus on actual art.
But I think it's a great idea.
You do!?
Suuure, you guys are young, you're building a name for yourself.
Promoting these big events is a great way to get yourself out there and build those connections.
FRAGILE

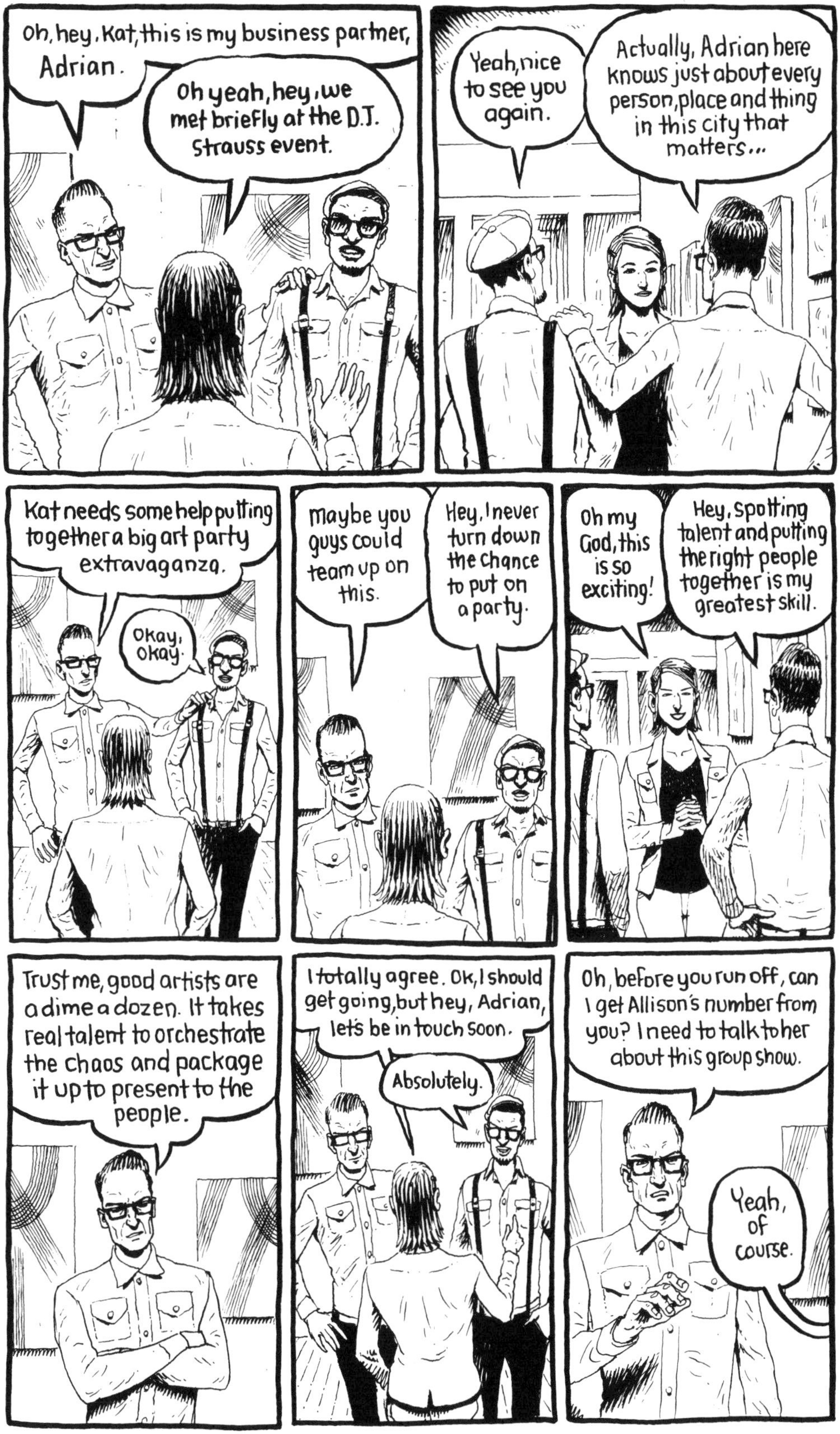
Oh, hey. Kat, this is my business partner, Adrian.
Oh yeah, hey, we met briefly at the D.J. Strauss event.
Yeah, nice to see you again.
Actually, Adrian here knows just about every person, place and thing in this city that matters...
Kat needs some help putting together a big art party extravaganza.
Okay, Okay.
Maybe you guys could team up on this.
Hey, I never turn down the chance to put on a party.
Oh my God, this is so exciting!
Hey, spotting talent and putting the right people together is my greatest skill.
Trust me, good artists are a dime a dozen. It takes real talent to orchestrate the chaos and package it up to present to the people.
I totally agree. Ok, I should get going, but hey, Adrian, let's be in touch soon.
Absolutely.
Oh, before you run off, can I get Allison's number from you? I need to talk to her about this group show.
Yeah, of course.

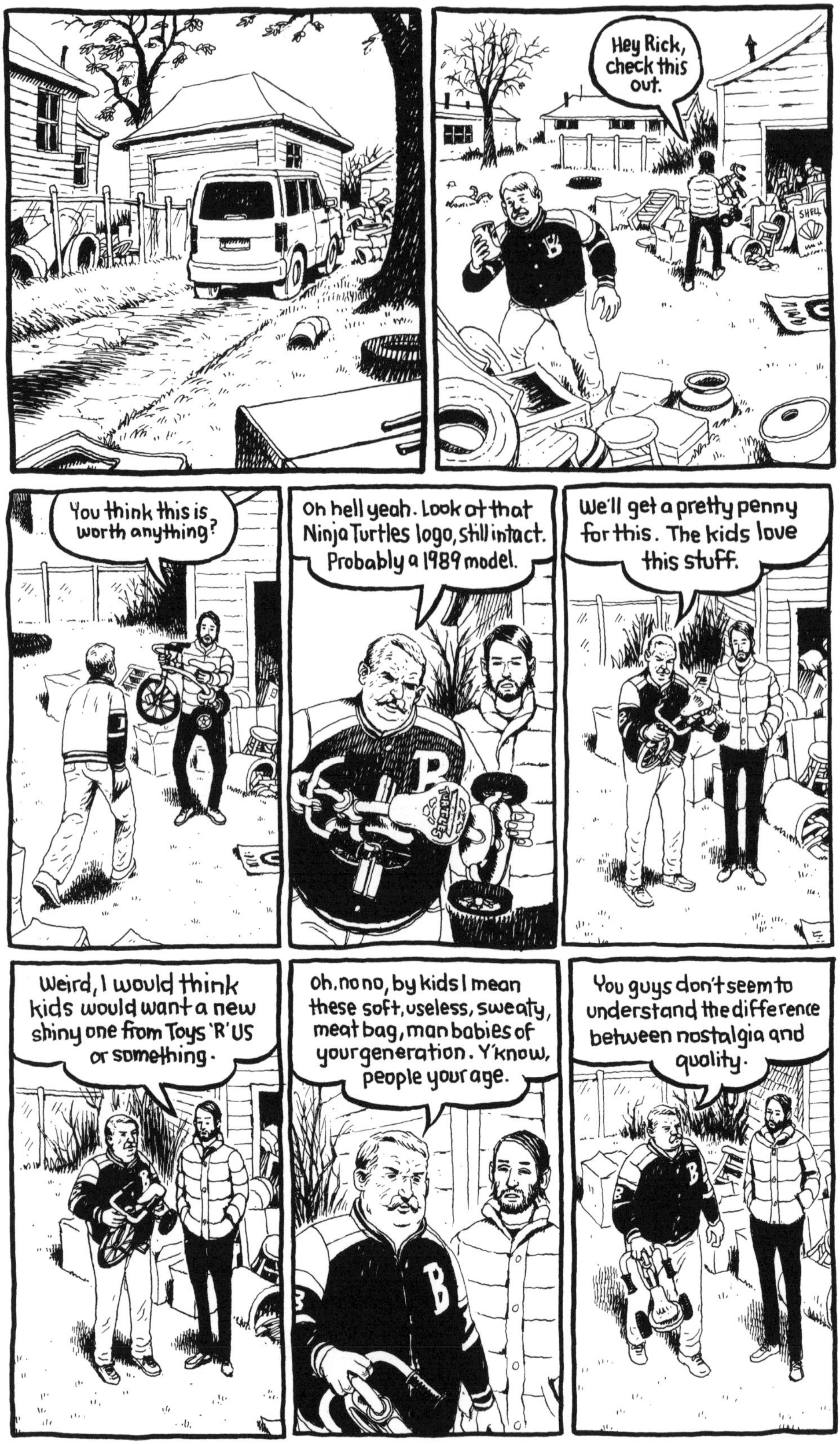
Hey Rick, check this out.
SHELL
You think this is worth anything?
Oh hell yeah. Look at that Ninja Turtles logo, still intact. Probably a 1989 model.
We'll get a pretty penny for this. The kids love this stuff.
Weird, I would think kids would want a new shiny one from Toys 'R' US or something.
Oh, no no, by kids I mean these soft, useless, sweaty, meat bag, man babies of your generation. Y'know, people your age.
You guys don't seem to understand the difference between nostalgia and quality.

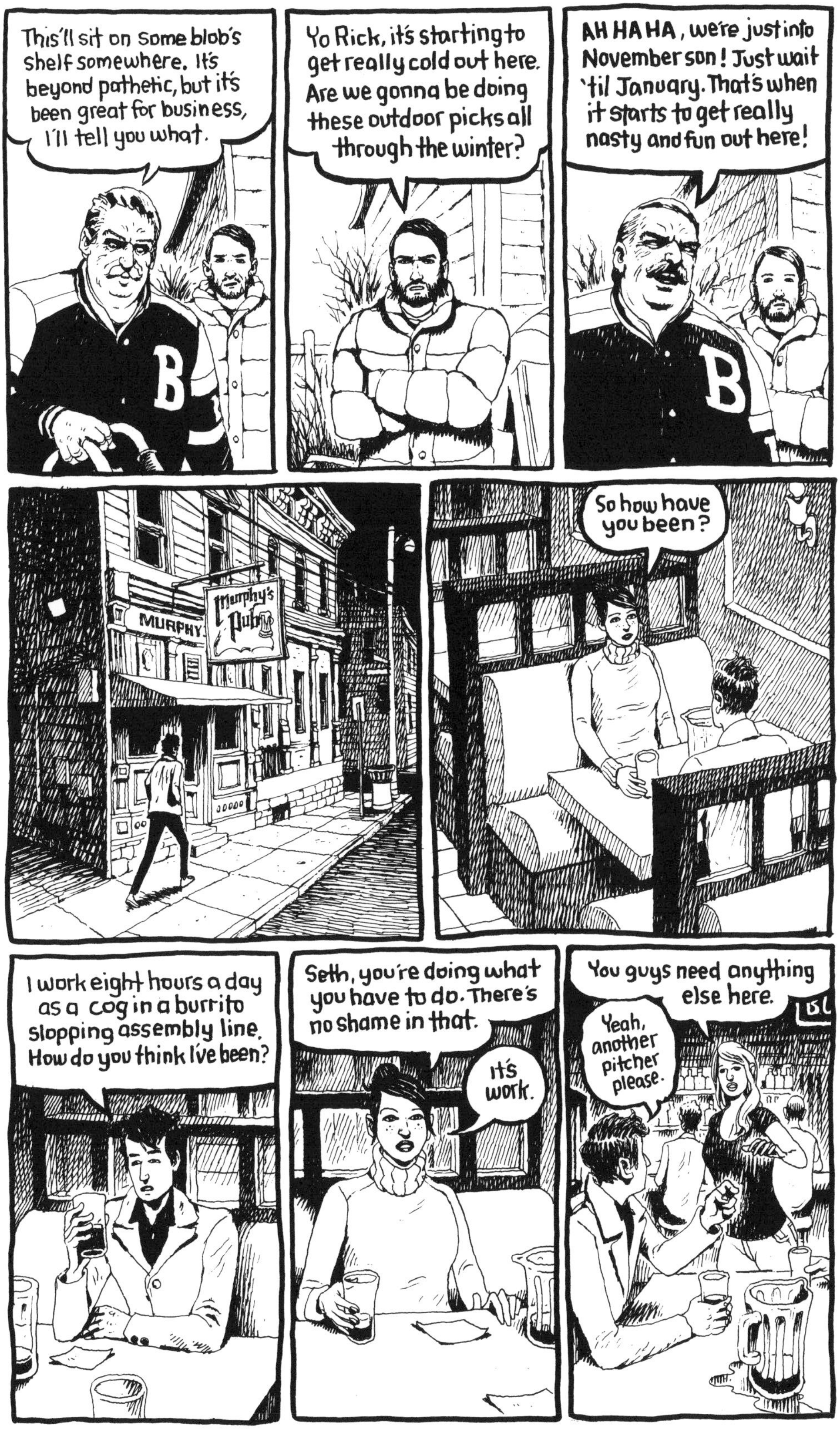
This'll sit on some blob's shelf somewhere. It's beyond pathetic, but it's been great for business, I'll tell you what.
Yo Rick, it's starting to get really cold out here. Are we gonna be doing these outdoor picks all through the winter?
AH HA HA, we're just into November son! Just wait 'til January. That's when it starts to get really nasty and fun out here!
B
MURPHY
Murphy's Pub
So how have you been?
I work eight hours a day as a cog in a burrito slopping assembly line. How do you think I've been?
Seth, you're doing what you have to do. There's no shame in that.
It's work.
You guys need anything else here.
Yeah, another pitcher please.

Oh, I'm probably not gonna drink anymore.

That's ok, I'll drink it.

What's that?

BZZZ BZZZ

oh that Colby guy keeps texting me about the show.

YEGCHH!

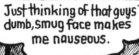

Just thinking of that guys' dumb, smug face makes me nauseous.

Just the worst combination of super confident and talentless.

He's probably one of those guys who says stuff like, "My greatest talent is spotting other people's talent," as if that's really a talent.

Like all those super wealthy guys in those VH1 documentaries, like David Geffen or Clive Davis.

Yeah, I guess he's kinda irritating, but his gallery is sort of a big deal, and he's showing my work so...

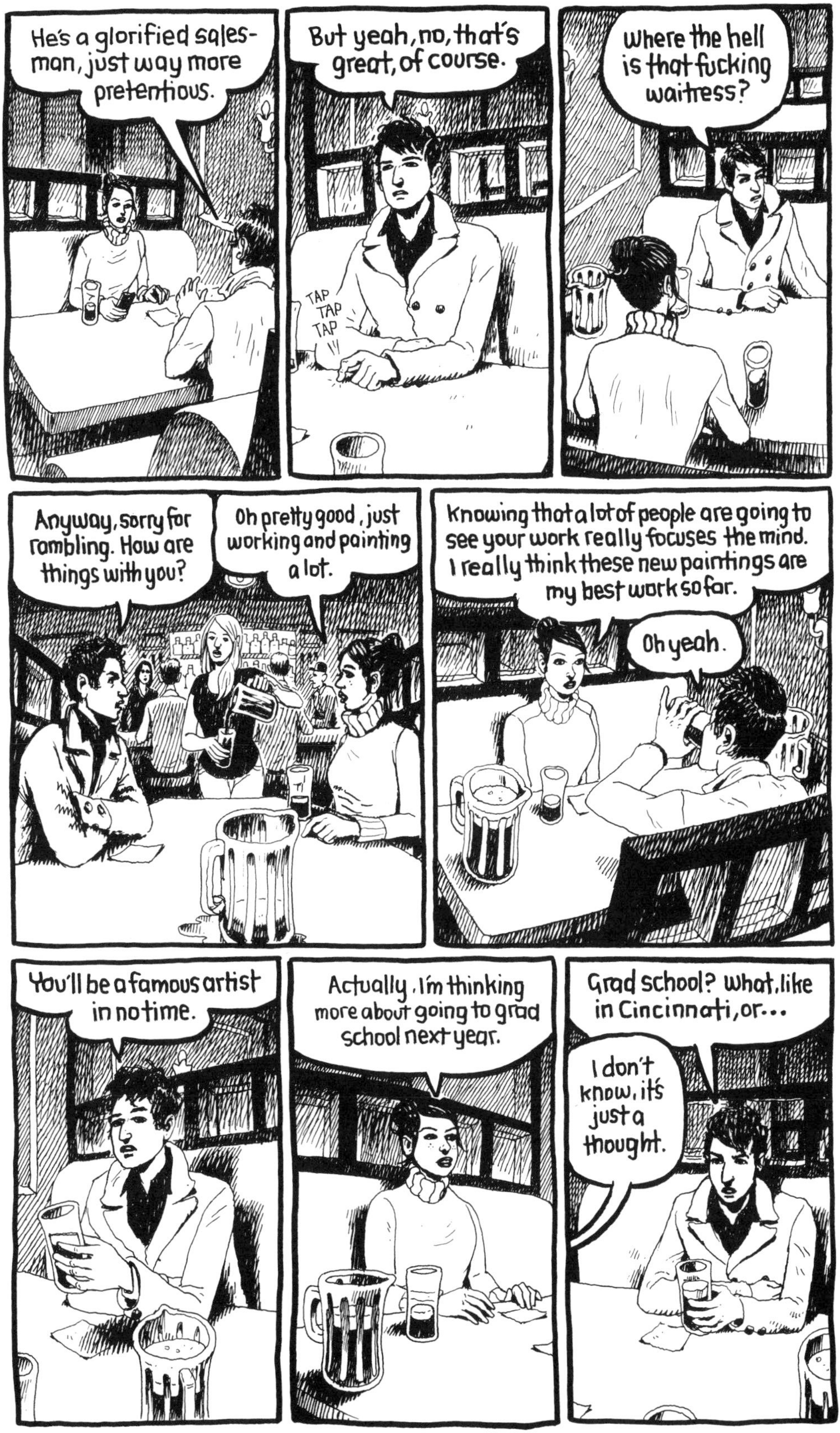
He's a glorified salesman, just way more pretentious.
But yeah, no, that's great, of course.
TAP TAP TAP
Where the hell is that fucking waitress?
Anyway, sorry for rambling. How are things with you?
Oh pretty good, just working and painting a lot.
Knowing that a lot of people are going to see your work really focuses the mind. I really think these new paintings are my best work so far.
Oh yeah.
You'll be a famous artist in no time.
Actually, I'm thinking more about going to grad school next year.
Grad school? What, like in Cincinnati, or...
I don't know, it's just a thought.

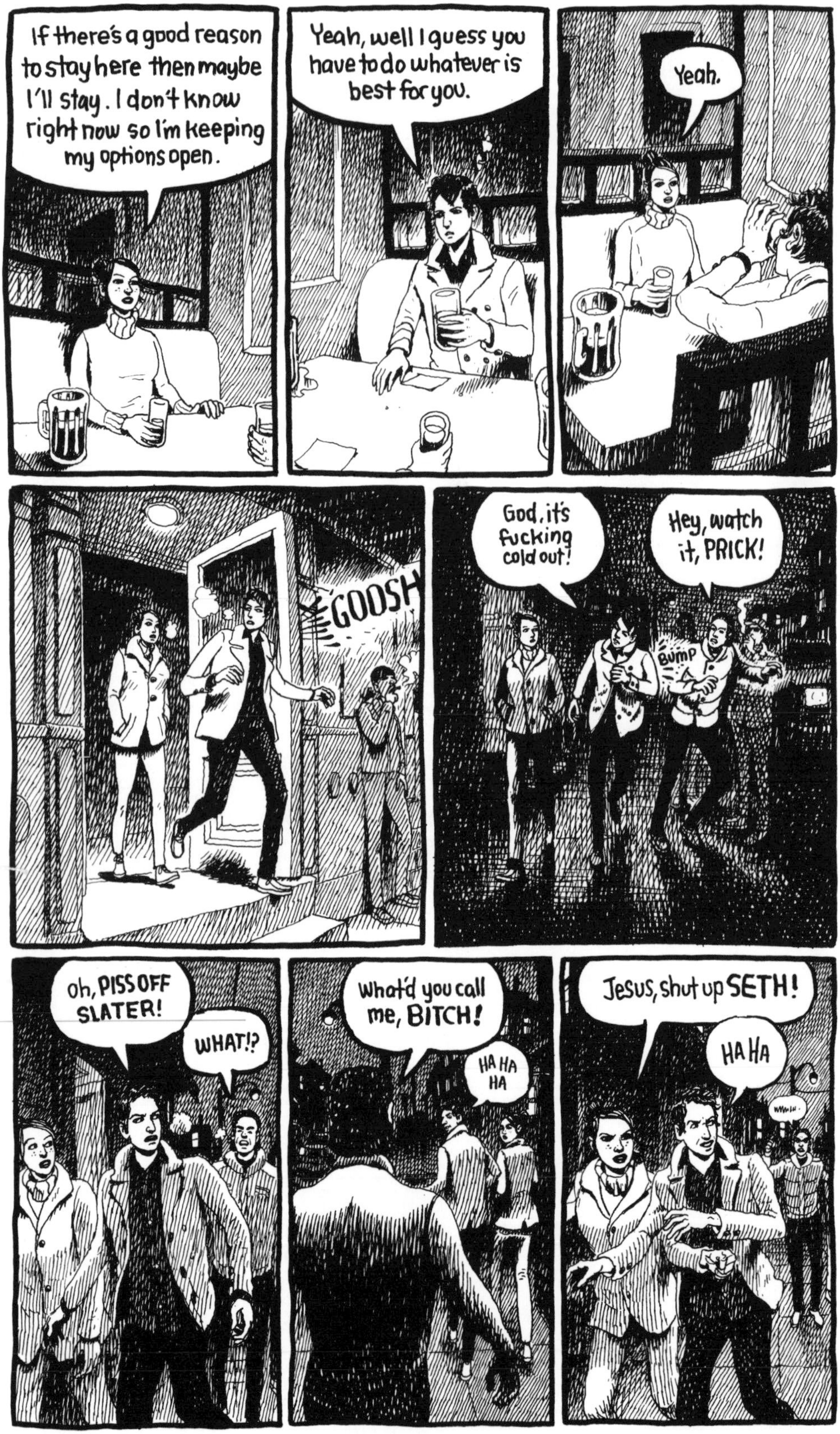
If there's a good reason to stay here then maybe I'll stay. I don't know right now so I'm keeping my options open.
Yeah, well I guess you have to do whatever is best for you.
Yeah.
GOOSH
God, it's fucking cold out!
Hey, watch it, PRICK!
BUMP
Oh, PISS OFF SLATER!
WHAT!?
What'd you call me, BITCH!
HA HA HA
Jesus, shut up SETH!
HA HA

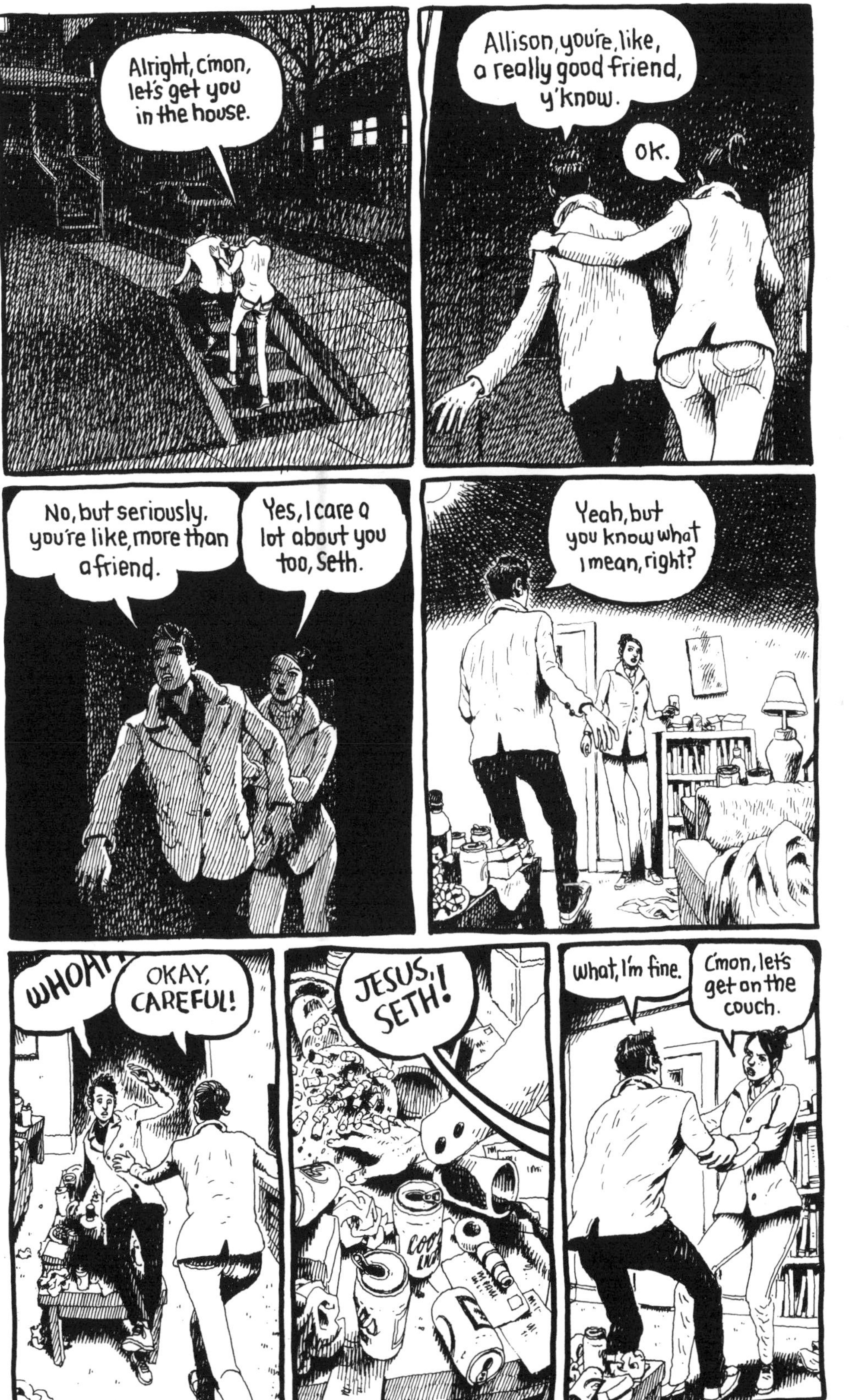
Alright, c'mon, let's get you in the house.
Allison, you're, like, a really good friend, y'know.
OK.
No, but seriously. you're like, more than a friend.
Yes, I care a lot about you too, Seth.
Yeah, but you know what I mean, right?
WHOAH
OKAY, CAREFUL!
JESUS, SETH!
What, I'm fine.
C'mon, let's get on the couch.

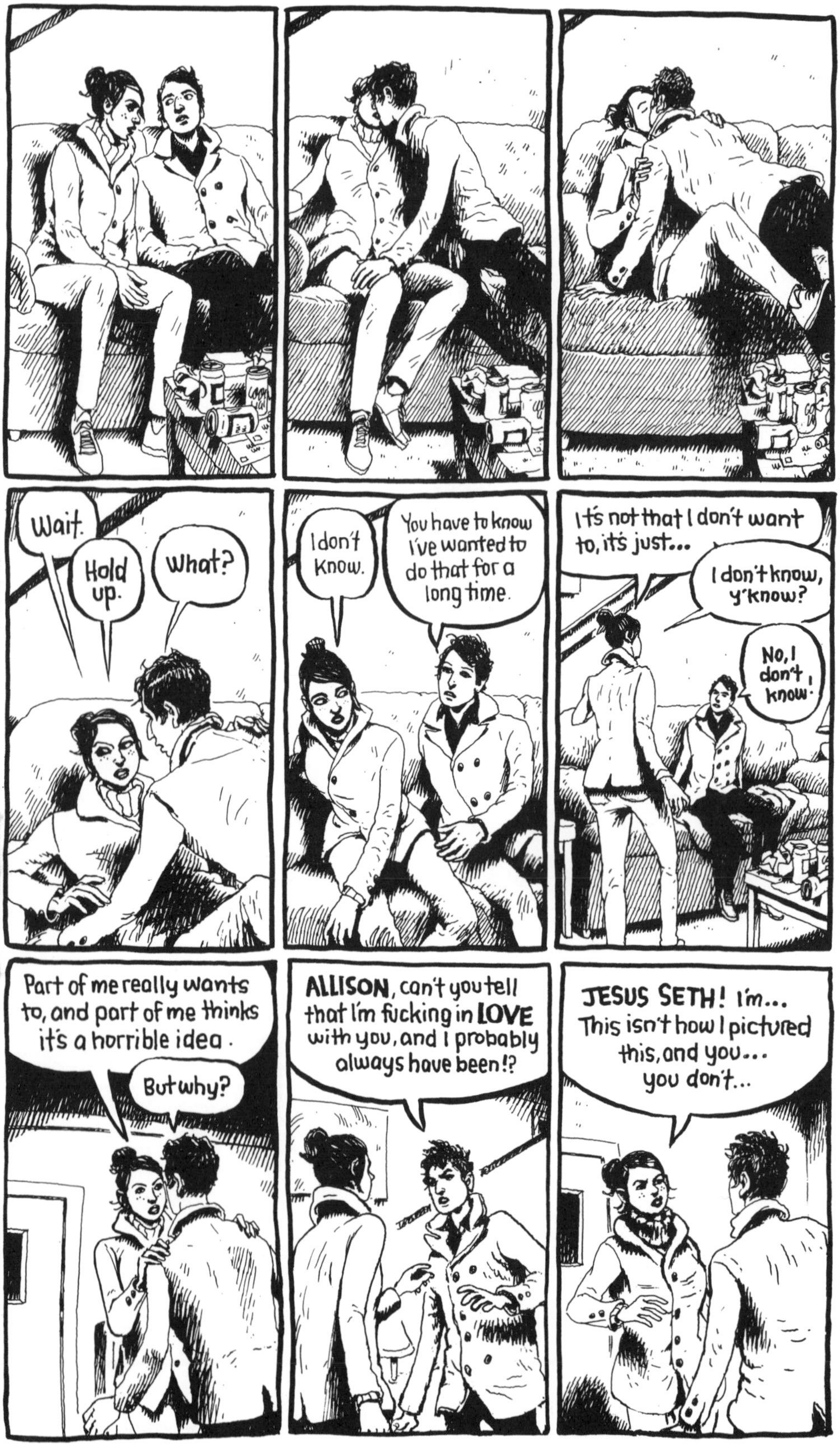

Wait.
Hold up.
What?
I don't know.
You have to know I've wanted to do that for a long time.
It's not that I don't want to, it's just...
I don't know, y'know?
No, I don't know.
Part of me really wants to, and part of me thinks it's a horrible idea.
But why?
ALLISON, can't you tell that I'm fucking in LOVE with you, and I probably always have been!?
JESUS SETH! I'm... This isn't how I pictured this, and you... you don't...

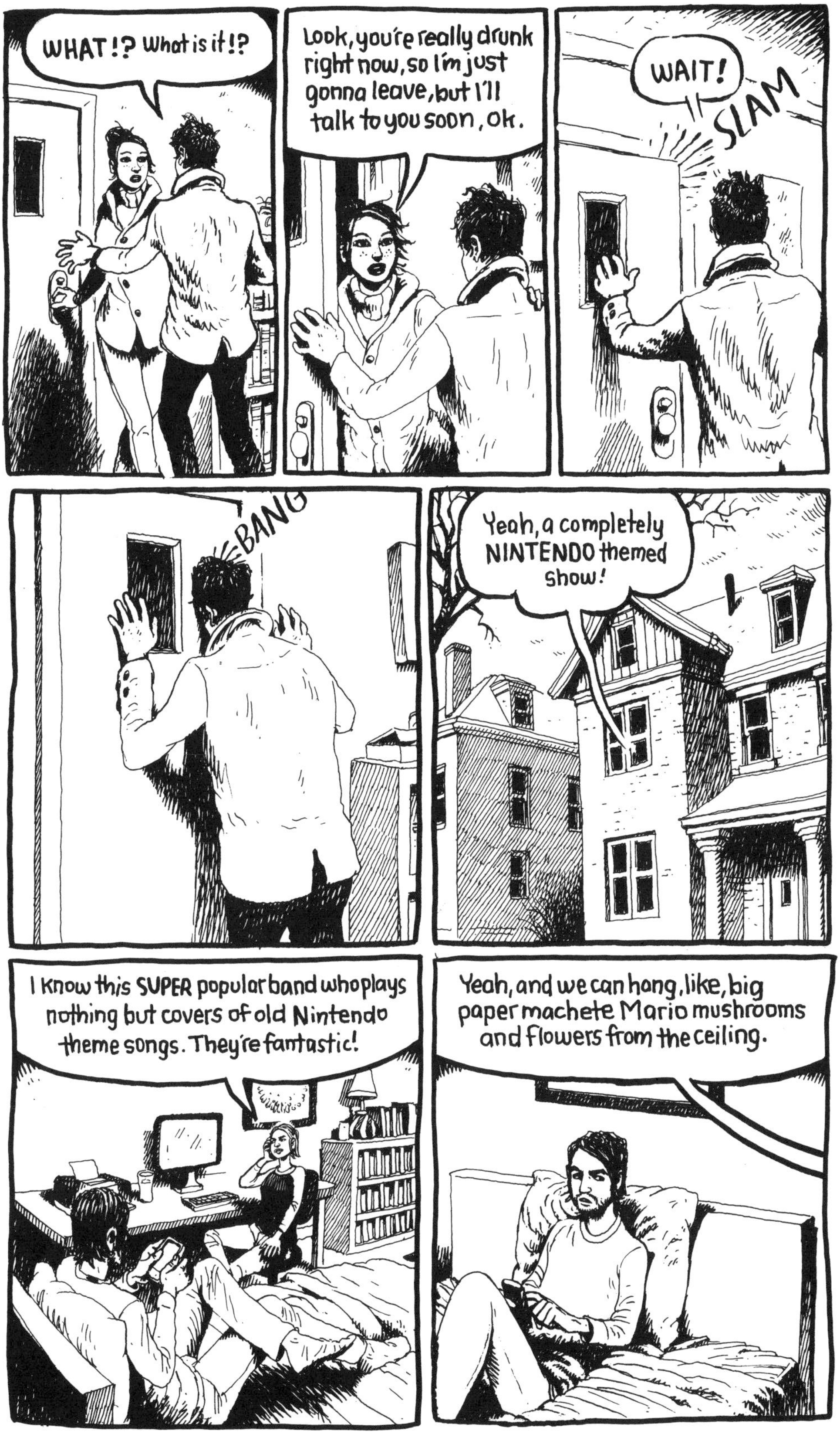
WHAT!? What is it!?
Look, you're really drunk right now, so I'm just gonna leave, but I'll talk to you soon, ok.
WAIT!
SLAM
BANG
Yeah, a completely NINTENDO themed show!
I know this SUPER popular band who plays nothing but covers of old Nintendo theme songs. They're fantastic!
Yeah, and we can hang, like, big paper machete Mario mushrooms and flowers from the ceiling.

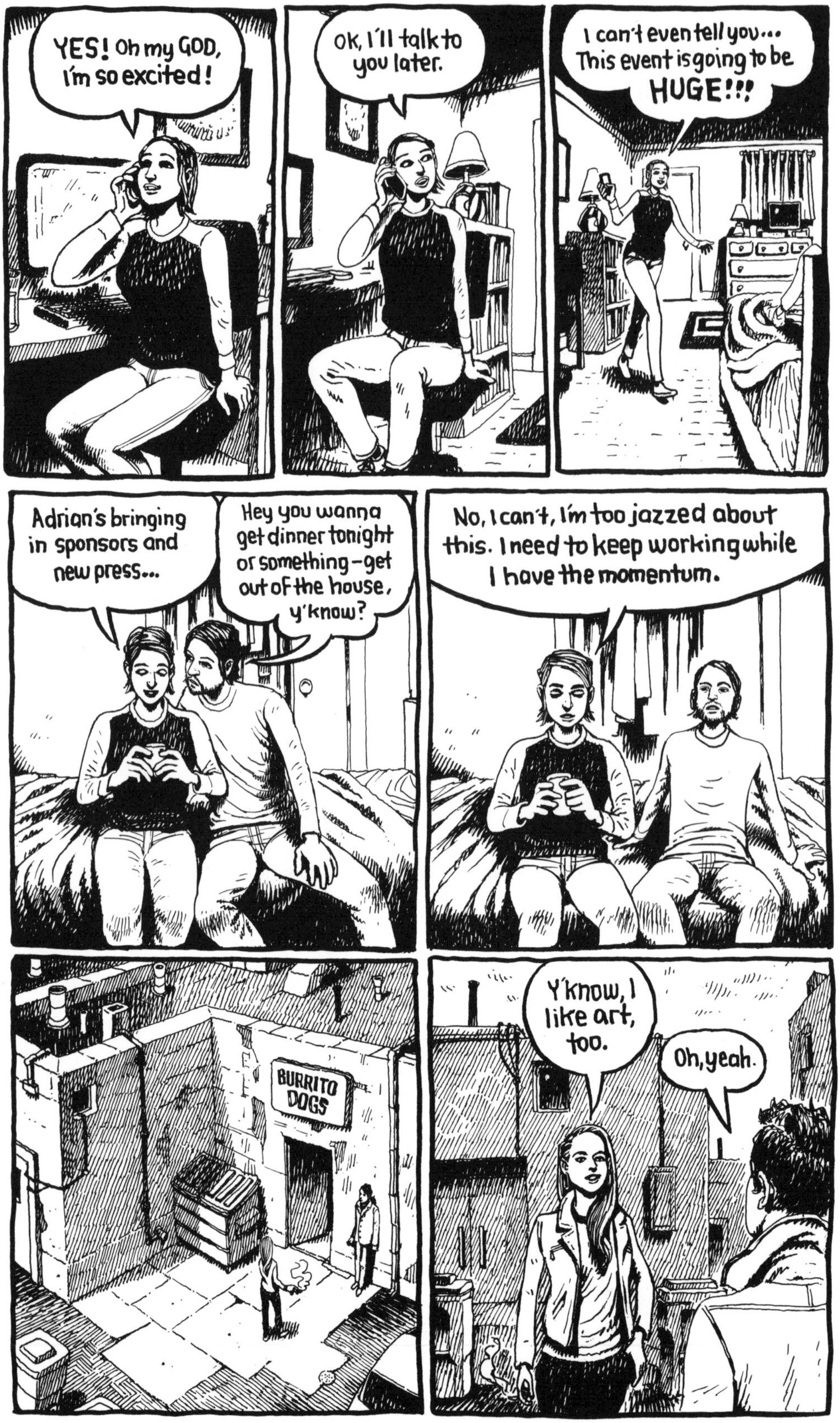
YES! Oh my GOD, I'm so excited!
Ok, I'll talk to you later.
I can't even tell you... This event is going to be HUGE!!!
Adrian's bringing in sponsors and new press...
Hey you wanna get dinner tonight or something – get out of the house, y'know?
No, I can't, I'm too jazzed about this. I need to keep working while I have the momentum.
BURRITO DOGS
Y'know, I like art, too.
Oh, yeah.

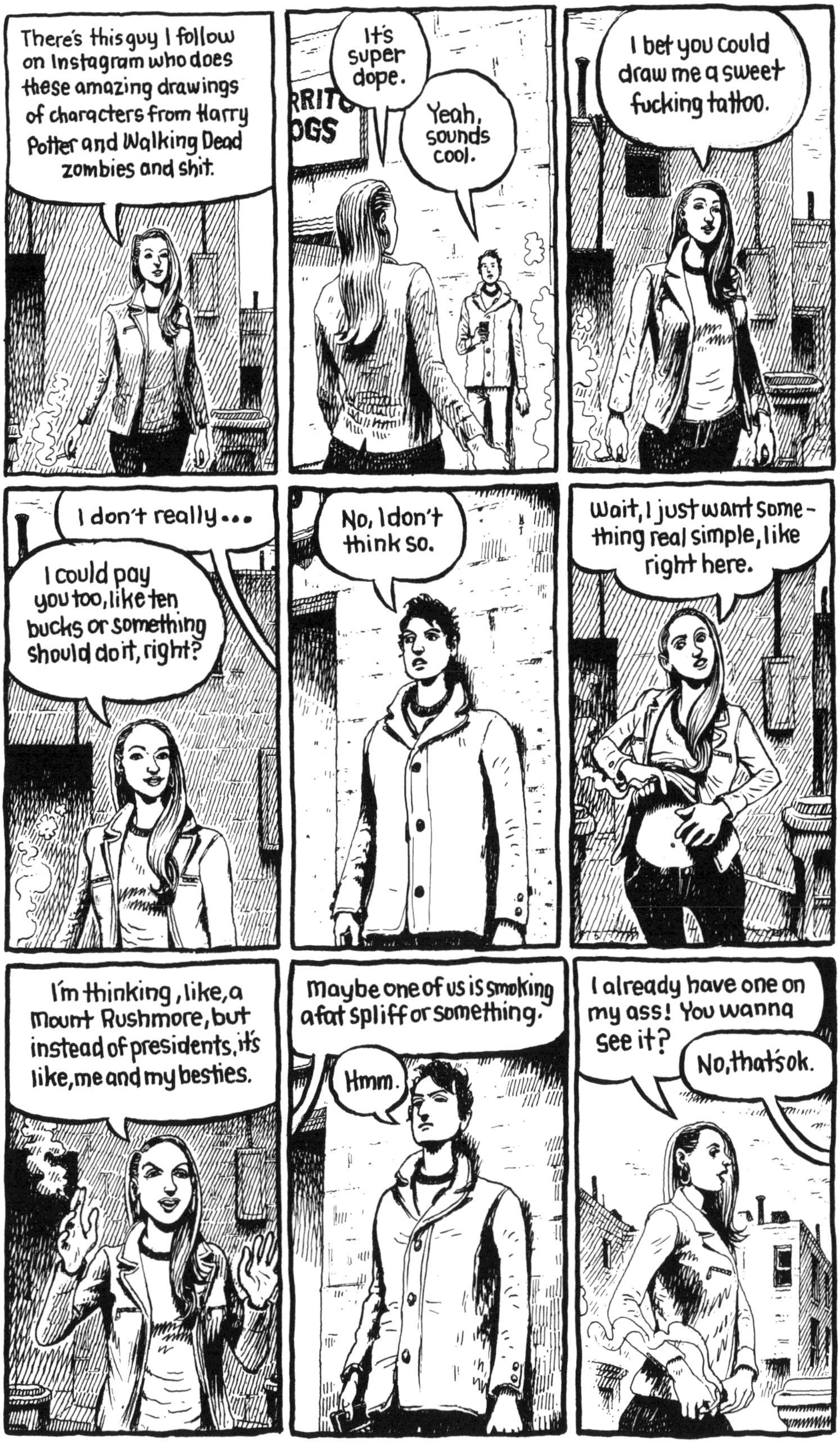
There's this guy I follow on Instagram who does these amazing drawings of characters from Harry Potter and Walking Dead zombies and shit.
It's super dope.
Yeah, sounds cool.
RRITO
OGS
I bet you could draw me a sweet fucking tattoo.
I don't really...
I could pay you too, like ten bucks or something should do it, right?
No, I don't think so.
Wait, I just want something real simple, like right here.
I'm thinking, like, a Mount Rushmore, but instead of presidents, it's like, me and my besties.
Maybe one of us is smoking a fat spliff or something.
Hmm.
I already have one on my ass! You wanna see it?
No, that's ok.

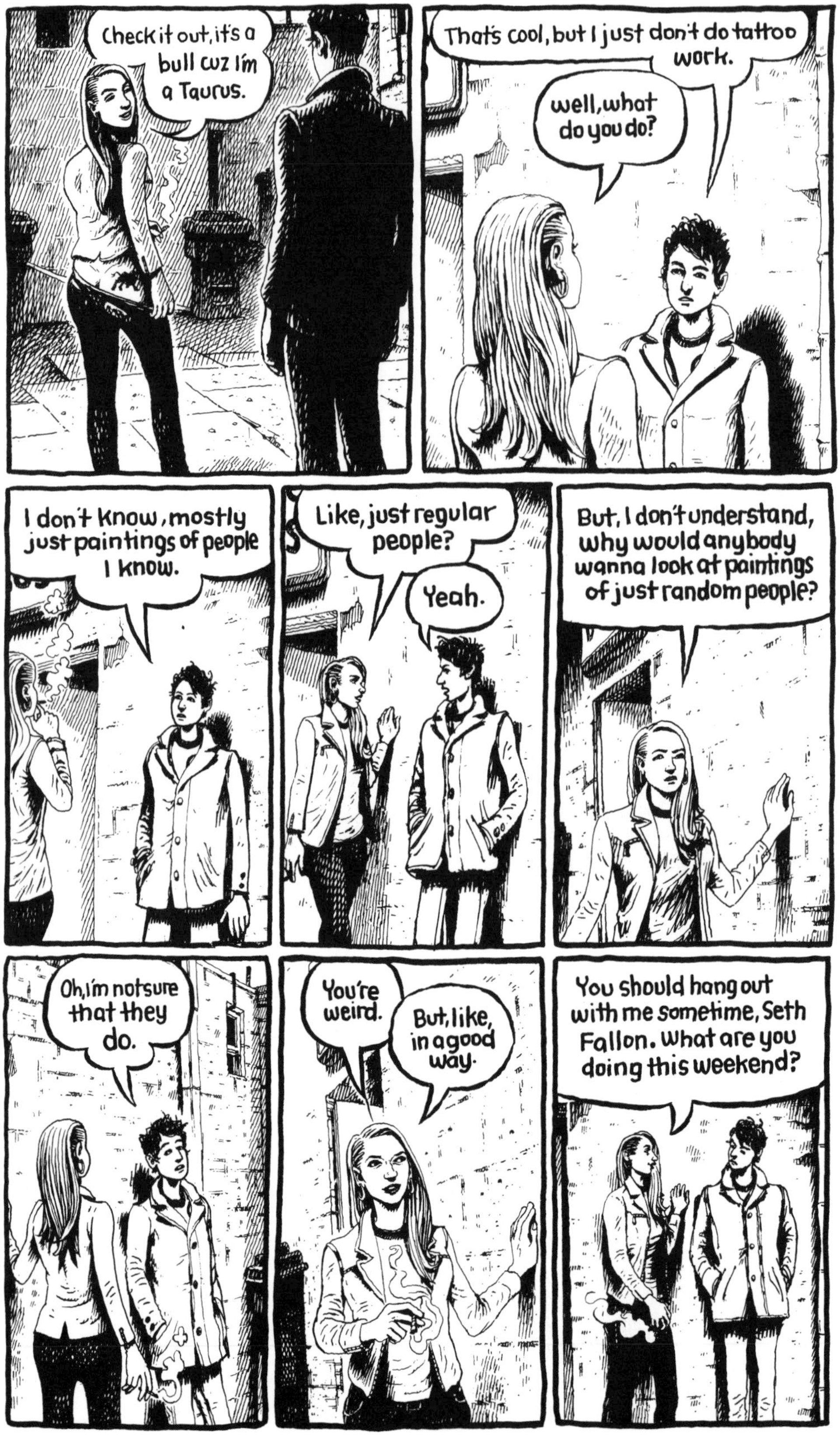
Check it out, it's a bull cuz I'm a Taurus.
That's cool, but I just don't do tattoo work.
well, what do you do?
I don't know, mostly just paintings of people I know.
Like, just regular people?
Yeah.
But, I don't understand, why would anybody wanna look at paintings of just random people?
Oh, I'm not sure that they do.
You're weird.
But, like, in a good way.
You should hang out with me sometime, Seth Fallon. What are you doing this weekend?

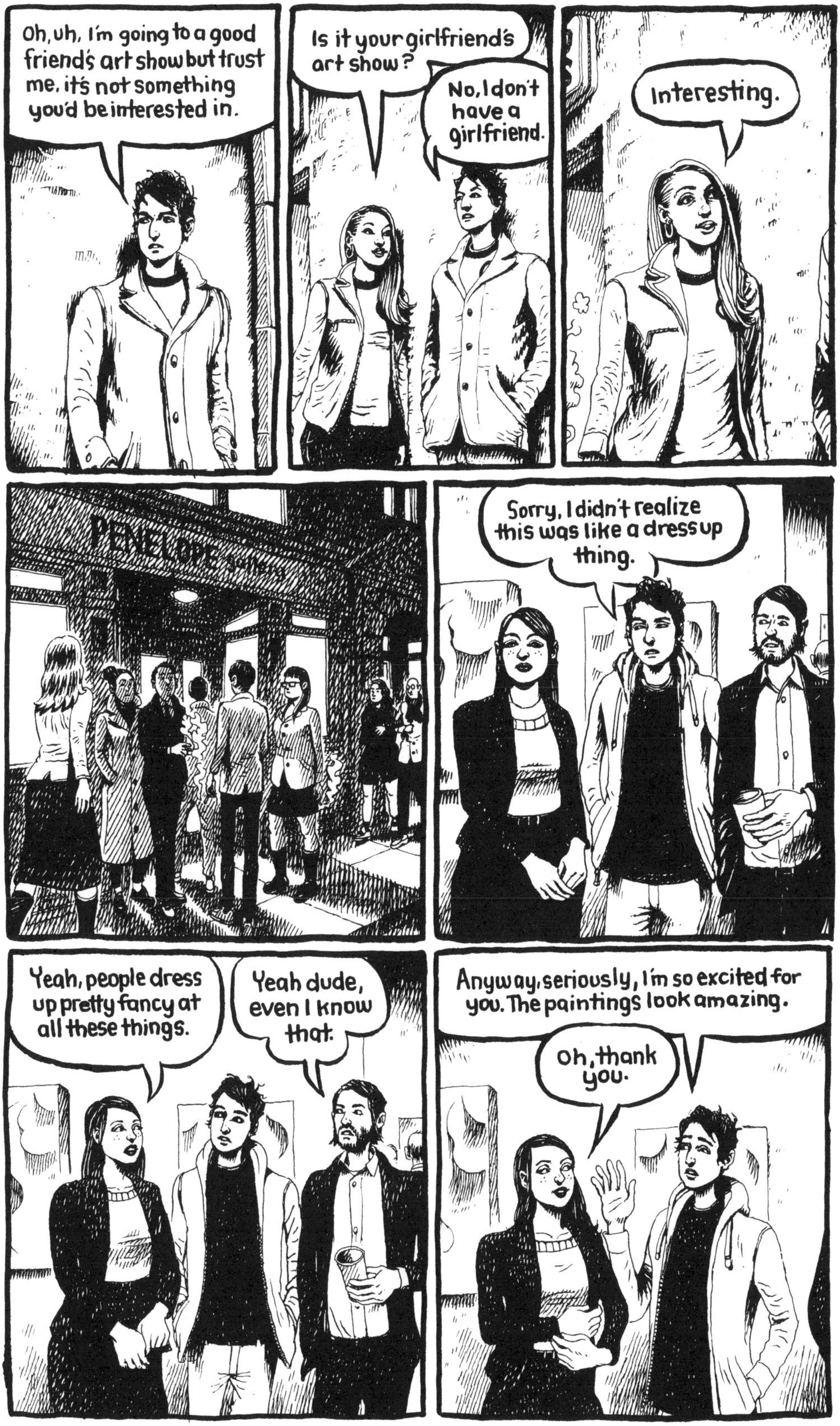
Oh, uh, I'm going to a good friend's art show but trust me, it's not something you'd be interested in.
Is it your girlfriend's art show?
No, I don't have a girlfriend.
Interesting.
PENELOPE gallery
Sorry, I didn't realize this was like a dress up thing.
Yeah, people dress up pretty fancy at all these things.
Yeah dude, even I know that.
Anyway, seriously, I'm so excited for you. The paintings look amazing.
Oh, thank you.

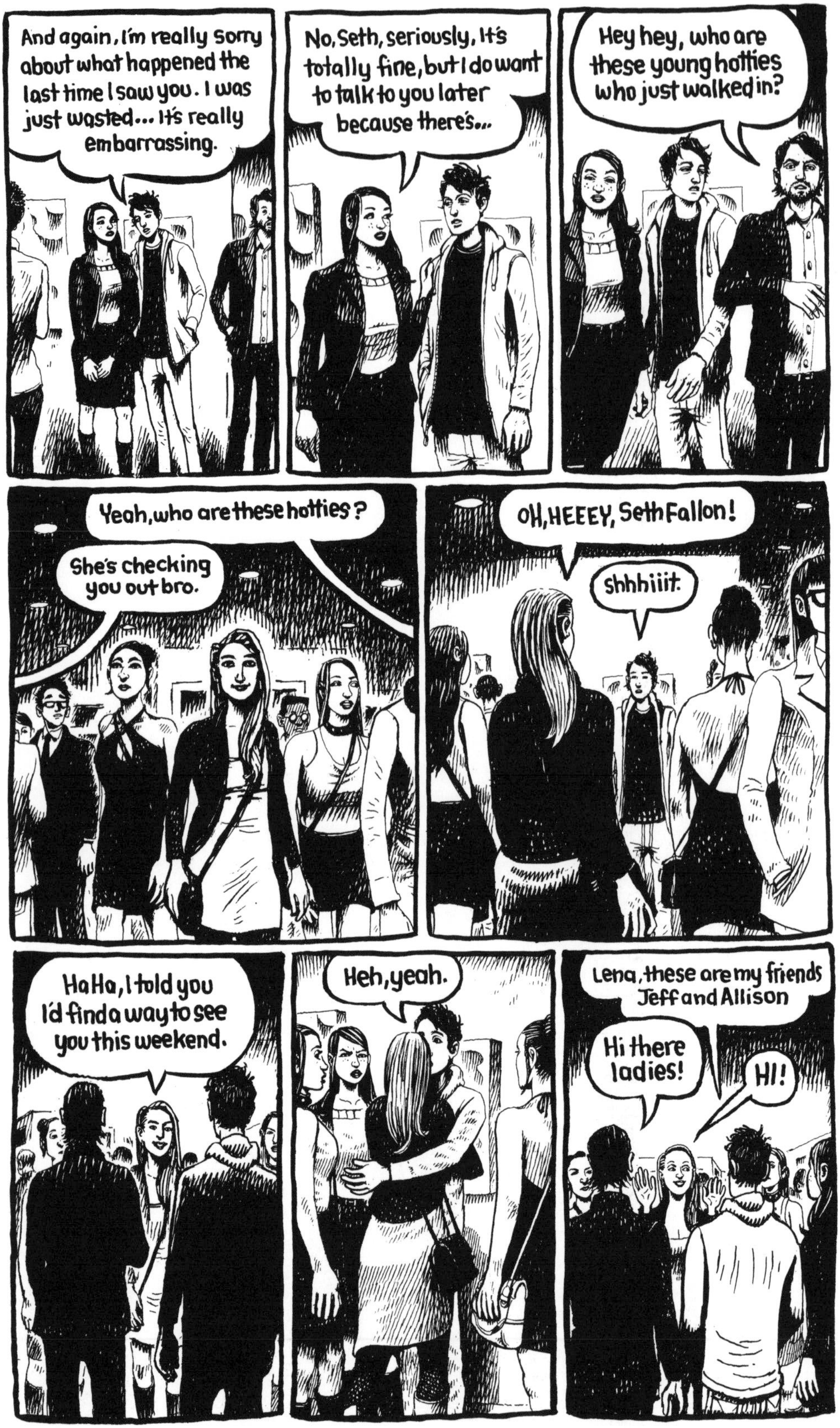
And again, I'm really sorry about what happened the last time I saw you. I was just wasted... It's really embarrassing.
No, Seth, seriously, It's totally fine, but I do want to talk to you later because there's...
Hey hey, who are these young hotties who just walked in?
Yeah, who are these hotties?
She's checking you out bro.
OH, HEEEY, Seth Fallon!
Shhhiiit.
Ha Ha, I told you I'd find a way to see you this weekend.
Heh, yeah.
Lena, these are my friends Jeff and Allison
Hi there ladies!
HI!

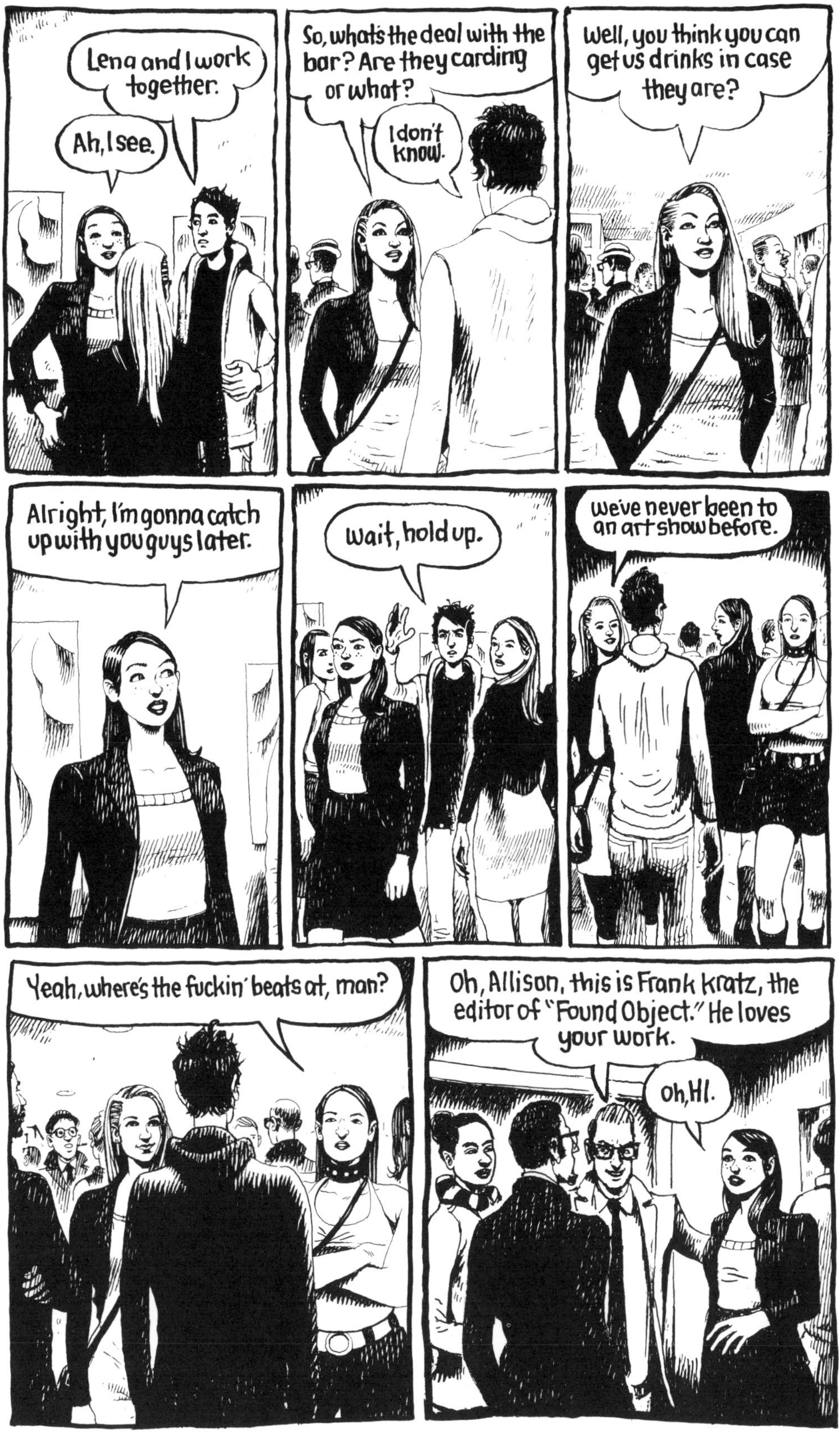
Lena and I work together.
Ah, I see.
So, what's the deal with the bar? Are they carding or what?
I don't know.
Well, you think you can get us drinks in case they are?
Alright, I'm gonna catch up with you guys later.
Wait, hold up.
We've never been to an art show before.
Yeah, where's the fuckin' beats at, man?
Oh, Allison, this is Frank Kratz, the editor of "Found Object." He loves your work.
Oh, HI.

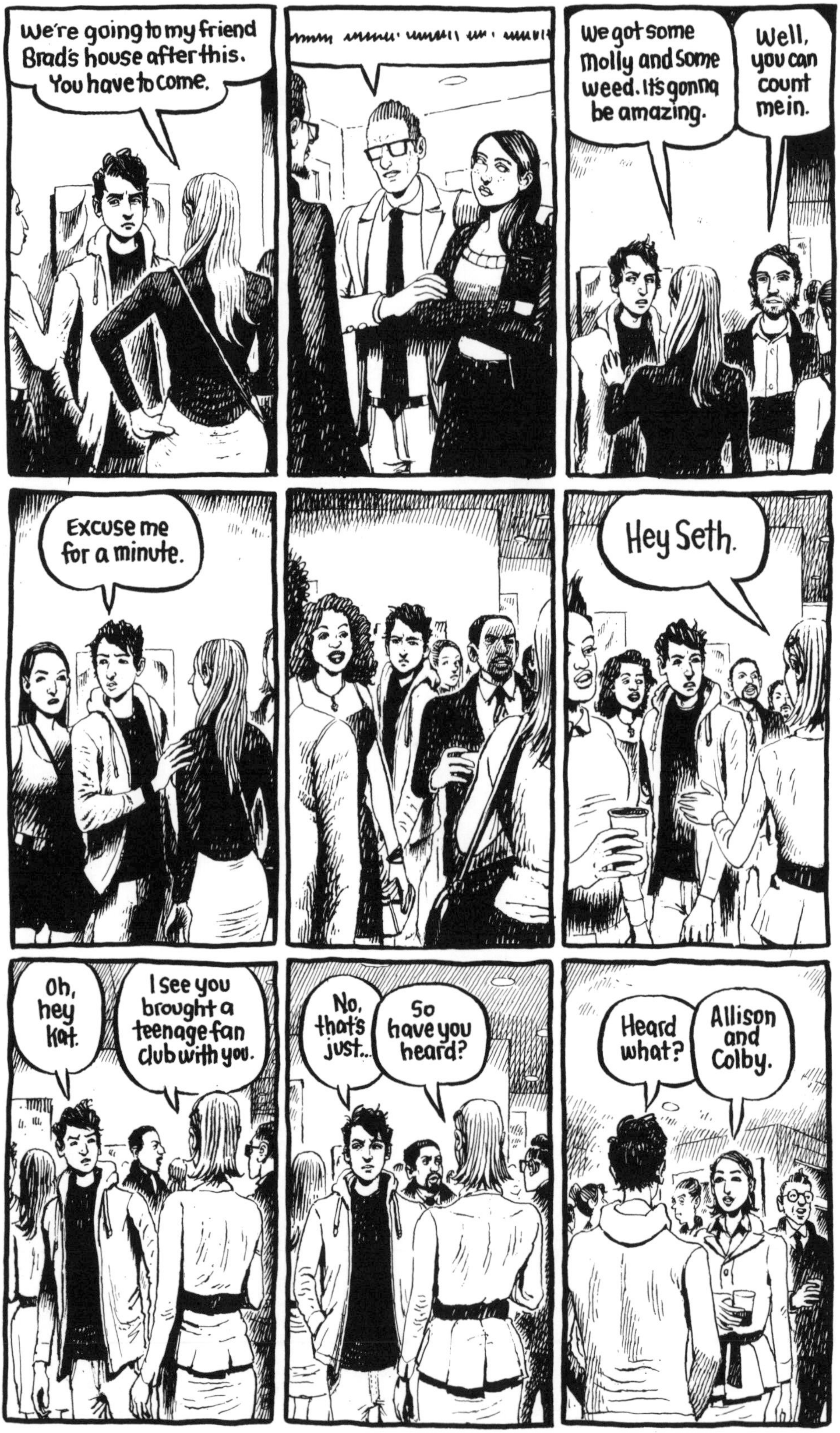
We're going to my friend Brad's house after this. You have to come.
We got some molly and some weed. It's gonna be amazing.
Well, you can count me in.
Excuse me for a minute.
Hey Seth.
Oh, hey Kat.
I see you brought a teenage fan club with you.
No, that's just...
So have you heard?
Heard what?
Allison and Colby.

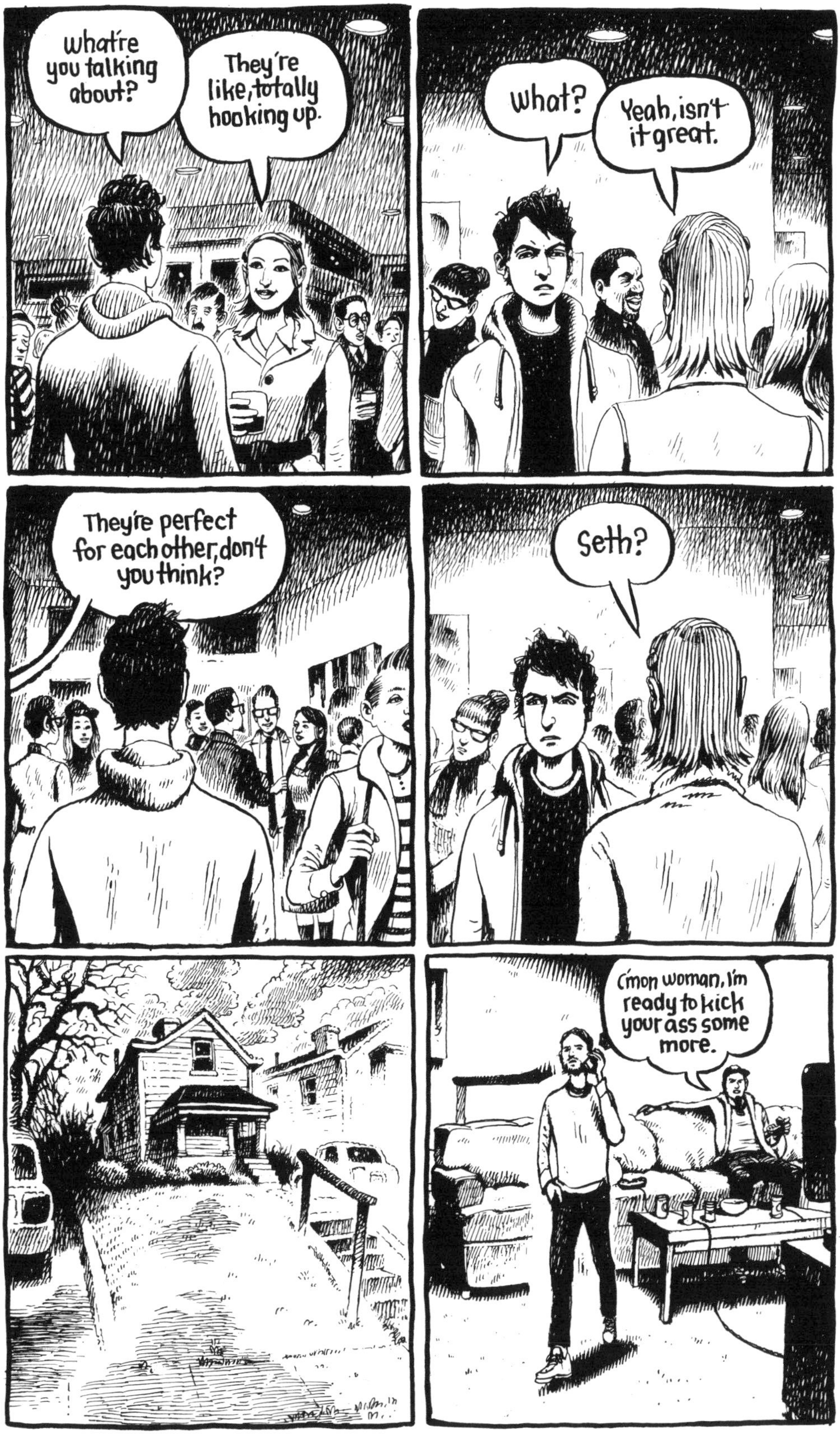
What're you talking about?
They're like, totally hooking up.
What?
Yeah, isn't it great.
They're perfect for each other, don't you think?
Seth?
C'mon woman, I'm ready to kick your ass some more.

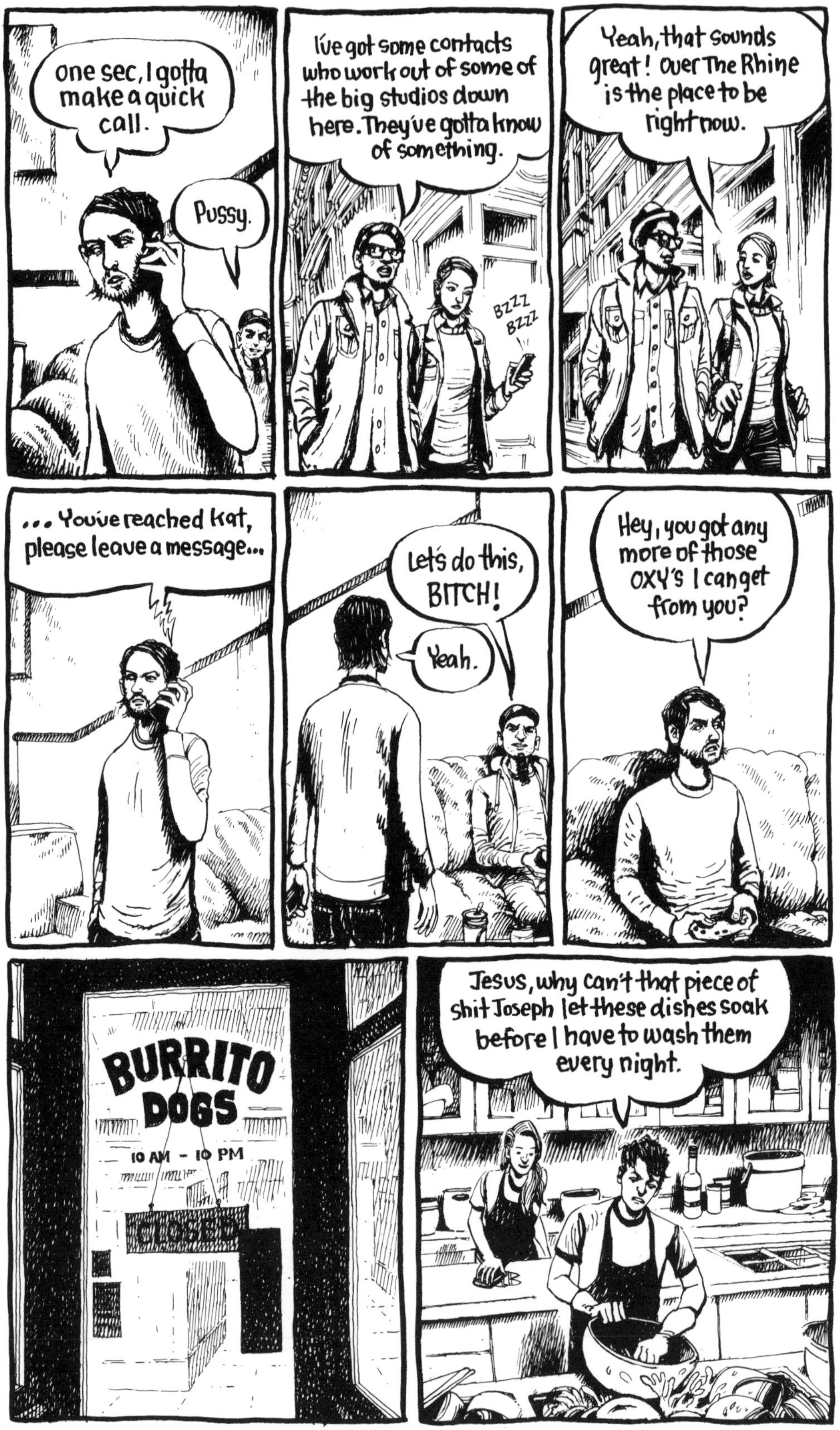
One sec, I gotta make a quick call.
Pussy.
I've got some contacts who work out of some of the big studios down here. They've gotta know of something.
BZZZ BZZZ
Yeah, that sounds great! Over The Rhine is the place to be right now.
... You've reached Kat, please leave a message...
Let's do this, BITCH!
Yeah.
Hey, you got any more of those OXY's I can get from you?
BURRITO DOGS
10 AM - 10 PM
CLOSED
Jesus, why can't that piece of shit Joseph let these dishes soak before I have to wash them every night.

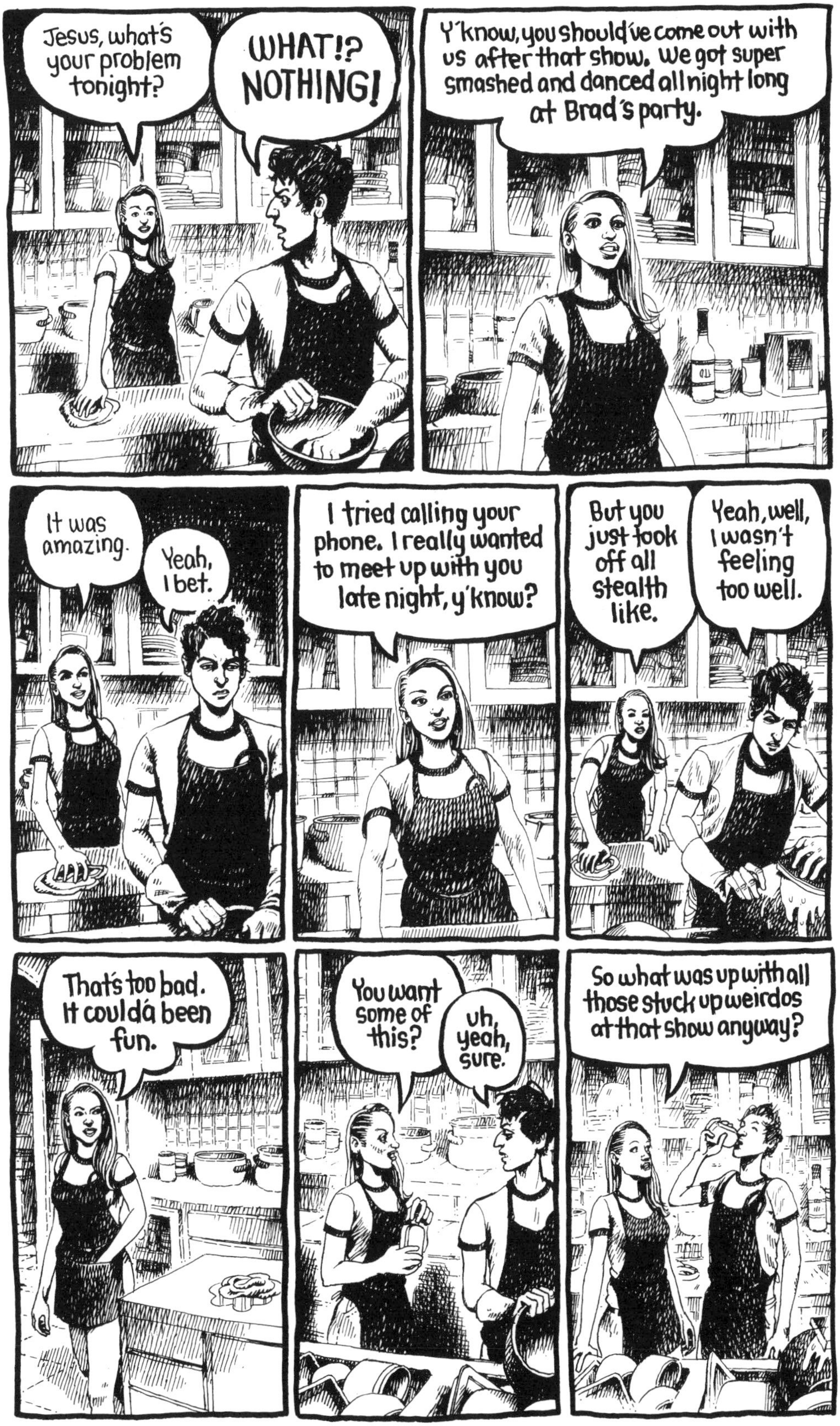

Jesus, what's your problem tonight?
WHAT!? NOTHING!
Y'know, you should've come out with us after that show. We got super smashed and danced all night long at Brad's party.
It was amazing.
Yeah, I bet.
I tried calling your phone. I really wanted to meet up with you late night, y'know?
But you just took off all stealth like.
Yeah, well, I wasn't feeling too well.
That's too bad. It could'a been fun.
You want some of this?
uh, yeah, sure.
So what was up with all those stuck up weirdos at that show anyway?

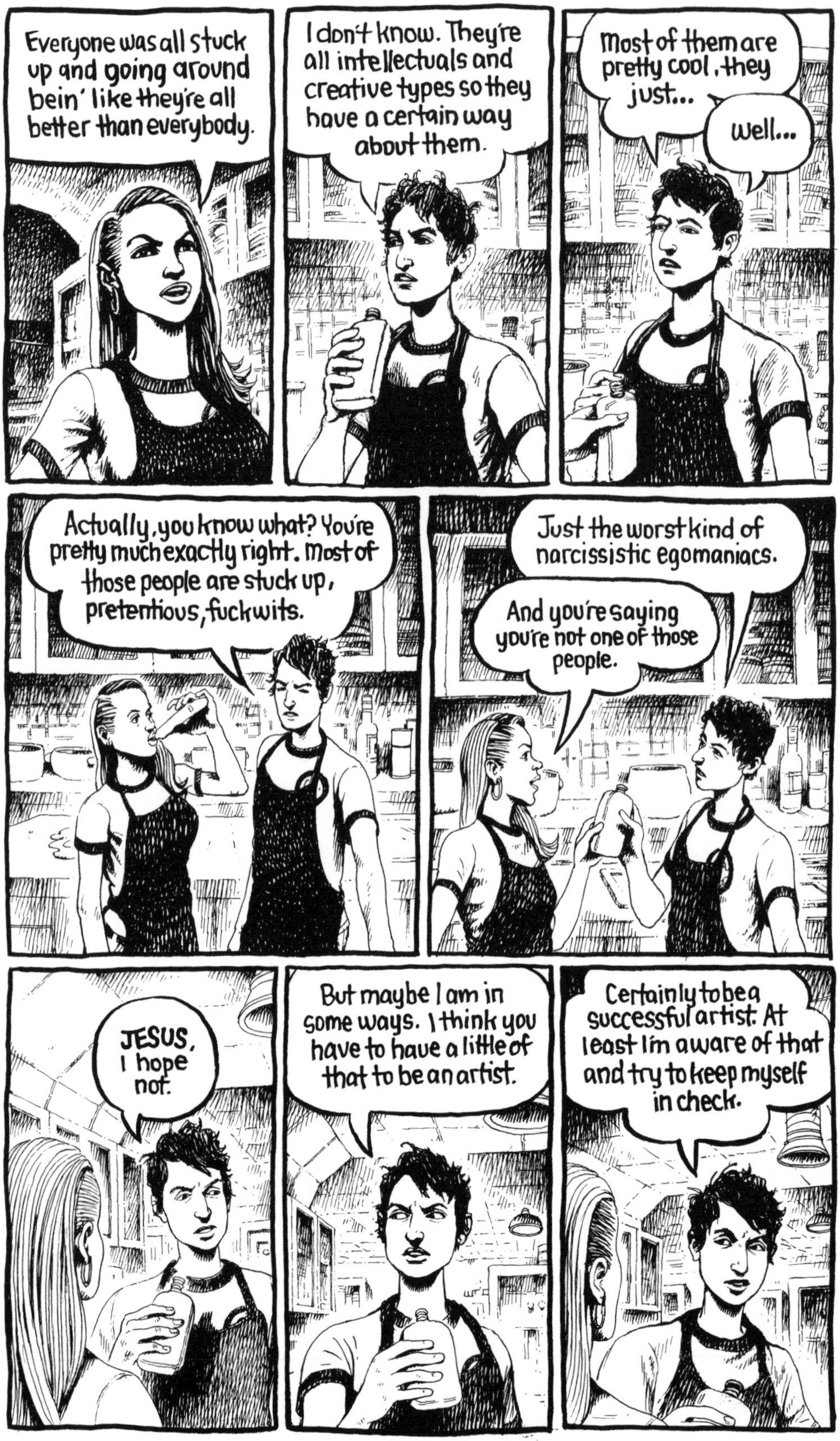
Everyone was all stuck up and going around bein' like they're all better than everybody.
I don't know. They're all intellectuals and creative types so they have a certain way about them.
Most of them are pretty cool, they just...
Well...
Actually, you know what? You're pretty much exactly right. Most of those people are stuck up, pretentious, fuckwits.
Just the worst kind of narcissistic egomaniacs.
And you're saying you're not one of those people.
JESUS, I hope not.
But maybe I am in some ways. I think you have to have a little of that to be an artist.
Certainly to be a successful artist. At least I'm aware of that and try to keep myself in check.

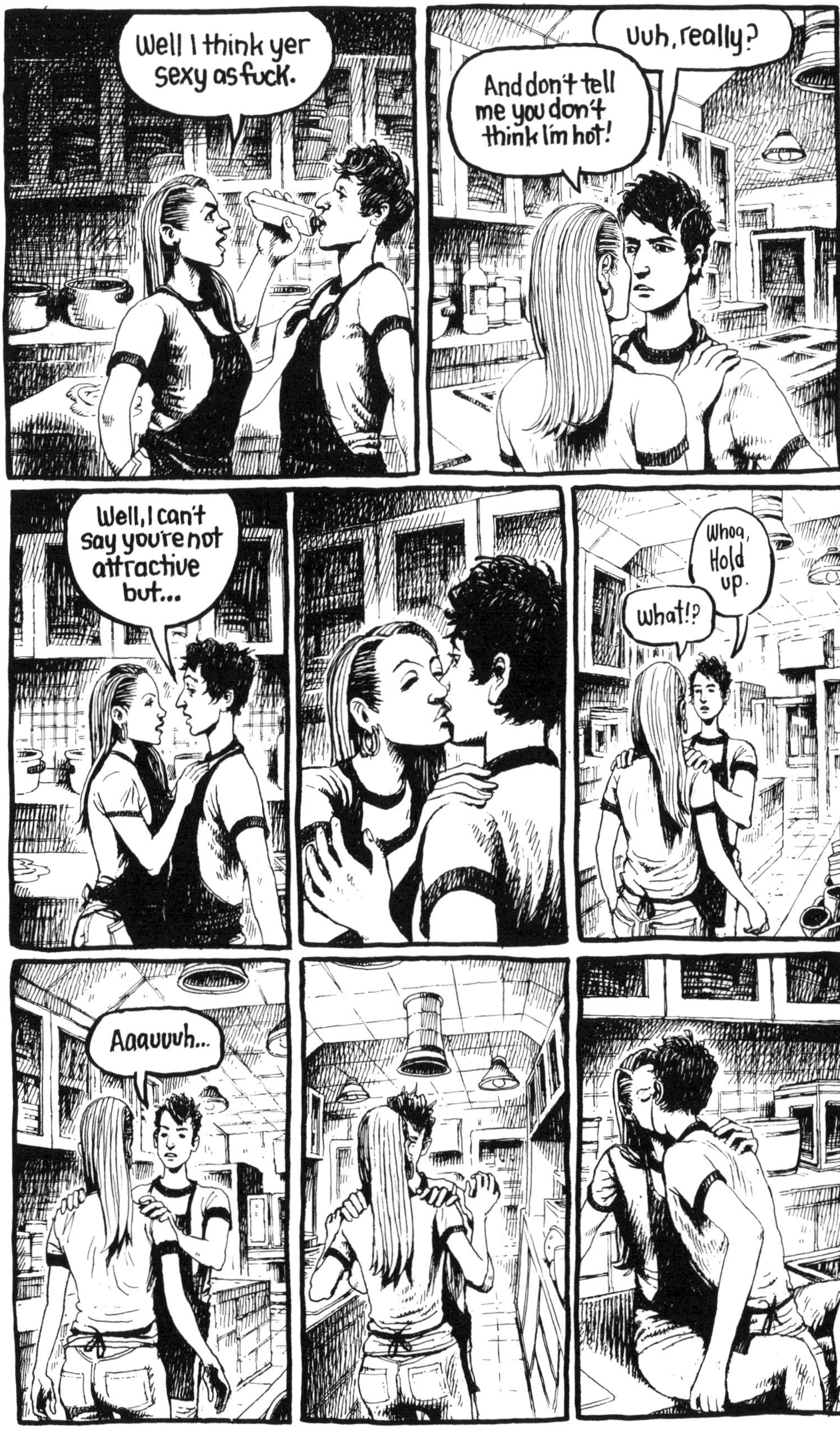
Well I think yer sexy as fuck.
Uuh, really?
And don't tell me you don't think I'm hot!
Well, I can't say you're not attractive but...
Whoa, Hold up.
What!?
Aaauuuh...

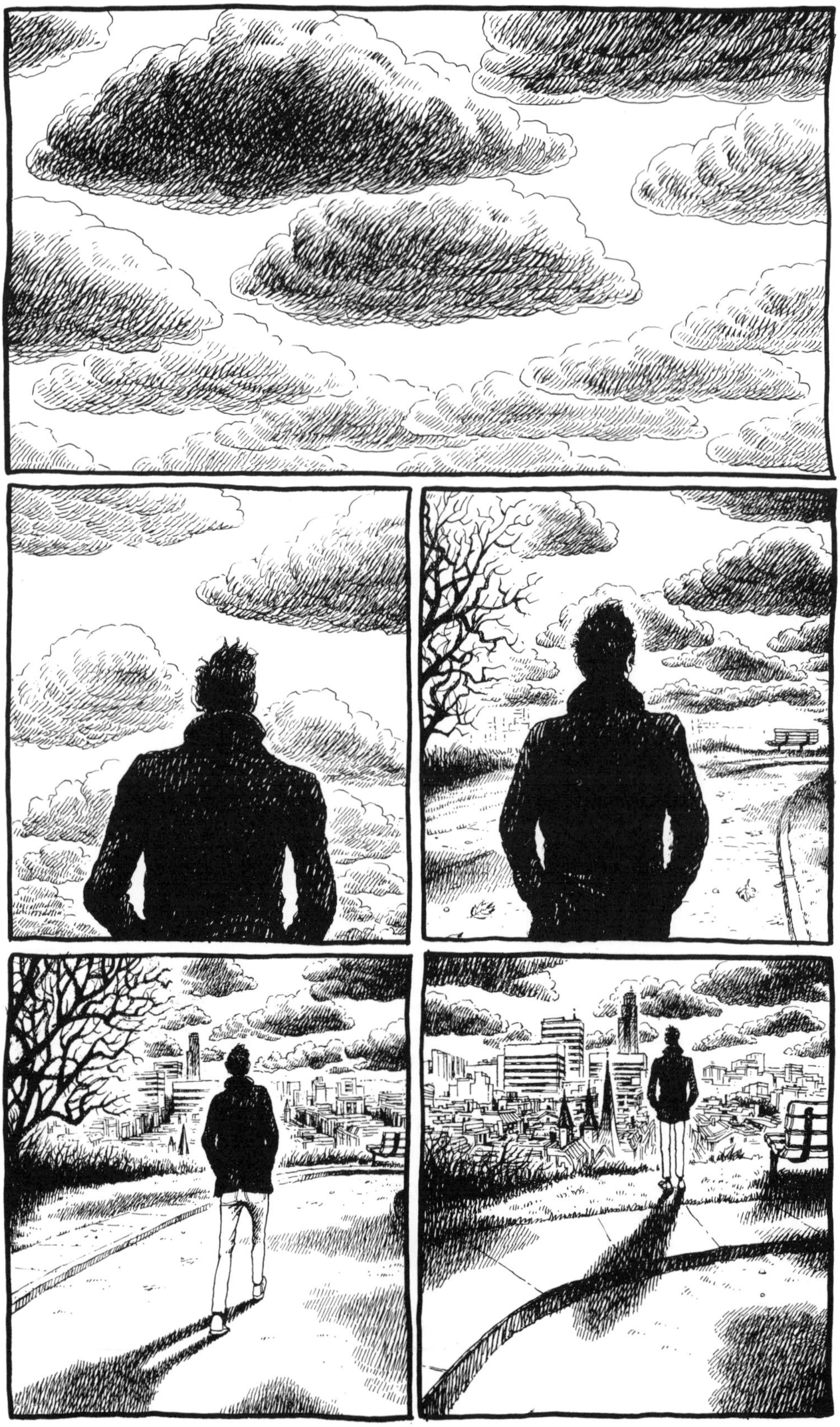

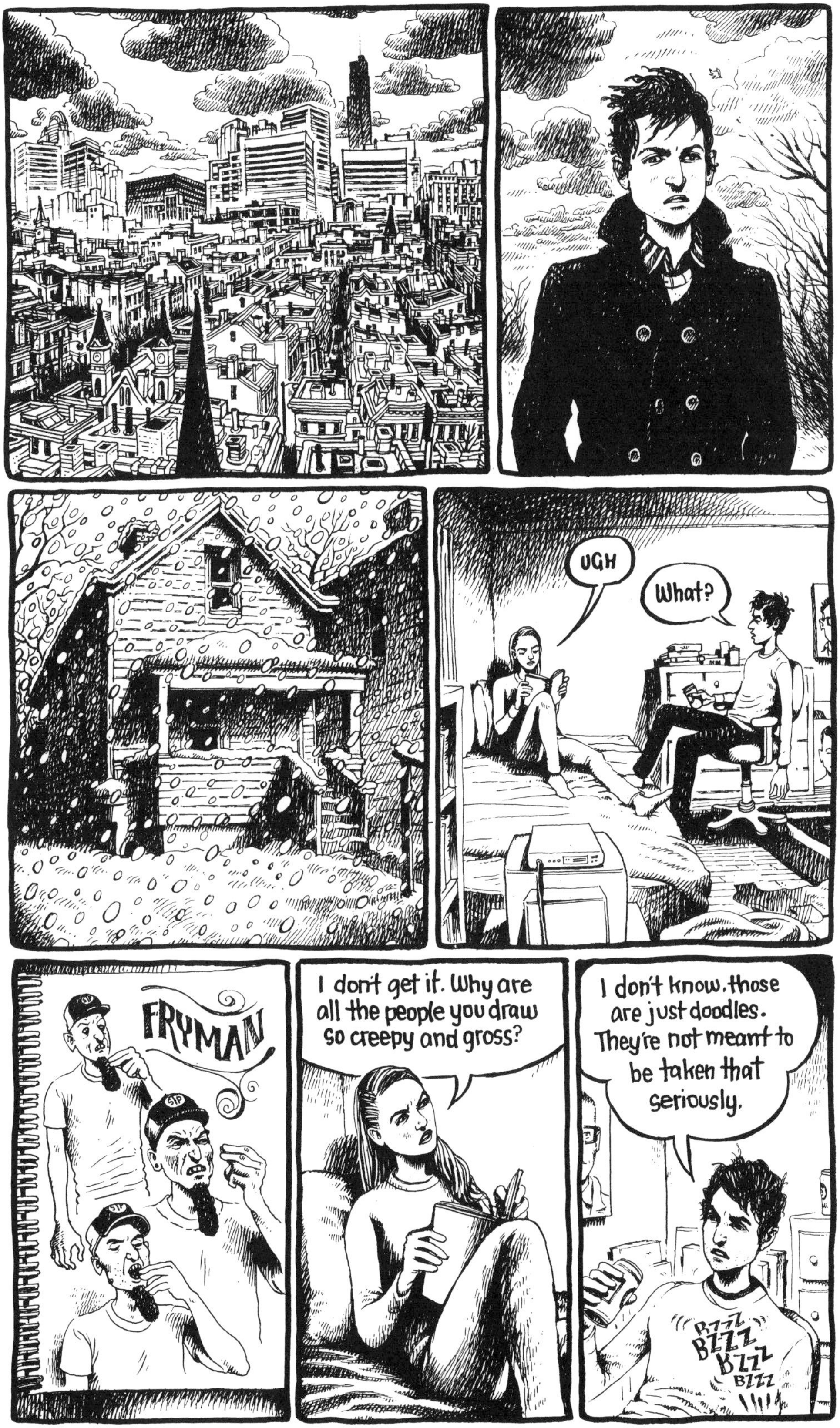
UGH
What?
FRYMAN
I don't get it. Why are all the people you draw so creepy and gross?
I don't know, those are just doodles. They're not meant to be taken that seriously.
BZZZ
BZZZ
BZZZ
BZZZ

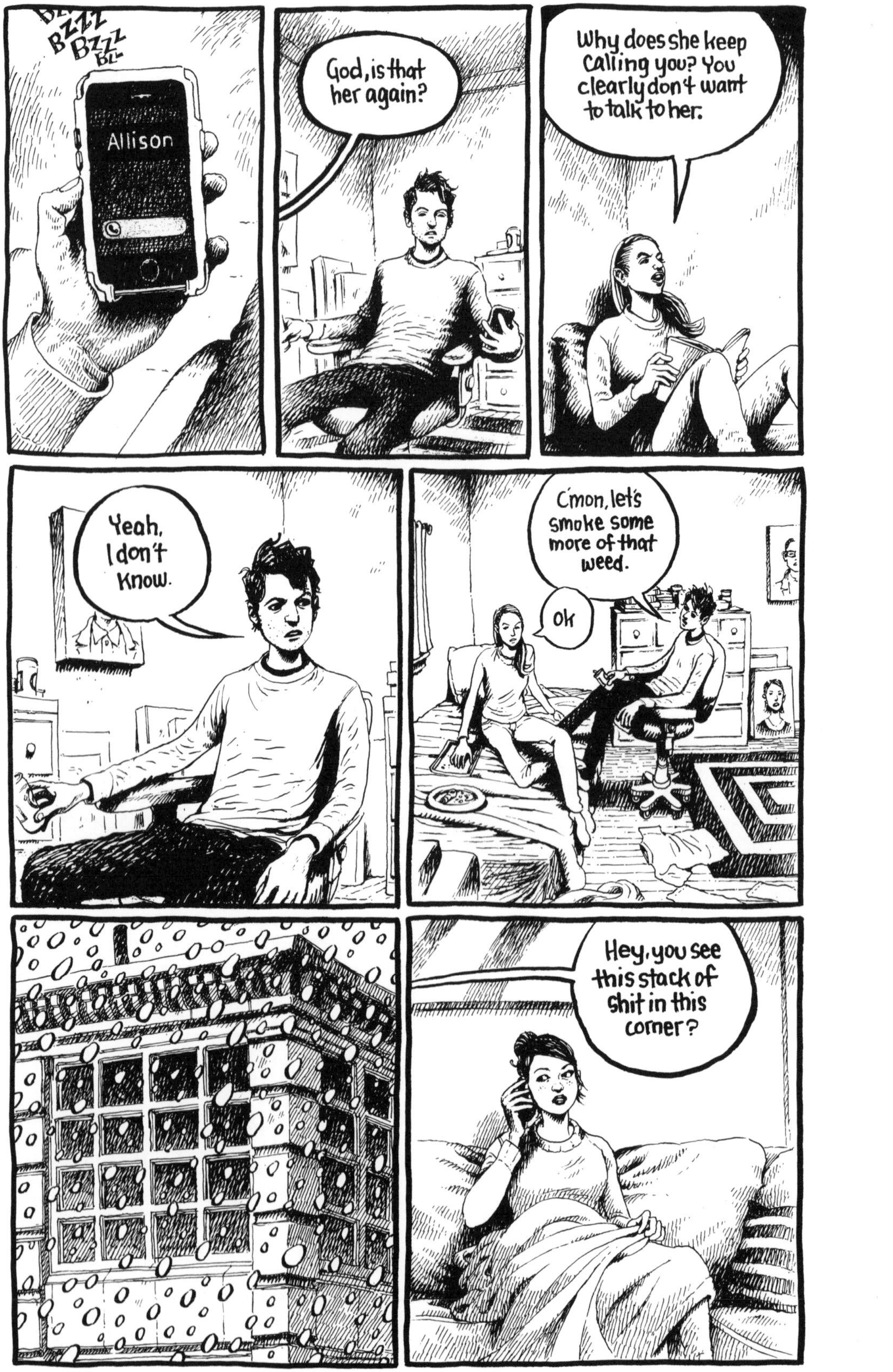
BZZZ
BZZZ
Allison
God, is that her again?
Why does she keep calling you? You clearly don't want to talk to her.
Yeah, I don't know.
C'mon, let's smoke some more of that weed.
Ok
Hey, you see this stack of shit in this corner?

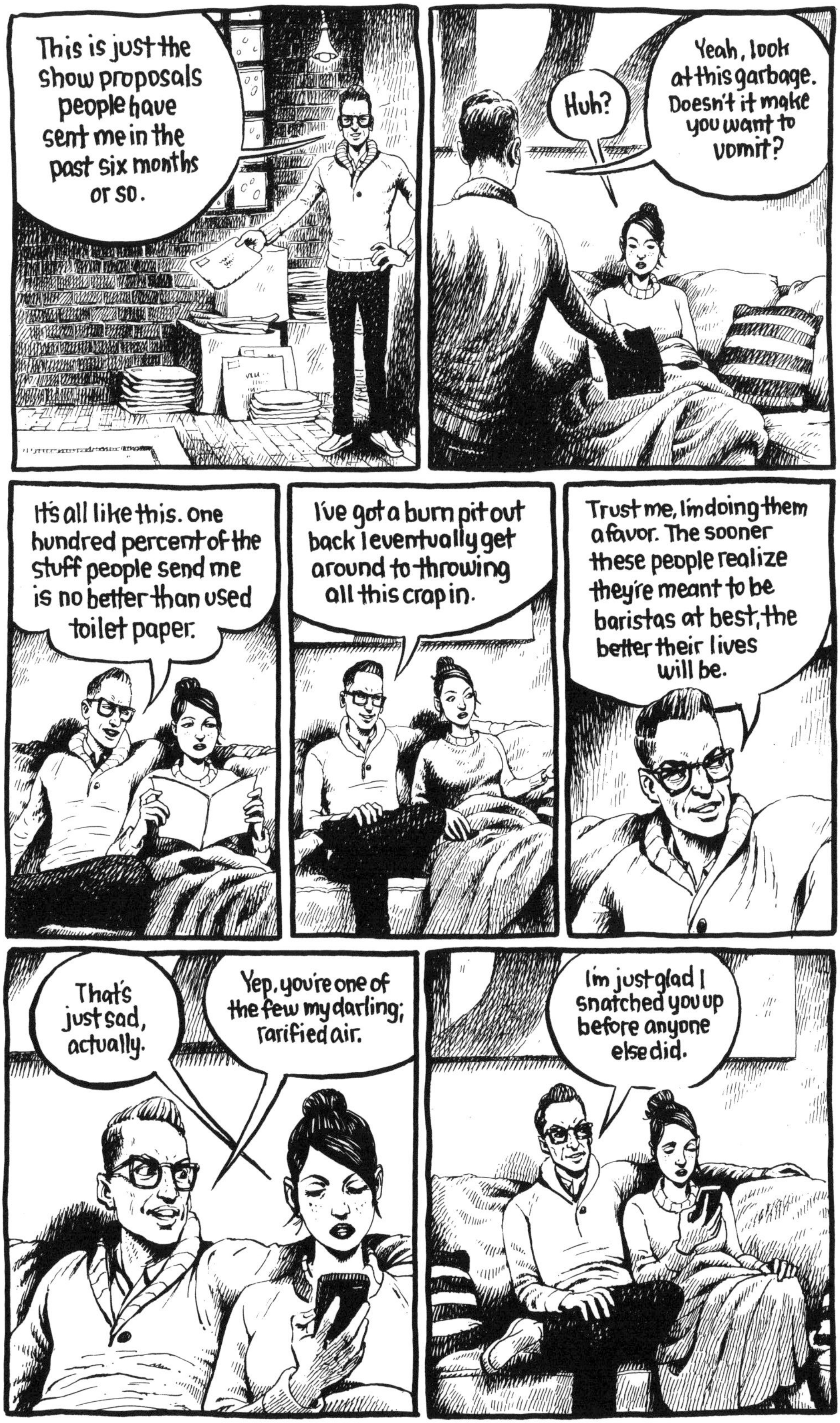
This is just the show proposals people have sent me in the past six months or so.
Huh?
Yeah, look at this garbage. Doesn't it make you want to vomit?
It's all like this. One hundred percent of the stuff people send me is no better than used toilet paper.
I've got a burn pit out back I eventually get around to throwing all this crap in.
Trust me, I'm doing them a favor. The sooner these people realize they're meant to be baristas at best, the better their lives will be.
That's just sad, actually.
Yep, you're one of the few my darling; rarified air.
I'm just glad I snatched you up before anyone else did.

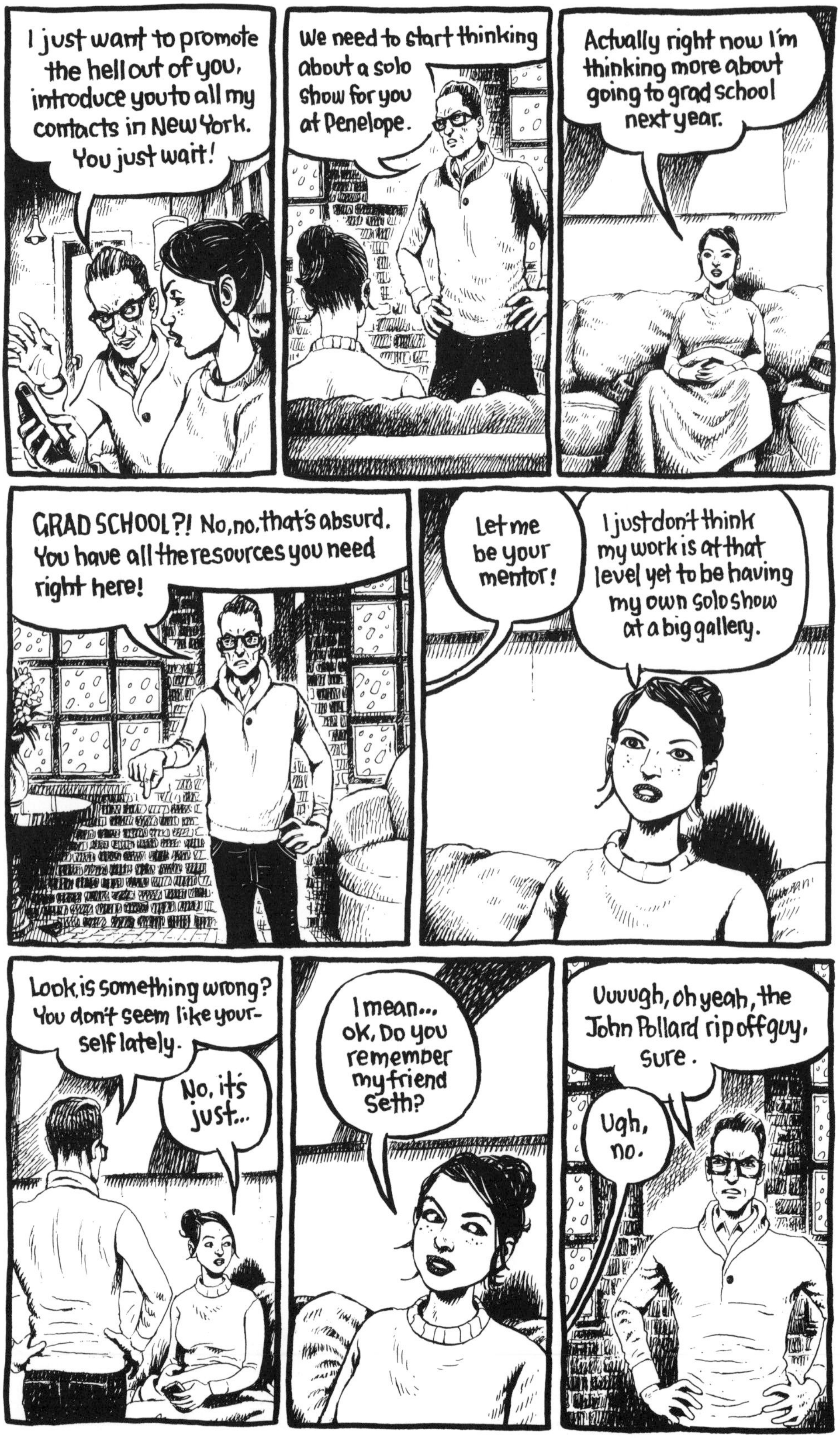
I just want to promote the hell out of you, introduce you to all my contacts in New York. You just wait!
We need to start thinking about a solo show for you at Penelope.
Actually right now I'm thinking more about going to grad school next year.
GRAD SCHOOL?! No, no, that's absurd. You have all the resources you need right here!
Let me be your mentor!
I just don't think my work is at that level yet to be having my own solo show at a big gallery.
Look, is something wrong? You don't seem like yourself lately.
No, it's just...
I mean... ok, Do you remember my friend Seth?
Uuuugh, oh yeah, the John Pollard rip off guy, sure.
Ugh, no.

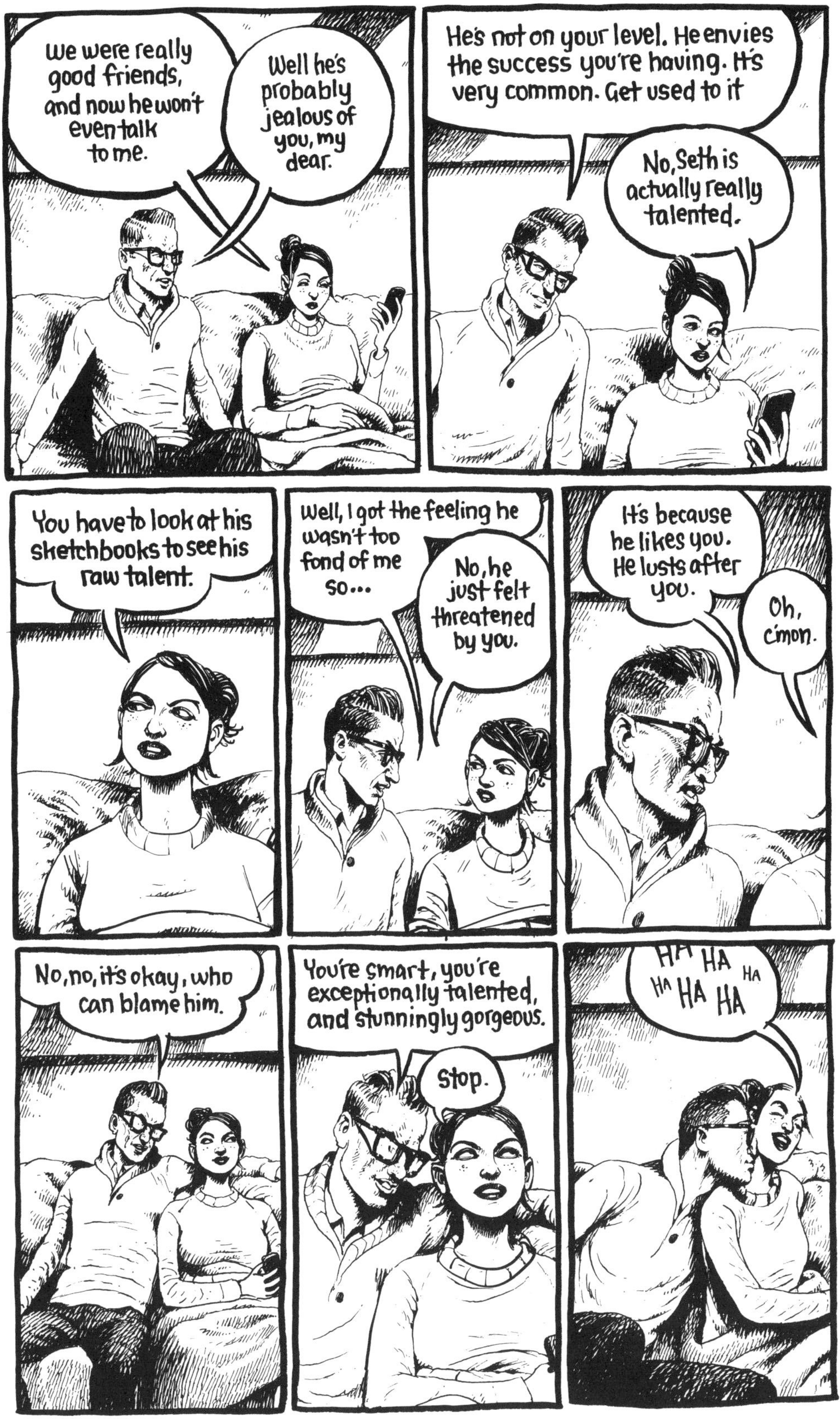
We were really good friends, and now he won't even talk to me.
Well he's probably jealous of you, my dear.
He's not on your level. He envies the success you're having. It's very common. Get used to it
No, Seth is actually really talented.
You have to look at his sketchbooks to see his raw talent.
Well, I got the feeling he wasn't too fond of me so...
No, he just felt threatened by you.
It's because he likes you. He lusts after you.
Oh, c'mon.
No, no, it's okay, who can blame him.
You're smart, you're exceptionally talented, and stunningly gorgeous.
Stop.
HA HA HA HA HA HA

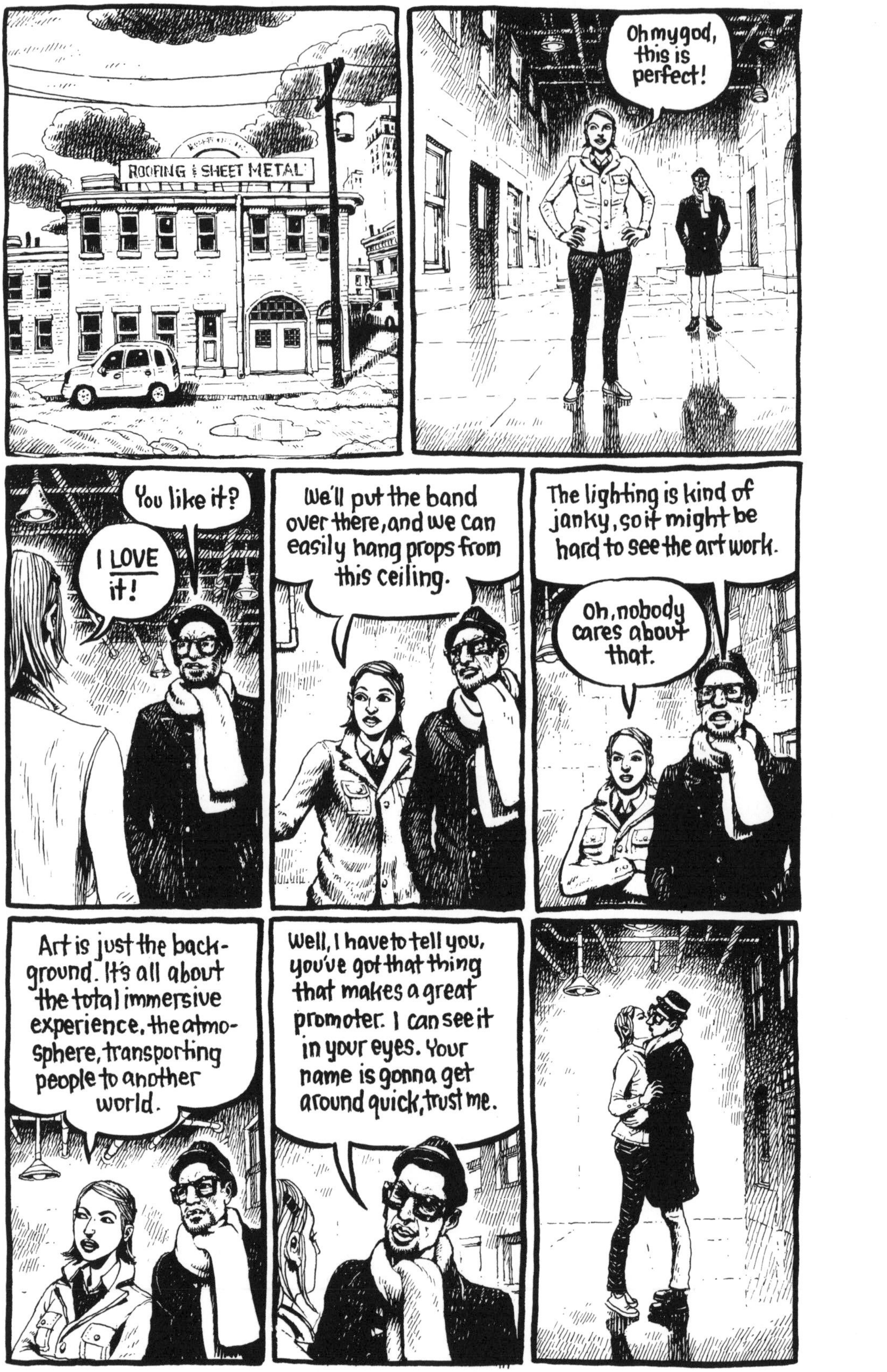
ROOFING & SHEET METAL
Oh my god, this is perfect!
You like it?
I LOVE it!
We'll put the band over there, and we can easily hang props from this ceiling.
The lighting is kind of janky, so it might be hard to see the art work.
Oh, nobody cares about that.
Art is just the back-ground. It's all about the total immersive experience, the atmo-sphere, transporting people to another world.
Well, I have to tell you, you've got that thing that makes a great promoter. I can see it in your eyes. Your name is gonna get around quick, trust me.

Is the overweight Santa sending the wrong message to kids? Is it time to put Ol' St. Nick on a diet? We bring the experts in next.

Goddamn Fryman won't answer his fucking phone, fucking PRICK!

Dude, listen to yourself. Why are you so concerned about hanging out with Fryman?!

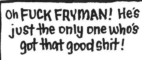

Oh FUCK FRYMAN! He's just the only one who's got that good shit!

Jesus, drink a beer and relax. Here, hit this bowl.

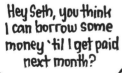

Hey Seth, you think I can borrow some money 'til I get paid next month?

Dude, you know I'm completely broke.

C'mon man, just like fifty bucks or somethin'!

Yo, I can't defer my loans any more, so I have to start paying $475 a month now.

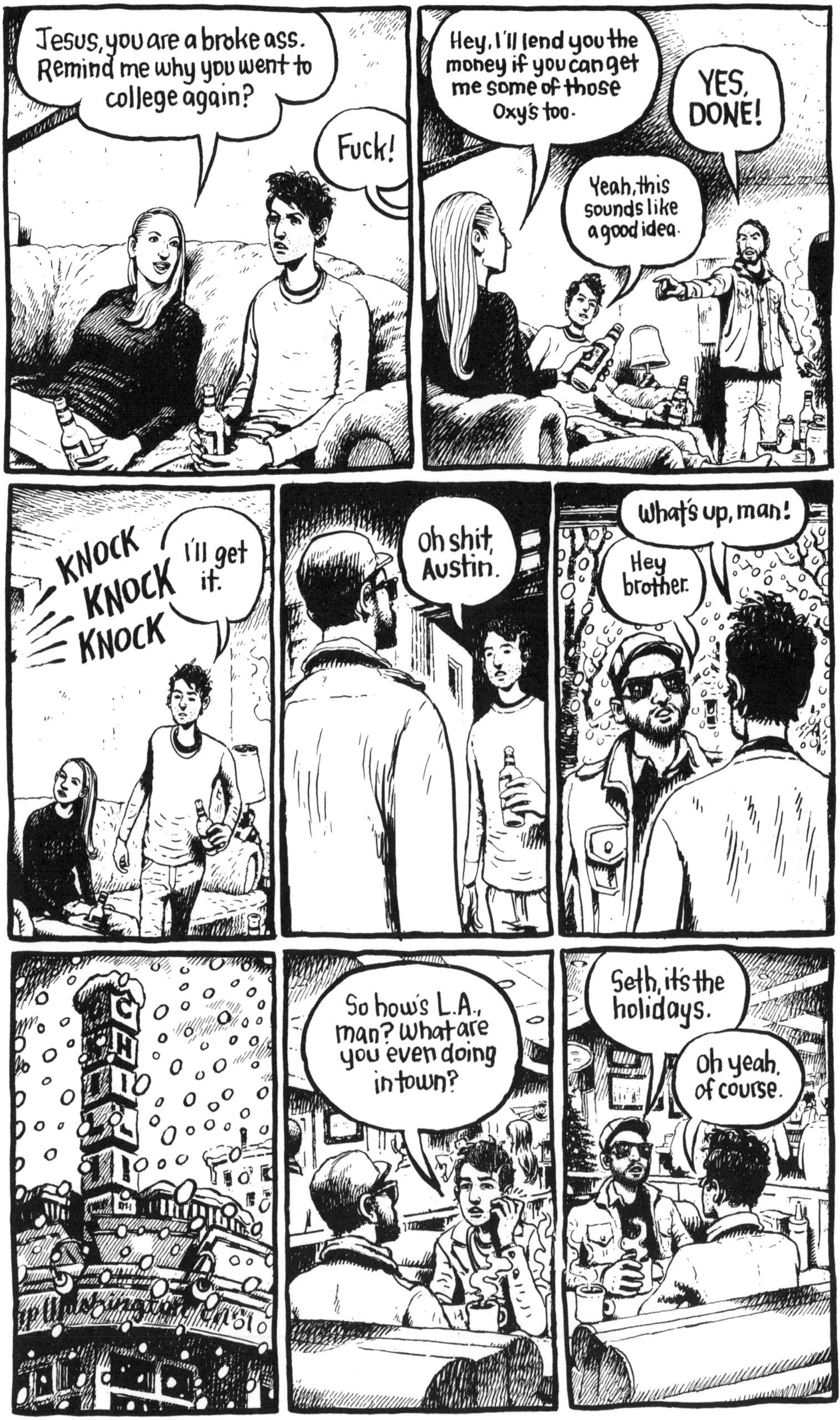
Jesus, you are a broke ass. Remind me why you went to college again?
Fuck!
Hey, I'll lend you the money if you can get me some of those Oxy's too.
YES, DONE!
Yeah, this sounds like a good idea.
KNOCK KNOCK KNOCK
I'll get it.
Oh shit, Austin.
What's up, man!
Hey brother.
So how's L.A., man? What are you even doing in town?
Seth, it's the holidays.
Oh yeah, of course.

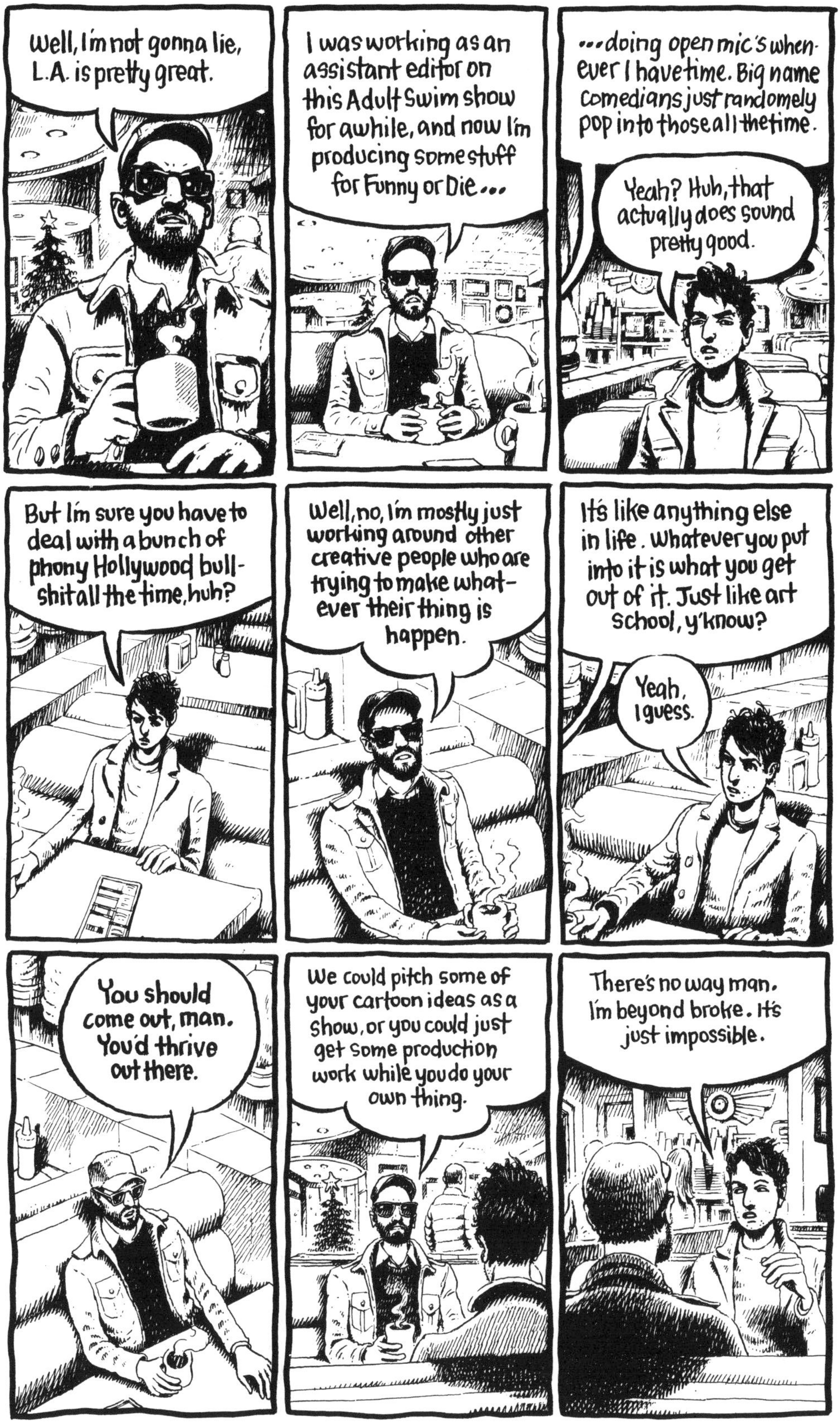

Well, I'm not gonna lie, L.A. is pretty great.
I was working as an assistant editor on this Adult Swim show for awhile, and now I'm producing some stuff for Funny or Die...
...doing open mic's whenever I have time. Big name comedians just randomely pop into those all the time.
Yeah? Huh, that actually does sound pretty good.
But I'm sure you have to deal with a bunch of phony Hollywood bullshit all the time, huh?
Well, no, I'm mostly just working around other creative people who are trying to make whatever their thing is happen.
It's like anything else in life. Whatever you put into it is what you get out of it. Just like art school, y'know?
Yeah, I guess.
You should come out, man. You'd thrive out there.
We could pitch some of your cartoon ideas as a show, or you could just get some production work while you do your own thing.
There's no way man. I'm beyond broke. It's just impossible.

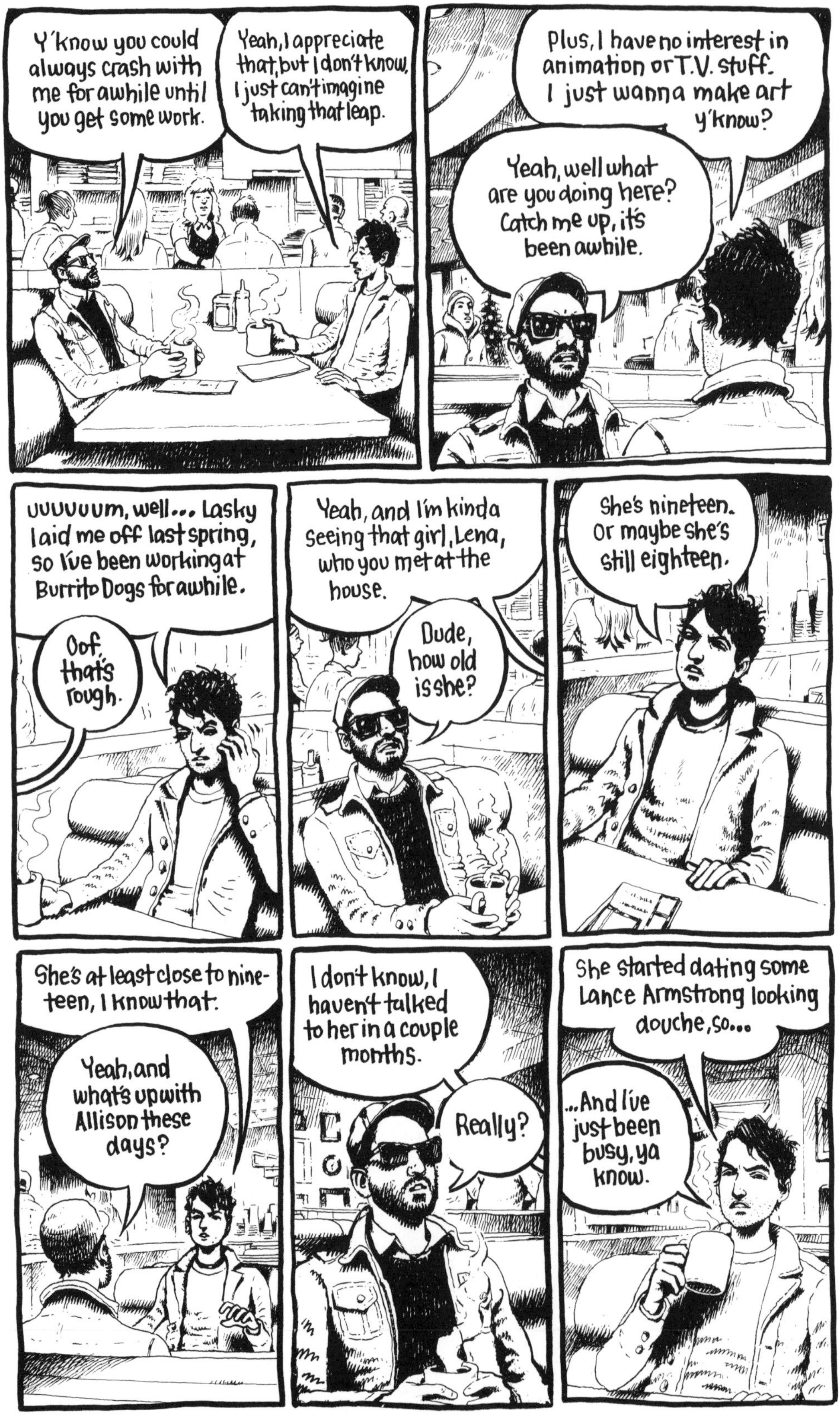
Y'know you could always crash with me for awhile until you get some work.
Yeah, I appreciate that, but I don't know, I just can't imagine taking that leap.
Plus, I have no interest in animation or T.V. stuff. I just wanna make art y'know?
Yeah, well what are you doing here? Catch me up, it's been awhile.
uuuuuum, well... Lasky laid me off last spring, so I've been working at Burrito Dogs for awhile.
Oof, that's rough.
Yeah, and I'm kinda seeing that girl, Lena, who you met at the house.
Dude, how old is she?
She's nineteen. Or maybe she's still eighteen.
She's at least close to nineteen, I know that.
Yeah, and what's up with Allison these days?
I don't know, I haven't talked to her in a couple months.
Really?
She started dating some Lance Armstrong looking douche, so...
...And I've just been busy, ya know.

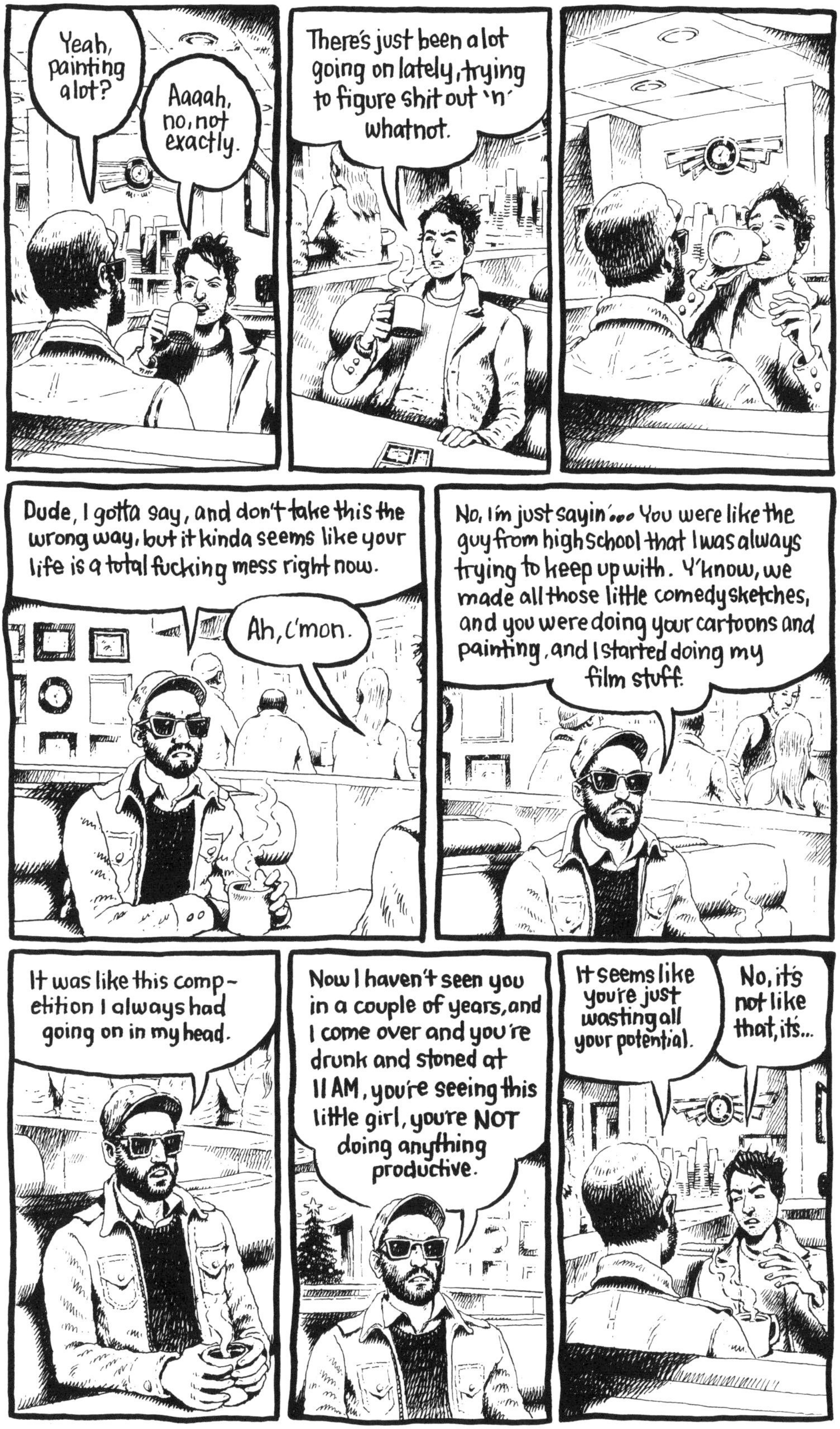
Yeah, painting a lot?
Aaaah, no, not exactly.
There's just been a lot going on lately, trying to figure shit out 'n' whatnot.
Dude, I gotta say, and don't take this the wrong way, but it kinda seems like your life is a total fucking mess right now.
Ah, C'mon.
No, I'm just sayin'... You were like the guy from high school that I was always trying to keep up with. Y'know, we made all those little comedy sketches, and you were doing your cartoons and painting, and I started doing my film stuff.
It was like this competition I always had going on in my head.
Now I haven't seen you in a couple of years, and I come over and you're drunk and stoned at 11 AM, you're seeing this little girl, you're NOT doing anything productive.
It seems like you're just wasting all your potential.
No, it's not like that, it's...

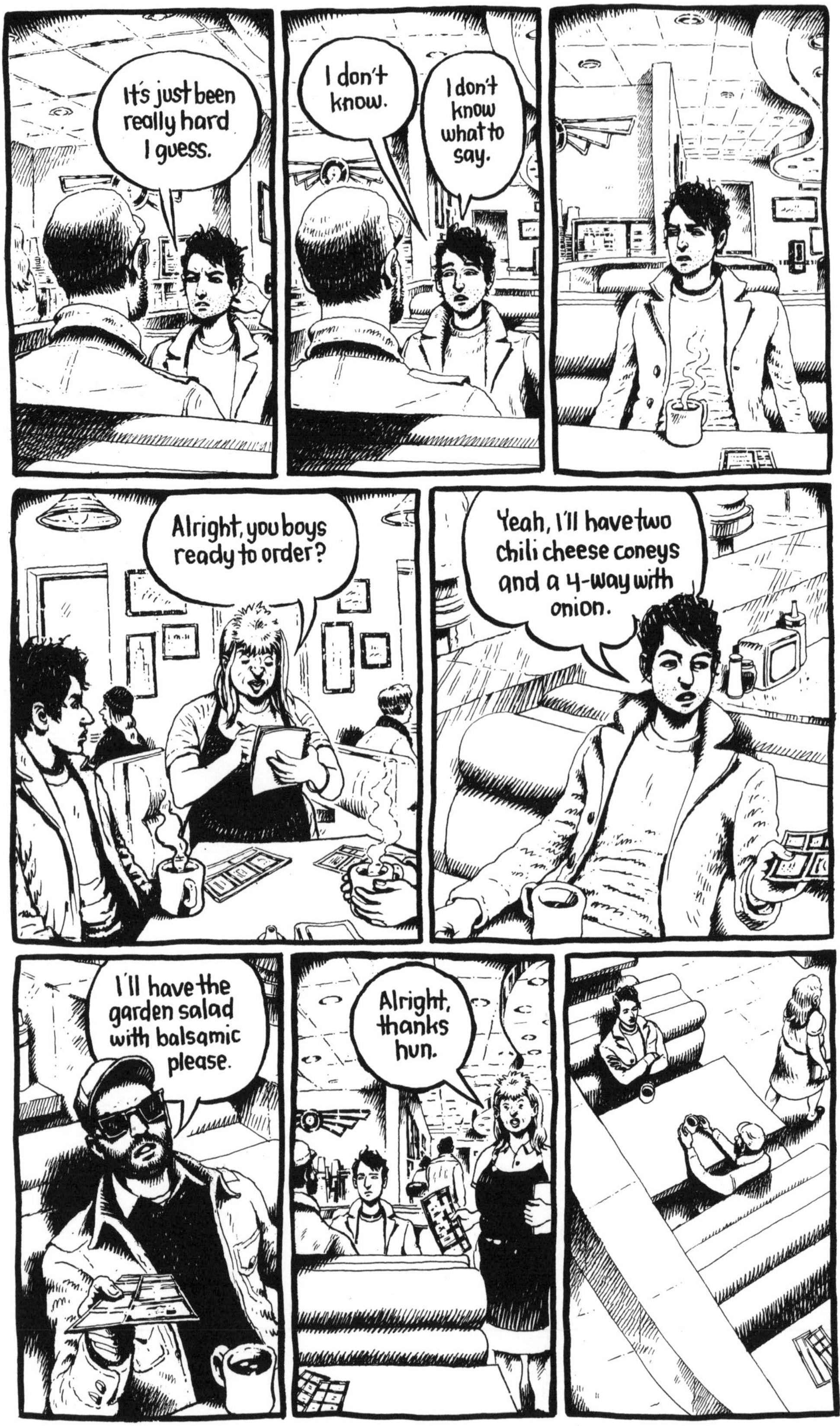

It's just been really hard I guess.
I don't know.
I don't know what to say.
Alright, you boys ready to order?
Yeah, I'll have two chili cheese coneys and a 4-way with onion.
I'll have the garden salad with balsamic please.
Alright, thanks hun.

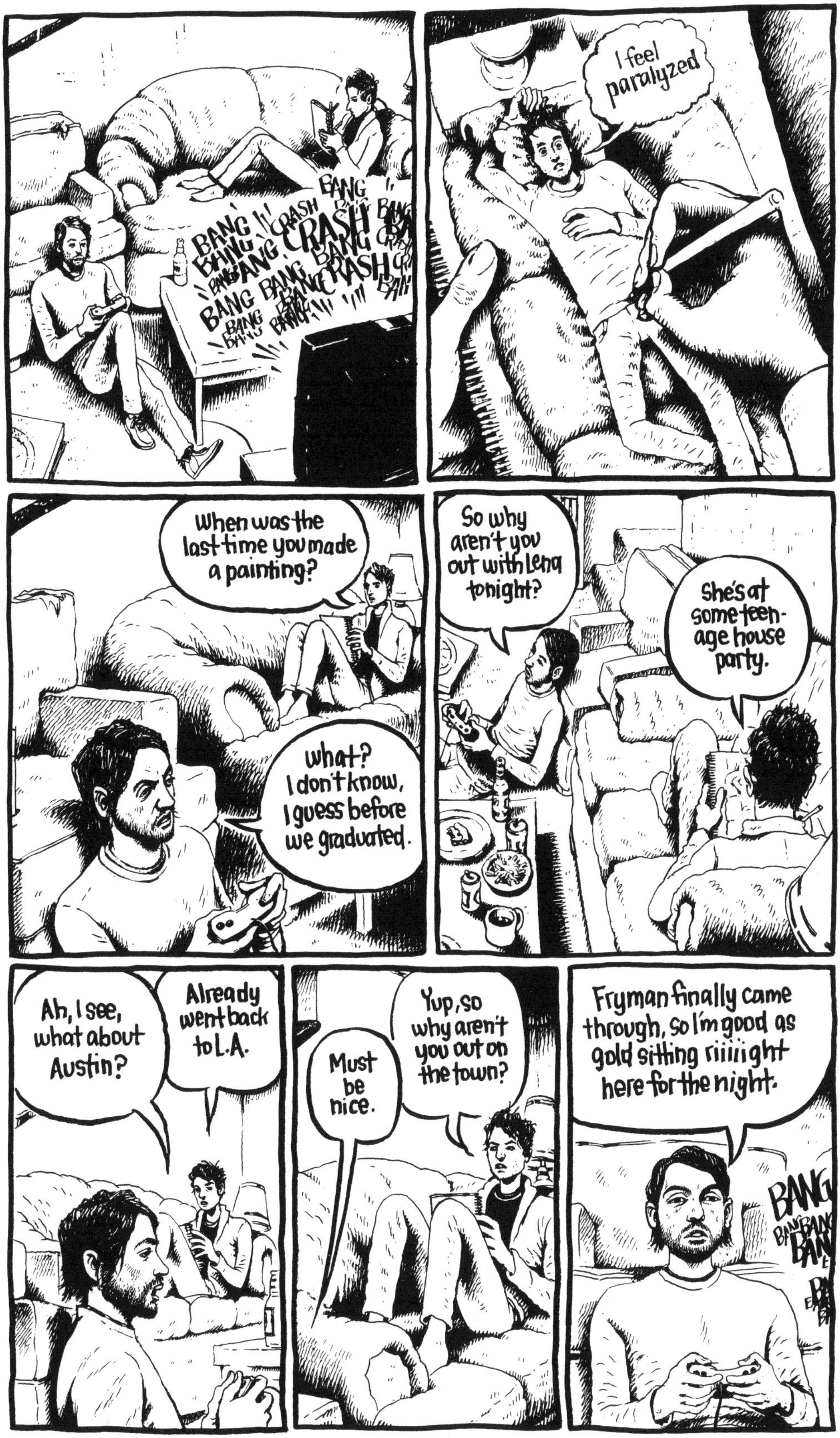
BANG
BANG
CRASH
BANG BANG
BANG CRASH
BANG BANG
BANG BANG
CRASH
I feel paralyzed
When was the last time you made a painting?
What? I don't know, I guess before we graduated.
So why aren't you out with Lena tonight?
She's at some teen-age house party.
Ah, I see, what about Austin?
Already went back to L.A.
Yup, so why aren't you out on the town?
Must be nice.
Fryman finally came through, so I'm good as gold sitting riiiiight here for the night.
BANG
BANG BANG
BANG

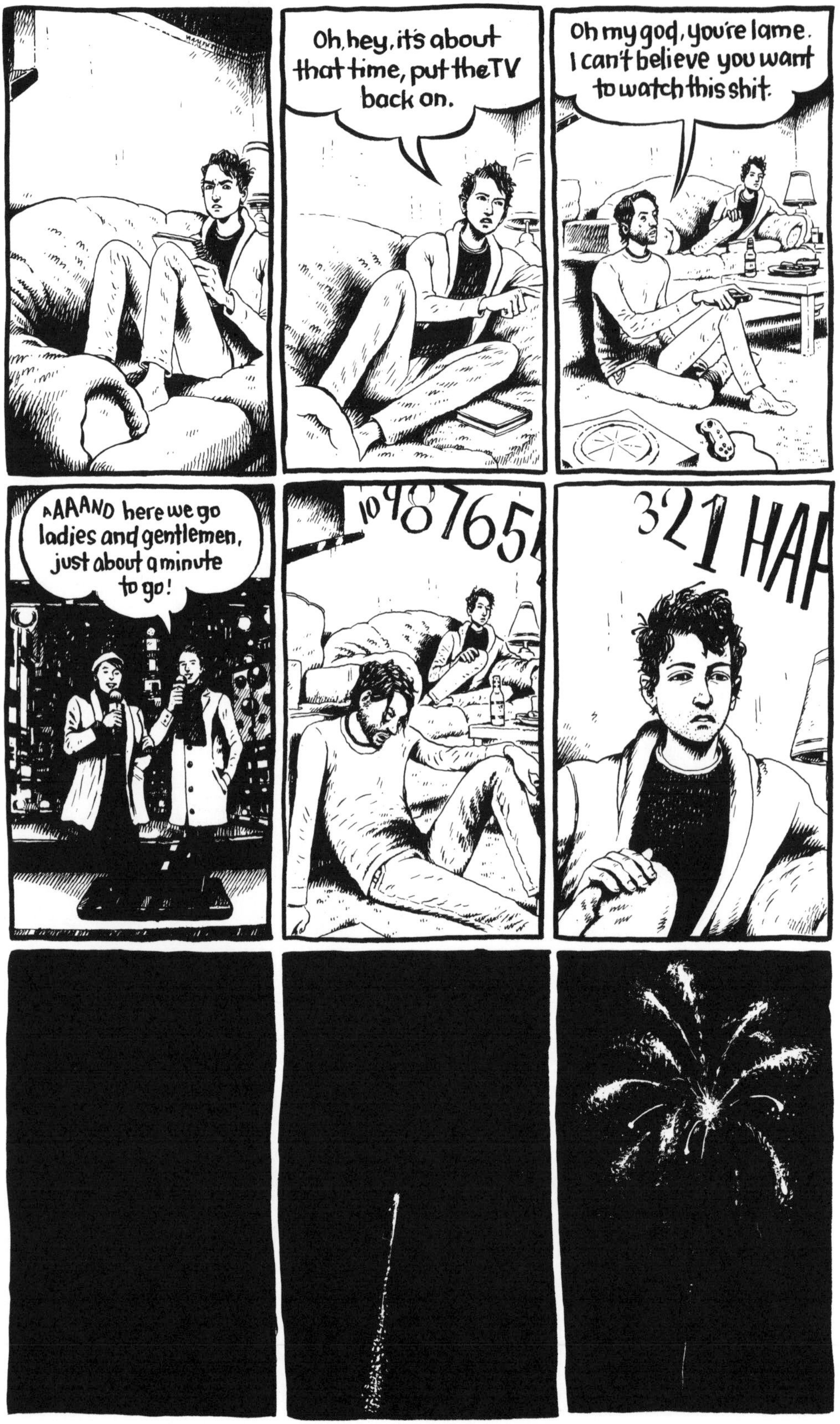
Oh, hey, it's about that time, put the TV back on.
Oh my god, you're lame. I can't believe you want to watch this shit.
AAAAND here we go ladies and gentlemen, just about a minute to go!
10 9 8 7 6 5
3 2 1 HAP

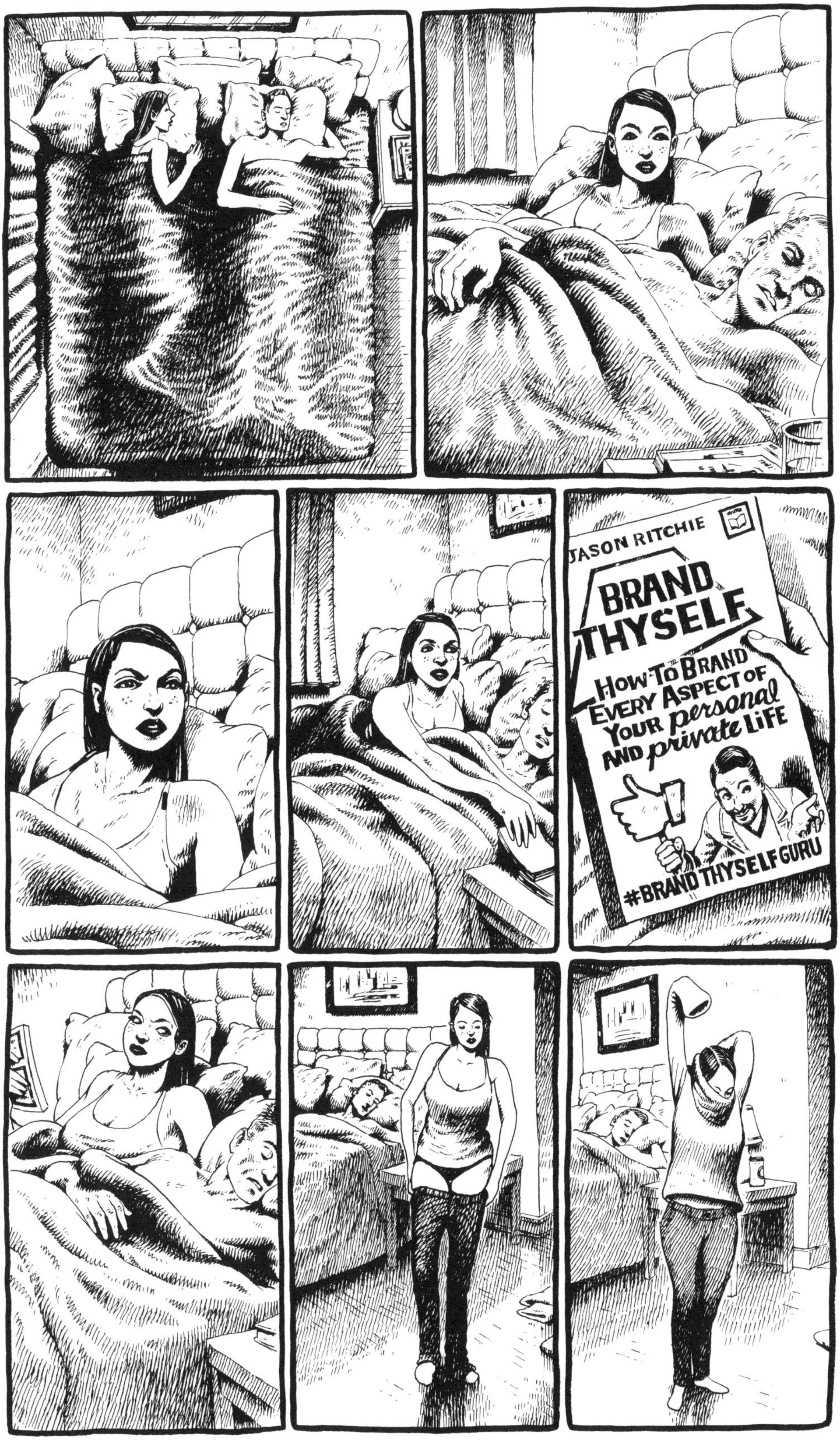
JASON RITCHIE
BRAND THYSELF
HOW TO BRAND EVERY ASPECT OF YOUR personal AND private LIFE
#BRANDTHYSELFGURU

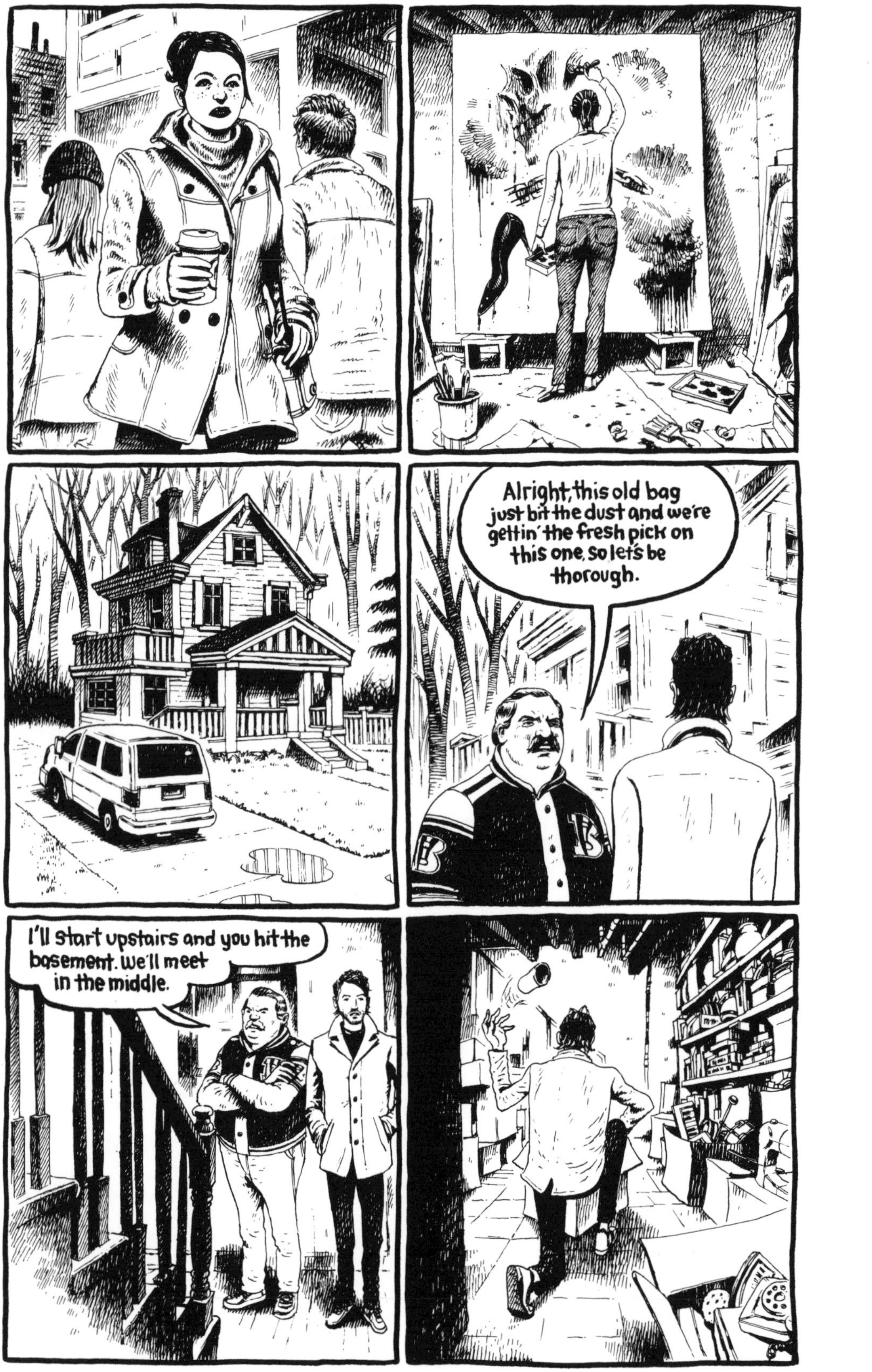
Alright, this old bag just bit the dust and we're gettin' the fresh pick on this one, so let's be thorough.
I'll start upstairs and you hit the basement. We'll meet in the middle.

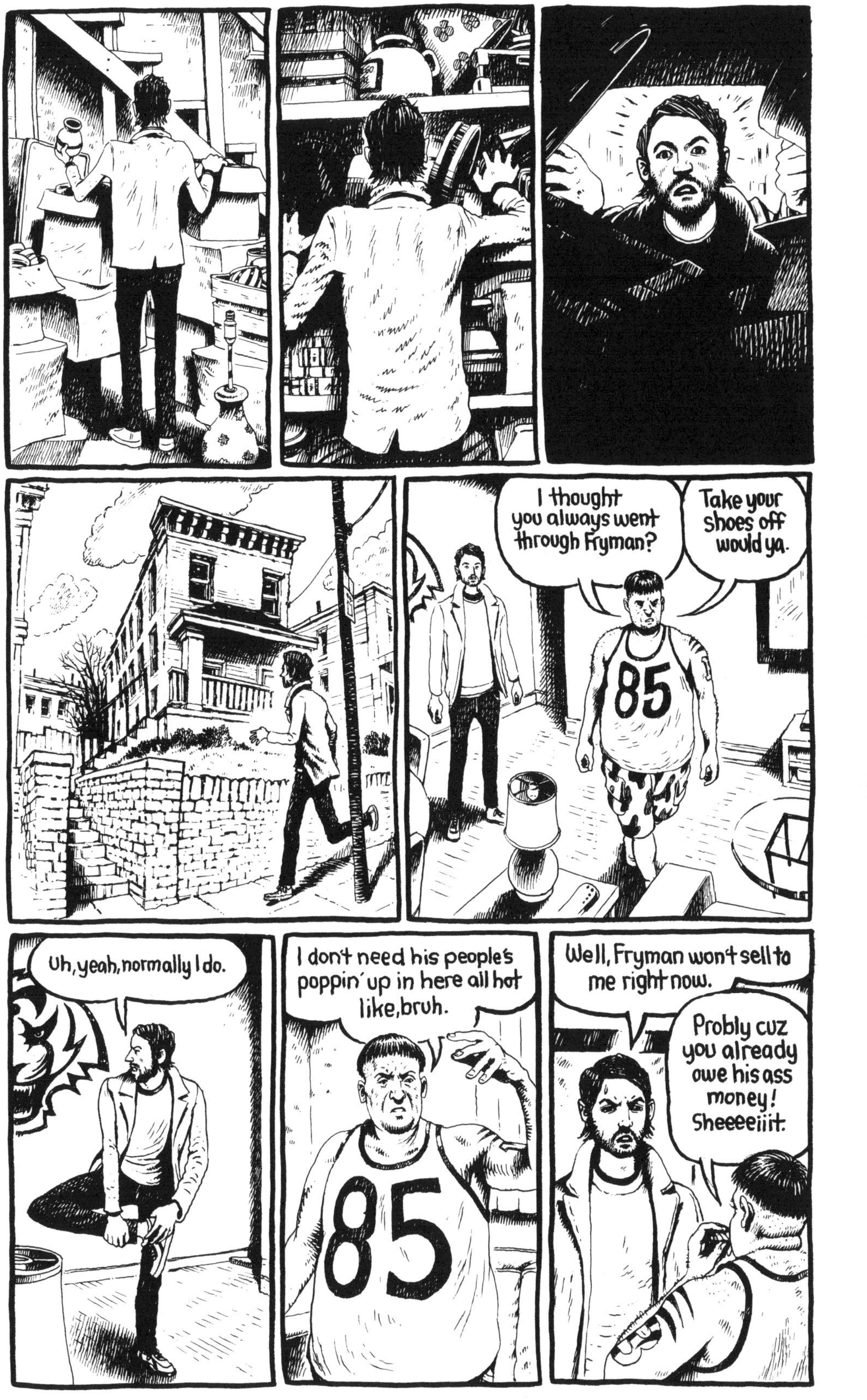
I thought you always went through Fryman?
Take your shoes off would ya.
Uh, yeah, normally I do.
I don't need his people's poppin' up in here all hot like, bruh.
Well, Fryman won't sell to me right now.
Probly cuz you already owe his ass money! Sheeeeiiit.

Nah Rufo, it's not even like that, check this out.

What the hell izzat?

That, my friend, is $12,000.

TIN MAN SODA

Man, get the fuck outta here with this bunk ass shit.

No, seriously, I found this at an estate sale today and look at this!

Man, get your grimey ass up off my leather!

Oh yeah, sorry!

The fug iz is?

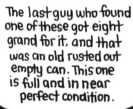
The last guy who found one of these got eight grand for it, and that was an old rusted out empty can. This one is full and in near perfect condition.

Cincinnati's Dirty Secret

Ah HELL NAH! They was slippin' glitter into that shit! That's straight up gangsta, dog!

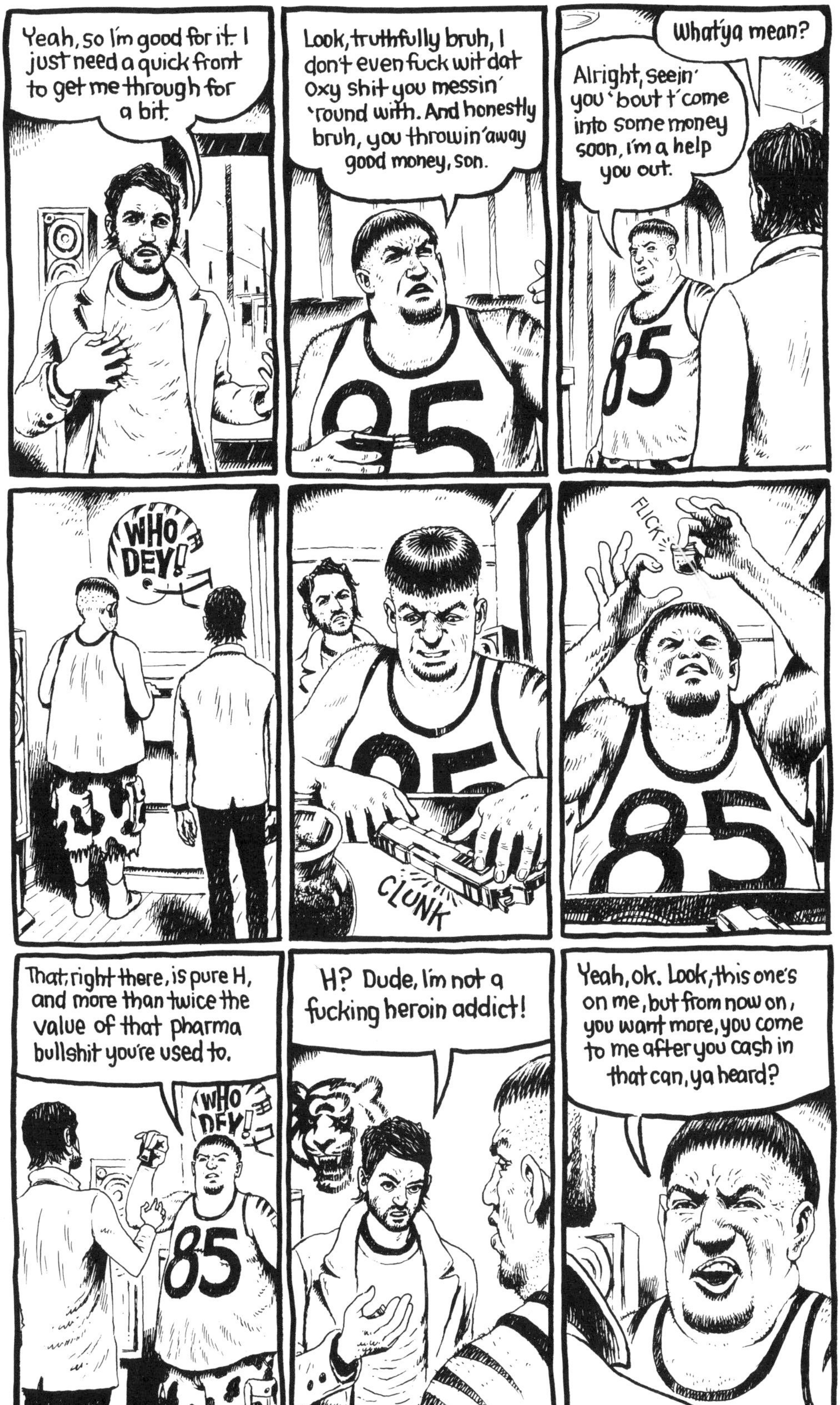
Yeah, so I'm good for it. I just need a quick front to get me through for a bit.
Look, truthfully bruh, I don't even fuck wit dat Oxy shit you messin' 'round with. And honestly bruh, you throwin' away good money, son.
What'ya mean?
Alright, seein' you 'bout t' come into some money soon, I'm a help you out.
WHO DEY!
CLUNK
FLICK
That, right there, is pure H, and more than twice the value of that pharma bullshit you're used to.
WHO DEY!
H? Dude, I'm not a fucking heroin addict!
Yeah, ok. Look, this one's on me, but from now on, you want more, you come to me after you cash in that can, ya heard?

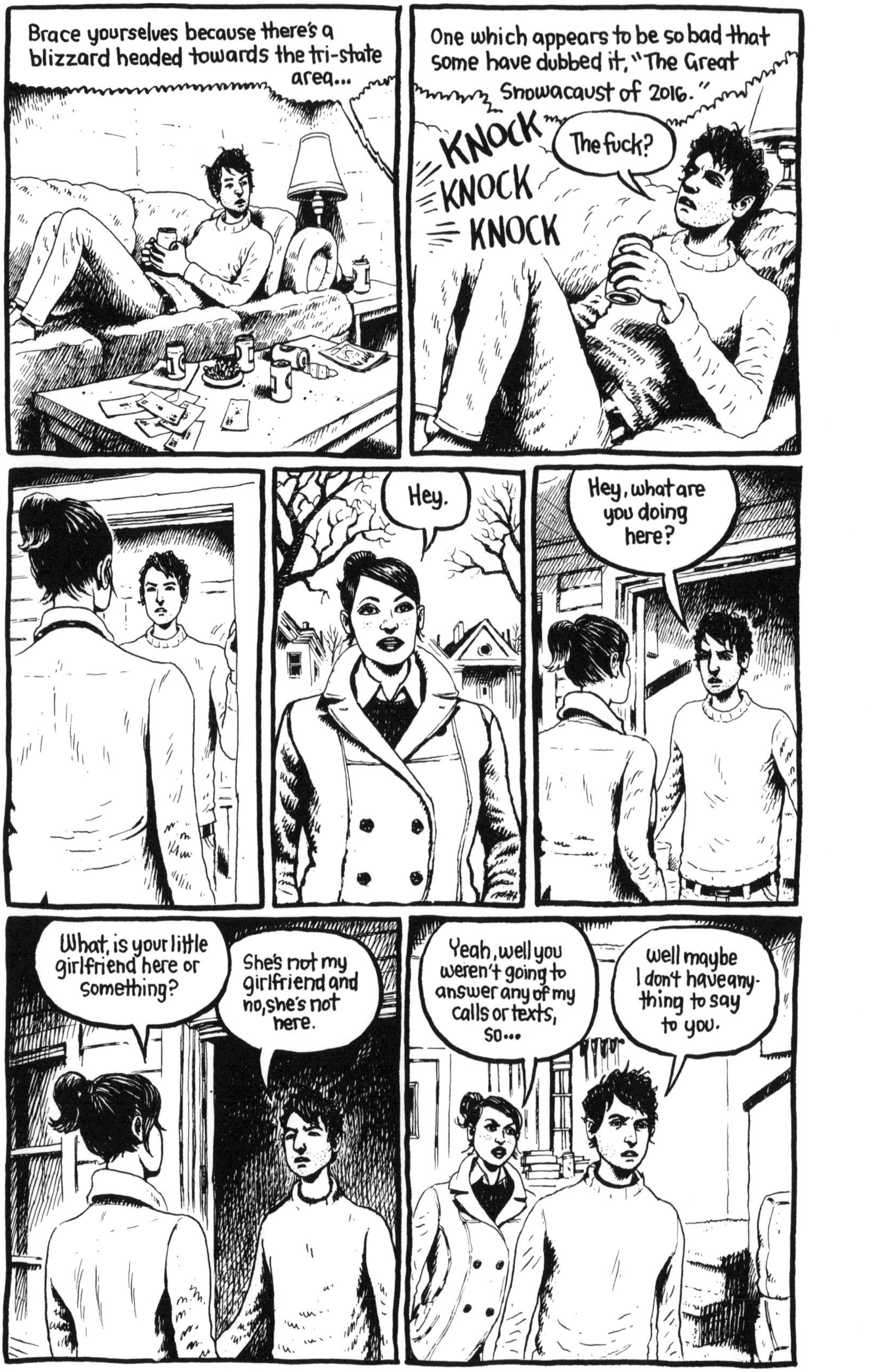
Brace yourselves because there's a blizzard headed towards the tri-state area...
One which appears to be so bad that some have dubbed it, "The Great Snowacaust of 2016."
KNOCK
KNOCK
KNOCK
The fuck?
Hey.
Hey, what are you doing here?
What, is your little girlfriend here or something?
She's not my girlfriend and no, she's not here.
Yeah, well you weren't going to answer any of my calls or texts, so...
Well maybe I don't have anything to say to you.

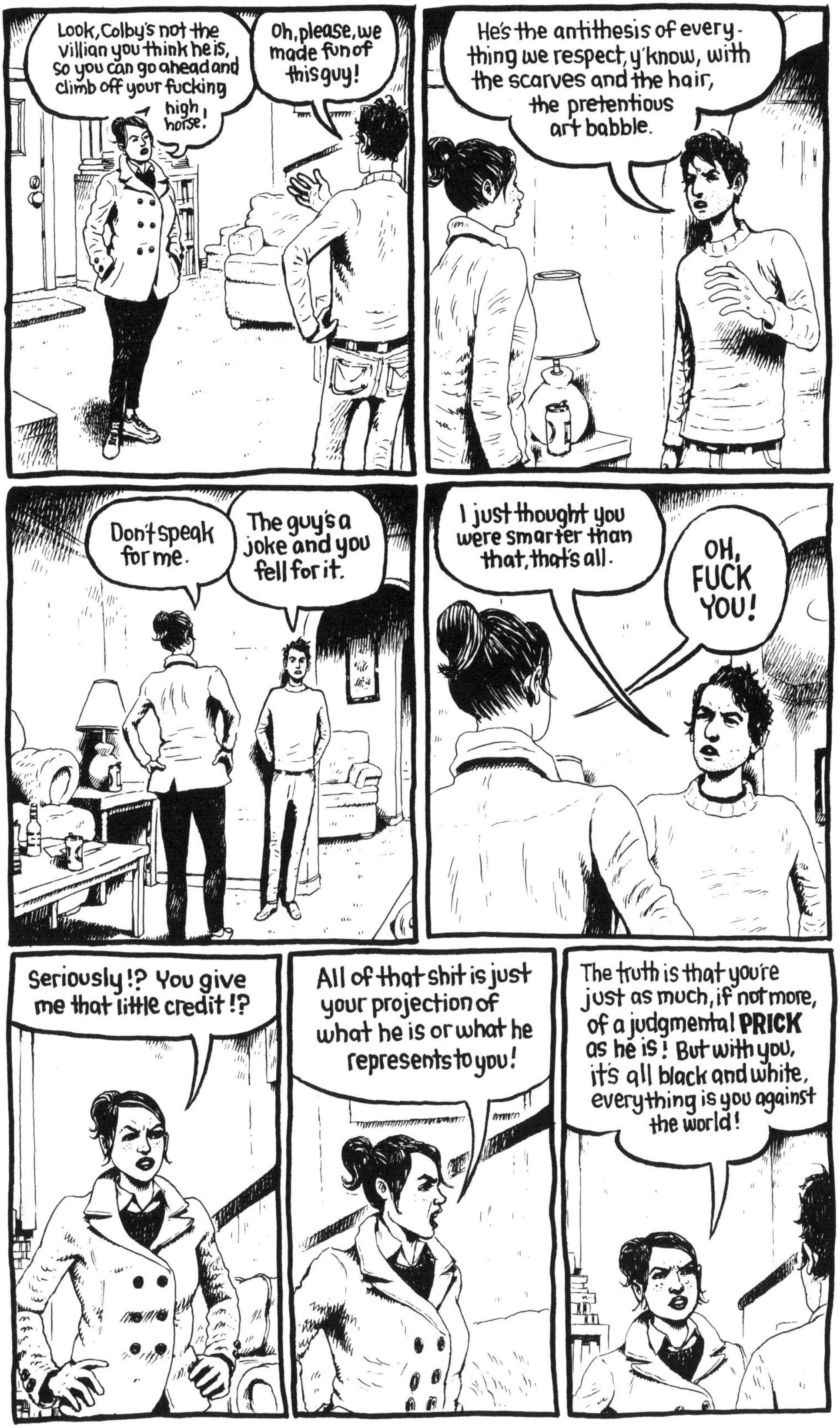

Look, Colby's not the villian you think he is, so you can go ahead and climb off your fucking
high horse!
Oh, please, we made fun of this guy!
He's the antithesis of every-thing we respect, y'know, with the scarves and the hair, the pretentious art babble.
Don't speak for me.
The guy's a joke and you fell for it.
I just thought you were smarter than that, that's all.
OH, FUCK YOU!
Seriously!? You give me that little credit!?
All of that shit is just your projection of what he is or what he represents to you!
The truth is that you're just as much, if not more, of a judgmental **PRICK** as he is! But with you, it's all black and white, everything is you against the world!

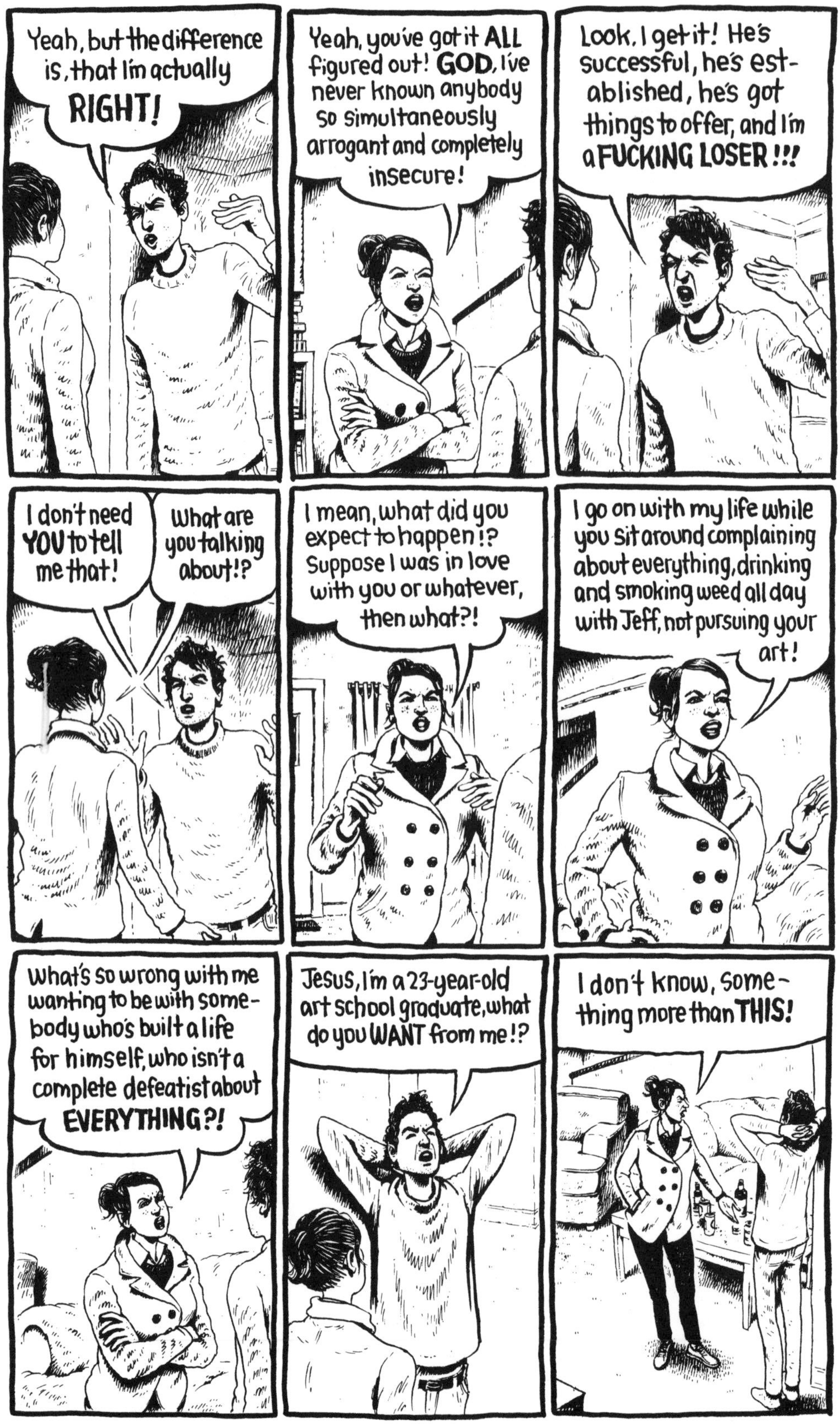

Yeah, but the difference is, that I'm actually RIGHT!
Yeah, you've got it ALL figured out! GOD, I've never known anybody so simultaneously arrogant and completely insecure!
Look, I get it! He's successful, he's established, he's got things to offer, and I'm a FUCKING LOSER!!!
I don't need YOU to tell me that!
What are you talking about!?
I mean, what did you expect to happen!? Suppose I was in love with you or whatever, then what?!
I go on with my life while you sit around complaining about everything, drinking and smoking weed all day with Jeff, not pursuing your art!
What's so wrong with me wanting to be with somebody who's built a life for himself, who isn't a complete defeatist about EVERYTHING?!
Jesus, I'm a 23-year-old art school graduate, what do you WANT from me!?
I don't know, something more than THIS!

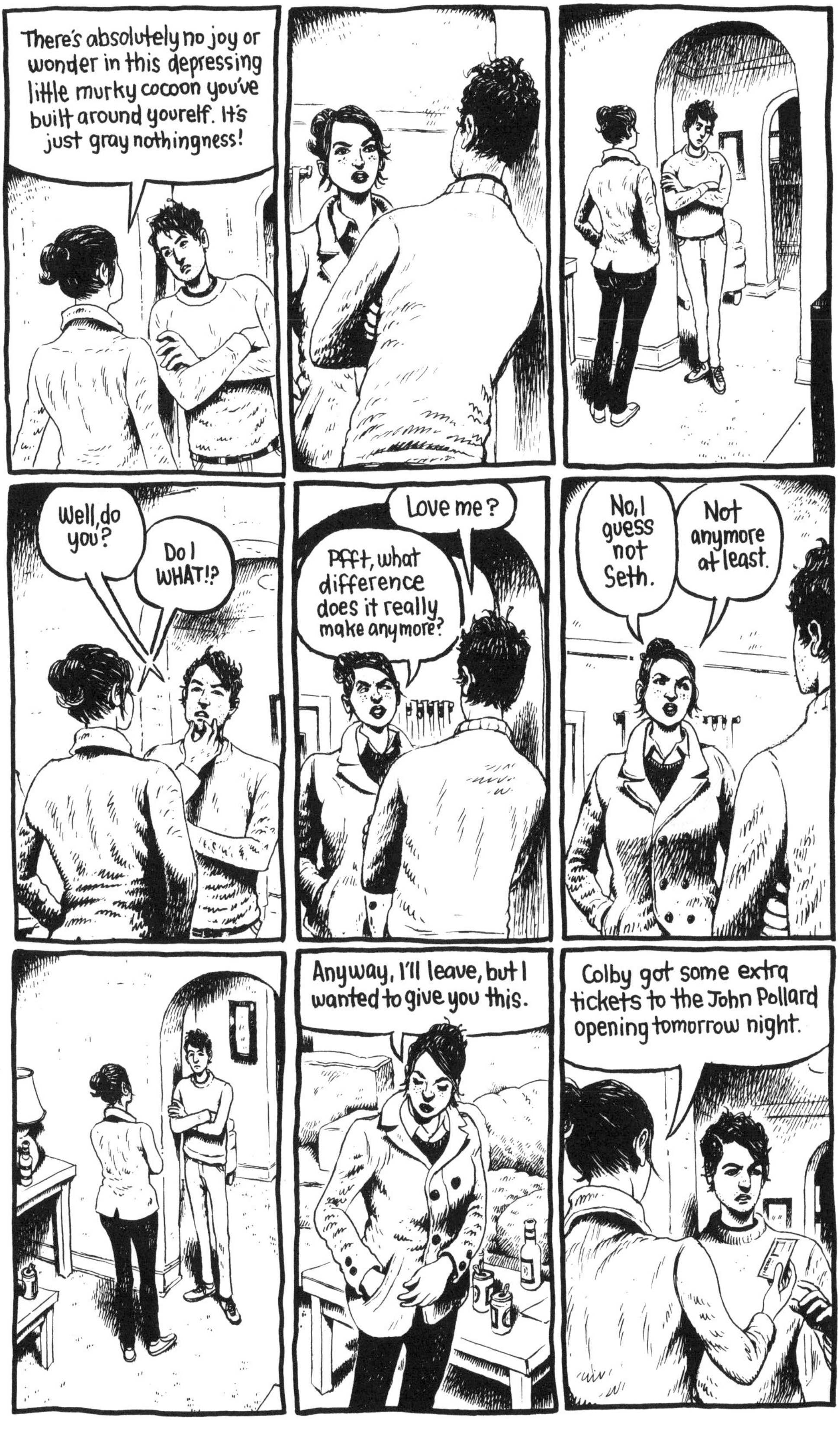
There's absolutely no joy or wonder in this depressing little murky cocoon you've built around yourelf. It's just gray nothingness!
Well, do you?
Do I WHAT!?
Love me?
Pfft, what difference does it really make anymore?
No, I guess not Seth.
Not anymore at least.
Anyway, I'll leave, but I wanted to give you this.
Colby got some extra tickets to the John Pollard opening tomorrow night.

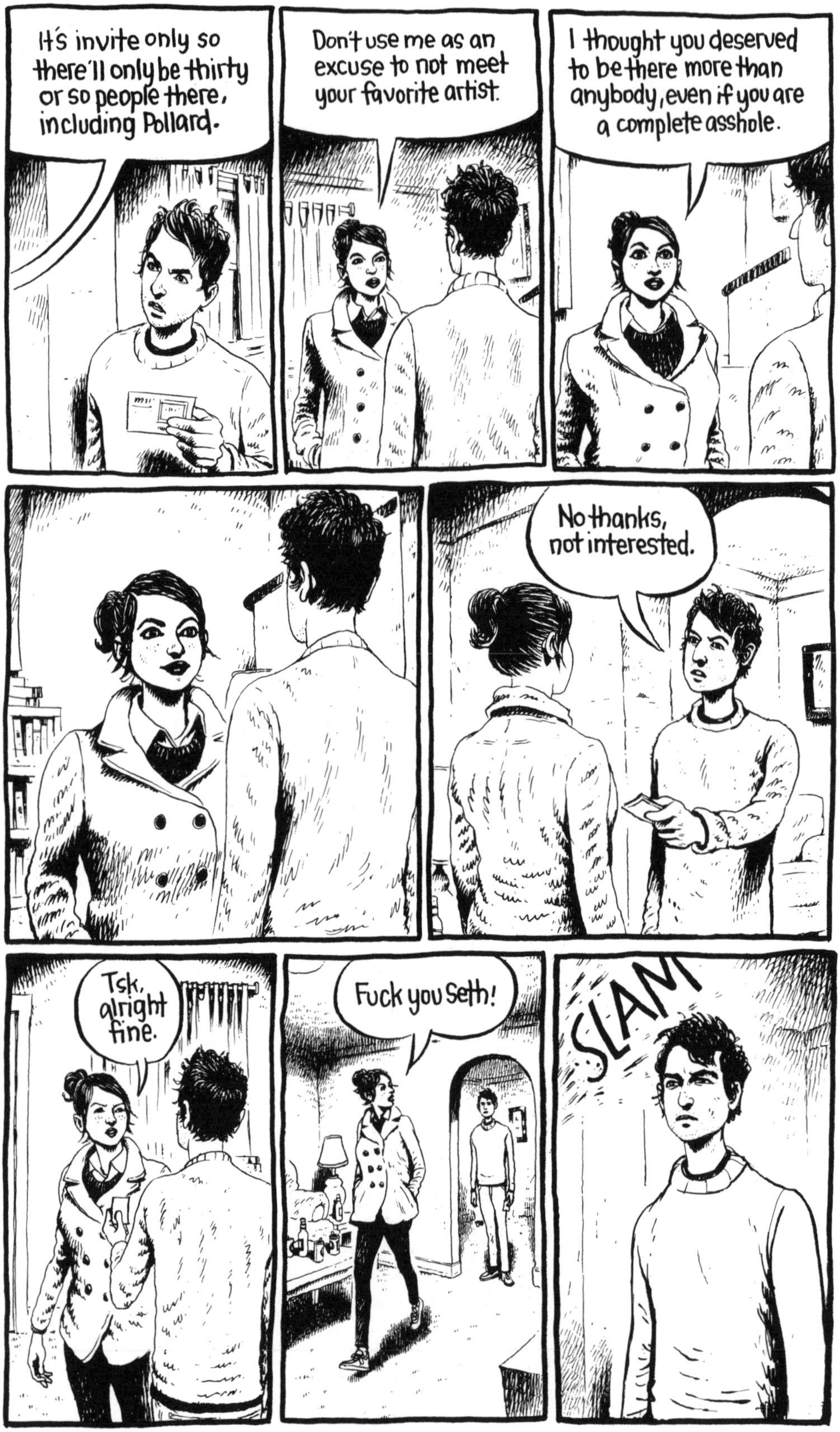
It's invite only so there'll only be thirty or so people there, including Pollard.
Don't use me as an excuse to not meet your favorite artist.
I thought you deserved to be there more than anybody, even if you are a complete asshole.
No thanks, not interested.
Tsk, alright fine.
Fuck you Seth!
SLAM

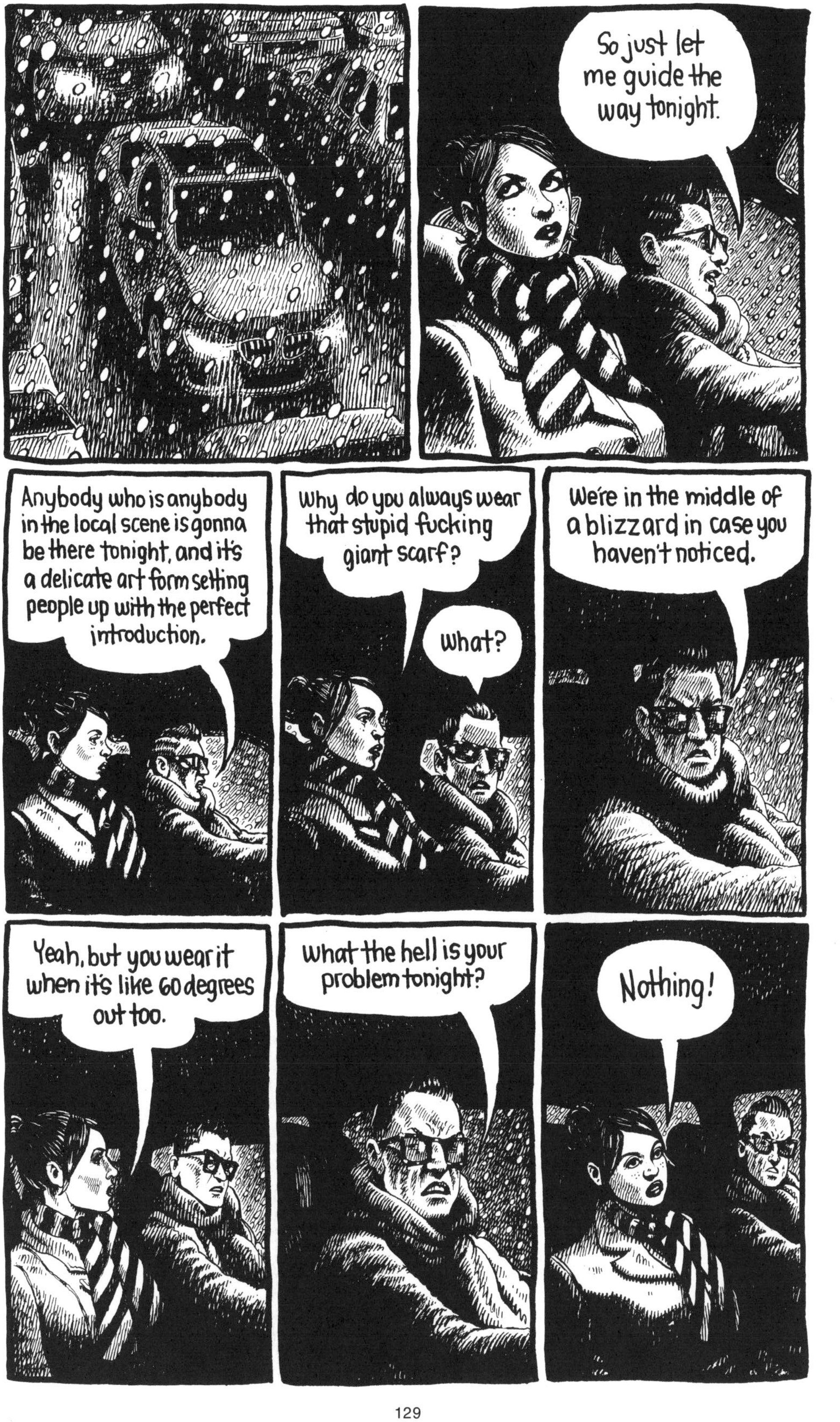
So just let me guide the way tonight.
Anybody who is anybody in the local scene is gonna be there tonight, and it's a delicate art form setting people up with the perfect introduction.
Why do you always wear that stupid fucking giant scarf?
What?
We're in the middle of a blizzard in case you haven't noticed.
Yeah, but you wear it when it's like 60 degrees out too.
What the hell is your problem tonight?
Nothing!

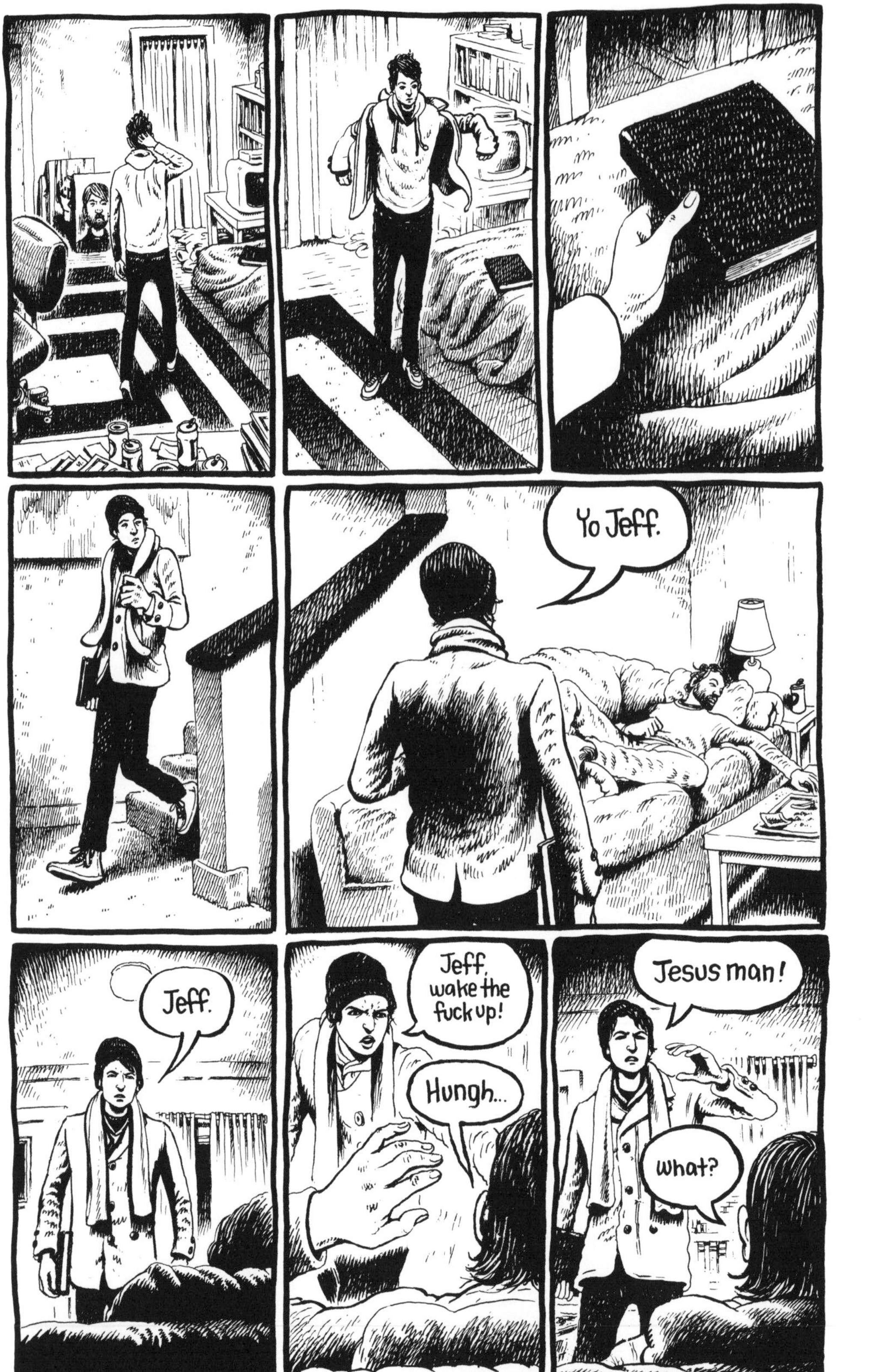
Yo Jeff.
Jeff.
Jeff, wake the fuck up!
Hungh...
Jesus man!
What?

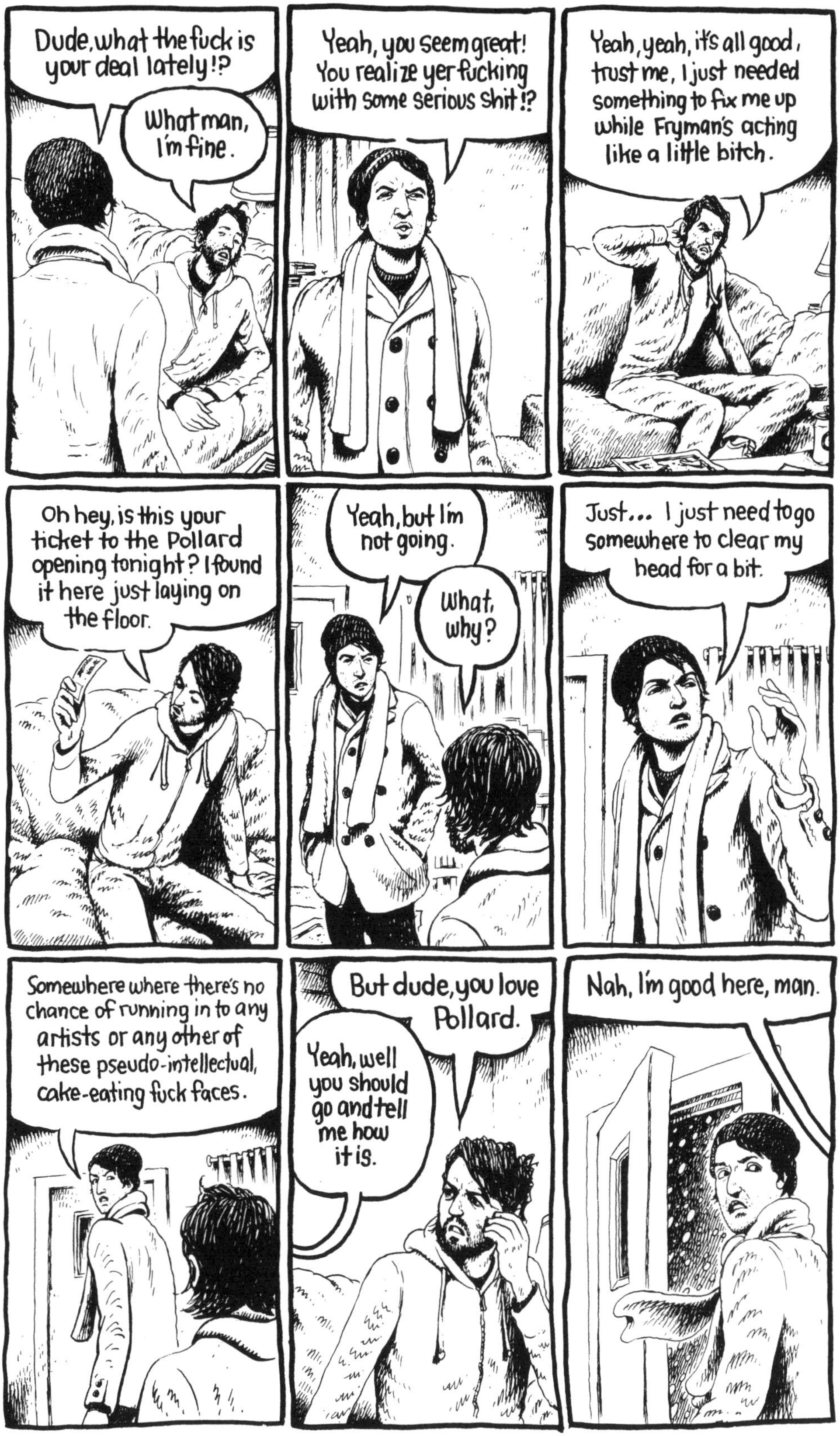

Dude, what the fuck is your deal lately!?
What man, I'm fine.
Yeah, you seem great! You realize yer fucking with some serious shit!?
Yeah, yeah, it's all good, trust me, I just needed something to fix me up while Fryman's acting like a little bitch.
Oh hey, is this your ticket to the Pollard opening tonight? I found it here just laying on the floor.
Yeah, but I'm not going.
What, why?
Just... I just need to go somewhere to clear my head for a bit.
Somewhere where there's no chance of running in to any artists or any other of these pseudo-intellectual, cake-eating fuck faces.
But dude, you love Pollard.
Yeah, well you should go and tell me how it is.
Nah, I'm good here, man.

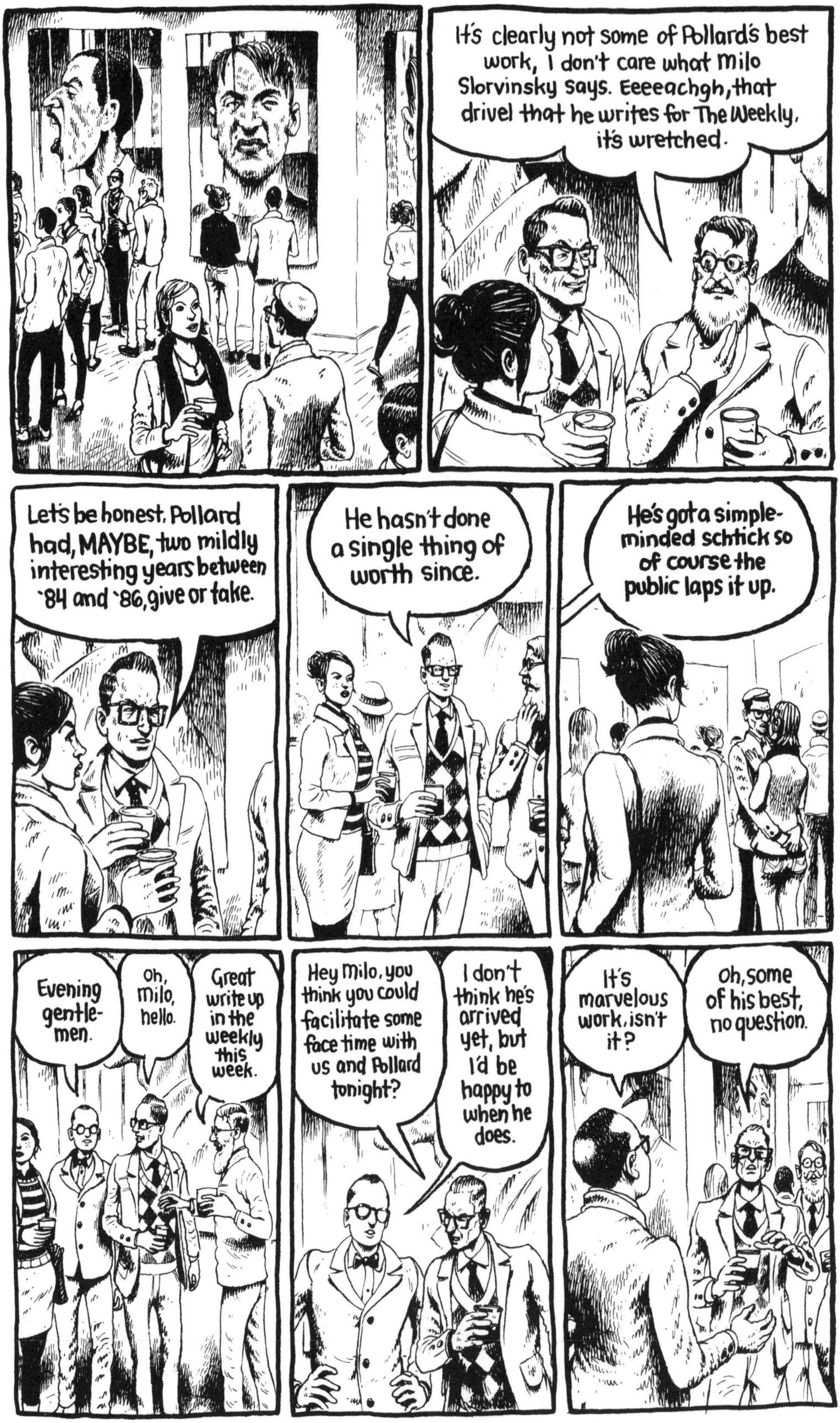
It's clearly not some of Pollard's best work, I don't care what Milo Slorvinsky says. Eeeeachgh, that drivel that he writes for The Weekly, it's wretched.
Let's be honest. Pollard had, MAYBE, two mildly interesting years between '84 and '86, give or take.
He hasn't done a single thing of worth since.
He's got a simple-minded schtick so of course the public laps it up.
Evening gentlemen.
Oh, Milo, hello.
Great write up in the weekly this week.
Hey Milo, you think you could facilitate some face time with us and Pollard tonight?
I don't think he's arrived yet, but I'd be happy to when he does.
It's marvelous work, isn't it?
Oh, some of his best, no question.

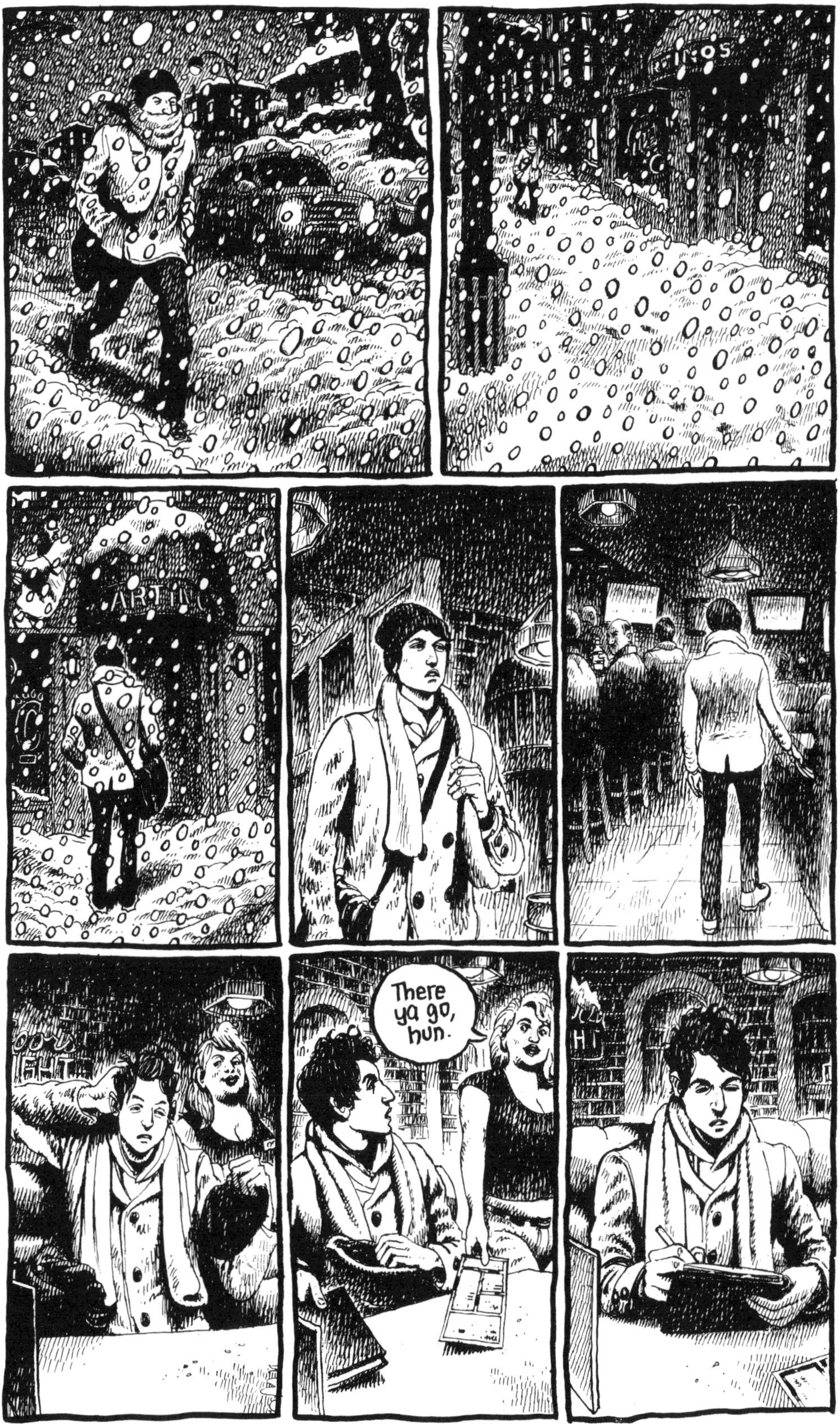
INOS
ARTIN
There ya go, hun.

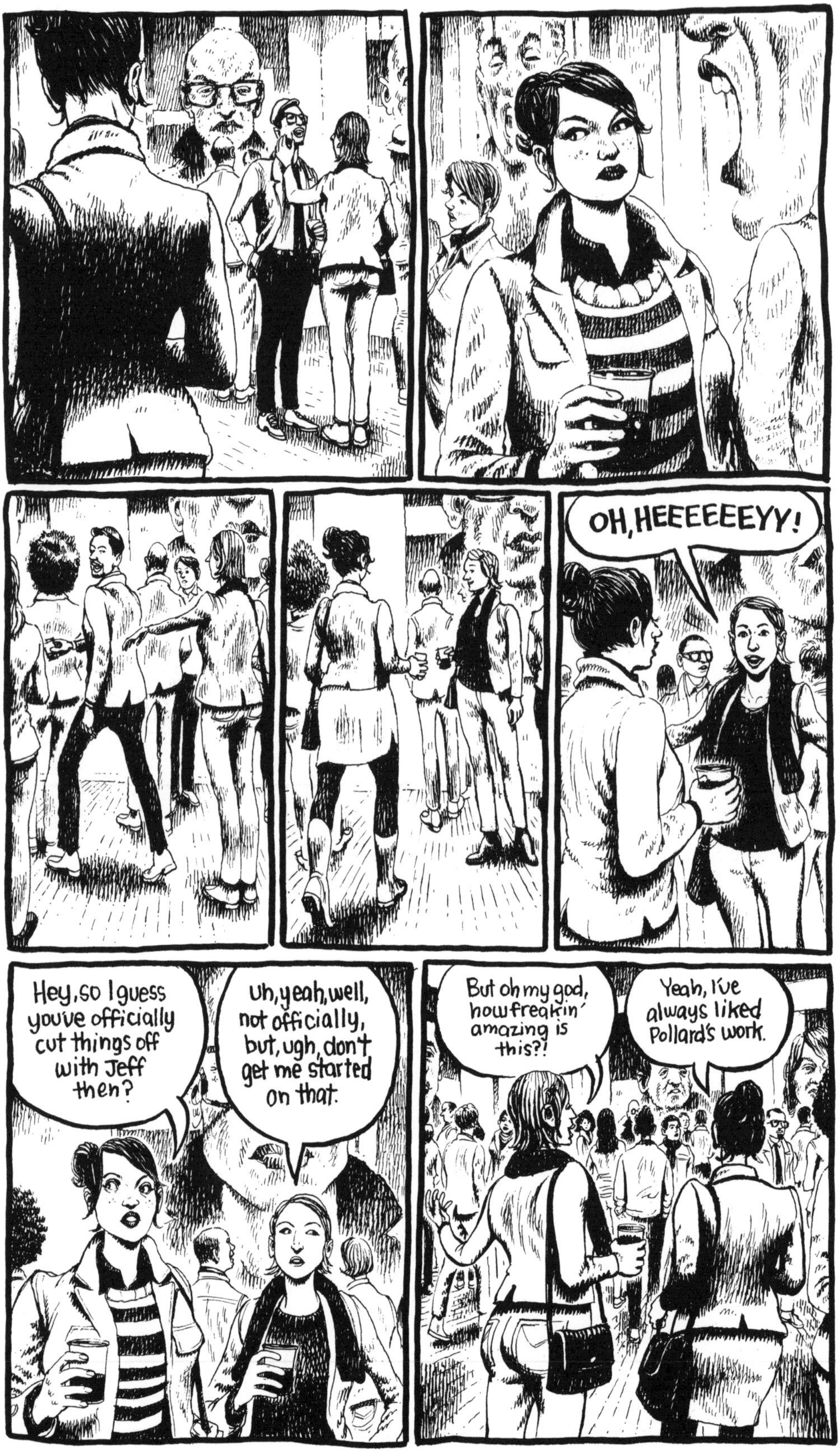
OH, HEEEEEEYY!
Hey, so I guess you've officially cut things off with Jeff then?
Uh, yeah, well, not officially, but, ugh, don't get me started on that.
But oh my god, how freakin' amazing is this?!
Yeah, I've always liked Pollard's work.

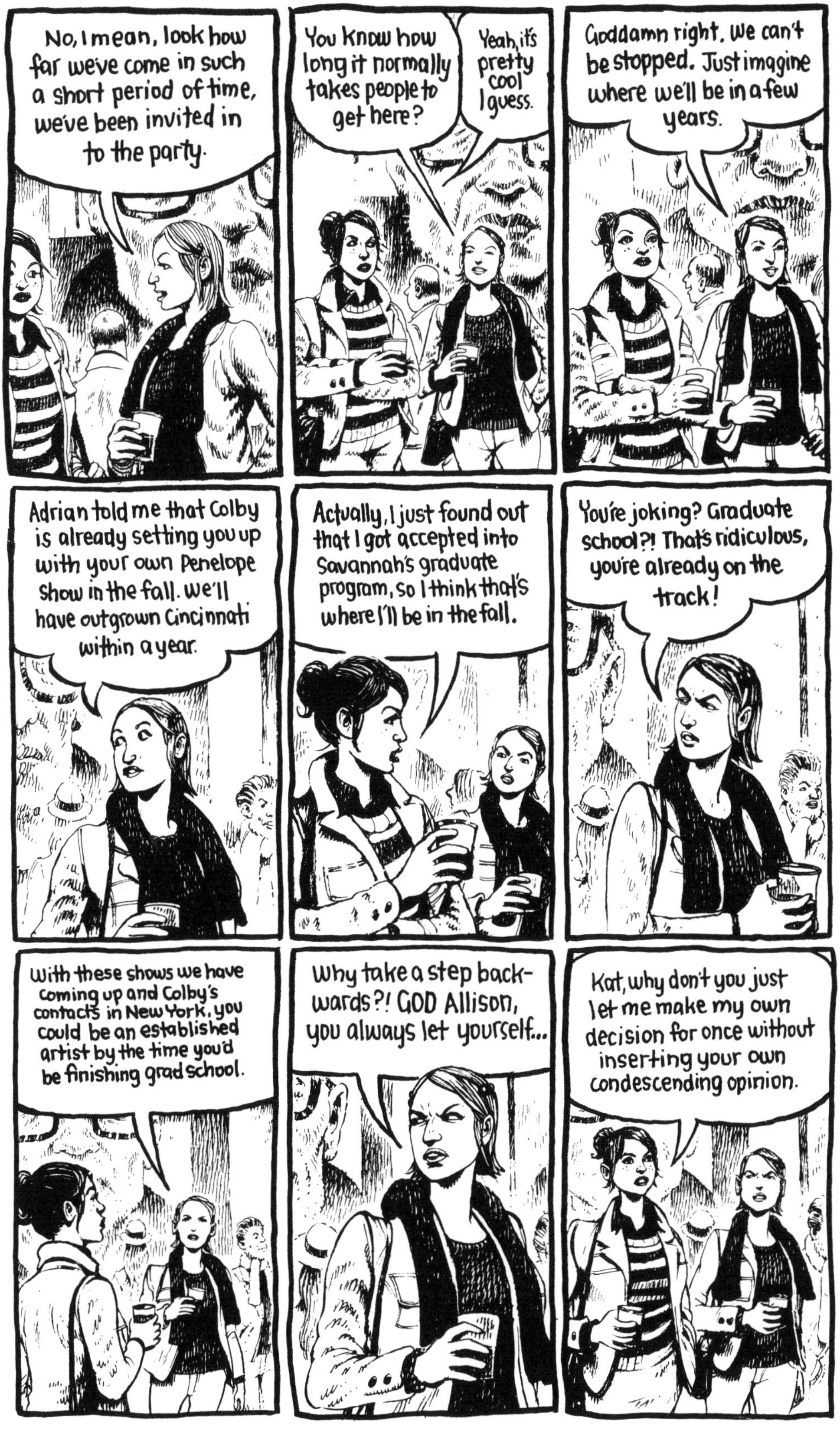

No, I mean, look how far we've come in such a short period of time, we've been invited in to the party.
You know how long it normally takes people to get here?
Yeah, it's pretty cool I guess.
Goddamn right. We can't be stopped. Just imagine where we'll be in a few years.
Adrian told me that Colby is already setting you up with your own Penelope show in the fall. We'll have outgrown Cincinnati within a year.
Actually, I just found out that I got accepted into Savannah's graduate program, so I think that's where I'll be in the fall.
You're joking? Graduate school?! That's ridiculous, you're already on the track!
With these shows we have coming up and Colby's contacts in New York, you could be an established artist by the time you'd be finishing grad school.
Why take a step back-wards?! GOD Allison, you always let yourself...
Kat, why don't you just let me make my own decision for once without inserting your own condescending opinion.

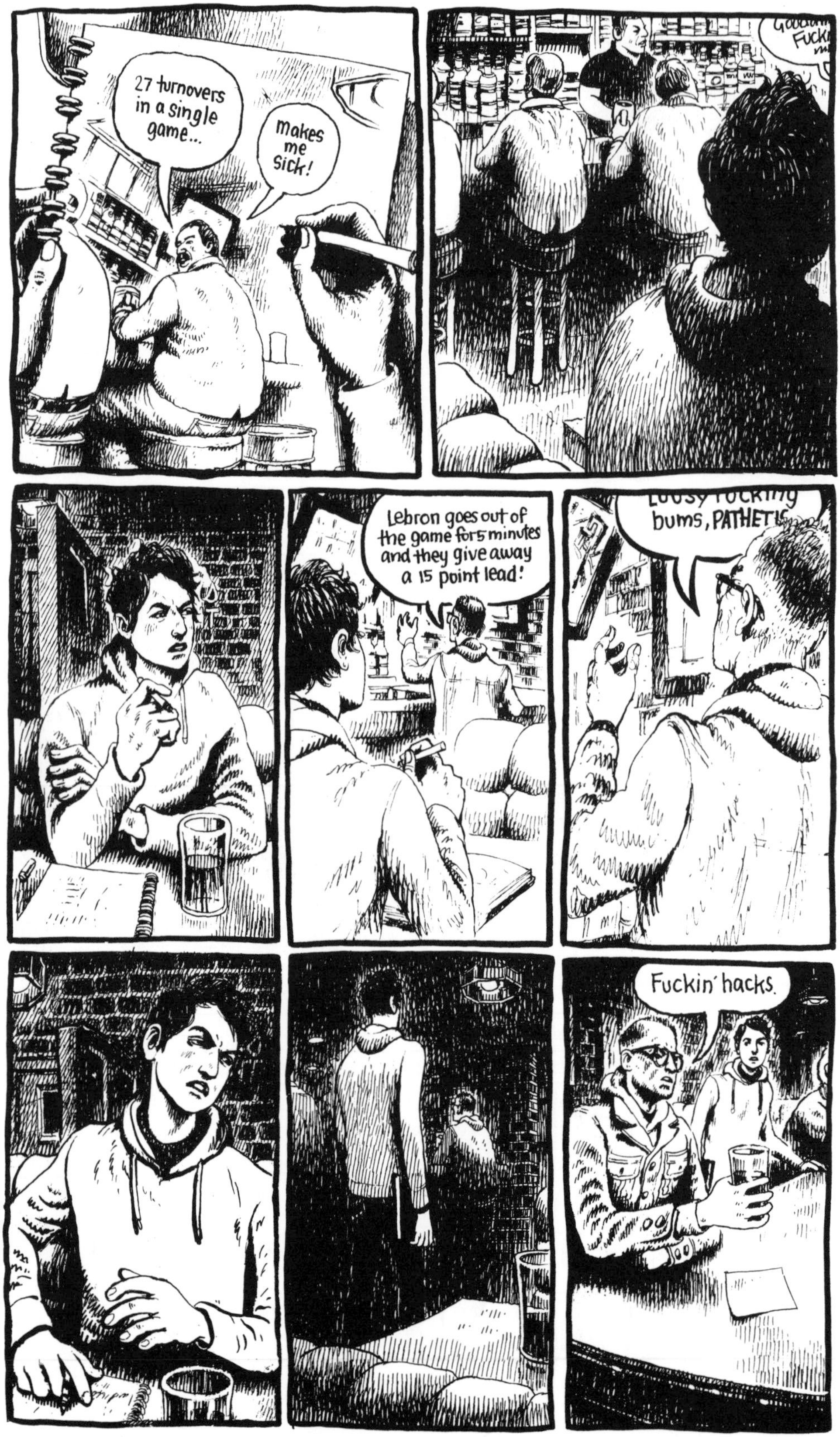
27 turnovers in a single game...
makes me sick!
Lebron goes out of the game for 5 minutes and they give away a 15 point lead!
Lousy fucking bums, PATHETIC
Fuckin' hacks.

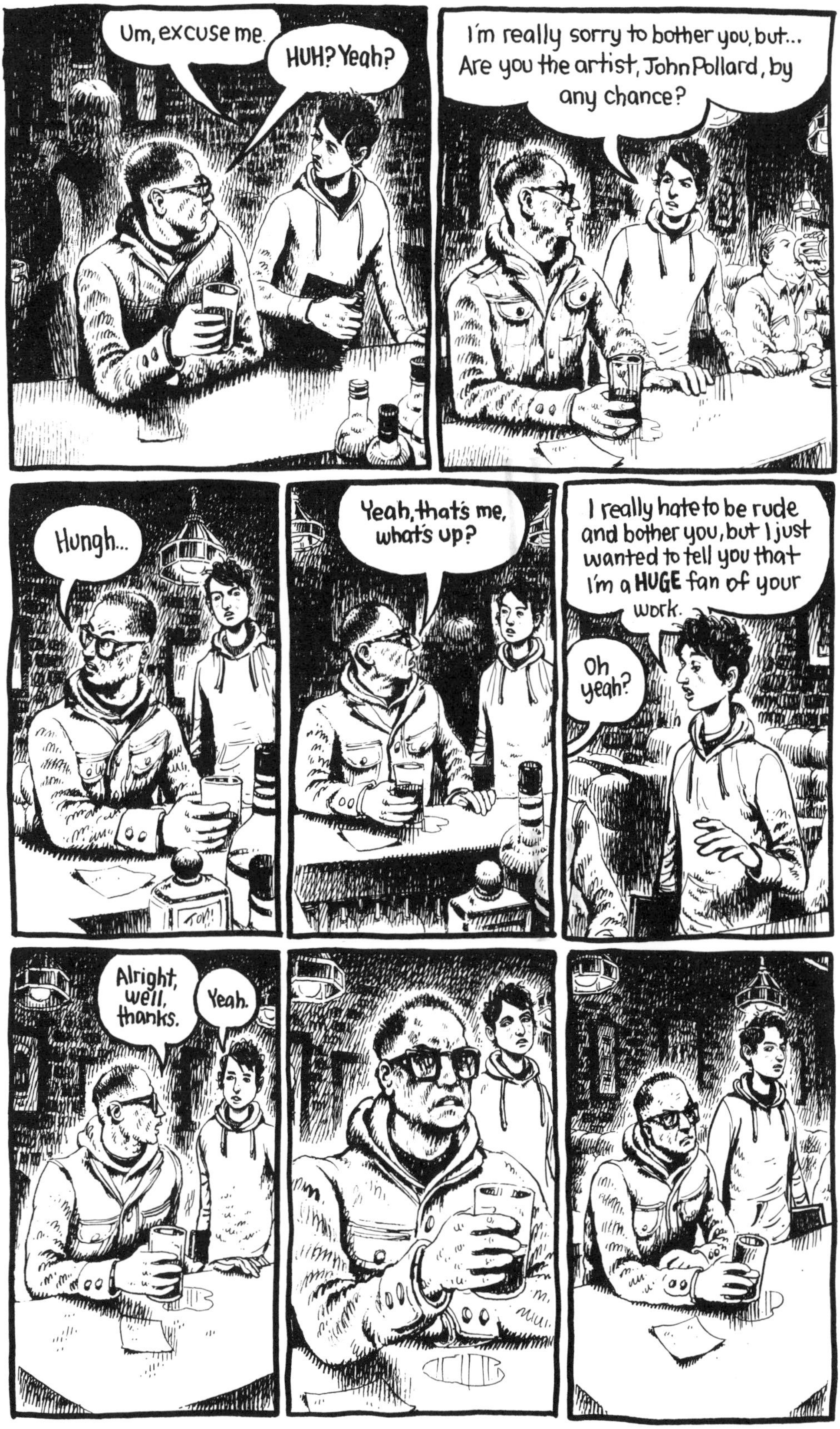
Um, excuse me.
HUH? Yeah?
I'm really sorry to bother you, but... Are you the artist, John Pollard, by any chance?
Hungh...
Yeah, that's me, what's up?
I really hate to be rude and bother you, but I just wanted to tell you that I'm a HUGE fan of your work.
Oh yeah?
Alright, well, thanks.
Yeah.

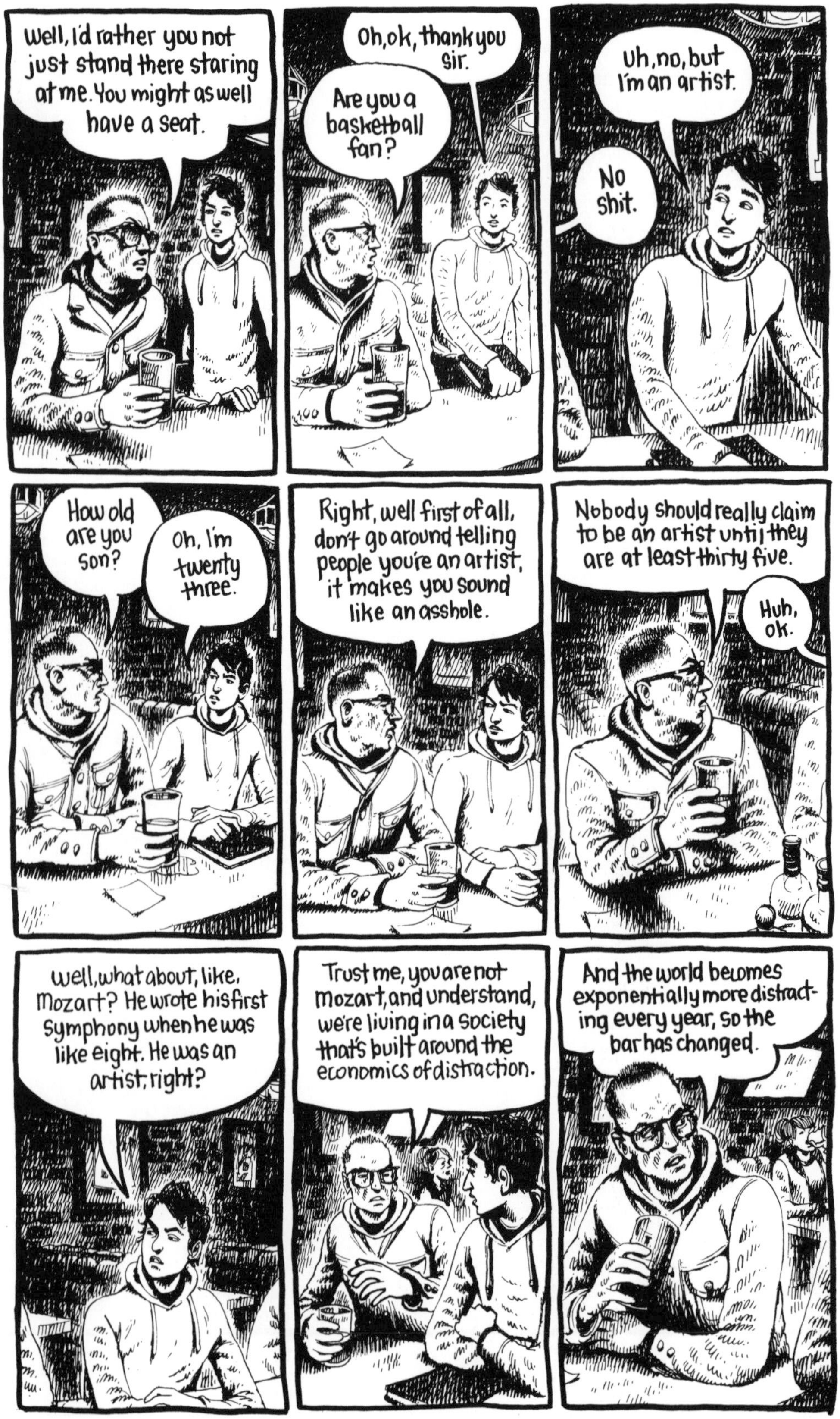
Well, I'd rather you not just stand there staring at me. You might as well have a seat.
Oh, ok, thank you sir.
Are you a basketball fan?
Uh, no, but I'm an artist.
No shit.
How old are you son?
Oh, I'm twenty three.
Right, well first of all, don't go around telling people you're an artist, it makes you sound like an asshole.
Nobody should really claim to be an artist until they are at least thirty five.
Huh, ok.
Well, what about, like, Mozart? He wrote his first symphony when he was like eight. He was an artist, right?
Trust me, you are not Mozart, and understand, we're living in a society that's built around the economics of distraction.
And the world becomes exponentially more distracting every year, so the bar has changed.

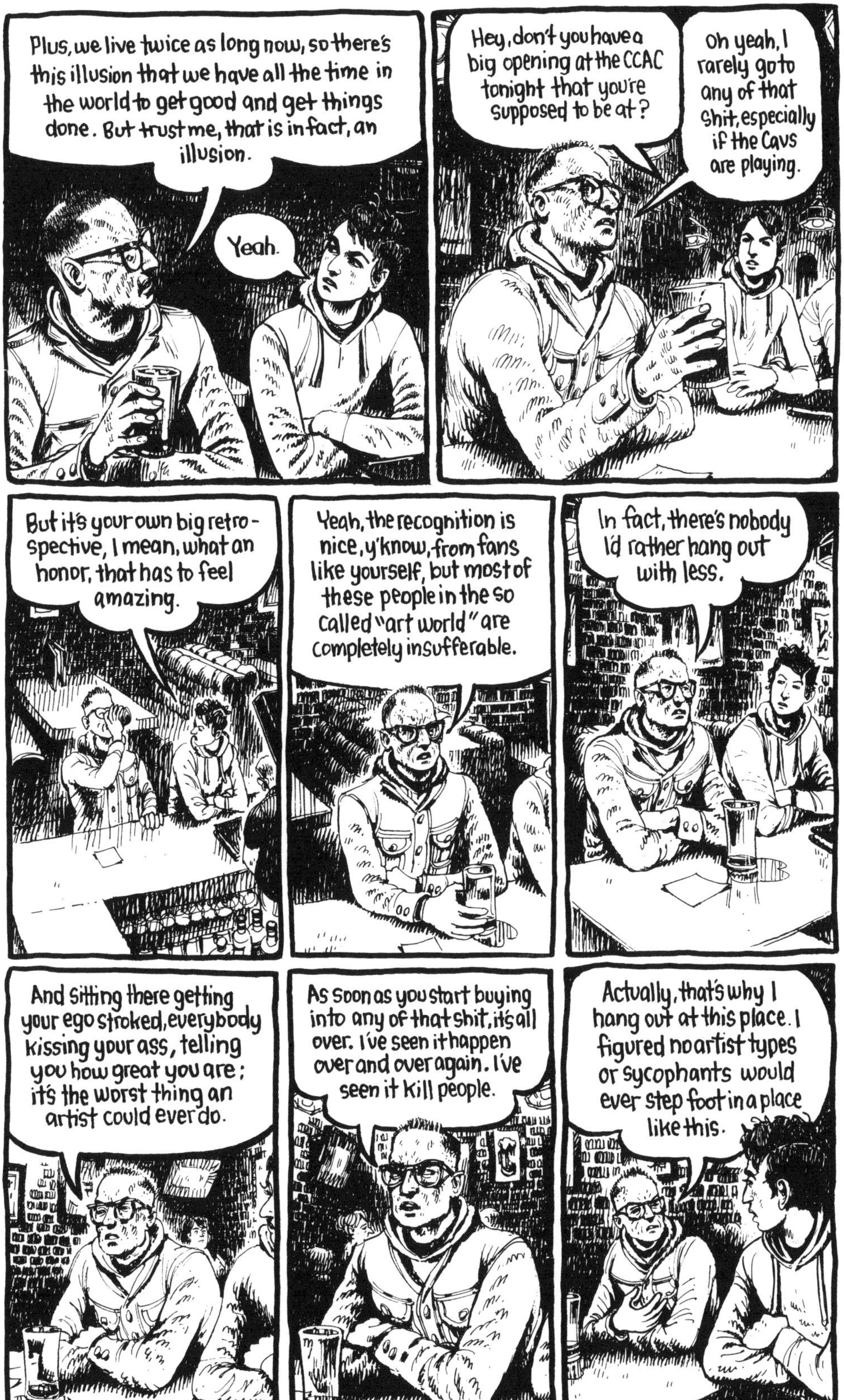
Plus, we live twice as long now, so there's this illusion that we have all the time in the world to get good and get things done. But trust me, that is in fact, an illusion.
Yeah.
Hey, don't you have a big opening at the CCAC tonight that you're supposed to be at?
Oh yeah, I rarely go to any of that shit, especially if the Cavs are playing.
But it's your own big retro-spective, I mean, what an honor, that has to feel amazing.
Yeah, the recognition is nice, y'know, from fans like yourself, but most of these people in the so called "art world" are completely insufferable.
In fact, there's nobody I'd rather hang out with less.
And sitting there getting your ego stroked, everybody kissing your ass, telling you how great you are; it's the worst thing an artist could ever do.
As soon as you start buying into any of that shit, it's all over. I've seen it happen over and over again. I've seen it kill people.
Actually, that's why I hang out at this place. I figured no artist types or sycophants would ever step foot in a place like this.

No offense, you're actually the first person to recognize me here.

Yeah, that makes sense I guess.

But... It's still kinda hard to understand cuz I feel like all I really want is an audience for my art. Otherwise, it's like, what the fuck am I doing this shit for?

I mean, you're living the dream.

You say "I mean" and "like" a lot. Stop doing that.

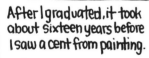

Oh, ok, sorry

Stop saying sorry.

Right.

C'mon mother-FUCKERS!

Look, it's true, I've got it good, but trust me, it took a long time to get any traction.

After I graduated, it took about sixteen years before I saw a cent from painting.

Until then, I worked just about every shit job imaginable. In fact, one of my jobs was actually cleaning up human piss and shit off the floor of of an elderly mental hospital.

Seriously?

Yeah, I did that for about seven years.

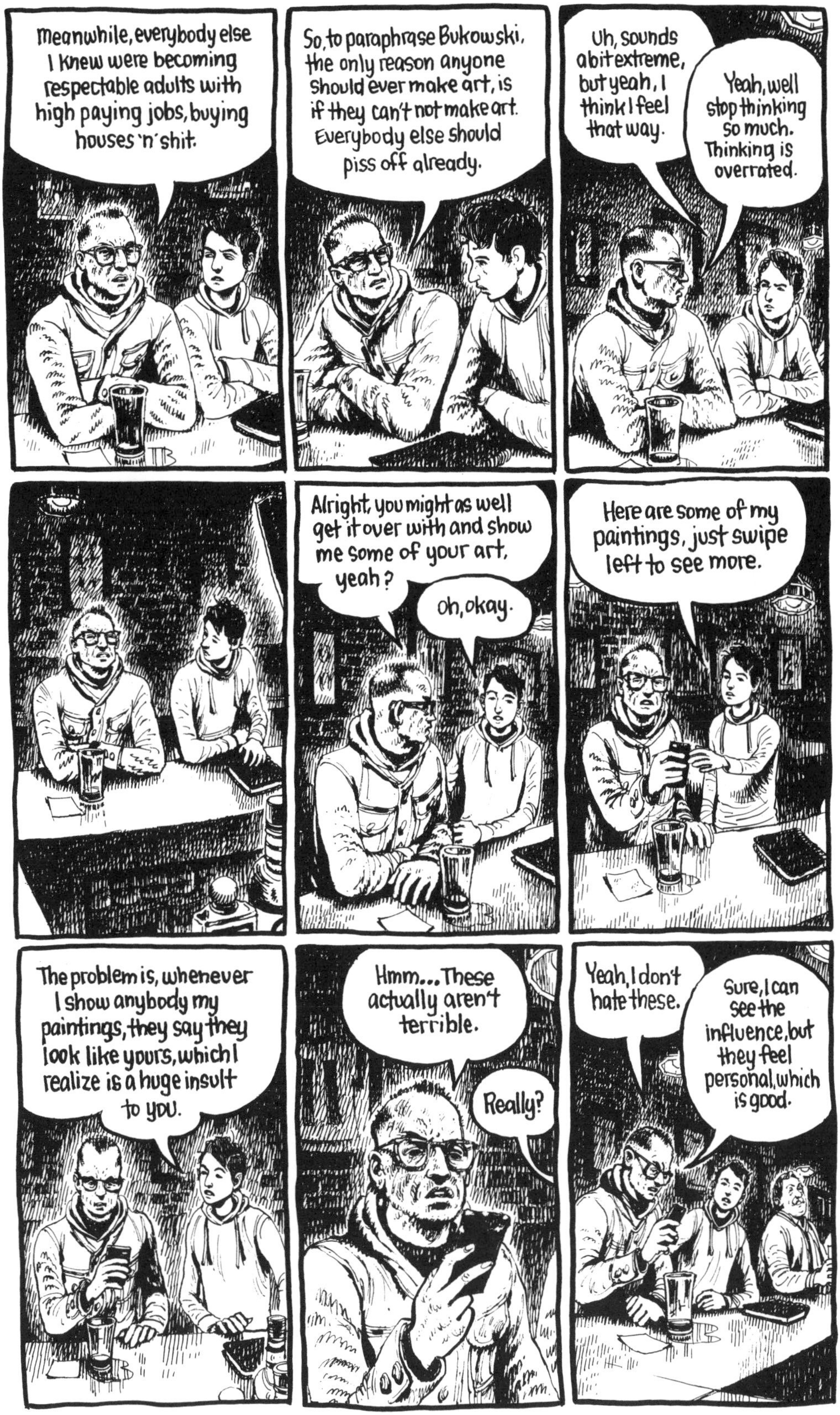
Meanwhile, everybody else I knew were becoming respectable adults with high paying jobs, buying houses 'n' shit.
So, to paraphrase Bukowski, the only reason anyone should ever make art, is if they can't not make art. Everybody else should piss off already.
Uh, sounds a bit extreme, but yeah, I think I feel that way.
Yeah, well stop thinking so much. Thinking is overrated.
Alright, you might as well get it over with and show me some of your art, yeah?
Oh, okay.
Here are some of my paintings, just swipe left to see more.
The problem is, whenever I show anybody my paintings, they say they look like yours, which I realize is a huge insult to you.
Hmm... These actually aren't terrible.
Really?
Yeah, I don't hate these.
Sure, I can see the influence, but they feel personal, which is good.

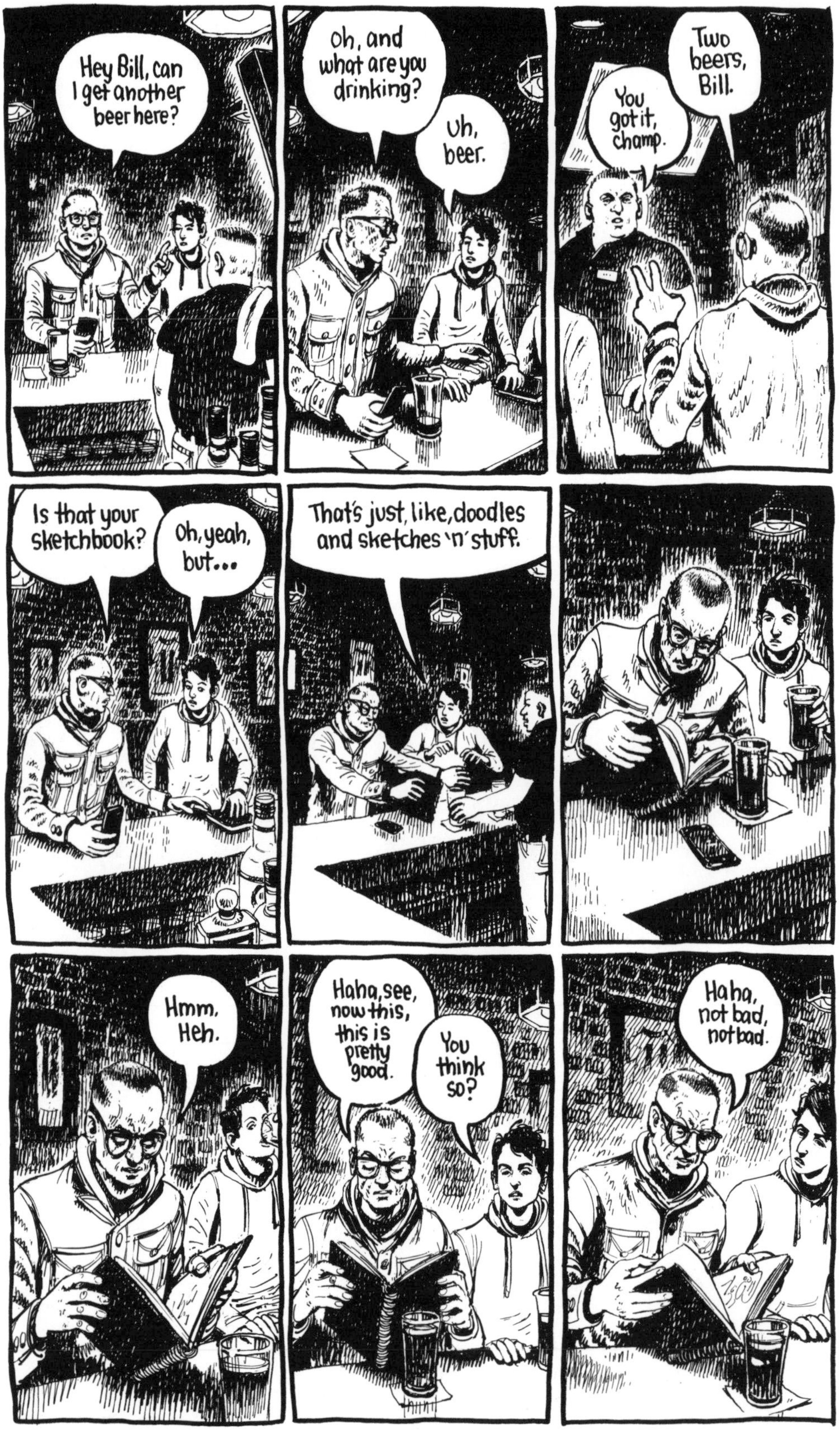
Hey Bill, can I get another beer here?
Oh, and what are you drinking?
Uh, beer.
Two beers, Bill.
You got it, champ.
Is that your sketchbook?
Oh, yeah, but...
That's just, like, doodles and sketches 'n' stuff.
Hmm. Heh.
Haha, see, now this, this is pretty good.
You think so?
Haha, not bad, not bad.

Jesus, this whole thing is filled to the brim.

Yeah, that's just from the past six months or so.

Seth Fallon, that's your name?

Yeah.

Well, you've definitely got something here Seth Fallon. The paintings are nice, but these drawings are more interesting to me.

These pop right off the page, just these little observations. You should do something with these, make little books or cartoons, I don't know.

Man, thank you, that means a lot coming from you. But, like, how do I go about starting a career? I don't even know where to begin.

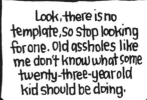

Look, there is no template, so stop looking for one. Old assholes like me don't know what some twenty-three-year old kid should be doing.

All you can do is keep making work and see where it takes you. Maybe get the fuck out of Cincinnati for awhile, work more shitty jobs and surround yourself with different kinds of people. Then let that inform your work.

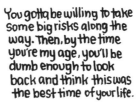

You gotta be willing to take some big risks along the way. Then, by the time you're my age, you'll be dumb enough to look back and think this was the best time of your life.

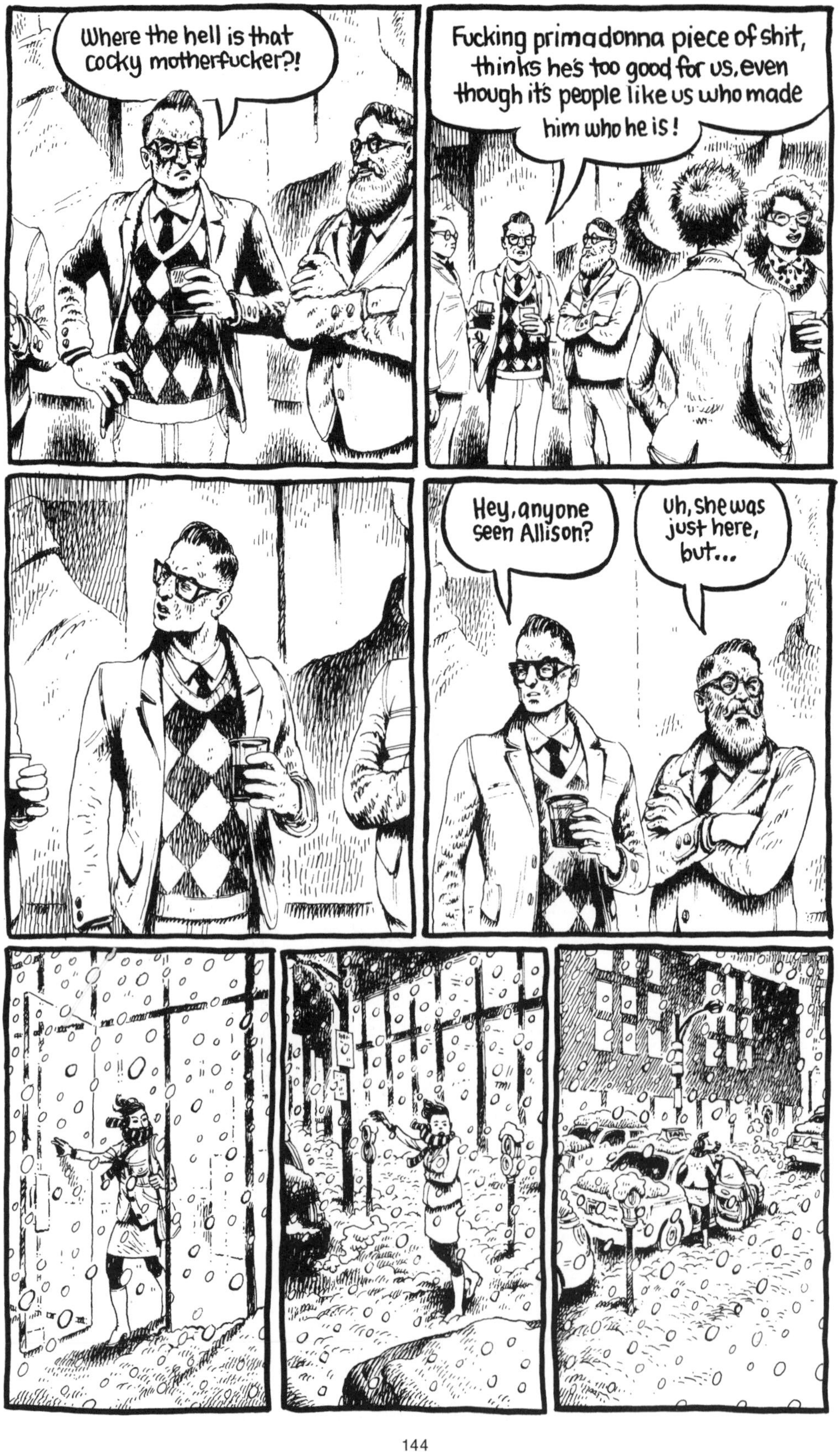
Where the hell is that cocky motherfucker?!
Fucking primadonna piece of shit, thinks he's too good for us, even though it's people like us who made him who he is!
Hey, anyone seen Allison?
Uh, she was just here, but...

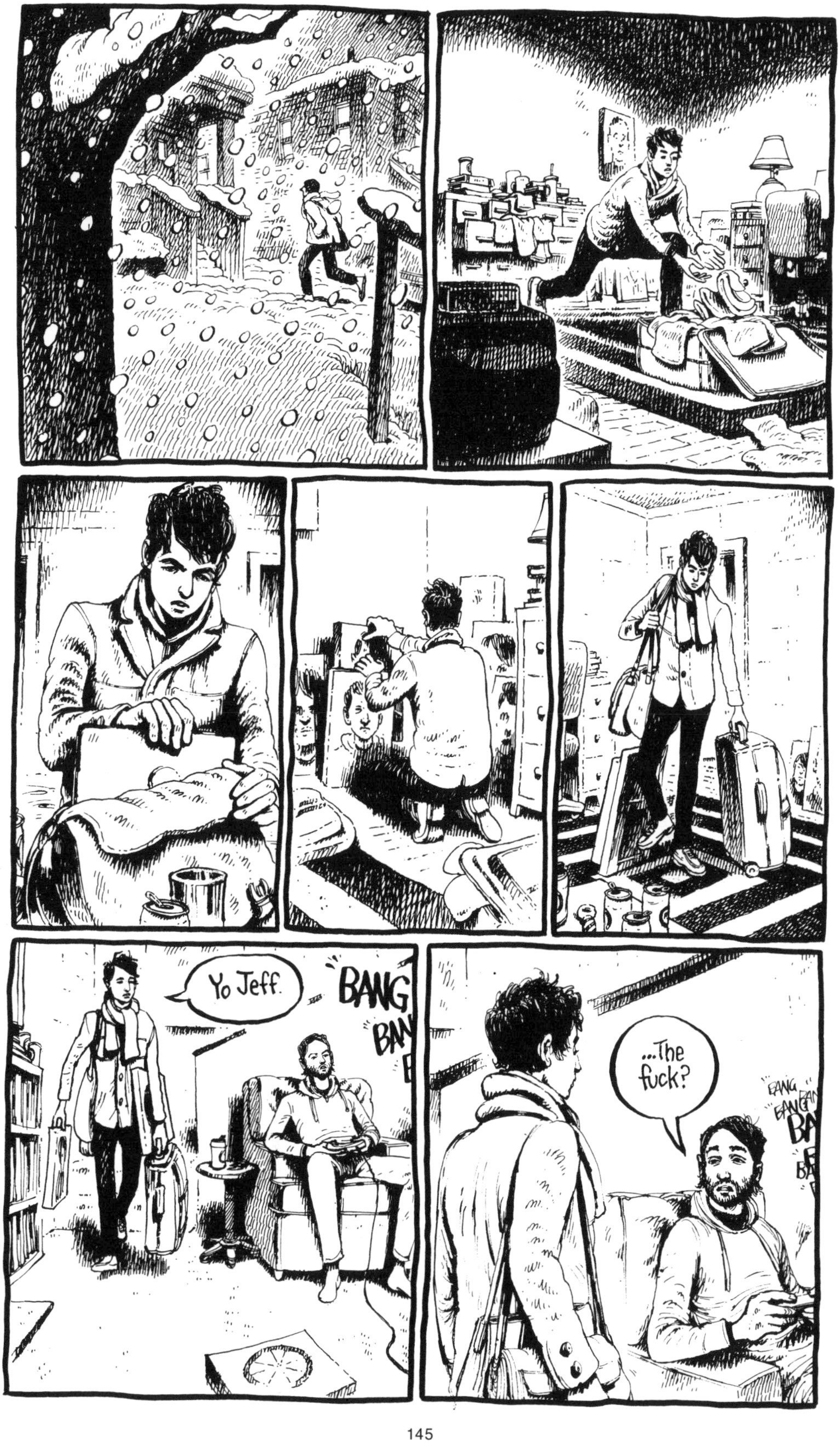
Yo Jeff.
BANG
BAN
...The fuck?
BANG
BANG
BANG
BA

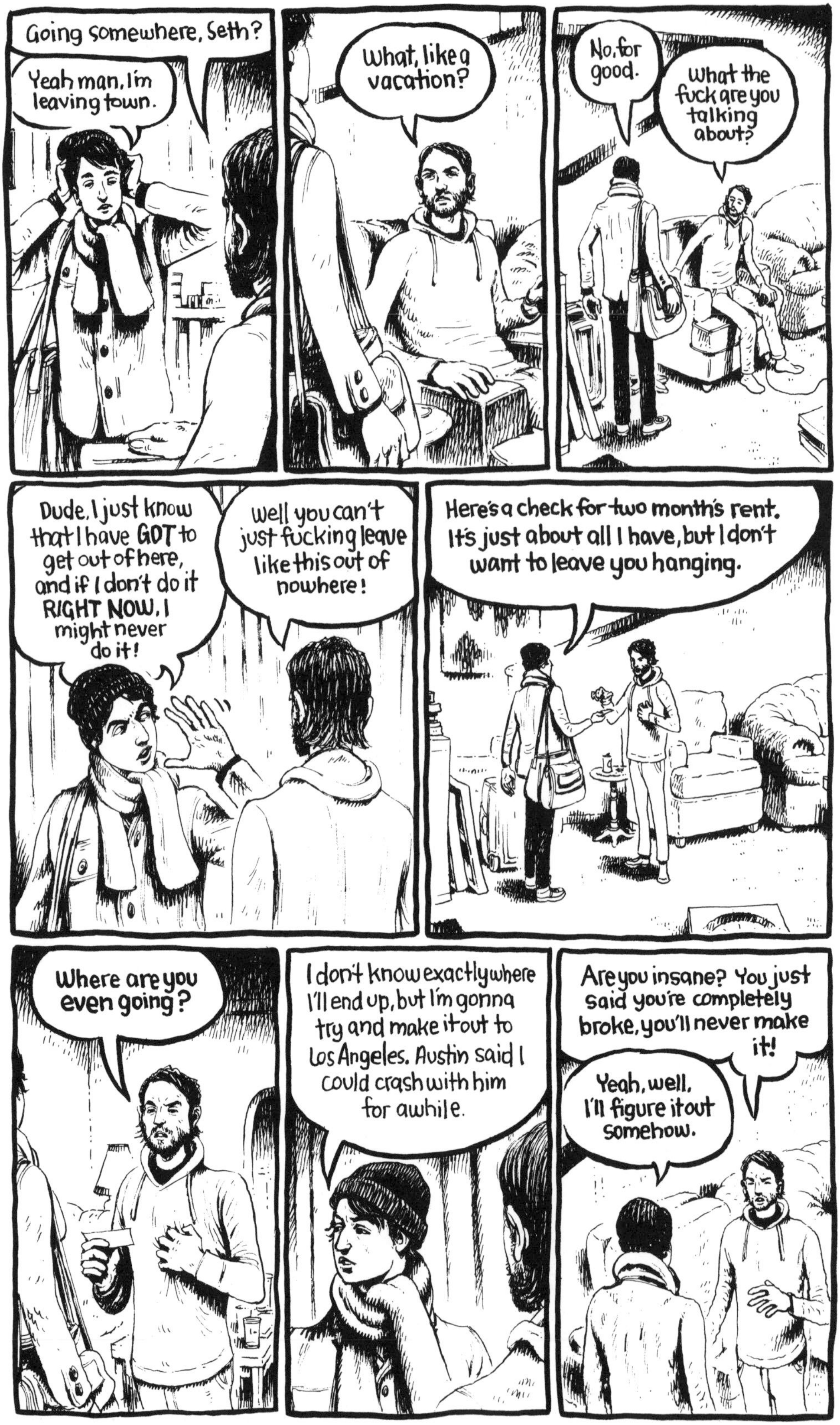
Going somewhere, Seth?
Yeah man, I'm leaving town.
What, like a vacation?
No, for good.
What the fuck are you talking about?
Dude, I just know that I have GOT to get out of here, and if I don't do it RIGHT NOW, I might never do it!
Well you can't just fucking leave like this out of nowhere!
Here's a check for two month's rent. It's just about all I have, but I don't want to leave you hanging.
Where are you even going?
I don't know exactly where I'll end up, but I'm gonna try and make it out to Los Angeles. Austin said I could crash with him for awhile.
Are you insane? You just said you're completely broke, you'll never make it!
Yeah, well, I'll figure it out somehow.

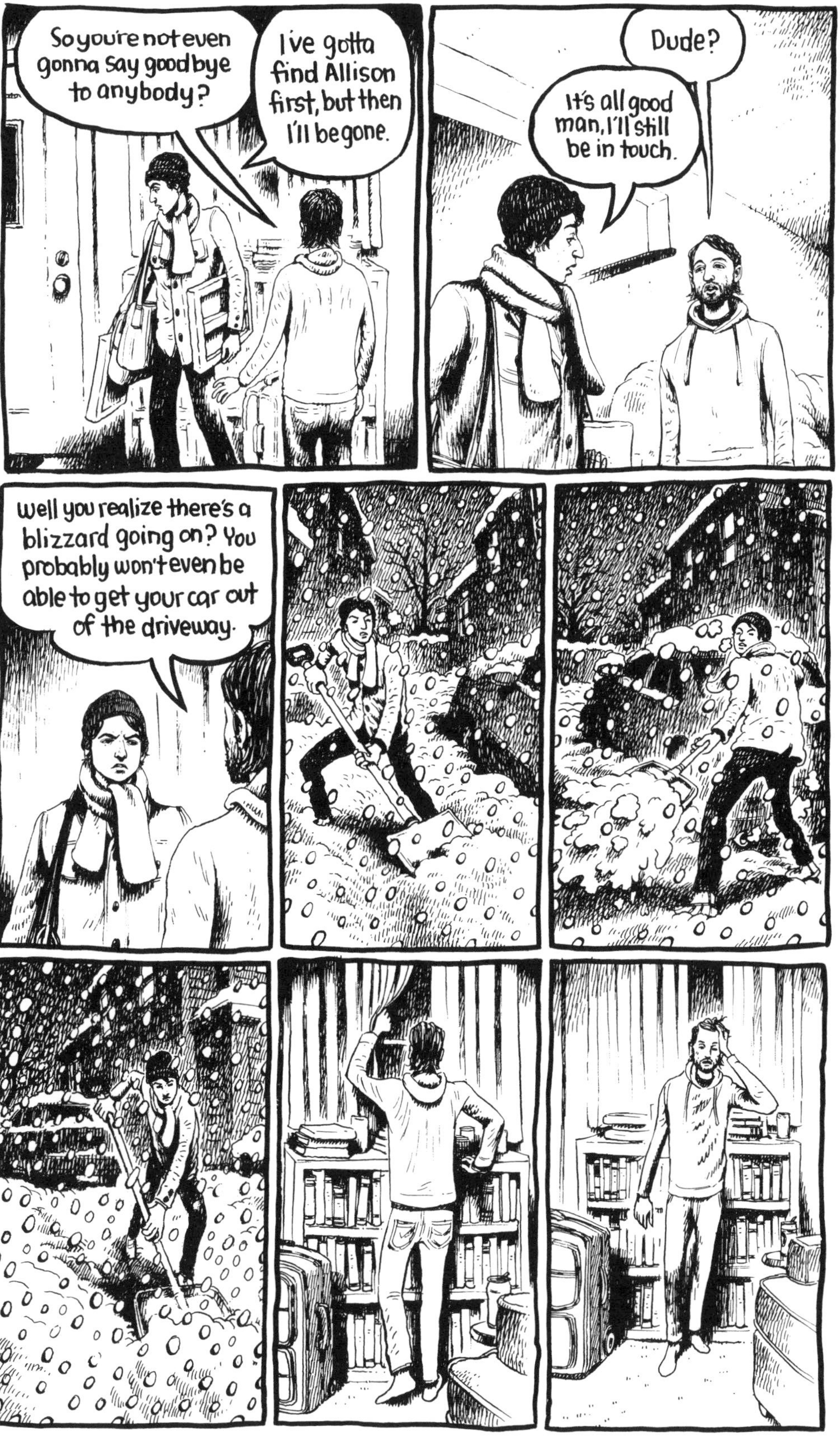
So you're not even gonna say goodbye to anybody?
I've gotta find Allison first, but then I'll be gone.
Dude?
It's all good man, I'll still be in touch.
Well you realize there's a blizzard going on? You probably won't even be able to get your car out of the driveway.

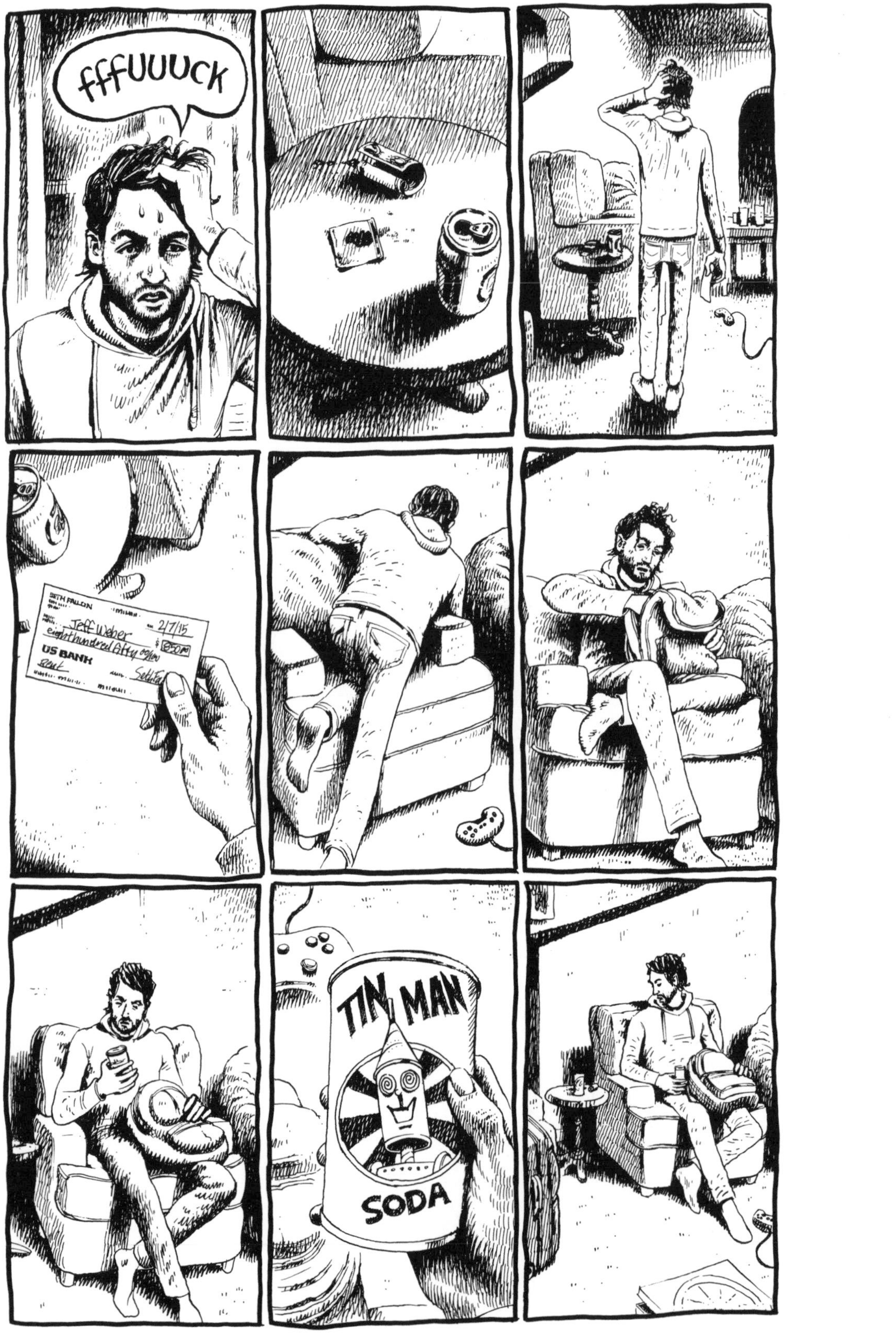
fffuuuck
SETH FALLON
Jeff Weber
2/7/15
eight hundred fifty 00/100
$850.00
US BANK
Rent
TIN MAN
SODA

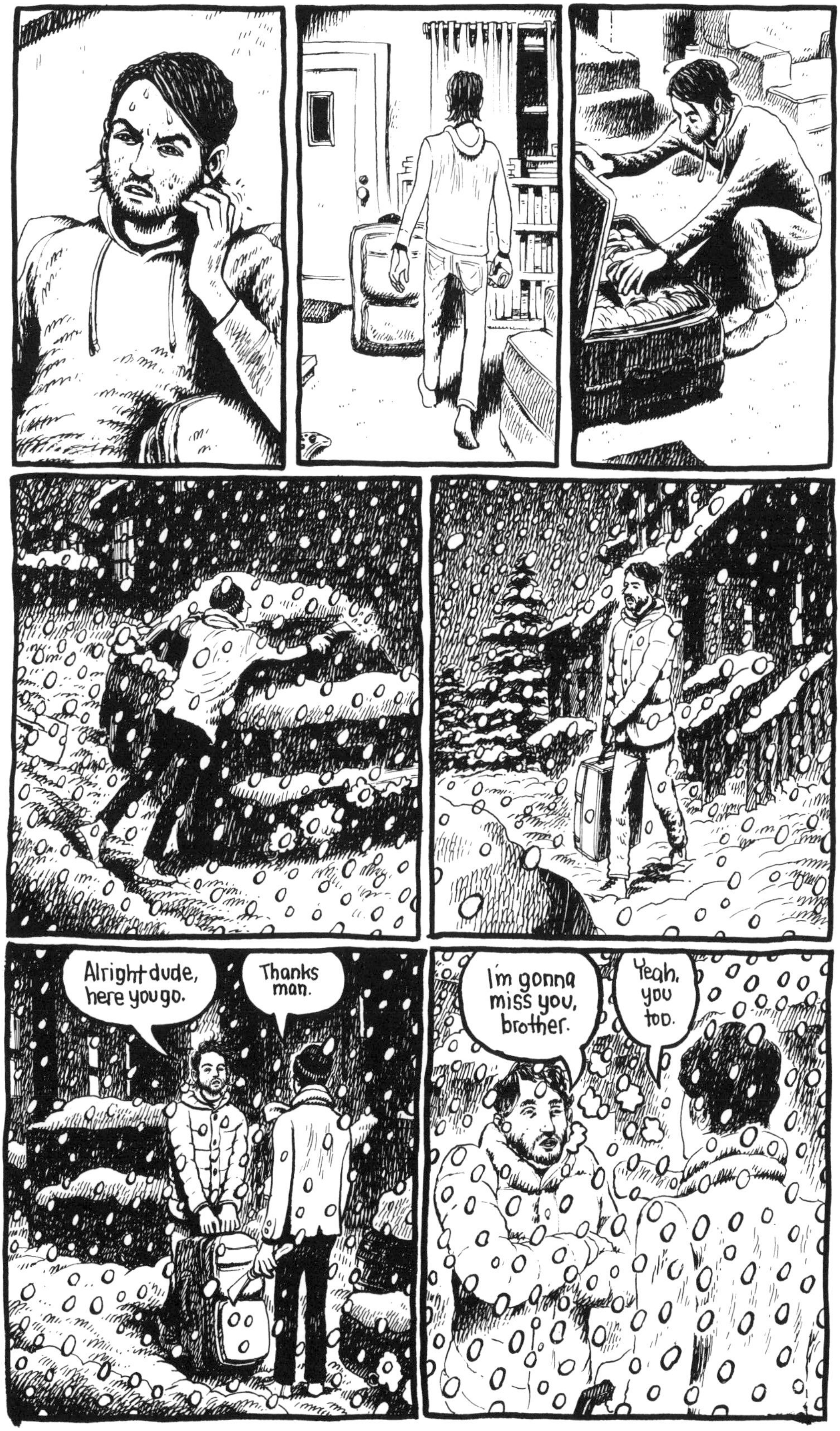
Alright dude, here you go.
Thanks man.
I'm gonna miss you, brother.
Yeah, you too.

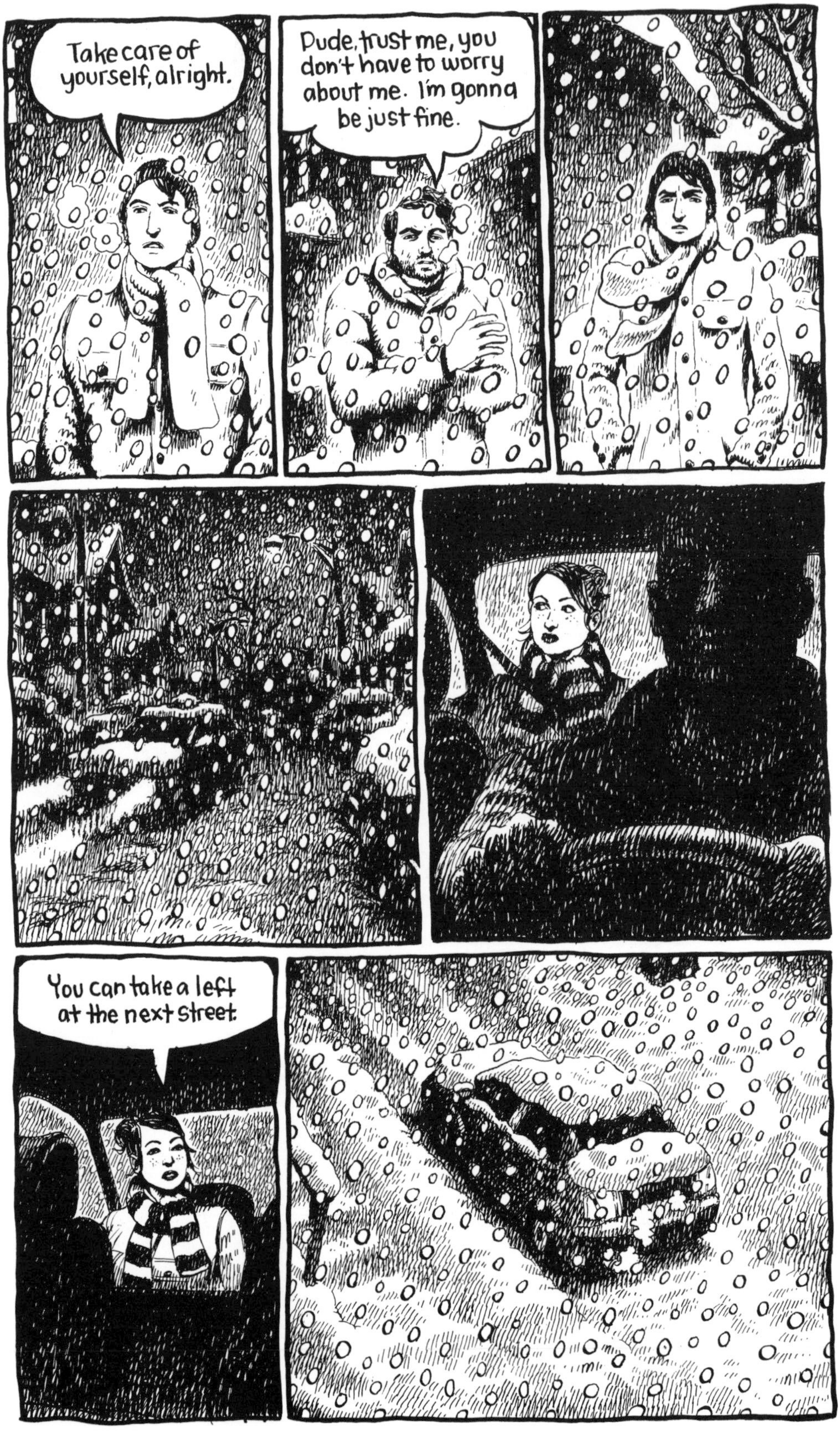
Take care of yourself, alright.
Dude, trust me, you don't have to worry about me. I'm gonna be just fine.
You can take a left at the next street.

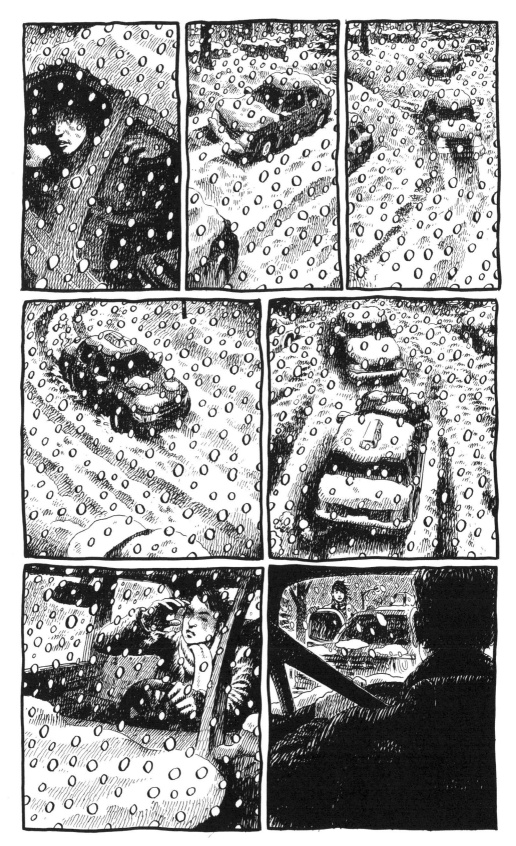

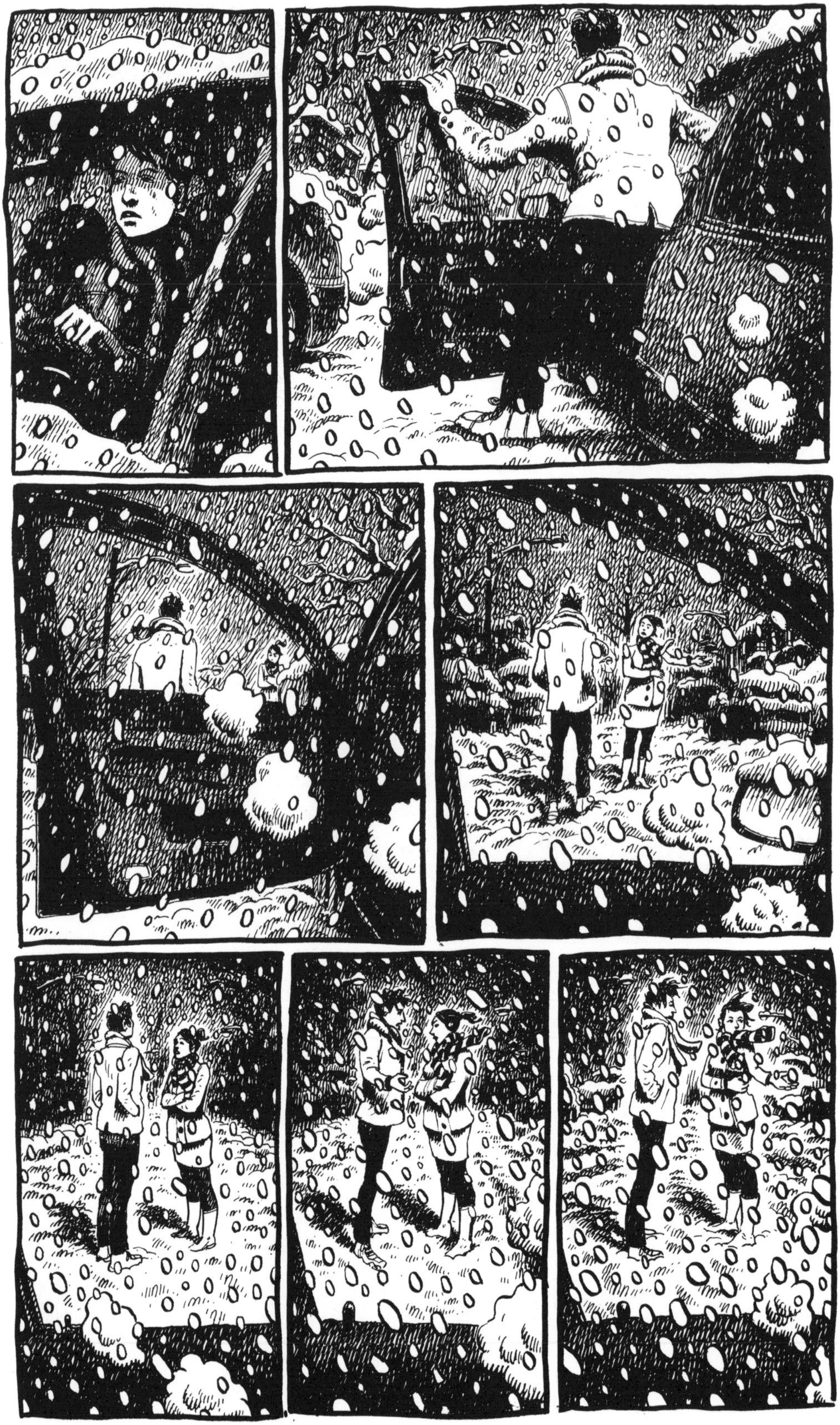

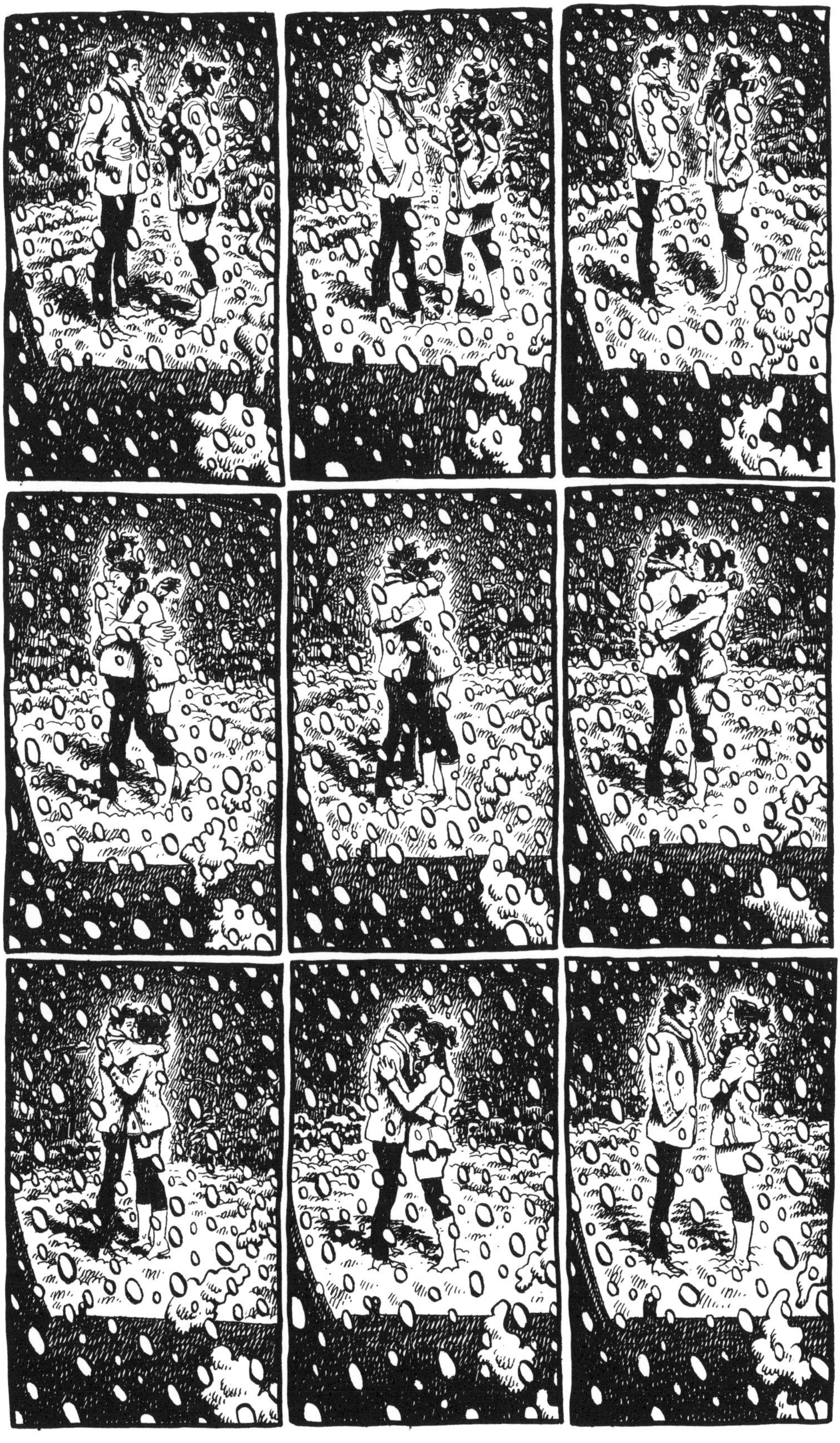

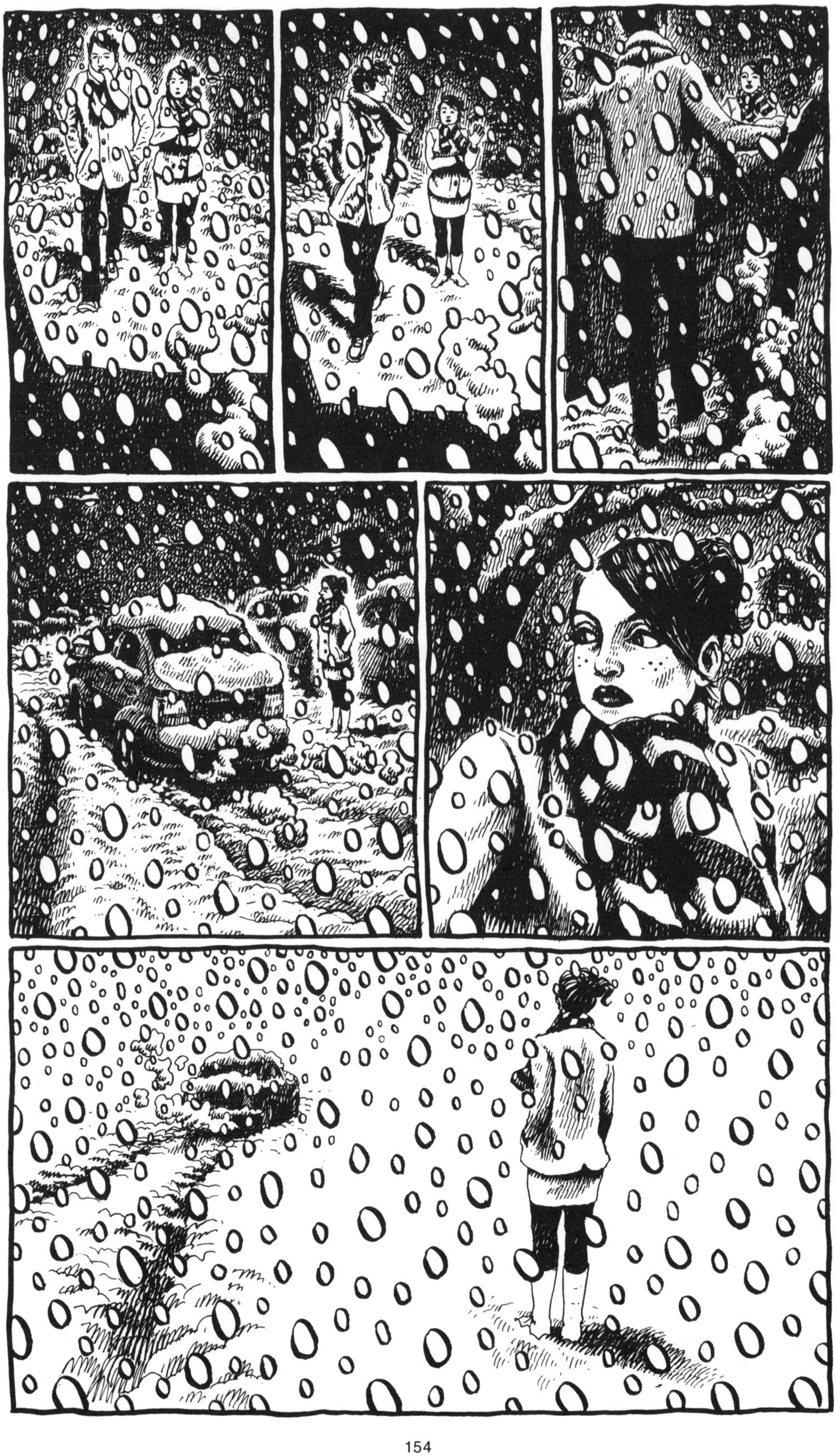

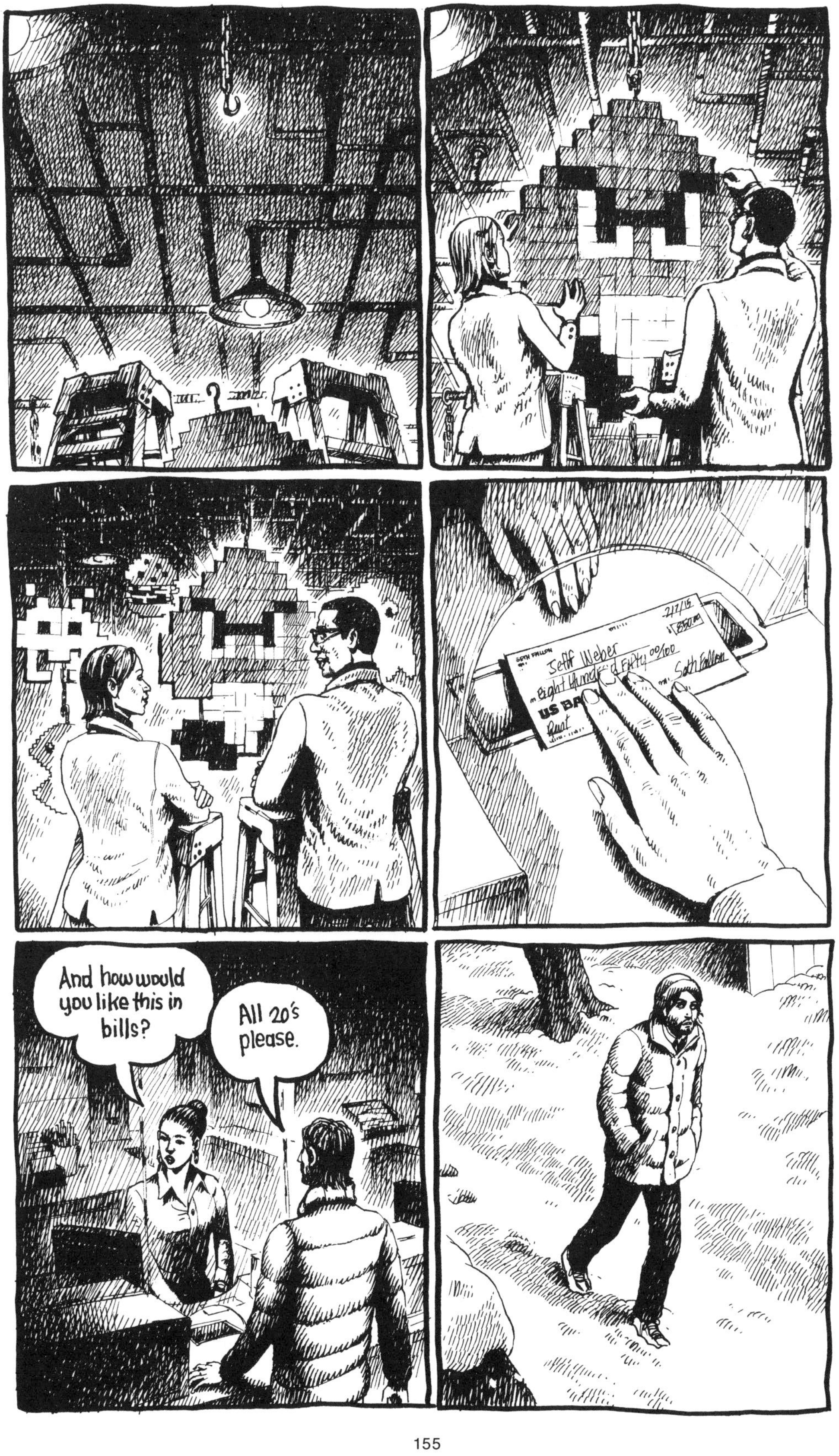
SETH FALLON
2/7/15
$850.00
Jeff Weber
00/100
Seth Fallon
Rent
And how would you like this in bills?
All 20's please.

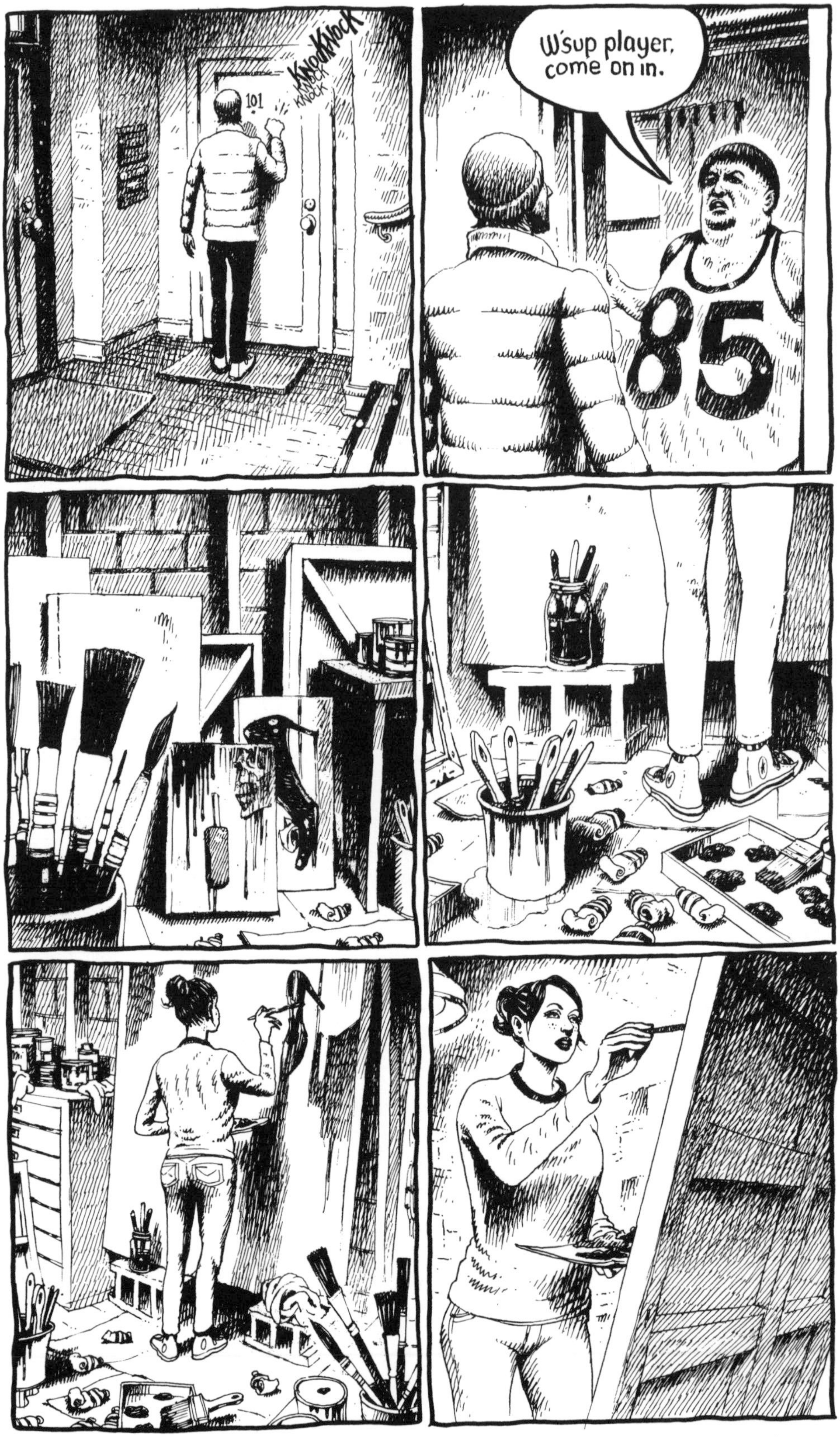
KNOCK KNOCK
KNOCK
KNOCK
101
W'sup player, come on in.
85

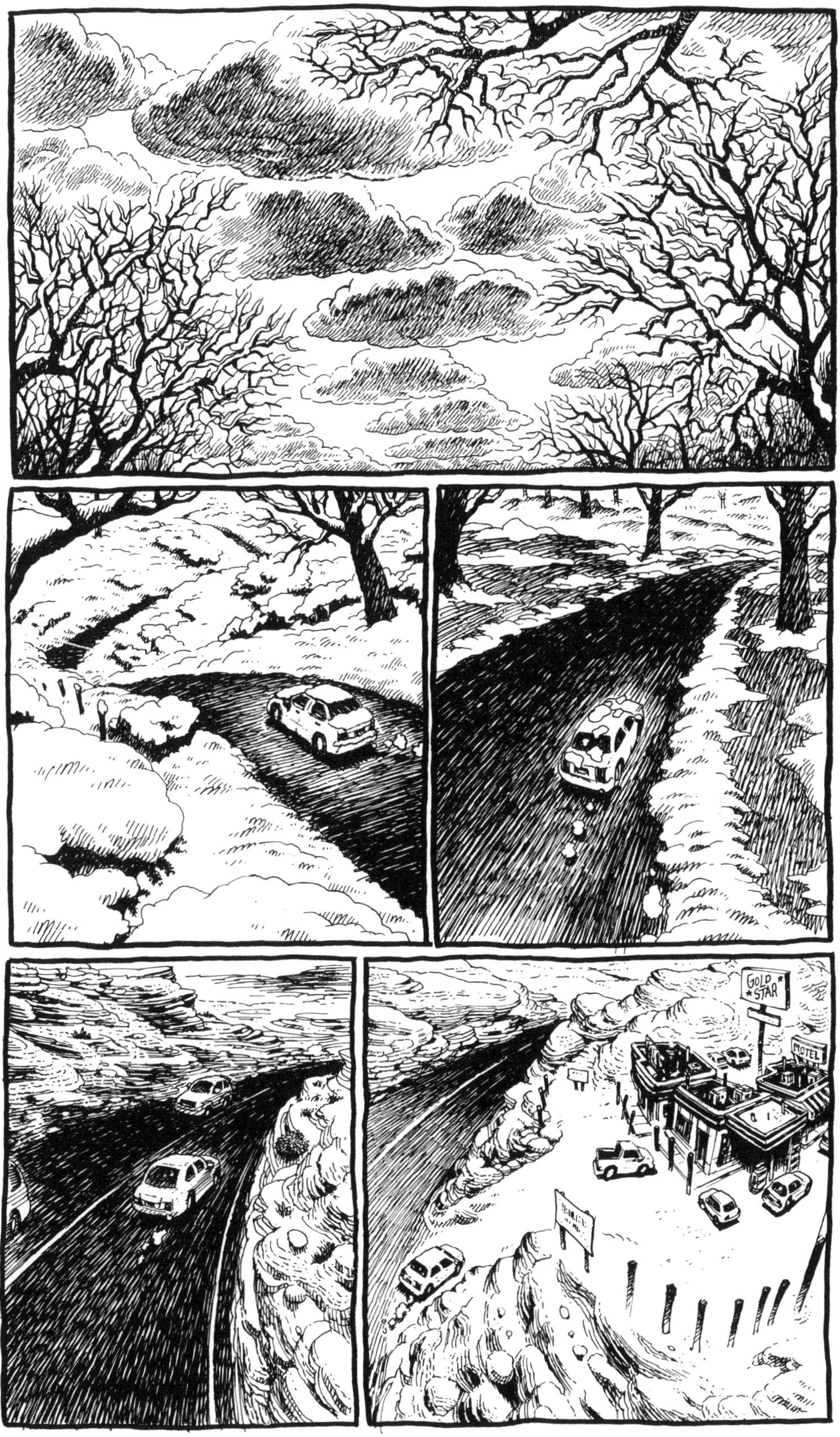
GOLD STAR
MOTEL

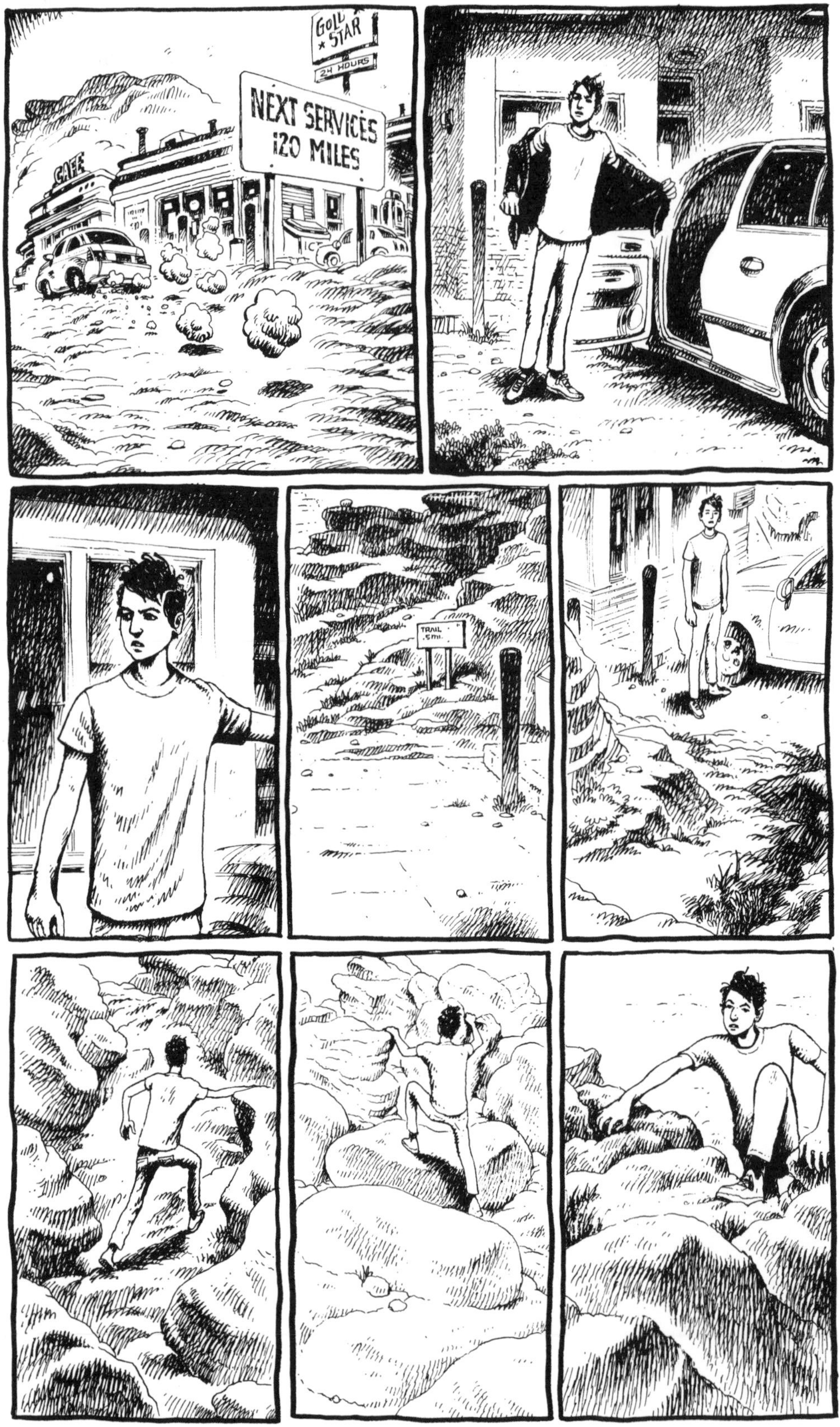
GOLD STAR
24 HOURS
NEXT SERVICES
120 MILES
CAFE
TRAIL
.5mi.